More praise for *Orpheus Lost*

"In *Orpheus Lost*, Janette Turner Hospital has written a warmly engaging and unnervingly timely love knot of a novel that moves with the fluidity of a timeless fairy tale." —Joyce Carol Oates

"One of the most powerful and innovative writers in the English language today." —*Times Literary Supplement*

"No book by this nervy, dynamic Australian-born author is ever anything less than intricate and deeply disquieting. . . . Reconnaissance into the storehouses of artistic tradition and the trenches of fearful contemporary life is . . . expertly accomplished in *Orpheus Lost*. . . . Lushly orchestrated, *Orpheus Lost* answered our grief and fear with an emotional expressiveness more visceral than words, with the candor of music—and of myth."
—Donna Rifkind, *Los Angeles Times Book Review*

"Janette Turner Hospital's new novel, *Orpheus Lost*, dramatizes harsh, current war headlines through the forebodingly resonant framework of Greek legend. Her hot-blooded, edgy characters scramble for survival and love in a world at odds with imagination, intelligence, and integrity. Hospital's twelfth book, like much of her work, is characterized by a rich, varied appreciation of place. . . . She leaves readers feeling hope and grief and a terrible sense of urgency about our own lives at this fragile moment in history." —Valerie Miner, *Boston Globe*

"[*Orpheus Lost*] will keep you on the edge of your chair or reading past your bedtime. . . . [It] should enthrall every kind of reader: a book full of intelligence and drama and compassion that is also a captivating page-turner." —*The Age* (Melbourne)

"Hospital shows her dazzling skill at thriller writing. [She is] a master-planner who never falters for an instant. Nor do the pace and intensity let up. . . . [A] consummate nail-biting example of a myth retold for modern times." —*Australian Book Review*

"By force of personal affinity and moral seriousness [Janette Turner Hospital] seems to be doing for fiction in a post–September 11 world something akin to what Graham Greene did for the dramatization of moral ambivalence during the Cold War." —*Australian Literary Review*

"A novel that grapples so thoughtfully with such resonant issues demands close attention." —*Kirkus Reviews*

"In a masterful manipulation of her characters, Hospital frames an intimate story of love and obsession. . . . Chapters riddled with paranoia and real danger, the Orpheus legend is acted out on a world stage. . . . Thrilling, compelling and utterly possible, Hospital speaks to our deepest fears and secret longings, offering redemption at the end of Orpheus's quest."
—Luan Gaines, Curled Up With a Good Book

"*Orpheus Lost,* beautifully written and disturbing, takes us from earth to underworld as a mathematician and a musician repeat the roles of Eurydice and Orpheus, with a few twists. . . . [She] deserves attention for the fine eye and mind she turns to the problems of our times. We should listen to her music."
—Claudia Smith Brinson, *Florida Times-Union*

Orpheus
Lost

Orpheus
Lost

A NOVEL

Janette Turner Hospital

W. W. Norton & Company   New York London

For information about permission to reproduce selections
from this book, write to Permissions, W. W. Norton & Company, Inc.,
500 Fifth Avenue, New York, NY 10110

For information about special discounts for bulk purchases,
please contact W. W. Norton Special Sales at
specialsales@wwnorton.com or 800-233-4830

Manufacturing by Courier Westford
Production manager: Anna Oler

Library of Congress Cataloging-in-Publication Data

Hospital, Janette Turner, 1942–
Orpheus lost : a novel / Janette Turner Hospital. — 1st American ed.
     p. cm.
ISBN 978-0-393-06552-7 (hardcover)
1. Women mathematicians—Fiction. 2. Musicians—Fiction.
3. Australians—United States—Fiction. 4. Terrorism—United
States—Fiction. 5. New England—Fiction. 6. Orpheus
(Greek mythology)—Fiction. I. Title.
          PR9619.3.H674O77 2007
823'.914—dc22   2007024023

ISBN 978-0-393-33414-2 pbk.

W. W. Norton & Company, Inc.
500 Fifth Avenue, New York, N.Y. 10110
                    www.wwnorton.com

W. W. Norton & Company Ltd.
Castle House, 75/76 Wells Street, London W1T 3QT

1 2 3 4 5 6 7 8 9 0

Acknowledgments

SECTIONS OF THIS novel, in slightly different form, have appeared in the following literary journals: *Nimrod International Journal* (where section IV.1, as "The Sword of the Lord and of Gideon," received the Geraldine McLoud award); *Southern Humanities Review*; *Hecate*.

Though Promised Land is the real and irresistible name of a small town in South Carolina (pop. 559 in the census of 2000), the Promised Land in this novel is entirely fictitious. Indeed, I have taken the liberty of moving the town from upstate, near the Georgia and North Carolina borders, to the coastal lowlands, somewhere between Charleston and McClellanville, but about thirty miles inland.

I wish to thank the Vietnam veterans, American and Australian, black and white, who shared with me their passionate memories. I take this opportunity to pay tribute to all those who have been called upon to put themselves in harm's way in conflicts with which they may or may not have agreed.

Orpheus crosses the boundaries not only between life and death and between man and nature, but also between truth and illusion, reality and imagination.

JOSEPH CAMPBELL

The language of music is quite different from the language of intentionality. What it has to say is simultaneously revealed and concealed. It is demythologized prayer.

THEODOR ADORNO

Contents

BOOK I

Leela

1

AFTERWARDS, LEELA REALIZED, everything could have been predicted from the beginning. Every clue was there, the ending inevitable and curled up inside the first encounter like a tree inside a seed. The trouble was that the interpretation was obvious only in retrospect.

Fact one: Mishka Bartok was an insoluble equation.

Fact two: Leela could never leave insoluble equations alone. Before Mishka, she believed that every code could be broken and codes which had yet to be deciphered were an irresistible provocation. They kept her awake at night.

She did sense from the start that Mishka was a question without an answer, but she could not accept this. Neither could she prove it. Not then. The riddle of Mishka was like Fermat's last theorem for which no solution exists. In 1630, Fermat himself could prove that all the way to infinity no solution would ever exist, but he kept his proof to himself and it hovered like marsh fire in algebraic and numerical dreams. It lured mathematicians for three centuries, almost for four. It drove them mad. Computations were exchanged between Oxford and Rome, between Berlin, Bologna, the Sorbonne, until finally, late in the twentieth century, someone at Princeton caught the proof of non-provability in his net. "I was ten years old," the Princeton genius said—Andrew Wiles was his name—"when I first read about Fermat. It looked so simple, his theorem, yet all the mathematicians in history couldn't solve it. From that moment, I knew I'd never let it go."

Obsession, wrote a seventeenth-century don who gave his life to the quest, *is its own heaven and its own hell.*

The words struck Leela like a blow. She copied them onto an index card which she thumb-tacked to the wall above her desk.

Sometimes, in dreams, when the beginning began again, Mishka would warn her: "Don't follow me, Leela." He would lift the violin to his chin and begin to play. He would turn his back and walk away from her, walk down into the subway tunnels, deeper and deeper, the bow rising above his left shoulder and falling again, the notes drifting back, plaintive and irresistible. "Leave me alone," he would say. "Don't follow me."

"Where are you going?" Leela would call, but he never answered.

Leela would push against the fog of underground air, her eyes fixed on the pale flash of bowstrings until the dark swallowed them. "Mishka! Wait!" she would call. "Wait for me!"

That always made him pause. "Don't call me Mishka." His sadness would speak in a minor key, two sweeps of the bow. "That's not my name anymore." He would wheel back then, briefly, to face her and she would see with dread—in dream after recurring dream—that indeed he was no longer Mishka, but a skeletal idea of himself thinly draped in a shroud. Some ghastly internal aura shone from the sockets that were his eyes. Humerus, radius and ulna, the bones of the arm, kept moving his bow across the strings. "Don't follow me, Leela," his skeleton warned.

The tunnel smelled of monstrous decay, but even so, even knowing within the dream that she should turn and flee back up into sunlight, Leela would be powerless. Mishka's music drugged her. Waking or sleeping, she could close her eyes and see him as she saw him that first time: not just the visual memory lurking entire, but the sounds, the sensations, the hurly-burly of Harvard Square, the slightly dank odor of the steps as she descended into the underworld of the Red Line, the click of tokens and turnstiles, the gust of fragrance from the flower sellers, the funky sweat of the homeless, the subdued roar of the trains, and then those haunting notes....

She stood riveted, her token poised above the slot in the turnstile. She had heard two bars, perhaps three, in the brief lull between trains.

"Would you mind?" said someone behind her.

"What? Oh... sorry." She let the token fall through the slot. She pushed against the steel bar and into the space of the music. There was another pause between trains, a few bars, a stringed instrument, clearly, but also a tenor voice. Was it a cello that the singer was playing? Surely not. No street musician would cart such a large and unwieldy instrument down into the bowels of the city, onto the trains, among the crowds; but the sound seemed too soft for a violin, too husky, too throaty. She could feel the music graphing itself against her skin, her body calculating the frequencies and intervals of the whole subway symphony: base throb of trains, tenor voice, soft lament of the strings, a pleasing ratio of vibrations. Mathematical perfection made her weak at the knees.

She was letting the music reel her in, following the thread of it, leaning into the perfect fifths. Crowds intruded, echoes teased her, tunnels bounced the sound off their walls—now the music seemed to be just ahead, now to the right—and two minutes in every five, the low thunder of the trains muffled all. The notes were faint, they were clear, they were gone, they were clear again: unbearably mournful and sweet. Leela was not the only one affected. People paused in the act of buying tokens. They looked up from newspapers. They turned their heads and scanned the walls and ceiling of the subway cavern for speakers. With one foot on the outbound train, a man was arrested by a phrase and stepped back out of the sliding doors.

"Where is that gorgeous sound coming from?" he asked Leela. "Is it a recording?"

"A street musician," she said. "Someone playing an early instrument, I think, a Renaissance violin, or something like that."

"Over there," the man pointed.

"Must be. Yes."

"Extraordinary," the man said. He began to run.

Leela followed him the length of the inbound platform to where a dense knot of commuters huddled. For a while the music was clearer as they approached, and then it was not, and then it seemed to be behind them again. Leela turned, disoriented. Her hands were shaking. The man who had stepped back from the outbound train leaned against a pillar with his eyes closed, rapt. Leela saw a woman surreptitiously wiping her sleeve across her eyes.

The violin itself was weeping music. Sometimes it wept alone; sometimes the tenor voice sorrowed along with it in a tongue not quite known but intuitively understood. The singer was singing of loss, that much was certain, and the sorrow was passing from body to body like a low electrical charge.

Leela recognized the melody, but although she could analyze the mathematical structure of any composition, she had trouble remembering titles of works and linking them to the right composers. It was an aria from some early opera, that much she knew. Gluck, probably. She had to hear all of it.

Ahead of her was an impenetrable cordon of backs.

Leela closed her eyes and pressed her hands to her face. She had a sense of floating underwater and the water was warm and moving fast and she was willing to be carried away by it. It was this way back in childhood in summer ponds in South Carolina, or on the jasmine-clotted Hamilton house veranda, or in deep grass, or lying under the pines with local boys; it was this way in later carnal adventures: body as fluid as soul. Everything was part of the euphoric storm surge which swept Leela up and rushed her toward something radiant that was just out of reach.

A fist of air punched her in the small of her back and a tidal wave of announcements drowned the music. Her hair streamed straight out in front of her face like a pennant. Words rumbled like thunder. *Stopping all stations to shshshshs clang clang for Green Line change at Park clang shshshshsh….* Bucking and pushing ahead of the in-rush of train, a hard balloon of air plowed through the knot of listeners and scattered them.

That was when Leela caught her first glimpse of Mishka Bartok.

His head was bent over his instrument, his eyes focused on his fingered chords and his bow. He was oblivious to the arrival of the train. His body merged with the music and swayed. He was slender and pale, his dark hair unruly. A small shock of curls fell down over his left eye. When he leaned into the dominant notes, the curls fell across the sounding board of the instrument and he tossed them back with a flick of his head. Leela thought of a racehorse. She thought of a faun. Incongruously, she also thought of a boy she had known in childhood, a boy named Cobb, a curious boy with a curious name, a boy who had been possessed of the same skittish intensity which somehow let you know that, if cornered, this was a creature who would not yield. The violin player had Cobb's fierce and haunted eyes.

There was no hat on the platform in front of him, no box, no can, no open violin case for donations, and the absence of any such receptacle seemed to bother the listeners. Someone tucked a folded bill into the side pocket of the violin player's jeans but he appeared not to notice. A student in torn denim shorts took off his cloth hat and placed it beside the closed violin case as tribute and people threw coins and placed dollar bills—ones, fives, tens even—in the hat but the musician seemed indifferent and unaware. Some listeners boarded the inbound train, some seemed incapable of moving. Leela let five trains come and go, bracing herself each time against the buffeting of air. She had now worked her way forward to the innermost circle. She was four feet from the man with the violin. She could feel the intensity of his body like a series of small seismic waves against her own.

Trains arrived and departed, some people left but more gathered, the crowd around the man with the violin kept getting larger. His instrumental repertoire seemed inexhaustible—he barely paused between pieces—but when he sang, it was always and only when he cycled back to the same aria that had first reached Leela's ears. When he sang, she could not take her eyes off his lips. She touched her own with the pads of her fingers. She had a sensation of falling forward, of free-falling into a well of melody without end. The cautionary words above her desk hovered at the edge of her mind: *Obsession is its own heaven and its own hell*, but she did not care if she stayed on the inbound platform all day. She wondered fleetingly if hours might have already passed. She gave herself to the wave of music. She wondered if she might have grown gills.

Perhaps because she was now so close to him, perhaps because of the heat that her body gave off, the musician glanced up as he began to sing the aria again. Their eyes met. Something fizzed and smoldered like a lit fuse along the line of sight. Leela let less than one second pass as the last note faded, and then, recklessly, interposed herself between the player and his next chord.

"What is that song?" she asked, or tried to ask, even as his bow hovered above a new beginning. There was a constriction in her chest.

"*Che farò senza Euridice.*" He lowered the violin from his left shoulder and stroked it with the fingers of his bowing hand. "Gluck."

"Ah." Leela's voice came back to her. "I thought it was Gluck." They stood inches apart. She could see two miniature projections of herself in his eyes.

"It's the lament of Orpheus," he said.

"When he descends into the underworld, right? To bring Eurydice back." Leela was babbling. To stop herself, she put one hand over her mouth and the gesture created a small obstruction in the flow of fixations. He dropped his eyes. He let the tip of his bow rest lightly against the top of one shoe. She studied the lace in his shoe and his hand on the bow. The half moons on his fingernails were white against the pale pink of the nails.

"Seems the right thing to play in the subway," he said. "For violin, anyway. If I were playing my oud, it would be different."

"Playing your—?"

"Oud."

"What is an *ood*?"

"Persian instrument originally. Like a Renaissance lute."

"Ahh…. Do you do this often? Play in the subway? I mean, there are always musicians, but I've never heard *you* here before."

"I normally never play here. Only on the Blue Line, where no one I know is going to see me."

Coins were showering into the donated hat. People moved into the space between Leela and the violin player, leaning forward, making appreciative comments, placing folded bills in the hat. This startled the musician, or even, perhaps, alarmed him. He seemed for the first time to become aware of the throngs of people.

"Don't," he said, distressed. "Thank you, but please don't. It isn't necessary. I don't do this for money. Thank you, thank you, please don't." In a nervous rush, agitated, he replaced his violin in its case. He removed the fistful of bills from the hat, stared at them, then stuffed them back again. He did not know what to do with the hat. He regarded it in puzzlement and then left it there, moving in urgent strides toward the exit.

Leela grabbed up the hat and ran after him, but he moved so swiftly that he was already through the turnstile and halfway up the steps into Harvard Square before she caught up. She reached for him and seized him by the sleeve. "You have to take this," she said, tugging. She was breathing heavily. "It's rightfully yours." She took a few gasping and shallow breaths. "It's a love gift from all those people."

His face creased in something like pain. "It's a misunderstanding," he said. "I do it for the reverberation. I do it for myself. For the sound."

He has the eyes of Orpheus, Leela thought. He has the eyes of Orpheus at the moment when Eurydice is bitten by the snake, or perhaps when he has lost her for the second time, when she is pulled back into the underworld, forever beyond reach. Leela thought she had never met anyone with such sad eyes, or someone so indifferent to his own sadness. She had an impulse to stand on tiptoe and kiss him. Instead she said: "You could donate the money if you wanted. To the Salvation Army, or a homeless center, or something."

"Yes," he said. "That's a good idea." But he made no move to take the hat.

"You have a funny accent," she said.

He raised one eyebrow, and for the first time Leela saw the shadow of a smile. "No I don't," he said. "You do."

"Ah well. Mine's Southern. I guess that's foreign in Harvard Square. What's yours?"

"Australian."

"Australian. You must be a student."

"Graduate student."

"Me too. Are you in Music?"

"Yes."

He looked around as though searching for escape. Leela noticed that the hand which pushed hair from his eyes was shaking. "Uh..." he said. "Today's an anniversary. A sort of... a private one. I didn't quite realize I was playing in public. That's why I'm—" he gestured at the noisy chaos of Harvard Square—"I didn't mean to be here. I usually play on the Blue Line."

"Want to go for a latte?"

"Oh," he said awkwardly. "Uh...." He looked at his watch. "It's a difficult day for me."

"An anniversary."

Alarmed, he met her eyes briefly, then looked away. "Yes."

"So you said. A sad one, I gather."

His hands were cupped over the thin end of the violin case. The fat curved end rested on the pavement between his feet. He pivoted the case, very precisely, in a half circle, as though navigating a passage through a reef.

"I can tell it's a sad one," Leela persisted. "That's why I'd like to offer a latte."

The violin case made two complete revolutions, then another half circle.

"I know it's inept," Leela said, "but it's the sort of thing we Americans do, we insist on doing."

He studied his shoe. He met her eyes momentarily and again a flicker of a smile touched his lips. "Enforced goodwill?"

"Exactly. You have to let us be generous and compassionate."

"Actually, I've got a rehearsal. I'm part of a West-meets-East quintet: violin, oud, cello, bass and tabla."

"Where? In Paine Hall?"

He raised his eyebrows.

"It figures, doesn't it?" she said. "I'm in math, not music, and I'm at MIT, but I did my undergrad work here and my particular thing is the math of music. I used to hang out at Paine Hall sometimes, pestering people. I'll come and listen."

He was drumming his fingers on his violin case. "That's never—No really, it wouldn't work. I don't think the others would accept it." He looked at her again, curious. "The math of music?"

"Specifically, changes in the employment of non-aligned wave frequencies from Monteverdi to Bach."

"That's my area," he said, his interest quickening. "Early to high Baroque. My area in *Western* music, at least."

"So I figured. From your instrument."

"Custom-made. Authentic reconstruction." He stroked the case as a proud father might stroke a child's hair. His eyes glittered. His nervousness fell away like a coat discarded. He hummed a few bars of Monteverdi. "I prefer Monteverdi's *Orfeo* to Gluck's, actually, except for that one aria."

"I thought you couldn't do performance at Harvard."

"You can't. My doctorate's in composition. But we all perform too."

"So can I?" she asked.

He broke off humming and frowned. "Can you what?"

"Be a fly on the wall in your practice room?"

"Oh... no, really. It would interfere. For me it would, anyway." He sighed, as though defaulting in advance on the ability to explain. "Look, the truth is, I'm a recluse. I live inside my music, really. I tend to shut out everything else."

"We're two of a kind, I suspect."

He smiled politely at this, patently disbelieving.

"Except I live inside pure mathematics," she said, "which makes less sense than living inside music, though in my own opinion, my private cave is just as beautiful."

"You don't understand." He hefted the violin case under his right arm and raked the fingers of his left hand, agitatedly, through his hair. "I listen to music, I play music, I compose it. I don't do anything else. I mean, I don't know how. I'm just no good at anything normal. I don't know how to have coffee with someone."

Leela did lean toward him then. "I could teach you," she said.

"Why?" He seemed genuinely curious to know the answer.

Why? Leela asked herself. A question of harmonics, perhaps, of vibrating at the same frequency. Or then again, because she could not bear to walk away from him. "I don't know," she said, though this was less than the absolute truth. Incongruously, she was awash in childhood sensations: the sense of an interlocking part.

"I don't know," she said again. "You remind me of someone I grew up with. That's not a good reason, is it? I don't know if this one's any better, but I just want to. I want you to want to."

Impulsively, she stood on tiptoe and kissed him on the lips.

He took a step back, affronted, but his eyes met hers again and they stood there, for seconds or minutes, and then he reached for her with his right hand and almost crushed her, the violin case pressed awkwardly between. He kissed her like a man starved for contact, and they stood there in the middle of Harvard Square, oblivious, devouring each other, crowds parting around them.

"Sweet Jesus," Leela gasped, coming up for air.

"Where can we go?" he asked.

She raised her eyebrows and gulped a little with laughter. "What about the rehearsal?"

"I don't need practice."

"I mean your East-West quintet."

"It's actually not until tomorrow," he confessed.

"In that case," she decided, "we could go to my place. It's close, if you don't mind a short walk. I'm just north of the Yard."

Hours afterwards, she said drowsily: "I don't know your name."

"I don't know yours."

"Mine's Leela."

He moved the bow of his mouth, as though feathering an instrument, lightly from her lips to her breasts, but said nothing.

"I could call you Orpheus," she said.

"You could."

"But what's your real name?"

"I don't know," he sighed. "Not really. The one I have isn't part of me."

"The one I'm stuck with isn't part of me either," she said. She wrote her name in cursive script across his chest with the tip of her index finger. He reached for her finger and sucked it.

"I was baptized Leela-May Magnolia Moore in Promised Land, South Carolina, and you can't get worse than that."

"Promised Land?"

"It's the kind of town you can't wait to leave. To this day, in Promised Land, I'm known as Leela-May. My daddy calls me LeelaMayMagnolia like it's one single word, but he's the only living soul who can say it and not get shot."

"The name on my passport is Michael Bartok."

"Bartok!"

"No relation to the composer. Or if we are, it's so distant, it doesn't count. Bartok was my mother's family name."

"Is she Hungarian?"

"My grandparents were. Hungarian Jews. My mother was born in Australia."

"Then there could be a link with Béla Bartók."

"My grandfather and my great uncle played the violin, so there's music in my genes, but as far as we know they're not Béla Bartók's genes. I get music from both sides. I get the Persian classical influence and the oud from my father."

"Yet you choose to go by your mother's family name. It can't hurt your career."

He recoiled and swung his feet to the floor and crossed the room. He pressed his forehead against her window and drummed his fingers on the glass. His agitation was violent. "I didn't *choose*—I was born out of wedlock, as they say. That's the name on my birth certificate. I'm legally stuck with it."

Leela went to him and put her hands lightly on his shoulders. She pressed her cheek against his back. "I'm sorry," she said.

"Forget it."

"I don't care about the history of your name. I just love the sound of it," she said. "Michael Bartok."

"No one has ever called me Michael. I was Mishka to the family and at school."

"Mishka Bartok," she murmured with her lips against his back. "That's even more beautiful. A chromatic melody. It's you."

"It isn't me. It doesn't feel like me. I don't know who it is. My visa says *non-resident alien*. That's me."

"Names are always a problem," Leela said. "They're never you. They're baggage from your parents."

"Mine is lost baggage," Mishka said.

"Wish I could lose mine. I thought about changing it. Changing the Leela, I mean. Obviously anyone who calls me Leela-May is dead on the spot."

"Today is my birthday," Mishka said. "My father died before I was born. The only thing I know about him is that he played the oud. I didn't even know his name until I was eighteen. Each birthday, I ask myself: how will I live without knowing who I am?"

"What I tell people here is that Leela is Sanskrit. Someone told me *lila* is Sanskrit for the Hindu gods at play. I like that. Sport of the gods. I thought of changing the spelling, but why bother?"

"Sport of the gods," Mishka Bartok said. "That's what we are."

2

AFTERWARDS, LEELA REALIZED, the sliver of years she spent with Mishka were radiant fog. That time was without fixed landmarks. He moved into her apartment and she could remember the way the horse-chestnut candles brushed the windows but not what the headlines were saying. There was making love and making music and studying. There were comprehensive exams and dissertations, then post-doctoral fellowships. There were undergraduate classes to teach. From time to time, dreadful news pushed its loutish way in from the street—news of war, terrorists, suicide bombers, random carnage in American cities—but Leela and Mishka muffled such noisy intrusions with passion and their passions were brainy and carnal in equal parts. Leela, high on discovery, would explicate the mathematics of the sound holes of violins; Mishka would demonstrate tonal mysteries of the lute and the oud. Skittish with words but profligate with melodic expression, Mishka composed their lives. "Listen," he would say. "Here is the sound of this morning before you woke up," and he would close his eyes and draw his bow across the strings of his violin.

And how, given Gluck's opening bars to the saga, could Leela have thought that the ending would be other than what it was?

Che farò senza Euridice?

What will I do without that which I cannot do without?

At night, after lovemaking, damp and satiated, Leela would light candles in the bedroom and Mishka would play: sometimes Persian music, sometimes early Baroque, sometimes his own compositions. He would sit naked in the chair by the gable window, backlit by neon updrafts of glare. Their apartment was on the third floor, tucked into the attic of an old Cambridge house. It was just far enough off the Square and off Massachusetts Avenue that police sirens and the urgent mating calls of ambulance vans were percussive but faint, as was the vulgar news of the nation and the world.

If Leela pulled at the sheet to cover herself, Mishka would protest, though not in words. *Please don't do that*, his eyes and the strings would beseech. She thought of him as a kind of musical version of Renoir, as a Modigliani. He worshipped flesh; he painted in cadenza and cantabile, in major and minor mode. She would find scribbled scores under a flower on her desk: sonatinas, rondos, études. *Portrait of Reclining Nude with her Face to the Wall. Nude in Street Light Turning Away.* Mishka's scoring was in heavy lead pencil with cross-outs and cloudy gray areas of erasure. The scores were signed: *To Leela, love Mishka.*

"But I don't turn away," Leela protested. "I never turn away. Why is your music about loss? Why is it always and only about loss?"

"Isn't that what music is for?"

Leela was envious of the oud, of its voluptuous inlaid curves, of the way he held it, of the way it brushed the silk skin of his crotch. She was envious equally of his violin when it nestled in the curve of his neck. She was jealous of his oblivion: of the way he would play a few bars, pause, close his eyes, hear silent and inner music, scribble down notes in a kind of frenzy, cross out, erase, play again. She would move languidly on the sheets and spread her legs. "Come back to bed," she would coax, and though Mishka kept his eyes on bow or plectrum, though he focused on the fingering of chords, his penis would thicken and he would play more violently, tilting at arpeggios, crashing through thickets of thirds and diminished fifths until all his defenses gave way and he surrendered and offered up his instrument as truce flag and laid it down and went to her.

"You shouldn't interrupt," he would reproach, "when I'm composing." He would touch his forehead to hers. "Can you hear the music inside my head? It gets loud when you interrupt."

"I prefer the music of your body."

"The music in my head is *Sonatina for Leela who Interrupts*. It gets loud for fear I'll forget it before I can write it down. If you lie still and quiet—"

"How can I lie still and quiet?"

"Put your ear against my heart.... Like that. Can you hear?"

"Mmm. Syncopation."

"Not my heartbeat. Concentrate."

"What am I supposed to be hearing?"

"The sonatina. Before I have written it down."

"Mishka, you're crazy," she would say tenderly, biting shoulder or buttock or thigh.

"I'm not crazy. Can't you hear it? What's that line about heard melodies being sweet, but those unheard being sweeter? Who wrote that?"

"Keats, I think."

"Keats was right." When he was a child, he explained, in his grandparents' house in northern Queensland, there was never silence. The house was a refuge, remote from the small sugarcane towns, tucked into rainforest. Bird calls by day were noisy; the night birds were sometimes shrill, sometimes muted, always haunting. But over and under the hubbub, Uncle Otto, his grandfather's brother, used to give a command performance every night. After dinner, once the dishes were cleared away, he would play his violin. "Mostly Beethoven or Mendelssohn. We always heard him by candlelight," Mishka said. "That was one of the family rituals. My mother would light the candles and then Uncle Otto would play, but he would never play in front of us. He would never come downstairs. He played in his room, and the door of his room was always shut, but we would stare into the candle flame and hang on every note."

"Why did he stay in his room?"

"He was a recluse. He taught at the Budapest Academy before the war. He was a concert violinist. You can still buy his recordings on the web."

"On vinyl?"

"On vinyl. On old 33s. Otto Bartok."

"And after the war?"

"He never performed in public again."

"Is your Uncle Otto still alive?"

Mishka tapped his forehead lightly with one finger. "Very much so. He's never quiet. I listen to his recitals every day."

"You're very strange, Mishka." She kissed him. She loved the taste of his lips.

"Listen to this," he might say. "It's not finished yet. I'm working on it." He would pull Leela's head toward his chest. He would start humming, but then stop. "Can you hear it?"

"Mmm," she would murmur, humoring him, but sometimes—so certain was his belief in the clarity of the music in his head, so confident was his light tapping of the beat on her skin—she would believe she heard music, but what she heard was always Gluck. When she closed her eyes, she always saw Mishka as she had seen him the first time.

Sometimes, when he sat at the window playing, he would pause, trancelike, and she would catch on his face a look of such sorrow it would alarm her. She would go to him and take his face in her hands. "Don't I make you happy, Mishka?"

"Yes," he would say, burying his face between her breasts. "You make me happy."

"Then why do you look so sad?"

He could not answer this question.

"Tell me about your mother and your grandparents and your Uncle Otto," Leela would prompt.

But he would pick up his violin and play something sweet and mournful. "That is my mother," he would say. "Those are my grandparents. This is Uncle Otto who is really my great-uncle in point of fact."

"How come you don't get letters from them?"

Mishka would bend over his violin. A lullaby, Brahms perhaps, would float across the room. Sometimes, if he did not have an instrument in his hands, he would finger imaginary frets and move an imaginary bow.

Leela reached for the framed photographs on his side of the dresser: his mother with a young man, his grandparents, Uncle Otto.

"Is the man with your mother—?"

"My father. Yes."

"But you said—"

"They never married and he died before I was born."

"You look like him."

"So my mother says."

"I was six when my mother died," Leela said, "but I do remember her. Sort of. Sometimes I still dream she puts lavender on my pillow. She used to do that. And you know what's odd? When I wake I smell lavender."

"My father smelled of spices. So my mother said."

"What else did she tell you about him?"

"He played the oud and sang. That's all I know."

"She's very beautiful, your mother. Is your family orthodox? They look as though they are."

"My mother's a botanist and a painter. She thinks of herself as a secular intellectual."

"But your grandparents and Uncle Otto. Are they orthodox?"

"Not orthodox, but they're observant. They keep Shabbas."

"Tell me about them."

"I'll tell you about the rainforest," he said, and he described the house made of mahogany and silky oak, built on stilts so that tropical cyclones and the flooded Daintree River could pass underneath. He described the verandas reaching out into the treetop canopy, the verandas vivid and noisy with parrots, surrounded by eyes that gleamed in the night. He described the peculiarities of the house, held to be a local wonder along the Daintree River in north-east Australia, because his grandfather had built it with turrets and minarets and gables. "Local people call it Chateau Daintree," he said. "It's not meant as a compliment. It's a regional joke. They even sell postcards of it."

"Do you have a photograph of the house?"

"I'll show you." But he would reach for his violin and play. "This is called *Sonatina for Quandongs and Parrots*."

"What are quandongs?"

"Rainforest trees with berries the color of cobalt."

Leela would close her eyes and hear birds and night creatures and the swaying of treetops hung with blue fruit.

"That is the house in the rainforest," Mishka would say.

"But I want you to show me pictures and give me details. I want you to tell me more about your family."

"I do. My music says everything."

3

"Mishka," Leela said, "tell me about your best friend when you were five years old." She was curled up against him, her breasts against his back, her thighs curved under his buttocks. The moon shone through their bedroom window.

"My best friend was my violin," he said drowsily. "I got it for my fifth birthday and I loved it so much, I used to take it to bed with me." He reached back with his left arm and stroked her leg. "I slept with my arm around it."

"I meant your best human friend."

"My mother, I suppose. Or Uncle Otto."

"I mean a playmate. Another child. Your closest friend."

"I didn't know any other children before I was six."

"Really?" Leela, startled, sat up in bed and leaned over him. "How come?"

"I was six when I started school. Before that, in the rainforest, we didn't live near anyone else."

"How strange."

"It was paradise," Mishka said.

"Well, tell me about your best friend at school."

Mishka sighed. "I didn't have one. There was a boy I wanted to have as a friend but mainly because I was scared of him. His name was Tony Cavalari. He came to play at my house one day and broke my heart."

"What did he do?"

Mishka slid from their bed and reached for his violin. He stood by the window looking out, a dark shape against the gold wash of the streetlight from below. For some time he simply fingered chords without moving his bow, spelling out a memory to himself, and then he began to play. He played so softly she had to close her eyes. Only then could she hear. The melody was slow and lush and full of anguish, the bow—so it seemed to her—damp with its own grief.

"What *was* that?" she whispered.

"That is what happened the day Tony Cavalari came to visit."

"I mean: what was that beautiful piece?"

"Schubert's *String Quintet in C Major*, the second movement. He wrote it weeks before his death. He knew he was dying."

"Oh Mishka," Leela said. She put her arms around him and kissed the nape of his neck. "You live inside a rain cloud. Isn't there anything I can do to shift it?"

"I don't mind rain," Mishka said. "I miss it. In the Daintree it rains every day."

"You remind me of Cobb Slaughter when you talk like that."

"Talk like what?"

"As though happiness is always out of reach."

Mishka turned, frowning slightly. "I'm happy," he said. "You shouldn't assume there's only your way to be happy."

"That's the sort of thing Cobb might say."

"All right," Mishka said quietly. "Since you want me to ask. Who is Cobb?"

"Cobb was *my* best friend when I was five." Leela began, with a strange excess of energy, to tidy up books on her shelves, bringing spines into alignment. "At least that's what I would have said." She offered this as though she had been challenged. "Cobb probably wouldn't have said the same. I'm not sure he ever liked me, even though we were blood brother, blood sister. I mean, we cut ourselves and traded blood, the way kids do. You know how it is."

"No," Mishka said. "I don't know how that is."

"He's like an amputated limb, a phantom limb. I keep thinking I see him, but I'm always wrong. I keep thinking he'll call me one day. When there's a wrong number and no one speaks, I always wonder if it's Cobb."

"What kind of a name is Cobb?"

"In high school, I think he had the hots for me, but he still didn't like me. Once you've traded blood though... well, you know...."

Mishka moved his bow on the strings. The sound was too low to be heard.

"I got into a fight for him once," Leela said. "Not that he thanked me. I could never figure him out."

"You like things you can't figure out."

"We were both fish out of water. Plus we both lost our mothers when we were kids. That was some sort of bond. And we both had this thing about math. I suppose that's why you remind me of him. The way you feel about music, he felt about math."

"Hmm," Mishka said. He closed his eyes and leaned into the music in his head. He fingered chords and moved his bow across the strings. There was no sound. "So what happened to Cobb?" he asked.

"I don't know. I haven't seen him since high school. He went to a military college and then he got into intelligence, code-breaking, that sort of stuff. I know he's done time in Iraq, but I heard he'd got out of the army."

Mishka stopped playing. He busied himself with his violin case. He rosined his bow and clipped it in place. He nested the instrument in its velvet-lined cradle. He snapped the case shut. "So you make inquiries about him?"

"Not really, but I get news. Promised Land's a very small place and everyone knows everyone else."

Mishka took his oud from the corner where it rested in the crook of the wall. His plectrum was as long as a quill. When he plucked at the strings, the sound was deep and resonant and he hummed as he played and the kind of song a peddler of silk carpets might hum filled the room. A thousand and one stories, none of them translatable by Leela, curled about her like smoke from an incense burner. Leela thought that if she rubbed the polished belly of the oud, a genie might suddenly appear. She would ask him if the riddle of Mishka could be solved.

4

THE NIGHT AFTER the Prudential Tower bombing was the first night that Mishka disappeared.

"There was another incident today," the news anchor said, "during the morning rush hour in Boston. Details were captured on security cameras in the underground garage of the Prudential. We warn viewers with children that coverage may be upsetting."

Leela and Mishka had watched the replays, over and over, on CNN, ABC, CBS. In hypnotic state, they seemed unable to stop staring at the same footage that coiled and uncoiled itself in endless loops. They had seen the driver of the cream Toyota— the suicide car—caught on video just before the boom gate went up. He was reaching for his parking ticket. He smiled and gave a victory sign the way a frat-boy clown might act up for a security camera in a dorm. Television close-ups, enlarging the face, were grainy, but the man was young, dark-haired, good-looking. To almost all viewers, in spite of the blurred focus, he looked distinctly Middle Eastern. Footage of the explosion, which occurred five minutes later, was peripheral, but was caught by another video-eye three levels down.

The Toyota had parked in a bay marked B3-C: third underground level in the basement, area C. Viewers saw the mangled cars and the bodies. Concrete pylons had collapsed and a sink hole had appeared in the main floor of the Prudential lobby. Down in the garage there were crevasses and mountains of rubble, flattened cars, hundreds of injuries, but only eleven deaths.

"Oh my God, oh my God," a woman with a bloodied face sobbed. "This isn't going to stop. It's going to keep happening, and no one knows where or when."

At Godiva Chocolates in the Prudential lobby, the store manager said: "Where next? First New York, then DC and LA, then Atlanta, and now Boston. Nowhere's safe." There was a splattered tide-line of chocolate wrack on the wall behind her. "Our stock is ruined," she said. "But what are truffles compared to a life? Not one of our sales clerks was killed. And yes, we'll be open tomorrow. If we folded our tents and crept away, we'd be letting the terrorists win."

"I heard about it on my car radio," a driver in downtown Boston said. "No, it won't make me avoid the Callahan Tunnel. This is just something we have to learn to live with. Suicide bombings are like traffic accidents. You know they could happen any time, but you believe they will always happen to someone else. If you hear about one, you make a detour."

"My daughter lives in Israel," a woman told the roving reporter. "They've had to deal with this kind of thing for years. What can I say? You grin and bear it. You can't let the terrorists win. You have to get on with your life."

A mother was interviewed in Massachusetts General beside the bed of her four-year-old son. An oxygen mask covered the child's face. "Ms. Dawson," the reporter said. "I understand that you were just getting into the elevator on underground level three and that your husband was killed. Do you think the government is doing enough to prevent terrorist attacks?"

The woman turned her ravaged face to the lens. She could not speak. The camera zoomed into a close-up of the little boy inside the oxygen mask, and a strangled sob came from Mishka. He had his knees hugged up to his chest. He rocked back and forth on the sofa like a child trapped inside a bad dream.

"Mishka," Leela murmured, holding him. She could feel him trembling. She turned the television off. "Let's go to bed," she whispered, and they made fierce and desperate love and clung to each other.

Afterwards, Mishka's sleep was turbulent. He groaned and cried out. He warded off blows with his arms. He talked in scattershot bursts, sometimes shouting and keeping Leela's nerves on edge. Most of his words were unintelligible. At certain moments he seemed to be pleading for his life. Twice Leela heard him cry out to his mother and once she heard him plead: *Uncle Otto, I promise I won't open your door.*

She stroked his hair, helplessly, until she too fell into fitful sleep.

Hours later, when she woke in the dark and reached for him, the bed was empty.

"Mishka?" she called.

She groped for the light and checked the bathroom. She checked the landing, the staircase, and the front hall at street level, but he had gone. She noted that his violin was also missing.

He did not answer his cell phone. He did not answer the phone in his office the next day. He did not return until nightfall.

"Where were you?" she asked, baffled, angry, and weak with relief.

"I'm sorry," he said. "I didn't want to disturb you. I went to the Music Lab and played for hours."

"I called the Music Lab. You didn't answer."

"I unplugged the phone. I just wanted to be alone inside my music."

"The entire day?" she asked, astonished.

"I'm sorry," he said. "It's what I do when I'm upset."

"You could play here, Mishka. I wouldn't mind if you played all night."

"I know that, but I have to be alone."

"Is it because of your grandparents and Uncle Otto? Because of the war?"

"I don't know. I suppose so. I'm sorry, Leela, but I did warn you. I don't know how to be normal."

"Normal people bore me to death," Leela assured him.

That was how the absences began.

5

MISHKA MADE LOVE as he made music.

When they made love, Leela believed whatever he said. She wanted to believe.

After each fresh incident, each scene of carnage, she came to expect his withdrawals. The absences grew longer. They grew more frequent. Always the violin or the oud went with him, sometimes both.

"Are you seeing someone else?" she finally asked.

Mishka was offended. "What kind of a question is that?"

"Last night, when you didn't come home, I went to the Music Lab. You weren't there."

"Leela," he said sadly, "I've never once asked you about all the other men before me, though I've heard plenty of gossip."

"They became irrelevant once I met you."

"That's why I've never asked," Mishka said.

"That's not true. You were awfully curious about Cobb Slaughter."

"You wanted to tell me. I didn't ask. I hear there were plenty of men between Cobb Slaughter and me."

"I swear to you, if that's got anything to do with anything, that I have been one hundred per cent faithful—"

"It doesn't have anything to do with anything," Mishka

said. "The boring truth is, I've been playing my oud at Café Marrakesh in Central Square two nights a week."

"The Marrakesh! I love the Marrakesh."

"You've been there?" Mishka seemed slightly alarmed.

"Of course I've been there. It's a stone's throw from MIT. I often meet colleagues there. I knew they had live gigs at night, belly dancers, Middle Eastern musicians and stuff, but I've only ever been there for coffee or lunch. Next time, I'll come when you're playing."

"I'd rather you didn't."

"Why not?"

Mishka sighed. "My music, especially my Persian music... it's just something I like to be alone with."

"You're not alone when you're playing in a club."

"Yes I am. I'm inside my music." He turned away from her. "Leela, I'll move out if you want. I'm afraid I take after Uncle Otto, better heard than seen."

Leela was stunned. "How could you think for a second—?" What she felt was pure panic. What would I do without Orpheus? she wondered. She touched him, hesitantly, and was reassured when the familiar sexual fever engulfed them. "I don't know how I would live without you," she murmured.

"You would survive," Mishka said. "Everyone does. People learn to do without whatever they have to do without." He reached for his violin. He hummed then began to sing. *Che farò senza Euridice....*

"Orpheus survived," he said. "Even though he didn't want to."

Leela realized with shock that she had never before been afraid of losing someone. She had never been jealous. She had never before gone through anyone's pockets or his violin case or his desk.

Not until Mishka's next disappearance had she ever thought of following him.

A few weeks later, there was the incident in the subway: evening rush hour, the Red Line, an explosion between the Park Street station and Harvard Square, chaos.

Leela heard about it in a delicatessen store in the Square. She bought wine and salad and salmon for dinner but as she walked home she was thinking that now Mishka would disappear again. Harvard Yard, and even Massachusetts Avenue, seemed subdued. She walked more slowly. Perhaps she should go back to the Square. Perhaps she should eat in bright company, in the jazz lounge at the Charles Hotel. When she turned into her own side street, which was dark and deserted, she decided: If he's not home, I'll go back to the Square.

Then a black car pulled up and she was ordered to get in. Her cell phone was confiscated. A wall sealed off the back seat from the front and the windows were covered.

There was a man in the back seat beside her. "You will not be harmed," he said, "provided you do not cause trouble. In case you do, as you already know, I have a gun."

Leela felt something cold, like the muzzle of a dog, against her cheek.

She could see nothing.

BOOK II

Cobb

1

SLAUGHTER HAD THE woman taken directly to the interview room. She was locked in and left there alone. A recessed spot in the ceiling cast harsh light on the chair where she sat; the rest was shadowy. Unseen, he watched closely. She did not know where she was, not precisely. She knew only that she must be somewhere in the western suburbs of Boston. She did not know why she had been brought in, but she was not afraid. Not yet. She had never been afraid, as far as he knew, and all his life he had wanted to make her afraid. His reasons were honorable.

Once, back in Promised Land, South Carolina, when they were both what?—fourteen probably, maybe fifteen—and she was still known to all as Leela-May, he'd dreamed they were impaled on thin wooden skewers on a grill. You look like a corncob, she told him. You've got a stick coming out of your head. So have you, he told her. You're a pointy-head know-it-all. In his dream, she couldn't stop laughing, and this enraged him. He shouted with a mouth full of basting sauce: You won't think it's so funny when we're burned to a crisp. His skin was blistering. The roof of his mouth was on fire. His father, the barbeque chef of all nightmares, wore an apron that said *Hot Devil* and his father kept squirting starter fluid—quite superfluously—on the coals. Clouds of flame, mushroom-shaped, rose in layers. They gave off popping sounds and sharp plosive bursts. Even as she roasted in his dream, in *his* dream, Leela couldn't stop making jokes.

Can't you be serious about anything? he demanded.

She should be burned at the stake, his father said.

Leela thought this hilarious.

Shut up! Cobb ordered her. He looked sideways at his father and caught his father's slow smile. Shut up! he said again for the pleasure of pleasing his father. You're non-stop trouble, Leela-May, but you never get punished and I do. It's not fair.

Instantly, within his dream, he regretted the outburst. He regretted the self-pity and the transparent wish. He knew he would pay for both. It was another of her thoughtless crimes: the way he lost dignity in her presence. She had no understanding, she had not the remotest inkling, of the differential: what recklessness cost her, compared with what it cost him. This was not right. Certain things should be required of all or required of none. She should be required to know fear the way he did: as enveloping fog. She should be trapped in it. She should flounder in soupy air so thick and heavy that it settled wetly in the very bones and turned them soft. She should feel the down-suck.

This time, he warned her in his dream, we're both going under.

Going *up*, I'd say, she said. Up in smoke.

Together, he emphasized.

He was almost glad, imagining the headlines: DUAL DEATHS IN BARBEQUE PIT. Or possibly TWIN TRIAL BY FIRE.

There's no escape, he told her; this is the end.

This is the beginning, she laughed, and I know what you're after. You're on fire. You've got smoke in your eyes. So here's what we'll do: I'll pull out your stick if you'll pull out mine and you can baste me with hot sauce and eat me. But first we piss on anyone who doesn't like us, especially anyone who's fanning our flames.

What did I tell you? she said. See how it douses the fire?

And indeed, when the dream-smoke cleared, they'd slithered free of the skewers and onto the coals, and she was sitting on the edge of his bed. He was aware, with shame, of sodden sheets and of the sordid mess of his room. There was a sharp and dreadful smell. Socks? Wet shoes? He prayed he was dead.

"Your father let me in," she told him. "I brought lavender for under your pillow. It's out of our garden and it cools you down."

He pulled a blanket over his head.

"You're burning up with a fever, Cobb. I'm going to get wet washcloths for your forehead and your neck—"

"Don't touch me."

"You're on fire. You need sponging down."

He burrowed under. He wanted the wet mattress to eat him.

"You've missed school for a week," she said.

"He's gone and wet the bed," Cobb's father growled, exasperated, from the doorway.

"Mr. Slaughter, Cobb's dreadfully sick. He needs someone here to look after him."

"You mind your own business, girly. Boy's fine. A fever never did anyone harm. Purifies the blood, is what, and burns off the trash in the brain. He needs sleep, is all, and more self-control."

"He needs praying for," Leela said. "My Daddy will come with the elders for the laying on of hands." She leaned down and whispered in Cobb's ear: "But I'm gonna call Dr. Rabon too."

"Needs self-control is what he needs," Cobb's father said. "You get on outta here, girly. He's stunk up the room."

Thus Cobb had legitimate reasons for wanting Leela to know the wet suck of fear. His motives were moral. He believed this. There were two kinds of people in the world: those who took safety for granted and those who never could because they knew on a visceral level that safety was a rare and capricious thing. The former often—and carelessly—put the latter at unconscionable risk. Survival lay in forcing the careless ones to understand. Cobb wanted to hold Leela's head under water (metaphorically speaking), let her gasp for breath, let her splutter, hold her under again. This is what abjection does to people, he wanted to say. Now you know. Now you can begin to understand.

From the control booth outside the interview room, he watched her for an hour through one-way glass.

"Just like old times," he murmured softly. His words settled as mist on the partition and he erased them with a sweep of his sleeve. In Promised Land, South Carolina, sometimes he had been the watcher, sometimes she had. Nevertheless, he could not have anticipated the present turn of events. It was a coincidence so huge that it was eerie. It was a provocation. What could he make of the sheer symmetry of chance?

This time Cobb Calhoun Slaughter was the one on the outside looking in and Leela-May was the one in the cage.

"Let her sweat," he told the handlers. "Let her stew."

So far, she showed no sign of sweat.

What she showed was the kind of curiosity that had led her into endless close shaves as a child. She still had, in fact, the birdlike demeanor of a child, tugged by a million stimuli. Sometimes he thought she did not know how to switch her nerve ends off. She pecked and darted. Sounds, scents, shapes all pulled at her. Her eyes flew about, she touched things, she smelled her fingertips, she was rarely still. She examined the bright light in the ceiling through half-shut eyes. Apparently this told her something. Apparently all splinters of data were of interest. She assessed the heat of the light on her upraised palms. She pressed her palms against her cheeks.

Now, as in childhood, Cobb envied and was afraid of her kind of indiscriminate curiosity, her *rapacious* curiosity, the kind that had exasperated teachers and rattled neighbors and made them all want to throttle her and made them love her, the kind that had made her own father and the entire congregation of the Church Triumphal of Tongues of Fire—Southern, white, and Pentecostal— hold all-night prayer vigils on her account, the kind that had ensured—to his chagrin—that her school projects were more attention-grabbing than his. In spite of this, in spite of his own fierce need to win, Cobb himself adored her in secret back then and she kept on gate-crashing his dreams.

He remembered their first year in high school when the Math Prize consumed them. His own project on Civil War firearms had demonstrated—with cross-sectioned diagrams and dioramas and hundreds of hours of work and with his father breathing down his neck—that the change from smoothbore muskets (and their paltry 100-yard range) to rifled muzzle-loaders that could kill from a half-mile away was the reason for casualty lists of such frightful dimensions, without precedent in the annals of war. In the lamentable Bloodshed Between the States, the kind of shoulder-to-shoulder Napoleonic charge that smoothbore small-arms required—and this he showed with toy soldiers and the firing of miniature guns, as well as with bar graphs and trajectory equations—was catastrophically retained as a battle technique though technology had gone marching on. The resulting slaughter of such close formations was worse than Waterloo.

He won second prize.

Her project, on the other hand, had involved mathematical pyramids (strange diagrams of numbers, dashes, greater than/lesser than symbols, digits in triangular formations, lines tipped with directional arrows) all of which connected two streams of descendants of the great cotton and rice plantations. One stream listed the black descendants of the white patriarchs and their sons; the other stream listed the descendants of the plantation slaves (that is, those descendants who had two black progenitors). Though both streams of descendants bore the plantation-family name—the Calhouns, the Slaughters, the Boykins, the Hamiltons and Hamptons and such—their paths in life had greatly diverged. Leela was thorough. With the help of the school librarian and of military historians and of black clergymen and schoolteachers, she tracked the offspring of slaves who enlisted (both of those who wore blue and of those who wore gray). She wrote to genealogical societies. She traced descendants of those who escaped and of those who stayed; of those who crossed the Ohio and of those who kept on keeping house for Confederate generals and brigadier-generals, kept on wet-nursing their wedlock children, kept on bearing them other ones too. She won first prize.

Her relentless curiosity, read the citation... *and especially her highly original "probability statistics" linking past family history with present occupation and welfare....*

In short, the judges had been dazzled and bemused.

Her numerical creativity, the citation continued, *is one more tribute to the extraordinary mathematical foundation laid down by the late Corinne Slaughter, a gifted teacher whose loss to this county some years ago is still greatly lamented by fellow teachers, and by parents and students alike*—though not mourned on this particular occasion, the citation might have added, by her mathematically gifted son, since Cobb forgave neither Leela nor his mother for his own second prize.

Cobb's father, a descendant of Confederate Brigadier-General James Slaughter, nephew to President James Monroe, had been incensed and had punched out two of the judges. "Which side are you turncoats on?" his father had shouted. His father stank of corn whisky at the time.

"You should have won, Cobb," Leela-May told him. "You're an engineering genius. These miniature muskets are unbelievable." Her eyes were shining. "Do you have statistics on all this? D'you have the number of smoothbores? Number of rifles? Did only white regiments have the rifles, and black ones the cast-off muskets? D'you know the percentages used in each battle? D'you have deaths from each kind of firearm at each battle? Will you let me see the statistics?"

There was something weird about the way that numbers turned her on. Numbers turned Cobb on too, but only after he had applied them to moving parts and tangible structures. Leela, on the other hand, seemed to find numbers themselves—the ciphers and cryptic symbols—strangely beautiful and full of narrative mystery. Cobb thought that she was slightly and seductively insane, the way his own mother had been. His mother had taught Cobb and Leela and everyone else in Promised Land their earliest math.

Listen to the cicadas, his mother—chalk-smeared and frail—used to urge the second- and third-graders. She would make the children beat out cicada-time with the palms of their hands on their desks. That rhythm is based on prime numbers, she would tell them. She showed them how math could describe the way leaves spiraled around a twig, and could predict how pine cones would fall from a tree, and how waves would make patterns on the sand. Math makes the world go round. Math is the Wizard of Oz, she would say. Math's the magician who pulls secrets out of his hat, but the best of all is, you can learn what his secrets are.

Math was Leela's favorite subject and in the second grade she would hang around after school to talk to Cobb's mother. In later years, in middle school and high school, Cobb began to do better in math than Leela. He had made a vow. He stayed after school and asked Miss Morrow for extra help, though the arrangements were complicated because Miss Morrow had spent years in the North.

"I can't ever let my father find out you're helping me," Cobb explained, "because he knows you taught school in Boston."

"I understand perfectly," Miss Morrow had said. "Your mother was an extraordinary math teacher, Cobb. I know you want to do her proud."

"We could do graphs for each battle, Cobb," Leela suggested on the night of the Math Prize in high school.

The school photographer nudged them closer together. "In front of your battle diorama," he said to Cobb. "Closer. Tilt your heads inwards. Closer. Yes, touching, like that."

Leela draped her arm around Cobb's shoulders. "We could write the Mathematics of the War Between the States," she suggested. "What do you say?"

He wanted to say: "You're nuts," but he could not afford such bald statements. This was the very big difference between them: she could blurt out whatever stray thought crossed her mind; he had to think first. He had to think very carefully. He had to assess consequences. In any case the words would have come out—he was afraid they would have come out—as shamefully thick with worship.

"One more time," the photographer said. "Cobb, put your arm around the winner."

Cobb's father was shambling toward them. Cobb was so nervous, so overcome by Leela's closeness and her praise, that he said the last thing he wanted to say. "You're a Yankee-lover and a nigger-lover, Leela-May. You won because you're full of liberal crap, and Miss Morrow loves that."

"What?" Leela said. "I don't believe you said that. You're nuts. What's the matter with you?"

"Nuts like my father?" he warned, his voice low. He tried to indicate the looming shadow.

"You're nothing like your old man. You're way too smart and way too nice. You're like your mother. You're a math genius like she was."

"Mumbo-jumbo with numbers," his father snarled. "Only judge who could make sense of your bullshit was that Yankee. What *you* need, girly, is a lesson instead of a prize, and I'm going to give it to you."

"You're drunk, Mr. Slaughter," Leela said politely, stepping aside. "You know Miss Morrow was born and bred in Charleston, and if you lay a hand on me, you know my Daddy and the elders will come and pray for you on your own front porch. They'll pray the Holy Spirit down and you'll get Jesused. But I do agree about the prize. I think Cobb should have won."

She never seemed to hold anything against Mr. Slaughter or against anyone at all, for that matter. Leela was strange that way, like all the Pentecostals. Preachers' leeches, Cobb's father called them. Never met someone they couldn't love. They applied themselves to it in the name of the Lord like wetbacks crossing rivers in the night, like Mexicans swimming the Rio Dreamtime because all were precious *etcetera* in God's sight, black, white, or brindle, sober or drunk. Suffocaters, according to Cobb's father, who had trouble breathing when Christian love was on the prowl. They'll pray you to death, he claimed. They're preachers' leeches. You gotta rub salt on them before they'll drop off.

"If one of them sets foot on my porch," Cobb's father regularly announced, "I'll shoot him dead."

"You know you don't mean that, Mr. Slaughter," Leela said.

Cobb felt winded whenever she spoke to his father. This was her primary offense, an act of blasphemy and insurrection on a monumental scale: she never took Calhoun Slaughter seriously. Such disregard endowed her with awesome power in the eyes of Cobb, but it also enraged him. Whatever sort of drunken buffoon his father could be, Cobb never could afford to take him lightly.

Something else: no other living person had the right to take him lightly. Cobb knew what he knew about his father. He did not forgive those who did not hold his father in high esteem.

Cobb was slight in build. There was something in his eyes, something that reminded people of his mother, some reflex of flinching in his muscles that invited taunts. Once, in the fourth grade, Leela intervened between Cobb and a clutch of older boys. Her ferocity was greeted with astonished glee and her underpants were pulled off for punishment and brandished like a flag.

"Just wait, Cobb," Leela promised. "We'll get them."

"Leave me alone," he said, shamed.

But she never left Cobb alone. She was, in fact, immensely curious about both Cobb and his dad. That was the problem. She asked if his father had nightmares about Vietnam. She wanted to know what the military discharge was about. *Dishonorable*, were the whispers that snaked around Promised Land. She asked Cobb point-blank: Was that true?

No, Cobb said. It was *not* true.

Cobb said his father was a hero, and if she didn't believe him—

She believed him, she said. She knew his father was afraid of nothing. She knew demons chased Calhoun Slaughter. She had heard him shouting at them, she had seen him fighting back.

She told Calhoun Slaughter himself that his demons could be cast out if he trusted in the Lord. She asked him what his demons looked like. She asked him if the pulpy hole in his cheek gave him pain. How had it happened? What did he take for it? She was dangerously curious. She was a threat, although she never did ask about Mrs. Slaughter's death.

Once, long ago, Cobb had seen Leela's face at their window, after dark, spying. He was mortified. It was his twelfth birthday and festive days were always dangerous because his father drank in high celebration until the moment—the werewolf moment— that always came. Cobb was expert at divining when that turning point was on the way and at coming up with reasons for leaving the house unobtrusively before the metamorphosis began. On his twelfth birthday, he sensed the moment settling in like a change in the weather and he moved toward the front door and was stunned to see Leela's face at the window. I was bringing you a present, she told him later, but she threw his timing off. He had never forgiven her, in spite of—because of— the stricken look in her eyes and the way she flinched at each lash.

That particular time, Cobb's hands splayed against the wall, his thumb had been broken. He wore a splint and a bandage for weeks, though both were somewhat inexpertly applied by Cobb himself. His thumb never set quite straight and he acquired a cleft nail. Pigfoot was one of his nicknames at school, Split Corncob another.

Mark of the Beast, ran the schoolyard murmur. Cobb's got a cloven paw. His father shot prisoners in the back of the head, the rumor ran. His father beat up on his mother till she killed herself. On nights when the moon is full, you can hear her weeping and you can hear Cobb's father howl like a wolf. One day Calhoun Slaughter will kill his son.

Or possibly, a parallel whisper warned, Cobb will kill the Old Man.

Don't make Cobb angry, children whispered.

Don't go near the Slaughter house after dark.

Neither Leela-May nor Cobb ever spoke of the night of his broken thumb. He knew that his disfigured hand, not Leela, bred the stories. After all, they both lived in crackbrained families; they both lived without benefit of mothers; they both navigated, daily, around highly unpredictable dads. They both could see the billboard thoughts and they could hear those thoughts turning, click click, inside the skulls of every person, child and adult, in Promised Land. There's a kid on a treasure hunt for trouble, people murmured. People read the signs. Old man's a lunatic, they whispered. Allowances have to be made.

So they had that much in common, Cobb Slaughter and Leela-May Moore. In another sense, they had nothing in common at all because on the derangement scale their fathers were at opposite ends.

The next day, after the night of her face at the window, Cobb Slaughter found in his desk a perfect single gardenia and a sand dollar taped to white card. On the card, block capitals in ballpoint ink announced:

THIS IS A LUCKY SAND DOLLAR. IT'S A FREAK. I FOUND IT AT
FOLLY BEACH. IT'S GOT SEVEN PETALS ON THE STARFLOWER
AND SEVEN SLITS INSTEAD OF FIVE. SEVEN IS GOD'S PERFECT

NUMBER. IF YOU PUT IT UNDER YOUR PILLOW, IT WILL
PROTECT YOU SEVEN DAYS OF THE WEEK.

The card was unsigned.

He knew it meant: *I'm a freak, you're a freak. So what?*

He knew it also meant: *Your protection needs are so great,
only magic and God can help.*

He was ridiculously comforted. He was ashamed. He was
furious. He loved her and hated her.

He still had the sand dollar. He kept it with him at all times,
wrapped in a silk handkerchief and protected inside a vintage tin
that had once held loose-leaf tobacco. The tin had been in his
desk drawer in the brief stint in Paris and with him in
Afghanistan and then in Baghdad and now in Boston. He kept
it in the inner pocket of his vest when he felt the need of totemic
power.

He studied Leela closely through the one-way glass. He
had not seen her for fifteen years but he could have picked her
out of a line-up in an instant. He noted that her mane of
coppery hair was shorter, though still unruly. She tossed it in
the same provocative way, daring all comers. Every boy in
Promised Land had wanted her. Many were lured; more than
a few were chosen. He felt abiding hostility toward every last
one of them. When she made out with boys in cars, or on the
veranda of the abandoned Hamilton house, he had hidden
and watched.

Even when Leela was still religious, she was wild.

Now, all these years and miles from Promised Land, she was
examining the interview room, plotting escape routes perhaps,
or calculating the ratio of walls to floor, who knew? Slaughter
could see her squinting, lining up points with her thumb,
assessing dimensions. There was not much to see: four walls, no

windows, a table, two chairs, a microphone, tape recorder, bare floor, everything a pale institutional green. Once the door was closed, the room appeared seamless. There was neither handle nor lock on her side. Inevitably, of course, she looked at—she looked through—the black plate of glass. All the detainees did that, as though staring would make it a window.

Slaughter savored this moment. The interview room, which was the phrase his team used in logs and documentation, gave him pleasure. He liked being outside and looking in. Whoever was in the interview room deserved to be there. They had given good cause. They needed to be shown—no, more than that, they needed to experience bodily the fact that carelessness in matters of national safety had consequences, and the consequences were costly. It angered Slaughter that certain kinds of people were so casual, so unaware. His duty was to make them aware and he took it seriously.

He liked the fact that whoever was in the room knew he was being watched, understood that she was being studied like a germ on a microscope slide, but as to *who* was watching or *why*... there the room's occupant was either uncertain or had no clue. Very quickly, however, that occupant—any occupant—dredged up likely and unlikely reasons by battalions. So the space and the waiting were like the forecourt of Judgment Day or like a Rorschach Test. Sins recalled or simply fantasized or buried deep in the mud of shame swarmed like bees. Sometimes detainees batted at them or covered their faces with their hands. Cobb himself called the room Bonbec, a private joke picked up on his NATO stint in Paris, and the nickname caught on though no one else knew what it meant.

Leela was looking at him so directly, so intensely, with such a well-remembered air of challenge, that he felt alarm. He had the uneasy sensation that she saw him and that she saw through him. Instinctively, he moved back from the glass. Leela crossed her arms and tipped her chair away from the table. She smiled slightly and nodded, as though she guessed the rules of this game. He was certain she would have written something sassy on the wall in lipstick if she'd had any with her.

She pulled the microphone toward her. "Is this how we begin?" she asked.

He did not answer.

"Am I supposed to get the ball rolling?"

Silence.

"What kind of confession are you after?" she demanded, and then she laughed. "Sexual? Social? Mathematical? You want a list of my speeding tickets? A list of equations I've never been able to solve?" She gave him the finger, but in a manner more flirtatious than obscene. She smiled and puckered her lips. She blew him a kiss. She pushed the microphone away from her again. She walked around the room and felt the walls, which were padded and gave slightly to the touch. After this, she sat again and folded her arms and closed her eyes. She was in—or appeared to be in—such a perfect state of repose that she gave the impression of sleep. He imagined her solving quadratic equations in her head.

We'll see who lasts longer, he thought. We'll see who blinks first.

This had always puzzled him: the way she could move from being wired to being still. The transition was always sudden. His theory was that she simply could not switch herself off until her batteries burned out. In the third grade, the fourth grade, other children would chant: *Leela-May's got ants in her pants.* And then, quite suddenly, she would be somewhere else, staring out the window in a brown study until a teacher, baffled, would loom beside her and slap a ruler against her desk and say

sharply *What planet are you on, Leela-May?* and Leela-May
would startle and say something predictably strange, such as
*I'm sorry, Miss Bostick, but I was thinking about the eleven-
times multiplication table and I was wondering what eleven
means and why it behaves the way it does.*

Slaughter looked at his watch. She had been brought in at
10 p.m. An hour had passed.

He looked at her lips. The lips, he had learned, were a
giveaway; the lips and the corners of the eyes. For those who
feigned indifference to cover their fear, it was the tiny muscles
and involuntary twitches that betrayed. As the minutes ticked
by, the twitching would increase and he would count the
convulsions of the nerves. Tapping feet were a further sign.
Some of his men—all of whom had had experience in
Baghdad and in Afghanistan and in other undisclosed
locations—kept scores and a record book: number of minutes
before fidgeting set in; number of hours before compulsive
jiggling of the legs.

At midnight, she remained as still as a lake becalmed.

He had done considerable preliminary research. He had
always kept tabs on her in a general sense and for purely
personal reasons. When he thought about it, he owed her a
lot, though the debt was, he supposed, perverse. The desire to
overtake and surpass her remained strong. His own curiosity
quotient—the furtive subterranean kind—was what drove his
career. There was always someone from Promised Land who
had seen someone who had seen Leela-May, or who had
talked to her sister or her father, or who had chatted to
someone who'd had a letter, and she was always that wild girl
who turned out, to the fond bewilderment of all, to be
practically a genius, it seemed: first Harvard, then MIT, no
one could understand what she did. There was never any

shortage of enlisted men from Promised Land—marines, navy, air force, grunts (black and white, but more often black)—and he would bump into them and have a drink and pick up news of back home. And now that Cobb himself, like so many, had graduated to a private security force—the financial perks being considerable, especially from those corporations rebuilding key industries in war-torn zones and from those which felt equally nervous and insufficiently safe from sabotage at home—now that he was corporate and private, getting news was simpler than getting good Southern grits. So, though he had not seen her since high school, Cobb had kept track.

They had both moved out of state: Cobb to Virginia Military Institute on ROTC money; Leela on a math scholarship to Boston. Cobb always had her current address. He had her number. From time to time, late at night, he would call. Usually he got her answering machine. Her voice smelled of browning gardenias and school cupboards and chalk and locker rooms. If she herself answered, he did not speak but he did not hang up. He waited. Cat got your tongue? she would say. Or she might ask, lightly: Are you a deep breather? When you call back, leave a message on my answering machine and I'll pass it on to Ma Bell.

He did not call very often, never more than three or four times a year, and always from different public telephone booths.

Now, however, was different. Now he had access to her emails, to incoming and outgoing calls, to transcripts of same, to her credit card transactions, her library borrowings. He had photographs. He was looking forward to the moment when he would say casually: You could have been a porn star. And then, when her eyes widened, he would say: I could get you started. I could post these on the net and you'd be flooded with calls. Bound to pay a lot better than teaching college kids math which is the only thing in store when your post-doc runs out.

She believed she was safely walled up in her ivory tower on a remote peak of higher mathematics. He wanted to tell her: Your grasp of reality has always been slight. You've always had your head in the clouds. You've never fully grasped the situation for people who live on the ground.

She had moved on from Pure Mathematics to the Math of Music. He had photocopies of articles that she had published: "Waves and Harmonics"; "Mathematical Frequencies and the Cultural Construction of the Twelve-tone Scale"; "Mathematical Signatures of Bach, Beethoven and Brahms"; "Trigonometric Identity in the Compositions of John Cage"; "Development of the Sound Holes in Violins: a historical and mathematical perspective". He'd read some of the pieces twice, hunting for intimate revelation, but the reasoning and the equations were opaque. Whatever she was talking about, it was not his kind of math.

What he did know was that numbers to her, as to him, were secret codes. She read messages in them. She used them to encrypt the notes she sent.

Cobb read, and listened to, thousands of messages every day. He collected codes. He deciphered them.

He believed that Leela—possibly without her own knowledge—was being used to encode information of a dangerous kind.

Watching her through the one-way glass, he focused on her lips and on her closed eyes. How could she manage such stillness? Was she counting? What could possibly be going through her head?

Cobb fingered the tobacco tin in the inside pocket of his vest. He studied Leela's lips as he had covertly studied them in junior high from two rows away. He had still wanted to please her in junior high. Then he had simply wanted to make her take notice. And then he had wanted to punish her for the casual way she flouted rules: meeting boys behind the derelict Hamilton house, making out with them on the weed-choked veranda, swimming in the creek with no attention to propriety whatsoever, swimming with black boys and white trash. He saw her day after day on the Hamilton veranda with Benedict Boykin whose father, after Vietnam, became the mailman and a member of the NAACP. Leela and Benedict Boykin smoked cigarettes. They sat on the rotting floorboards and leaned back to back against each other. Sometimes they kissed. Cobb, behind azalea bushes, could hear them laugh. They rode buses with banners on the side. They marched on the State House in Columbia and listened to speeches about the Confederate flag. Back then, it still flew above the State House dome. The flag must come down, they chanted.

The demonstrations enraged Cobb's father. "Sherman's thugs," his father said, "may have burned our fields, but they can't burn that flag from sacred memory. Or off of our bodies either." He flexed the tattoo on his arm.

Leela put a sticker on her locker: *Take it down! The war ended in 1865.*

The day after her sign was posted, Cobb shaved his head. He had a flag—a Confederate flag—and a rattlesnake tattooed on his arm and that worked.

It worked spectacularly.

Leela stared at him, at his right bicep, and at the coiled rattler on his right forearm, all through math class. The rattler was the *Don't Tread on Me* snake of the Sons of Liberty flag.

Leela penciled a question mark on her notebook and flashed it at Cobb. The interrogative curve was a snake, the dot below it a drop of poison from its fangs.

Sons of Liberty, Cobb wrote on his own notebook. *Revolutionary flag*. He held up the page.

Duh! Leela wrote. *I know that. But why?*

Cobb turned away to hide his smile. He never looked at her again but he could feel her watching him all afternoon.

She caught up with him after school. She drew alongside on her bike. He pedaled faster, but so did she. It became, pure and simple, a race, with the finish line at the Slaughters' front porch and the result a dead heat.

"You better watch out for my father," he said.

"Why, Cobb? *Why?*" she asked.

"Because he'll shoot anyone comes on our porch before he even thinks about it, especially preachers' leeches and types who suck up to the NAACP."

"I mean, why'd you shave off your beautiful hair? And why did you get the tattoos?"

"Doesn't heritage mean anything to you?"

"It just isn't you, Cobb." She was genuinely puzzled. "It doesn't make sense. It isn't you."

"You don't know anything about me. You don't know me at all."

"I know you go nuts every once in a while. I know you take after your mom."

"I do not take after my mother. I'm nothing like her. You think you're smarter than I am at math, but you're not."

"I don't think that at all. I know you're smarter. But Miss Morrow thinks we'll both get into Ivy League."

"I wouldn't go to a Yankee college if they paid me."

"What's got into you, Cobb? What's happening to you?"

I saw you kissing Benedict Boykin, he might have said.

And she would have said: *So?*

"Don't tread on me," he warned. "You don't know the first thing about me."

"I know you're not making sense. But I admire the way you're always loyal to your dad even though—"

"Get out!" he shouted. "Get out before I get my dad's gun."

She could not think of a single joke. She could think of nothing to say. She stared at him and then she turned her bike around and rode away.

2

LEELA OPENED HER eyes when he entered the room but she did not otherwise move. The ski mask startled her—he saw the widening of her eyes—but otherwise her body was relaxed. Her ankles were crossed and her arms folded. She leaned slightly back in the vinyl chair which gave a little under the pressure though her weight was slight. In all the years since he had seen her, Cobb thought, she could not have put on more than five pounds. He, on the other hand, was considerably heavier. He knew that the shape of his face had changed. His body, which was hard and muscled, bore no relationship to that of the skinny kid he had been at school. One glance was enough to reveal, back then, that he was the kind of child who got picked on.

No one would pick on him now.

Leela focused on the eye holes in the mask. Her gaze was intense and unwavering. His face felt naked. On his left hand, he wore a close-fitting leather glove.

Even if he were to remove the mask, he thought it possible she would not recognize him, particularly since he had a military buzz cut (although it was true she had once seen him—for several weeks—with shaven head.) That act of attention-getting having served its purpose, he had let his thick hair grow back. It was dark and wavy and a hank always fell across his brow and she had turned one day and collided with him as he passed her locker. He had been avoiding her for weeks, ever since the standoff when he'd threatened to get his father's gun, but on this day he walked past the girls' lockers by design. She was reaching for her books, her back to the hallway, at the moment of impact.

"Hey," she said, "watch where you're—oh, Cobb!" She put her hand on his arm. That was something she did instinctively: she touched people when she spoke to them.

"I'm so glad you let your hair grow back. You look great." She stood close and he could smell her breath, sweet and citrusy, as though she had just drunk orange juice. "You look like you again," she said.

He wanted to do something intense and passionate and possibly violent. He thought of biting her lips. He thought that he could not bear for the searchlight of her attention to flicker or move on.

"I've missed you," she said, and then he thought of what to do.

He held her gaze steadily and coldly until her warmth turned to uncertainty and she withdrew her hand from his arm and stepped back a little, and then he walked on without speaking. His heart was racing. He felt that a victory had been chalked up. He felt something as decisive as a power surge in every nerve. There had been a transfusion, a reverse flow of energies: he was soaked with her power; she was flooded with his anxiety. He felt in such a state of excitation that he barely reached the men's bathroom in time. He did not even have to touch himself before he came.

He invented a word for the sensation: *switch-flow.*

In the interview room so many years later, watching her bounce lightly against the back of the vinyl chair, languorous, swaying as a waking sleeper sways, he felt the old blood-rush coming on. He was addicted to switch-flow. He had the sensation that his ears were on fire. Hot needles, in small battalions, were pricking his extremities—his fingers, his toes—and advancing like shock troops toward his crotch. Adrenalin lurked in odd places when the switch-flow tide was on the rise.

He was skilled at feeding his addiction.

In high school, he had become an enigma to her. This was the weapon he could always count on because he knew she could not leave puzzles alone. He bothered her. She was preoccupied with him. He knew it from her perplexed smile when she looked at him. He did not return her smile and this puzzled her further. His status was assured. He settled into his niche and was warmed by it. It felt permanent.

Knowledge was power: she had taught him that.

Secret knowledge—knowledge illicitly gained and kept private—was absolute power, and for that awareness also, he had Leela to condemn and to thank. Her face at the window on the night of his broken thumb, the night of which she never spoke, not to him nor to anyone else (he was confident of that), had given sudden meaning to his life. It had shaped his career.

If I were to tell… her silence said, *though I never would….*

He knew with absolute certainty that she would never even be tempted to tell, that the possibility would never enter her head, that she could no more think of telling than she could fly. Nevertheless, the hold she had over him because of that night was intolerable. It was also the very thing that made the tripping of the switch so intense. She would come to understand that. Lesson One was about to begin.

"I keep reading about this," she said, coming to life.

"Random interrogations. A lot of bloggers claim they're not official at all, they're rogue vigilante groups, ex-military types, that kind of thing." She leaned forward and rested her elbows on the table. "Everyone's understandably paranoid these days, it's a national epidemic, isn't it? Still, I've assumed the bloggers were conspiracy nutters." Her focus on the eye holes in his mask was intense. "But then, it's never happened to me before. I've never had a gun held against my head before." She waited for his response, and when there was none, she said, "And then again, suicide bombers tip us all toward conspiracy theories."

She was turned on again.

So was he.

They were at the lip of the switch-flow falls.

Would she recognize his voice? Unlikely. Did he want her to? Yes. No. Not yet. Not until he was ready. *I know things about you that no one should know. When you know that I know them, you will squirm. You will find the situation unbearable but there will be nothing you can do.*

"This is all very strange," she said. "I suppose it's to do with yesterday's subway bombing?"

"I have some questions. Your answers will be recorded."

She frowned, her monitoring of details unwavering. "You remind me of someone. Do I know you?"

He did not look at her. He said nothing. He took the chair opposite, on the other side of the table, and switched the tape recorder on.

"Name," he said.

"Have we met somewhere? Your voice sounds familiar."

"Name."

"You mean you don't know it?"

"State your name."

"Obviously you already know it. You don't arrest people in the middle of the night and put them in a car with blackened windows and take them on long rides in circles around Boston and to God knows where without knowing who they are."

"You are not under arrest."

"I'm glad to hear it. You would have been in multiple violations of due process if I were. So what exactly am I under, apart from duress?"

He busied himself with knobs and dials, his voice bureaucratic. "You have been brought in for questioning on issues pertaining to terrorist acts."

"You mean the Park Street incident." She leaned closer, intimately conspiratorial. "If you bring in people at random, that's okay. Well, it's not okay, but these days it's better than being on the casualty lists. On the other hand, if I'm supposed to have any information on the incident, I regret to tell you somebody must have screwed up because I'm a dead waste of your time. But if you tell me who you think I am and what murky connection you think I have to the bombing, then I'll tell you who I really am and what I actually do, and I'll state my full name for your machine there. Then maybe you can figure out who screwed up."

She was behaving the way she behaved in his dreams. Was this a dream? In a small spasm of anxiety, he applied tests: he pushed REWIND and PLAY.

You are not under arrest, his own voice said.

I'm glad to hear it. You would have been in multiple violations of due process due process due process—

He pushed STOP.

He had the dream-sense of moving underwater, of wading through sand, of being unable to make things happen, of being impotent. He could never make the dream scripts come out right. He could never make switch-flow happen in his sleep. *You won't think it's so funny*, he kept warning in dreams, but she kept on insisting it was.

He almost shouted at her: *A normal person would be alarmed*. A normal person, at the very least, would be either frightened or outraged. What was the matter with her fear index? How was it possible, given what had happened to her in the course of the last few hours, to be so unperturbed? He wanted to ask: *What's your trick?*

But he probably knew the answer. Her trick was that there was no trick. She would not know what he meant. She had the alarming sort of innocence and the wide-eyed insatiable curiosity available only to the genius, the idiot, and the child. She could be all or any of those. In that instant of realization, he felt something shift at the bottom of the deep well where his own sorrows and angers roiled. He saw that he had never been an innocent child. That luxury had never been his.

"Your machine's stuck," she said helpfully. "It's in a loop. Loops are fascinating phenomena, especially to mathematicians, which is what I am. Do you know what a 'strange loop' is, mathematically speaking?"

"Ma'am, this is not a game." He spoke sharply but his voice caught and he had to clear his throat. "State your name."

"*Ma'am!*" She laughed. "You're a Southerner." She reached across the table and touched his arm. "I know you. I know you from somewhere. Where are you from?"

"Don't touch me." His gesture was violent.

"Hey," she said, eyebrows raised. "Sorry. I'm not infectious with anything except the Deep South, but you'd be immunized. Hard to shake off, isn't it?"

"State your name," he shouted. The shout was involuntary, and shocked him.

"Gosh, okay," she said. "Take it easy."

She did this every time: made him lose dignity. He wanted to strike her. There were always and only two outcomes: switchflow or surrender.

"My name is Leela-May Magnolia Moore, per my birth certificate. My driver's license, which I'll be happy to show you, says only Leela Moore and anyone who calls me Leela-May these days is dead on the spot. But since you've also left the South and tried to disguise your accent, none of that will come as any surprise. I bet you have at least two names yourself."

"Place of birth?"

"Promised Land, South Carolina. Know it? Small town near the coast, but close enough to the capital—"

"Subject states for the record—"

"What record am I stating for? Are you FBI or Homeland Security or one of those rogue vigilante forces or what?"

He opened a drawer on his side of the table and extracted a loose-leaf ring binder. "For the record: interrogator has introduced the folder of photographic evidence to show subject and to gauge her response."

"Where am I, by the way?"

"I am going to show you a series of photographs," he said, "and I'm going to ask you whether or not you can identify the subjects in the photographs."

"Sure," she said. "Fire ahead. I'm terribly curious to find out who I'm supposed to know and what I'm supposed to have done. But before I look at your photographs, I would like to know where I am."

She was like a pit bull. He felt challenge and irritation in equal parts. "Bonbec," he said without thinking.

"Bonbec?" She frowned and made a compass with her hand on the table, her thumb as fulcrum. She described an arc, calculating something. "I know I'm still somewhere in Greater Boston, not far off 128, I'd say. I know we took the Mass Pike because we slowed for the toll, and even though your driver had an EZ pass I kept count of the slowdowns and booths. My specialty happens to be the mathematics of sound—well, of music in particular, which is simply one highly codified branch of the mathematics of vibrations—and there's a precise mathematical relationship, you know, between the sound of tire revolutions per minute on the pike and on 128, where they are quite different, and on the secondary roads, where they are different again, and on the off-off roads to the secondary, and so on. I'd say we made at least one complete revolution of the city on Route 128 in a rather silly attempt to confuse. And now I'd say we're west or north-west of Boston on one of those off-off roads, out beyond Waltham is my guess. So is Bonbec a new subdivision? Or is it some sort of private bunker? One of those empty warehouses taken over by rogue security corporations, as some bloggers claim?"

He was studying a photograph in the binder. Perhaps it was taken in her bedroom, perhaps the room of her lover. Because of the darkness, there were green shadows at the pillowy edges, but the curves of flesh were like cream.

"The only Bonbec I actually know of is in the Conciergerie in Paris," she said. "Not a helpful association."

"On the contrary."

She stared at him. "Bonbec is the tower where they tortured people to make them talk."

"Correct."

"You intend a connection?"

Silence.

"I'll take that as a yes," she said, "though I can't think of anything sicker. D'you know what *bonbec* means? The word itself?"

He had imagined her often in tangled sheets, as in the photographs. He had imagined her with various lovers, himself included. He had watched her, sometimes, from behind the azalea bushes, cavorting on the Hamilton veranda. He had seen boys tearing at her clothes.

"*Bonbec* means 'good beak'," she told him. "That is, a beak that sings well, a mouth that won't shut up under torture."

"Yes." He looked up from the photographs. "You are sweating," he noted. Mentally, he put a checkmark in his own column on the switch-flow scoreboard.

"That excites you," she observed, fascinated. She was watching him closely.

One: one, he thought.

Switch-flow was a switchback ride, and because it was never simple, the thrill was high. Switch-flow took focus; it took concentration; it took skill. It was like whitewater rafting. A player could drown.

"You have beads of perspiration on your upper lip," she said. "Of course, the ski mask itself must make you sweat, but I'd say there was also some excitation involved."

He said vehemently: "Freedom and safety have a price tag." He would have preferred calm. He would have preferred ironic disdain. He would have preferred not to have sounded so furious. "That's the meaning of Bonbec. Bonbec is where traitors were induced to confess before they undermined the public good."

"*Induced* to confess. That's one way of describing torture."

"I take it that the rash of recent incidents and civilian deaths don't bother you."

"They horrify me."

"But you don't believe atrocities require strong measures."

"I *do* believe atrocities require strong measures."

"That's what we're engaged in at Bonbec. Taking strong preventative measures."

"Strong measures are one thing. Torture is quite another. If I were you, I wouldn't call an interrogation room Bonbec. That's pretty sick. Not to mention bad PR for democracy and civil rights."

"There are people who put themselves outside the pale. You've been brought to Bonbec for good reason."

"I see," she said, shaken. "And of course mistakes are never made."

"No one is brought in without substantial cause. Interrogation determines what comes next."

"I see." She put her elbows on the table and leaned her chin on her interlaced hands. She flexed her fingers so that her fingernails and the backs of her digits touched her cheeks. She took in a long deep breath and released it slowly. She studied his eyes. She nodded with the air of a puzzle solved mournfully. "You like making people afraid." Her body relaxed. "That's what this is about."

"It is about national security," he said.

"Oh right. I forgot."

It was the dismissiveness which got to him. He thumped his fist on the table. "Why aren't you scared?"

Her eyebrows shot upwards. "What have I got to be scared about *here*? I'm scared of suicide bombers, but I don't know the slightest thing about the Park Street incident, so I know this is all a big mistake." She frowned. "But of course I've been assuming all this is legitimate and therefore rational.

Do you mean why aren't I scared of *you*?" She pondered the question, taking it seriously. "I think I might be now, as a matter of fact. At least a bit. I think you are scary, and that makes you interesting, because when weird things happen, I get curious. I can't help myself. The unexpected turns me on, the way scaring people does you. Why is that? I mean, why do you enjoy trying to make other people frightened? Is it just the power?"

"No," he said. He could see a wall of high-school lockers behind her. She was extremely interested in his answer. She was waiting. "I want to know what happens when other people believe they've done nothing wrong, but sense they'll be penalized anyway. When they realize deep down they are powerless." He had not meant to say this. He had not meant to say anything at all.

"Fascinating. But we are never without power," Leela said. "Especially when we know we've done no wrong."

Agitated, he raked the gloved fingers of his left hand over his head, a reflex, expecting to feel the soft stubble of his hair. He had forgotten the mask. He fumbled with the photographs in the folder—they were all eight by ten, black and white, with a matte finish—and extracted one. "Do you know this person?" he asked.

Leela was surprised. "That's Berg. He was my PhD supervisor and now he's supervising my post-doc. What's he got to do with anything?"

"You meet with him regularly."

"Of course I meet with him regularly. We're working on a grant proposal together."

"Are you aware of the nature of his work?"

"I just told you. We're working on a joint project. We're in the same field: the mathematics of sound, vibration patterns, harmonics. It's not exactly rocket science. It's not exactly national security either, for that matter, unless you happen to think Bach or the history of violin construction is of interest to the CIA."

"The mathematics of vibration patterns is of considerable interest to the CIA."

"Come again?"

"Don't be disingenuous, Dr. Moore. It doesn't wash. Intelligence agencies employ mathematicians for codes and code-breaking."

"So professors and post-docs in math are a security threat?"

"The following recruiters have approached you—"

"Okay, okay," Leela admitted. "They trawl all the Ivy League schools. Like most of my colleagues I've been approached, and I'm sure you know I turned them down. So did Berg, I happen to know. Turn them down, I mean. Is that why I've been brought in?"

"Why does Berg stalk you?"

"Don't be ridiculous."

Cobb placed another photograph on the table: an urban street scene. In the foreground, at a table in a sidewalk coffee shop, Leela was lifting a tiny cup of Turkish coffee to her lips. Across from her, his back to the camera, was a man.

"That's Café Marrakesh," she said. "So? And speaking of stalking, who's taking pictures of me?"

Cobb extracted a magnifying glass from the drawer on his side of the table. He handed it to her. "Examine the reflection in the coffee-shop window at the extreme right edge of the photograph," he said.

Leela focused through the curved lens. She could see a shadowy doorway: the entrance to a small shoe-repair store on the other side of the street. In the doorway, half-hidden, was a man. She squinted. She moved the lens closer to the image then further away. The man was Berg.

"This means absolutely nothing," she said. "This is Central Square, for God's sake. Hundreds of MIT students and faculty are there every day. So Berg took his shoes to be repaired while I happened to be across the street. He probably never even saw me. And what if he did?"

Cobb put another photograph on the table.

The shot was an aerial one. It appeared to have been taken at dusk: a deserted street, store fronts, huddled three-decker houses, an empty lot. There were only two figures in the street. One was walking down the middle of the roadway itself, level with the empty lot; the other was two blocks behind, on the sidewalk, a shadow that clung to the houses.

"And now the close-ups from this aerial shot," Cobb said. "First of you, in front. You recognize yourself, I'm sure. And then of your follower, Berg."

"This doesn't make sense," Leela said. "What proof do you have that these close-ups are of the figures in the other photo? Those blobs could be anyone."

"You remember this street? What's the name of this street?"

"I have no idea."

"You remember that you walked there alone?"

"I often walk in the evening. I like walking. I'm getting exercise. I'm thinking. I'm solving equations in my head. I'm not reading street signs."

Cobb reached for the magnifying glass and handed it to her. "Look at the aerial shot. Look at the second figure. Look at the doorway of that house he's huddling against. Look at the length of the man's shadow. Now look at the doorway and the shadow in the close-up."

Leela's concentration was intense. She studied each image in turn. She held the glass at varying heights.

"Well?" he prodded. "Do they match?"

"They match," she said quietly. "I don't understand why he'd be following me. It doesn't make sense."

"You were both going to the same place," Cobb said.

"When I'm walking, I'm just walking for the exercise. I'm not going anywhere."

"This is a back street a few blocks north of the T stop in Central Square," Cobb said. "You were going somewhere that night. You were going to the mosque on Prospect Street."

Leela stared at him and in the flicker of surprise and unease that crossed her eyes, he knew the seesaw had begun to tip. He had an odd and intense sensation of water swirling about his ankles: the switch-flow tide on the rise.

Leela said quietly, "I didn't *know* that's where I was going. I was—" she skipped two beats; he could practically see the quick editing inside her head—"meeting a friend."

"You were following someone who was going to the mosque and Berg was following you."

Leela met his eyes steadily; or rather, she stared at the eye holes in his mask, unblinking. She said nothing.

Cobb drew another photograph from his folder and placed it in front of her. "You were following this man," he said. "Who is he?"

Leela seemed reluctant to look. Instead, she gazed at the wall above her interrogator's head but her focus was clearly not in the room. Cobb noted the tic at the corner of one eye, the twitching nerve in her lip. He picked up the photograph—a view of the back of a walking man—and held it in front of her face. The man's hair was thick and dark, as Cobb's used to be, though the hair of the man in the photograph was dense with loose curls. He wore jeans and a white shirt. There was nothing to give a sense of scale. There was no way to tell if the man was tall or short.

"Who is he?" Cobb demanded.

"I haven't a clue," she said. "He could be you."

"You were following him. Who is he?"

Leela looked at Cobb through half-closed eyes as though she were succumbing to a drug. "How can I tell? I can't see the face."

"We both know his name," Cobb said.

"Do we indeed?"

"Unless you don't know the name of the man you've been living with for the past few years."

Leela put her elbows on the table and laced her fingers and leaned on her interlaced hands. Cobb observed a slight tremor at her fingertips. "I had no idea my private life was so important," she said. "Do tell me the name of the man I'm living with."

"Mikael Abukir."

"What?" She burst into involuntary laughter.

"Though it's possible you know him by a different name."

Cobb had her now. Certainty was leaving her like air from a punctured balloon. Nothing gave him more pleasure than to watch confidence ebb from the supremely self-assured.

"What name do you know him by?" he asked.

She tapped the photograph. "This is a picture of the back of a man who could be anyone. I can't see the remotest connection with the man I live with."

"Hmm," he said. He extracted two more photographs from the folder. "Here is a frontal view of the man you were following to the mosque. And here's yet another view in which I would have said you were intimate." He saw the flash in her eyes: the shock of invasion and violation. "But perhaps they all look the same to you," he said. He could feel a power surge beginning at the soles of his feet. "You could have been a porn star," he added lightly. He was electric with switch-flow. His nerves sucked energy from the air. He placed more photographs of intertwined bodies before her. "You know him as Mishka Bartok," he said. "You've been living with him for several years, but he has a tendency to disappear from time to time. To be absent for an entire night or even longer."

"He's a musician. He plays at the Marrakesh."

"He has another life. He's involved with a Muslim Youth Association which has ties to Hamas and to assorted extremist groups."

"That is impossible," she said. "That is absolutely ridiculous. He's Jewish!"

Cobb produced another photograph. "Then it's very strange, don't you think, that he's so warmly received by this group of young men?"

"Who are we kidding? Anyone can engineer that sort of photograph these days, on a computer. Mishka's not in the least religious, and he's not political. He's a composer. He's a violinist. He plays the oud."

"An Islamic instrument."

"He has a scholarly interest in the difference between Western and Eastern music. He has a post-doc at Harvard and teaches there, for heaven's sake."

"That is his cover."

"His *cover?*" She stood abruptly and knocked over her chair. She laughed nervously. "I feel as though I've been kidnapped by Cloud Cuckoo Land. Music is Mishka's passion. It's his whole life. I have never known anyone less political. I have never known anyone less connected to the real world at all. Mishka's not like ordinary mortals."

"No, he's not like ordinary mortals."

"Why are you doing this?"

"He keeps disappearing for hours and days at a stretch, doesn't he? Which is why you followed him. And now you know he goes to the mosque off Central Square. Which, by the way, was behind yesterday's incident at Park Street."

"It's the *music* he's interested in."

"The bomber's body has been identified. He's another Harvard graduate student named Jamil Haddad. Haddad is an engineering student, but strangely enough, he's auditing the same course in Persian Classical Music that your lover is auditing, and Jamil Haddad's involvement with the Prospect Street mosque is well documented."

Leela, agitated, gathered up the spread of photographs as though they were contaminated and turned them face down. She slammed the palm of her hand on the white backs of photographic paper. "Who took these? Did you take these?"

"No," he said. "I receive and interpret the data. I don't gather it."

"Who gathers it? Who took these? Who's been following me?"

Cobb leafed through yet more photographs in his folder.

"Answer me," Leela demanded. "Who's spying on me?"

"Your Dr. Berg is obviously spying on you." Cobb smiled. "Which interests us greatly. We've got him under surveillance too."

He watched the impact of this information.

"Your hands are shaking," he said. Leela was flustered; but he had yet to make her afraid. "The question that troubles me is this," he said. "How much of your affecting ignorance of Mikael Abukir's true identity is real and how much is fake? How much of it is your cover?"

"My—?" She began to laugh but the sound turned into something like a hiccup and she seemed on the point of choking. He had, for an instant, rendered her speechless.

She recovered. "I guess you'll just have to keep stalking me to find out," she said tartly. "You'll have to keep paying your goons to take photos with a telescopic lens."

"Oh, we have been," he said quietly. "We've been making inquiries. We have quite a list of former lovers. You really could have been a porn star."

"Those relationships are far in my past."

"We're well aware that your proclivities for sexual cruising changed quite suddenly once you picked up Abukir and bedded him." He smiled. "I could, of course, post the recent erotic scenes on the net. Or I could mail them to MIT to demonstrate, let's say for a tenure committee, how truly multi-talented you are."

"Clearly you are not restrained by a sense of decency."

"Clearly, neither are you," he said with more bitterness and energy than he'd intended. "Of course, none of this publicity will be necessary if we have your cooperation."

"Oh, now we get to the point of all this. Now we get down and dirty. My cooperation in what?"

"In our ongoing inquiries into the activities of Abukir."

She pushed the stack of photographs raggedly toward him. "Am I free to go?" she asked quietly. "Or do I spend the night here?" Her dignity was intact but strength was ebbing from her, switch-flow in full flood. He thought she might be in shock. He was aroused.

"Abukir must be quite a fuck," he said. "You don't even cheat when he's AWOL."

Leela met his eyes levelly.

"I regret," Cobb said, "that we can't say the same for him."

"I don't believe you."

"Perhaps you'd like to see some more photos?"

"If you had any, you'd have shown them."

Cobb studied the clenching of her interlaced hands. Her white knuckles made his body heat rise. "I'm saving them," he said. The words were husky, like a declaration of love. "A little treat for the next time we meet."

Slowly, he pulled off his glove and laid it on the table between them. She stared first at the glove and then at the thumb of his left hand, the nail of which was deeply scored by a blackened groove. Their eyes met and held above the photographs.

"Cobb?" she said uncertainly.

He pulled off the ski mask. He would have liked to fuck her violently.

"Cobb! It *is* you." Spontaneously she leaned across the table and touched or almost touched his wrist but malaise caught up with her unguarded pleasure and her hand wavered like a bird bucked by an updraft of air. Her body also wavered before curling back into the chair. "I often think about you. I often wonder...."

He met her gaze with intense coldness.

"From Promised Land, you know, the only news...." She looked behind her, as though hearing the click of a shutter. Cobb's attention returned to his folder. He leafed through photographs, absorbed. He ignored her completely. "My little sister and I—you remember Maggie?—we talk on the phone. I hear your father's quite frail." Leela's voice faltered and fell silent then rallied again. "Would you believe I had a call from Benedict Boykin not long ago? He was in Boston on leave and we met for drinks in Harvard Square. Hadn't seen him since high school either."

Cobb extracted a black-and-white image from his folder and played it, without emotion, like an ace.

"I see you knew about that already," Leela said. She curled into herself the way a sea creature does. She looked smaller. She looked like a sand dollar, Cobb thought. She looked sick. She hugged herself with folded arms to keep herself warm.

Cobb lifted the photograph and held it in front of her face and she saw a man and a woman in joyful embrace, the logo of the Harvard Coop above their heads. The man, who was black, was in uniform. His white teeth flashed. There was a small jagged scar, that showed pale, below his lip. Leela's chin rested on his shoulder.

"Benedict said you were in the same unit in Iraq." Her voice sounded strangely drowsy. Cobb believed he could make her skin smolder and blister if he wished. He could make her twist in the wind and float away. Her voice was barely more than a whisper. She could have been talking to herself. "He said you were both with Special Forces." Cobb focused on the pulse in her neck. "Of course, you would know what he told me."

Cobb felt slightly and dangerously drunk. He kept his eyes on the hollow above her collar bone. He saw the bleat of a pulse beneath her skin and the way a blue vein throbbed and jumped about. He knew that Benedict would say as little as possible about Iraq. Benedict played by the book. He reported only to his superior officer, Cobb Slaughter.

Sir, I have to report, sir, that gross irregularities are taking place.

Gross irregularities, sergeant?

Yes, sir.

You have observed these irregularities yourself?

Yes, sir.

Are you making charges, sergeant?

I am reporting incidents, sir.

If charges were to be laid, sergeant, would any kind of evidence exist?

Some of the men have taken videos, sir. And there are photographs.

Have you seen these photographs?

Yes, sir. Whenever I could, I confiscated them. There's a stack in this envelope, sir.

I see. Thank you, sergeant. Leave the photographs with me. The matter will be investigated.

"Benedict said you were awarded a Bronze Star in Afghanistan. That's wonderful, Cobb."

Cobb was absorbed in the photographs of Benedict Boykin and Leela. He picked up the magnifying glass and studied segments of the images closely.

"Benedict heard...." Leela's voice was faltering. "After Iraq, he heard you'd left the army."

"Is it true what they say about black cocks?"

Leela asked quietly: "Why can't you look at me, Cobb?"

He did then. He held her gaze icily until bewilderment made her drop her eyes. Then he pushed up one sleeve to reveal the tattooed snake on his arm. *Don't Tread on Me.*

Leela pondered the rattler. It might have been a trick question or a rune. "I don't understand," she said. "Is it possible you feel I've trodden on you, Cobb?"

Cobb placed one more photograph in front of her: two young men were talking in front of a mosque. The sign at the street corner was Prospect Street. "You'll recognize your lover, Mikael Abukir," Cobb said, pointing. "The other one is Jamil Haddad, yesterday's subway bomber. Which would make your lover, at the very least, material witness for an atrocity and possibly accessory to mass murder. Which, in turn, makes your mathematical transcriptions of your lover's musical compositions of interest to us."

He smiled and walked out of the room and locked the door behind him and left her there.

BOOK III

Leela

1

AFTERWARDS.

After the night spent talking to Cobb Slaughter....

The black car stopped but Leela could not open her door. She would not ask. She waited. Through the thick glass partition, she saw the driver's hand move, heard the click of central unlocking. She opened her door and stepped into wet forsythia. The blossoms were massed on the sidewalk, thick as pillows. This seemed of immense but obscure significance as she stood there, uncertain, the car door open.

The driver did not cut the engine, but his window rolled silently down. "Close the door quietly," he ordered. He did not move on.

Leela wrote a question mark in wet petals with the toe of her shoe. The brick paving, exposed and interrogated, gave no answer. With her foot, Leela prodded at the heave of the sidewalk over tree roots: she knew this particular tree, this sprawling beech, this humped wave of brick. She had walked these undulating cobbles yesterday and the day before. She had walked this street day after day for several years.

You cannot step into the same street twice, she thought.

She was several blocks from her Cambridge apartment. She had not been asked for directions. The driver, not Leela, had chosen this stopping point. It was at precisely this spot that a different driver had forced her into a different car the night before. Her digital watch said 5.20 a.m. It was still dark. The purring car had not moved. Under the streetlight, she studied its license plate. The registration was Massachusetts. There was a bumper sticker displaying the coiled image of a rattlesnake and beneath it were the words of the early South Carolina flag: *Don't Tread on Me*.

This could be a bad dream, Leela thought. She considered possible tests. She bent over and touched the black outline of the snake. Immediately, the driver got out of the car. "What are you doing?" he demanded.

"Nothing," Leela said. "I was just wondering what your bumper sticker meant."

"It means we bite." The driver laughed with a short barking sound. He wore dark glasses. He wore a cap pulled low over his eyes. "When your boyfriend asks where you've been," he said, "remember that we'll be listening in." He got back into the car. "Now that you've followed your boyfriend to the mosque, you're radioactive. Every Boston incident, from last year's Prudential bombing to this week's big bang at Park Street, has been traced to that mosque. Think about it. We've got you both under surveillance."

The car moved off without a sound.

Leela stirred the wet forsythia petals with her foot as though this might reveal the laws of what to do next. She felt dizzy. She reached for the tree and leaned against it. Black circles floated across her vision in small clusters and the edges of things were frayed. There were odd jags of light, like fireflies or fizzy atmospheric disturbances, off to one side. She blinked rapidly and turned but the fireflies turned too. The street looked utterly foreign. She did not recognize any of the houses. It was as though something had changed overnight. It was as though the laws of mathematics had defaulted. She could no longer remember which apartment was hers but she thought that if she started to walk, she would find it. She thought that if she could re-establish a fixed point in her life—a known intersection, perhaps, or the routine comfort of one of her classes, or a debate on prime number theory—she could calculate her angle of deviance from the norm.

She walked until an outline of sunrise touched the trees and then she recognized a STOP sign, she identified the oak that lightning had struck two years ago, she saw a set of stairs leading up to a front porch, the door to a triple-decker house, the third-floor gable that was her living-room window.

When she let herself into her apartment, Mishka stirred and sat up in bed, half awake. "You're safe," he said. "Thank God for that."

Am I safe? Leela wondered.

"Where have you been?" he wanted to know.

"I don't know how to answer that," she said. She moved slowly around the bedroom, running her fingers along the windowsill, opening and closing the Venetian blind, probing the potted fern. Where were the microphones? Where was the digital eye?

"I was afraid something dreadful—" Mishka said. "I had a horrible dream."

"Really?" She did not want to look at him. She did not want to talk. Cobb Slaughter's final photograph still assaulted her: two men in front of the mosque. *You'll recognize your lover.... The other man is Jamil Haddad, yesterday's subway bomber.*

"Where were you?" Mishka asked. "Why didn't you call?"

Leela opened the sash window and leaned out into the dawn. She could smell late hyacinths. She felt Mishka behind her, trailing a sheet. He pressed against her, naked, and kissed her on the nape of the neck. She felt her body seal itself up to ward him off.

"It was one of those dreams where you hope you're dreaming and you prove to yourself you're awake," he said. He ran his fingers through her hair. He covered her neck with kisses. "I was so afraid." He bit her shoulder.

"Don't," Leela said. She moved away from him, into the kitchen.

Mishka followed. He left the sheet on the bedroom floor. Leela was conscious of his sweet-smelling skin, of the hair that fell across his eyes, of his erection. She would not look.

"What happened?" he demanded. "What's wrong?"

"Isn't that what I should be asking you?"

"What do you mean?"

"I think you know," she said.

She felt Mishka's withdrawal like a drop in temperature and she felt instantly, paradoxically, bereft. He said nothing. She realized how rarely they needed words. They were more like a convergence of atmospheric fronts: they made a new and turbulent weather.

"Are you leaving me?" he asked quietly.

She stared at him. I have no idea who he is, she thought. I have no idea if he means what he says. She filled a mug with water and opened the microwave door. She pressed the one-minute tab. She studied the shelf of teabag packets with great concentration: lime blossom, chamomile, green tea, ginseng, mint.

"Something's happened," he said. "Something's changed."

Indeed, Leela thought. She took her cup from the microwave oven. "Tell me your dream," she said.

Mishka left the room and picked up the sheet and wrapped it around himself. He closed the bedroom door. After a little while, she heard his violin, low and plaintive, and the apartment was billowing with Gluck: *What will I do without Eurydice*? Extravagant sorrow fogged the kitchen and leaked under the door and down the hall. Leela steeped the chamomile sachet in boiling water.

The music changed.

Now he had switched from the violin to the oud: a low intense plea, a ghazal love song, or else one of Rūmī's mystical poems, one of Mishka's own settings, a hymn of abject religious devotion which nevertheless sounded erotic. What seduced Leela was not the mood but the convoluted math: it was like Western notation on mescaline, a whirling dervish of song. Now the music was mournful again. Now it wept.

The chamomile teabag steamed with exasperation, but when Leela moved jerkily, angrily, hot mug in hand, to pull open the bedroom door, she saw that Mishka was sitting huddled on the bed like a child with a stomach ache. She saw the violin case in its usual place: on top of the bookshelf. She saw the big-bellied oud propped in the corner of the room. She saw his totemic objects in his hands: the two diptyches, the two hinged frames of family portraits. They were as much a fetish as his instruments.

She had intended to say: *Why do you have to play tragic hero to the hilt? And why do you keep playing Gluck and those neurotic hymns on the oud? And why do you go to that mosque in Central Square?*

She blinked, disoriented, and asked instead: "Where's your violin?"

"My violin?"

"I thought I heard you playing."

"I wasn't playing."

I am having hallucinations, Leela thought with panic. And last night?

A wave of chamomile tea splashed the floor.

Mishka stared at the puddle. "You've spilled your tea."

I'm no longer sure of what's real, Leela thought. I'm contaminated. Mishka's stories have seeped into my brain. I'm having his fantasies.

We kept Uncle Otto in the attic, he had told her so often. *He played for us after dinner every night.*

Was he real? she would ask.

Extremely real. I had to tiptoe around him all through childhood.

And then Leela would lick the chord calluses on Mishka's fingers, one by one. *You're crazy*, she would murmur. *I've always been partial to crazy.*

You've hit the jackpot, he would tell her.

Did you dream Uncle Otto up?

I sometimes think Uncle Otto dreamed me.

Leela had heard theme and variations. She had heard Uncle Otto doubling and tripling himself in descant, in ornamentation, in counterpoint bass. She had almost heard Uncle Otto play. She studied Mishka warily: the way he sat hunched on the bed, the way the violin and the oud were not in his hands.

"I heard you playing," she said stubbornly.

"You've spilled your tea."

"So this dream then." She was irritable and aggressive. "This dream that you had last night."

"It was a nightmare. No, worse than that. A night terror."

"Well?"

"We were coming home from Symphony Hall—"

"*We.* Who's we?"

"You and I. We were coming home on the T. We'd just left the Park Street stop."

He put one diptych back on the dresser and pressed the other one—the one that displayed his Hungarian grandparents and his great-uncle Otto—against his forehead.

"Yes?" she prodded, annoyed.

"There was a sound like a bass string snapping and the train lurched like a shot animal. It was an explosion."

Leela looked at him sharply then looked away. She moved to the window and set her mug on the sill. "There *was* an explosion yesterday, as you well know."

"Of course I know. In my dream, it was close, the next car, but *our* car reared up like a horse and we all slid into a writhing heap like eels. It was horrible."

"They've identified the bomber's body," Leela said. She looked at him now. She kept her eyes on his. "He's a Harvard grad student. Engineering, but apparently he audits a course in music. He has connections to that mosque in Central Square."

"What?" Mishka snapped the diptych shut and pushed it under his pillow. "How do you know that?" He looked wild-eyed. He began to feel for the chords on an unseen violin. He was agitated. His fingers moved on invisible frets at frantic speed. "How do you know they've identified the bomber?"

"I heard it on the news."

"No you didn't," he said. "There were no details last night. Not even online. I went looking."

"Why?"

"Why what?"

"Why'd you go looking?"

Mishka's fingers reached for the chords of a turbulent passage. In Gluck, no doubt. He was playing the moment of the snakebite perhaps, the first death of Eurydice. His right hand swept the bow back and forth, his head was bent low. He rocked himself on the bed like a frightened child.

She did not understand why the rocking made her so angry. "Why are you doing that?" she asked.

Mishka finished whatever passage he was hearing in his head and laid his ghostly instrument down. "I got a call from that store on Tremont yesterday," he said. "The one across from the Common by the Park Street stop. My sheet music arrived. I went in after teaching my class, picked it up and got the next train back. I'd just got home when I heard the news. I kept flipping channels. How many were killed? Where were *you*? I called your office and got no answer. I was afraid you'd already left. I was afraid you were on that train. I wanted to know where you were. I wanted to know which train.... And I wanted to know how close I'd been to death."

"How close were you?"

"I must have been on the train before the death train. What if I'd missed that one...? And I almost did. It was such a close thing. The doors were closing when I got on the platform. I could have been dead."

"But you had no idea."

"Death breathing hot air in my face. I'm still—" He felt his cheeks. "I feel as though I shouldn't be alive. And then I was terrified that *you* were on that train."

"And you didn't hear that they identified the bomber's body?"

"No! There was nothing. I kept flipping channels. I went online. Nothing."

"But you were expecting—"

"I didn't know what to expect. When I couldn't get hold of you, I was too shaky for anything except my violin. I played for hours. I must have played till I fell asleep."

"And fell into your nightmare."

Mishka's fingers were frantic, racing across frets that were not there. "The train was full of street musicians, scores of them—in my dream, I mean—all playing cellos or basses or percussion." He jumped up and paced the small bedroom. He took his violin case from the bookcase and lifted the instrument out. The *actual* instrument, Leela noted. "There were drums, tympani, cymbals."

"Must have been noisy."

"I have the sound of the whole thing in my head. It's writing itself. I'm calling it *Incident in a Nightmare*." Leela listened to the low violent notes. "It was pitch dark. There was a meteor coming at us down the tunnel." Leela closed her eyes. Mishka's music came thudding down the tracks, the chords sharp and discordant, as though the strings of the violin had snapped. "And then *boom*! Arms and legs everywhere, it was like wrestling an octopus, and gouts of blood. I couldn't breathe. I kept hearing your voice, I kept hearing you calling *Mishka, Mishka!* but all I could see was a leg with your sandal on it. I grabbed at your foot and I pulled, but what came free was your leg. Just your leg. I woke and you weren't in bed. I was terrified."

"And then you realized it was just a dream and went back to sleep."

Mishka went to his desk and scribbled notes onto the lined staves at a furious pace. "What?" he asked, distracted. "Sleep? Are you kidding? I was calling your office and leaving messages from the moment I got home. I was calling your cell phone." He was blacking in notes with a lead pencil, feverish and intent. "I kept calling your cell. I spent the rest of the night working on this." He finished setting down the sounds that he heard in his head—"Got it!" he said—and then went to her and took the cup of tea from her hand and set it down. "Why didn't you answer?" He did not wait for her to speak before closing his mouth over hers. Leela felt her body turn soft, she felt herself yield and respond. Then, as his tongue met hers, she imagined the blink of a shutter. She saw the two of them in a black-and-white photograph in someone's folder: Mishka's buttocks and thighs in the glow of the streetlight, herself leaning into him with want.

She swiveled out of his arms and picked up her tea. "I had my cell phone turned off," she said.

"What happened? Where were you?"

"I ran into an old school friend. We got talking."

"Until six o'clock in the morning?"

"I hardly think you are in a position to complain about secret excursions at night."

"But you know where I go. To the Music Lab or the Marrakesh."

"I'm exhausted," Leela said. "I have to sleep."

I need my passport, Leela thought urgently. I've got to have it. I can't find my passport.

She was rummaging, panic-stricken, in her underwear drawer. She was still in the country of bad dreams. Where am I? she wondered, holding a silk camisole up to the light. Beyond the window, the maple was in earliest leaf. On one desk, in the corner of the room, were the typed pages of her grant proposal. On the other desk, in a messy heap, were pages scribbled with the score of Mishka's *Incident in a Nightmare*.

The bedroom came into focus.

The outlines of yesterday grew sharp. There had been an incident, yet another one. Leela had first heard of it about nine the previous evening in a deli in Harvard Square. She listened to customers talking: the death estimates, the body parts, the disruption. People had begun to speak of incidents the way they spoke of accidents on the pike: the frequency was distressing, but such things always happened to someone else. There was a certain *frisson*, a low-level hum of anxiety that was more or less constant, especially in crowds, especially at sporting events, or in concert halls, or in the subway, but one had to get on with one's life.

"Were you delayed?" the deli owner asked her. She was a regular in his store. "I heard the Red Line's completely blocked."

"I missed the whole thing," Leela said. "Pure chance. I walked home along the river instead."

"Jesus." The deli owner shook his head, wondering. "All the way from MIT? That's gotta be ESP."

Was it? Leela asked herself. Was this premonition? In retrospect, she thought it must have been, though when she had veered away from the Central Square T-stop and headed down to the riverside footpath, it was the spring weather, pure and simple, that had lured her. She wanted to be out in the night air, not buried in an underground tunnel. She remembered thinking exactly those words: *not buried in an underground tunnel.* Besides, the constant rush of traffic on Memorial Drive meant the riverwalk was totally safe, safer than the subway at night.

At the deli in Harvard Square, she had bought smoked salmon and Greek salad and a bottle of wine. She had walked home, thinking languidly of a late supper and of passing Kalamata olives from her own mouth to Mishka's, of licking red wine from his lips. "There's been another incident," she would tell him, and he would say, "I know," and they would make boisterous love because they were alive and unharmed.

But then he would toss in his sleep. He would cry out. He would disappear again, and where would he be, and how long would she have to wait before he turned up, and what explanation would he give?

Perhaps he would already have gone missing.

She felt a sudden precipitous chill in the air.

A few blocks from her apartment, just as she was shifting the grocery bags to ease the drag on one arm, a black car had pulled up at the curb and a man in the passenger seat had got out and pushed something small and hard against her back. *Get in*, he had ordered. None of this had seemed real. She had spent the night talking to Cobb Slaughter, which seemed even less so. She learned that Mishka might or might not be her lover's name. She learned that the mosque on Prospect Street in Central Square was said to have terrorist links, perhaps the night's least surprising piece of news.

She remembered a headline from many months back in the *Boston Globe*: MOSQUE'S TREASURER APPLAUDS ANTI-ISRAELI VIOLENCE. MOSQUE'S LEADER ENDORSES STATEMENT BY YUSUF ABDULLAH AL-QARADANI: "WE WILL CONQUER EUROPE. WE WILL CONQUER AMERICA. WE WILL CONQUER THE WORLD."

She remembered drawing the article to Mishka's attention. Mishka had shrugged. "One rotten apple doesn't wreck the whole crop. It's like judging all Jews by Meir Kahane, or all Christians by the Ku Klux Klan."

This was long before she had any inkling that one night she would follow him to that mosque.

In her back-into-focus apartment, Leela looked at her watch. It was one o'clock in the afternoon. The apartment was empty. On the fridge door, behind the Mozart magnet, were two notes. The first one said:

Berg called. He wants you to call him back.
You missed your session at 10 a.m. and he was pretty worked up. He said, and I quote: "I trust she remembers the grant proposal is due next week, but revisions are

necessary first." I told him you were sick. Too sick to let him know you were sick. I thought that was the best excuse. Mishka.

The second note said:

I'll be working late again in the Music Lab.
Don't wait up. Mishka.

Leela removed this note and set it beside the coffee machine while she measured water and ground espresso. *Late again at the Music Lab,* which was where he had claimed to be the night she had followed him to the mosque. She made coffee and sat staring out the window at the horse-chestnut tree. She had a word for this stage of new leaf: the parsley stage. Frilled ruffs of green, baby green, celery green, sprouted from every knuckle on every branch, the spacing always perfect. Like the stops on a flute, mathematically ideal, as Berg—who had called—might say.

Berg called? Berg never called her at home. He left notes, scrawled in thick black pencil, on pale yellow sheets.

Need to discuss passage on harmonics.
This section flawed. 10 a.m. Thursday.
Berg.

She would find these peremptory messages in her departmental box. She gulped at her coffee. She pulled the telephone toward her and dialed his office. She imagined microphone ears in the drapes and promptly hung up.

She got up from her chair and left the room. In the bedroom, she pulled down the blind. Would that help? She stood on a chair and draped a pillowcase over the light fixture that dangled from the ceiling in one corner. She looked in the closets. She looked under the bed. She could not see any foreign object.

She gathered up sheets of paper from the messy pile on Mishka's desk. The sheets were lined with staves and scribbled over with the draft notes of the composition in progress. In one of the margins, Mishka had scribbled: *Bach meets Saladin*. On another page, beneath the heading *Rūmī*, he had copied the lines of a poem:

> At the time when we shall come into the garden, thou
>   and I.
> The stars of Heaven will come to gaze upon us:
> We shall show them the moon herself, thou and I.
> Thou and I, individuals no more, shall be mingled in
>   ecstasy...

Below this there were notes:

1. *Check Rūmī translations with Siddiqi.*
2. *Prepare critiques of ghazal compositions for Siddiqi's seminar.*
3. *Persian Classical CDs in Music Lab. (Catalog; make copies.)*
4. *Write paper for conference: Comparison of Persian dastgah system with Western octave.*
5. *Incident: experiment with fusion of Western octave and dastgah system. Possible in same piece?*

Leela went to her own computer and summoned up Google and typed in *Rumi*.

Jalāl al-Dīn Rūmī, she read on a website, *who died in 1273, was the greatest mystical poet of Persia and also one of the supreme masters of Sufism. In current brands of fundamentalist Islam, Rūmī and Sufism are condemned as Western-influenced corruptions.*

She then visited the Harvard School of Music website and scrolled through the faculty listings. She found Siddiqi, Abdul-Hakeem, Distinguished Professor, who was teaching a course in History of Persian Classical Music. She clicked on his email address. *Dear Dr. Abdul-Hakeem Siddiqi*, she typed. She stared at her screen. If Cobb's information was reliable, Mishka, along with the suicide bomber, was auditing Dr. Siddiqi's course. Perhaps Mishka went to the mosque as part of a course assignment. It might be that simple.

Dear Dr. Abdul-Hakeem Siddiqi:

I am curious to know, she typed, *whether your junior colleague Mishka Bartok, whom you possibly know by the name Mikael Abukir—he has a post-doc, but I believe he is auditing your course—has ever discussed....*

But what did Mishka ever discuss besides music?

She erased her message. She clicked CANCEL.

She knew everything and nothing about Mishka Bartok.

She knew the taste of his skin. She knew the sweet smell of him before and during and after making love, she could summon up those fragrant stages at will. She knew what it was like to be enclosed in the haunting cocoon of his music—early Baroque, high Baroque, his own compositions, which Leela could only describe as Baroque Postmodern—and she would simply sit with her eyes closed and listen.

Then he would switch to the oud and play for hours. He would sit cross-legged on a cushion on the floor.

"Is that required?" Leela joked. "Oud players have to sit on the floor?"

Mishka smiled but did not deign to answer as his left hand fingered the chords. In his right he held not a bow, but a long pick shaped like a quill. "It's called a *risha*," he told her.

"When did you learn to play the oud?"

"I've been playing for years."

"The math of the rhythm blows my mind, but you never play chords on your oud. No harmonics."

"No. Persian music's melodic and rhythmic, not polyphonic. Totally different system."

"So what's the attraction? I don't understand."

"My father played the oud. He was a singer."

"Ah, I'd forgotten. But he died before you were born."

"Right."

"Do you have relatives on your father's side?"

"I do, yes."

"Are they in Australia?"

"No."

"Where are they?"

"Beirut, I believe. We have no contact."

"Aren't you curious? Don't you want to meet them?"

For answer, Mishka played complicated rhythms on the oud.

"That's not a wholly adequate answer," Leela teased.

"Music's the way I talk."

"Want to play me again?"

But exactly what game was he playing?

She knew everything and nothing about him.

She also knew everything and nothing about Cobb Slaughter.

Apparently.

He had told her years ago that she knew nothing about him. He had told her that many many times.

She knew it was true and yet she realized she had never believed it.

She opened her wallet. Behind the clear plastic window which showed her ID was a hidden pocket. She reached in with her index finger and thumb and pulled out her contraband: three photographs, old ones, dog-eared, the color fading. She had not looked at these photographs for a very long time, though she was always aware of their presence. One photograph showed her father and her mother seated rather awkwardly on chairs beneath a pecan tree. Her parents were laughing. Leela, a child of six with fiery corkscrew curls, was nestled into her mother's lap and was leaning toward her father and pulling at the pocket of his shirt. She remembered with the utmost clarity what she expected to find: the brownie in her father's pocket. This brownie was not something to eat; he was related to goblins. "He's very shy," her father said. "He always hides. His name is M'sieur de Crac de Bergerac."

Leela's little sister Maggie was present in this family photograph as the bulge beneath her mother's shift.

"Only the baby can see the brownie," Leela's father said.

He always laughed and winked when he said this, and Leela had kept the photo for two reasons: it was the only one she had of her mother, and it was proof that once upon a time, her father laughed.

In the second photograph there were three people, all standing, in the shadow of the pecan. Leela's father looked somber, his thoughts on eternity. Though he had his hands on the shoulders of his daughters—Leela was on one side, Maggie on the other—he was thinking of something else. His eyes were half closed. He might have been praying for his wild and wayward ten-year-old and for four-year-old Maggie. Leela was gesturing to someone outside the photograph, to Cobb, on whom she had pressed the Kodak instamatic and her orders.

The third image was of Leela and Cobb, arms entwined. They were fourteen years old and had just placed first and second in the Math Prize.

Leela tucked the photographs into her bra and lay on her back on the bedroom floor. She felt the thump-thump of her heart against the glossy-paper image of her mother. What she smelled was the rotting floor of a veranda in Promised Land, a sweet fungal smell. She heard birds calling. Her eyes followed the slow curve of wasps through magnolia trees.

"Have you ever been stung by a wasp, Cobb?" she asked drowsily.

"Yes," he said. "Have you?"

"On my eyelid once. It swelled up as big as an egg. I couldn't see."

They were on the floorboards, side by side on their backs, studying stains on the pulpy ceiling of the veranda of the derelict Hamilton house. They were seven years old.

"What can you see?" Cobb asked.

"I can see a parallelogram."

Cobb said, "It's not a parallelogram. It's a coffin."

"It can't be a coffin. You can't have a crooked coffin. It would have to be a rectangle to be a coffin and it's not."

"I'm not looking at that one. The one I'm looking at is a coffin."

What he saw, Leela knew, was the box where his mother lay, still open for viewing.

Leela rolled over and stroked Cobb's hair. "I'm so sad about your mama, Cobb."

"I can see a rattlesnake," he said.

"Where?"

"Up there near the post. The curly brown stain."

"That's not a rattler, it's a river."

"It might be the Styx," Cobb conceded. "Like Mr. Watson told us. When people sail over it they don't come back."

"It's the Jordan River," Leela said. "After you cross it, you're in heaven."

Cobb pulled a soft chunk of wood from a floorboard and threw it at the River Styx. "D'you remember *your* mother?" he asked.

"Sort of."

"Like what? What do you remember?"

"I remember she smelled of lavender."

"No one smells of lavender."

"My mama did."

"No she didn't. I remember her. She didn't smell of lavender, she smelled of fried eggs and soap."

"She used to pick lavender every day and crush it up in her hand and put some in her pocket and give me some too. Sometimes she comes and puts it under my pillow and under Maggie's pillow while we sleep. Yours will come back too, Cobb. Maybe she'll leave something different. Maybe she'll leave Confederate jasmine, 'coz she loved jasmine, didn't she? Or maybe she'll leave math answers under your pillow."

"Did you see your mama when she was dead?"

"No," Leela said. "Children aren't allowed to see dead people." She tried to summon up the image of her mother, but all that came was the sensation of softness, the lavender smell, and the shadowy woman in the photograph. There was always a blur like a too-bright light where a face ought to be. "She died in the hospital."

"My mama told me that yours died in childbirth."

"Yeah. When Maggie was born."

"How come Maggie didn't die?"

"Daddy says that Mama's soul went straight into Maggie, so we brought her home, but Mama went to be with the Lord and that's where she's waiting for us."

"I saw mine."

"You mean, you saw your mama when she was dead?"

"Yeah."

"Children aren't supposed to. They're not allowed."

"It was me who found her."

"Oh." There was a long silence. Leela's eyes wandered along the bends of the river on the ceiling. She was searching for the coffin Cobb had seen. "What did she look like?"

"She looked like a fish on a hook."

Leela thought of fish, white and twitching, at the end of a line or in the bottom of a boat. She could not connect this to a mother. "But she isn't dead really, Cobb. She's gone to be with the Lord."

"She's dead. And she's not in heaven. She's at Thompson's Funeral Parlor."

"Well, she's going to be in heaven soon," Leela said. "After they bury her, that's when people go to heaven. There's your mother's face, see? With angel wings. She's watching us. And after the funeral, she'll be in heaven."

"There's not going to be a funeral."

"There's always a funeral."

"The minister told Dad we couldn't have one."

"There's always a funeral. Why did he say you couldn't have one?"

Cobb had rolled over and poked a stick through the softened veranda boards. There were acres of cobwebs and spiders down there. "I hope the spiders get her," he said savagely. He began to sob, or rather, a tornado of strangled sounds touched down on him. Leela was frightened. She did what she did when her baby sister cried and would not stop. She put her arm around Cobb and sang the song her own mother had left behind: *Hush, little baby, don't you cry, Your mamma's gonna sing you a lullaby-ay. All my troubles, Lord, soon be over.*

Cobb stopped crying abruptly and sat up. "I'm not a baby," he said.

"I know you're not."

"Don't sing me baby songs."

"I'm sorry. It's what I do when Maggie cries."

"I'm not a girl."

"You're allowed to cry for dying, Cobb. Even my daddy cried."

"My daddy would never cry," Cobb said.

"I bet he does when you're asleep."

"I bet he doesn't."

"I feel like crying, Cobb. I don't know why."

"I do too."

"Let's cry. I promise I won't tell."

"You wanna be my blood sister?"

"Yes," she said.

He took his pocketknife then and drew blood from his middle finger and from hers. They pressed their fingers together.

"Till death do us part," Leela said.

"If you ever tell that I cried," Cobb said, "your blood will spurt out and you will die."

"Cross my heart," Leela said. "I'll never tell."

At school, when they stood for one minute of silence, Leela heard one of the teachers whisper: "What a dreadful business this is. I just hope that poor child will be all right."

* * *

In her Cambridge apartment, Leela tried to reconstruct her mother's face but the jigsaw pieces were fuzzy. Mrs. Slaughter's face, suspended from a ceiling fan by a sheet, always looked like a fish. Leela could summon up blurred flashes of her father and Maggie and Mr. Slaughter. She had a fleeting image of Mishka with a ferryman in a boat, crossing to somewhere. She saw Cobb, then and now, and the pieces would not match up.

"Do you ever see Cobb?" she'd asked Benedict Boykin, a month or so back, in Harvard Square.

"Yeah," Benedict said. "We've crossed paths."

"Where?"

"Afghanistan. Iraq. Major Slaughter."

"How is he?"

Benedict shrugged. "He was in his element, I guess."

"It's hard for me to imagine Cobb as a military officer."

"He's in intelligence. Special Forces. We both were. We were in the same unit."

"That figures, I guess. Does he look the same?"

"No. You wouldn't recognize him."

"That I don't believe," Leela said. "I'd know Cobb anywhere."

Benedict said nothing.

"So... between you two, how was it?"

"It was fine."

"Ben, don't do this to me. Give me something more substantial to go on. I mean, how *was* he?"

"He's distinguished himself," Benedict said.

"Meaning what?"

"He got a Bronze Star."

"Wow. For what?"

"Our unit pinned down a Taliban stronghold. Slaughter himself did the high-risk stuff."

"That's fantastic. I've always loved that about Cobb. Someone who's scared shitless but doesn't back off, it's the most impressive kind of courage, don't you think?"

"I wouldn't say he's scared shitless anymore," Benedict said.

"Where is he now?"

"Couldn't say. But I know he's left the army. He's running a private security force."

"You mean he's a mercenary?"

"We don't call them that anymore. The army's outsourced now. Lot more money to be had. He offered me a slot, as a matter of fact, but I turned it down."

"Are you serious?"

"Leela, I'm on leave. I don't want to talk about the war."

"Sorry. Let's talk about Promised Land. How are your folks?"

"They're fine. How're yours?"

"Fine." Leela grimaced. "Maggie and I talk once in a while. I avoid talking to Daddy. I don't feel good about that, but I can't talk to him without getting exasperated."

"I know the feeling only too well."

"Really? I never ever saw the slightest splinter of anger in your family. You all seemed to be *blessed*, as we used to say back in Promised Land."

"Blessed. Yeah. Exactly. Anger was a sin. We didn't believe in it."

"Do you remember that time you came rushing onto our porch—?"

"The night we got shot at."

"They hit the pipe from the well and you had a waterspout."

"That was the turning point for me."

"Your father was laughing."

"We had a fight. We've never really been close since that night."

"Are you serious? But Ben, he didn't really think it was funny. That was his way—"

"*Yessuh, Lord Jesus, Thy will be done.* It still infuriates me."

"That's really unfair," Leela said. "He was NAACP. And we were... what? Nine years old? We were little kids."

"We were ten."

"You can't still be angry—"

"Yes I can."

"But that was years before we were marching, before the flag rallies.... Your father was so proud of you. And you. You were *fiercely* defensive of him. No one hadn't better say one bad word—"

"Right. Just like you on the subject of your father."

"Touché," Leela said.

After a time she asked: "Do you go back when you're on leave?"

"No. Do you?"

"Are you kidding?" After a time, she added: "But I get homesick. Do you?"

"All the time. But it's... you know, sentimental. Pathetic, really."

"I know. Remember the time the bus broke down—"

"Outside Summerville."

"Right. Banners on the side. From Charleston to the State House—"

"And we all piled out on the side of the road—"

"And we sang—"

Slightly drunk by now, they began singing in unison, *We Shall Overcome*.... And, to the same tune, *The flag must come down to-day-ay-ay-ay*....

People in the bar turned to stare.

"This is sick," Benedict said. "Nostalgia. And black schools are still falling apart."

"The flag *did* come down."

"Right. Let's drink to Major Cobb and the good old days."

Leela lifted the receiver in her apartment. She wanted to ask Benedict questions. She wanted to talk to Cobb. She had no idea how to reach either of them. She replaced the receiver. She crawled onto her bed and hugged her pillow and trawled through riddles. She fell asleep and dreamed she heard a violin in the subway. She followed the sound into the tunnel, deeper and deeper.

"Mishka!" she called. "Wait for me."

"Don't follow me, Leela," he called back.

2

WHEN THE TELEPHONE rang, Leela could not remember where she was. She seemed to be in a canoe and there were swamp channels with streamers of Spanish moss trailing in the water and Cobb had left her without a paddle or gone for help perhaps. She could dimly see a dock where Mishka was stranded, and behind him was a shack, and the telephone would have to be in that tumbledown place but it was too dark to see. Leela propelled herself toward the dock by pulling her bare hands through the water and then she stumbled over floating paddles and a pair of shoes and yesterday's mail and found the source of the ringing.

"Yes?" she said. "Cobb, can I just ask you—?" but the voice was not Cobb's, it was a young woman's voice. "Maggie?" she repeated, puzzled. "Oh my God, *Maggie!*"

"We saw the subway bombing on TV," her sister said. "We've been worried sick."

"What time is it?" The swamp had turned into bedroom floor, but it was still too dark to see.

"Wasn't that your stop?" Maggie asked. "We've been so afraid. Are you okay?"

Leela moved to the window and raised the shade and was almost blinded by afternoon sun. "I'm all right, I'm fine. I didn't take the T yesterday."

"You sound funny."

"I'm groggy. I had a very bad night."

"Were there delays getting home?"

"No. I don't know. Actually, I could have been on that train, but I walked home instead. And then this very strange thing—" *Just remember that we'll be listening in.* "Uh, Maggie, listen," Leela said. "I'm in a rush. Can I call you back?"

Fifteen minutes later, from a pay phone in Harvard Square, Leela called back.

"Maggie? Sorry about that, but I can't take calls in the apartment. Don't ask me to explain because it won't make sense."

"I kept trying your cell last night," Maggie said.

"I don't keep it on. I hardly use it. I only have it for emergencies."

"I would have thought an explosion qualified. You must have known we'd be beside ourselves with worry. You're the most unreachable person."

"Sorry. Didn't mean to make you worry."

"Well, I figured we'd have been notified if anything dreadful... if you'd been carted off in an ambulance or something worse."

"Maggie, it is really really good to hear your voice. You have no idea...." Leela was aware of the numbness of shock wearing off. She was aware that her hands were shaking. She could feel a crying jag coming on, as overwhelming as it was shaming. The phone booth felt like a coffin. She pushed the door open, gasping air, and clapped one hand across her mouth.

A passing jogger paused in consternation. "Are you okay?" he asked.

Leela, embarrassed, nodded and waved him on.

She lifted the receiver to her ear. "Leela? Leela?" Maggie was saying. "Are you there? What's the matter with you? What's happening?"

I don't know what is happening, Leela thought.

"Leela, are you there?"

"Sorry," Leela said, her voice thick. "I'm on the edge of Harvard Square. Too much traffic. How's Daddy?"

"How do you think? He's been a nervous wreck, mostly on his knees by the porch swing, praying for you. How's Mishka?"

"What do you mean, how's Mishka?" Leela asked sharply.

"Well, I don't mean anything. I just mean, is everything okay?"

"You'll never believe who I saw yesterday."

"Why are you changing the subject? Is Mishka okay?"

"I just don't want to talk about Mishka right now."

"Because of the bombing?"

"What do you mean, *because of the bombing*?"

"I don't mean anything. I mean, I suppose it's hard to think of anything else."

"It is, yes."

"But you thought I meant something else."

"Everyone's rattled here, Maggie. I can't deal with this third degree."

"Well, I hope nothing's gone wrong with Mishka."

"What do you mean by that?"

"Why are you so touchy?" Maggie wanted to know. "I meant I liked the sound of you being in love and settled. If it's over already, it's still the longest relationship you've had. That's a good sign."

"Of what?"

"Of you turning out normal."

"Thanks," Leela said. "Guess who I saw yesterday."

"Who?"

"Guess."

"Benedict Boykin."

"Funny you should mention Benedict," Leela said. "I *did* see him, but that was about a month back."

"Mr. Boykin told me. He heard from Benedict."

"Hmm. That's interesting. I got the feeling from Benedict that he was keeping a certain amount of distance from his family."

"Yeah. He does. Same as you. But he calls them when he's on leave. Mr. Boykin and I have tried to figure out why you two won't visit."

"Good grief. People in Promised Land still got nothing better to talk about than me and Benedict?"

"Promised Land has a limited range of topics. By the way, I get my teaching degree next month."

"Wow. Where does the time go? My little sister with a master's degree."

"You *will* come home for my graduation, won't you?"

"Sure. Well, if I can get away." What Leela felt was an onset of claustrophobia so extreme that she had to push open the door of the phone booth again, taking deep breaths.

"What are you doing?" Maggie asked. "You sound funny again."

"I'm in the middle of Harvard Square. It's noisy."

"Will you fly down or drive?"

"Will you promise Daddy won't hold a prayer meeting on my behalf?"

"Beyond my power. I won't forgive you if you don't come."

"I'll try, Maggie."

"You won't just break Daddy's heart. You'll break mine."

"Maggie, you don't understand. You weren't ever the black sheep, the way I was."

"People who make a career out of being black sheep just like to be the center of attention."

"You haven't guessed who I saw," Leela prodded.

"Someone from Promised Land."

"Otherwise I wouldn't ask you to guess."

"Cobb Slaughter."

Leela was startled. "How could you know that?"

"Not very difficult. You can count on one hand the folks who've left Promised Land to live with Yankees."

"Cobb left Promised Land to join the army."

"I know. But now he's in Boston, and I knew that because Benedict told Mr. Boykin he was there."

"He did? That's weird. When I ran into Benedict, he said he didn't know where Cobb was now. What else did Benedict tell his dad?"

"Don't know. Mr. Boykin sends his love."

"D'you ever see Cobb's dad?"

"Sometimes. Never see him sober. He's in worse and worse shape. I've heard that he's diabetic and his liver's shot but he's too damn stubborn to die."

"I believe it. How's Daddy's business?"

"It's fine. I still help out with sharpening knives and mower blades on weekends. He's never short of work. People drive all the way out from Columbia with stuff to be fixed."

"Sword of the Lord and of Gideon," Leela said.

"You're smiling."

"What?"

"I can hear the smile in your voice," Maggie said.

"Is that sign still on the truck?"

"Still there. One of the Boykins, the painting and

sign-writing uncle, gave it a touch-up. Everyone loves Daddy, you know."

"I know that. They also think he's slightly crazy, which he is."

"You were his biggest defender."

"He's my father, isn't he? He's only got us and magic numbers, Maggie. But that doesn't mean you have to chain yourself for life."

"I've got no complaints."

"Don't you want to escape? Try your wings?"

"Escape from what? From where I belong and where I'm happy?"

"What about after graduation?"

"I'm staying," Maggie said. "Got a teaching post at DeLaine Elementary. It's only ten miles, so I'll live at home. I don't want to leave Daddy alone."

"Accusation noted."

"None intended," Maggie insisted. "If you take it as one, you'll have to ask yourself why."

"DeLaine Elementary. Isn't that where Daddy used to donate all the maintenance work?"

"Still does."

"Big changes, I imagine, since my day."

"Not many. Still mostly black kids. Still shockingly underfunded, like all the schools in Clarendon County. The buildings are falling apart and the governor and the legislature don't give a damn. It makes me furious."

"Next thing I know, you'll be running for office."

"I might."

Leela sighed. "It would be easier to come home if you and Daddy weren't quite such good people."

"Oh please," Maggie said. "Don't make me throw up. I'm doing this because the kids give me pleasure. I enjoy teaching the way Daddy enjoys fixing things and you enjoy math. We're all the same."

"Maggie, we're so different I can't even begin...."

"We're really not, you know."

"You and Daddy think about other people all the time, and Daddy thinks about God. I only think about math. Plus I've got an intensity addiction."

"Like Cobb."

"What?"

"Face it."

"A bit like Cobb, I suppose. You mean our math obsession?"

"Math and everything else. Obsessive, intense, tunnel vision. The way you two used to go at each other... *whooo*, talk about electrical storms! I remember watching you on the Hamilton veranda—"

"You what?"

"I used to hide in the azaleas. You were quite the show. You used to give off blue sparks."

"Glad you found us so entertaining," Leela said. "Give Daddy my love."

"How about you tell him yourself?"

"You'll do it better. Bye, Maggie."

3

BERG'S OFFICE WAS in the late Paleozoic wing of MIT and alpine collisions were constant. There were books, dissertations, student term papers, sheaves of lecture notes, off-prints, mathematical journals, all of them piled on desk and floor, all of them collapsing and cascading and folding into each other in seismic rearrangements of rift valleys and peaks. Entering the office was hazardous. One incautious step could kick off an avalanche.

Leela cleared a space, moved a pile of papers from a chair, and sat down. There was a shifting of tectonic plates: a tower of books teetered and slithered forward in a perfectly calibrated arc, the books overlapping like dominoes. Leela re-stacked them on the floor.

Berg's secretary called through the door: "He should be back from class any minute, if he's not waylaid by a student."

"I've found a spot on the shore of the Tethys Ocean," Leela said.

"Pardon?"

"Joke. It's where the alps happened, when Africa rammed into Europe."

"Oh. Got it." Berg's secretary laughed. "I don't dare touch a thing for fear of starting an earthquake. Speaking of which, there was a bit of a crisis this morning when you didn't show up.

Much flailing of arms and cascades of stuff from his desk. Your section of the grant proposal is probably deep under last term's rubble."

"No. I can see it on top of the earthquake," Leela said. "But that's not a good sign. It means he doesn't think much of it. He's going to make me rewrite."

"It doesn't mean anything," the secretary said. "He freaks out at least once a day."

"I've always sort of liked that about him," Leela admitted. "Things that matter, *matter*."

"Hmm," the secretary said. "He makes me think of my two-year-old."

"What I know," Leela said, "is that when I've done something that ascends into his calm zone, I've done something really first-rate."

She studied the photographs on Berg's desk. The one of Berg with his wife and the children as toddlers had disappeared, though Leela remembered it from her first year as a graduate student. It seemed to her a sound working strategy: to expunge from consciousness those who caused pain. The gossip was that Berg's divorce was very messy. Did removing a photograph help? Suppose she tore up or threw out the photograph of Cobb in her wallet? (And why had she kept it all these years? The answer seemed zigzag and murky and she did not want to go where it might lead.) She would have liked to take a photograph of her muddled emotions at this moment and then burn it. As for Mishka: he lived in sound and sensation, he lived in melodies trapped in her head. She would have liked to blank them out with white noise. She would have liked to take a photograph of the sense of dread that was closing in like fog. She would have liked to tear that photograph to shreds.

One by one, she picked up the framed images that were still on Berg's desk. There was an elaborate filigree border around his daughter at her college graduation and another around his son's wedding. There was a photograph of Berg on an archeological dig, somewhere in the Middle East. Leela studied it with interest, noting the brush in Berg's hand, his painstaking attention to the detail in a carved fragment of pediment, mud-crusted. The site was somewhere in the Sinai desert. Berg had gone there, Leela knew, a few summers back, the summer of his son's wedding. His son and daughter-in-law, he had told her, lived on a kibbutz.

Berg entered his office and she set the photo down guiltily. "Sorry. I was just—"

"Where were you?" Berg demanded. "The deadline is this week, and you give me this inadequate, this insufficient"—he lifted it and let it fall back to the desk, a dead weight—"words fail me."

Leela winced. She felt bruised. She despised female students and junior faculty members whose desire to please their male mentors was as great as their desire to excel. Apparently she was one of them and the knowledge shamed and infuriated her. To compensate, she protested with undue combativeness, "I've done a *substantial* survey of harmonics and violin construction, and the history and math of the f-holes—"

"This isn't a history department. Where's the math on resonance?"

"I've got a whole section on that." Leela picked up her proposal and flipped through it. "Here. Page five. Factors affecting volume of air in the violin and Helmholz resonance: the f-holes; placement of the sound post; placement of the bridge; thickness of plates in the body of violin."

"It's not enough to get us the grant. There's a technique to writing proposals that rake in funding. Diagrams, equations, graphs of the changes in sound. Stay up all night if you have to and add some dazzle to this."

"I'll get it done."

Berg was scribbling notes furiously on a legal pad. "And what about the matter of your boyfriend?"

"Excuse me?"

Berg tore the top sheet from his notepad and crumpled it violently and hurled it at a waste paper basket several feet from his desk. He missed. "I believe I spoke to him on the phone."

"He said you'd called."

"It's none of my business," Berg said, "but do you know what you're getting into there?"

Leela said evenly: "Is this relevant to our grant proposal?"

Berg gestured vehemently, precipitating small convulsions in the unstable files on his desk. "Do you know the kind of company your boyfriend keeps?"

"Dr. Berg, may I ask why my partner is of such interest to you? And why you think you know what company he keeps?"

"You may well ask," he said—his words were staccato, hard and sharp—"and I will tell you." But the intention to tell seemed swamped by agitation or anger. Elbows on his desk, head in his hands, Berg clutched handfuls of his own hair and pulled.

"Dr. Berg," Leela said, alarmed.

Berg stood abruptly and paced the small section of office floor not covered with books. "I've been getting hate mail," he said. "Anonymous. It's been going on for months."

"That's shocking."

"It's not pleasant. *Death to Israel. Death to Jewish imperialists and racists.* That sort of thing. In my departmental box. So either from a colleague or a student or staff."

"Wait a minute," Leela protested. "Anyone could hand the secretaries a letter addressed to you. Or they could just stick it in the departmental mail slot and it would wind up in your box. Anyone could walk in off the street and do that."

"It was on Math Department letterhead."

"Oh."

"It gives you a very sick feeling, but you figure, you know, the sender's unbalanced."

"Before you go any further," Leela said, "in case you're implying this has anything to do with... with my boyfriend, as you call him, Mishka is Jewish."

Berg stopped pacing and turned to look at her, startled. "I didn't know what his name was." He sat down at his desk again and stared at Leela. "I thought he was Muslim."

"You can't possibly have thought that *Mishka*...?"

"No, no. I found out who was doing it. Not your boyfriend."

Leela said: "So why have you been following me?"

Berg raised his eyebrows. "Following you?"

"Please. I happen to have photographic evidence. Why were you doing it?"

"In fact, I wasn't following you. I was following my personal hate-mail correspondent and then his contacts."

"I don't understand."

"Your boyfriend is one of my hate-mailer's regular contacts. I learned that before I found out he was your boyfriend. And then when I discovered that *you*... which was something I discovered entirely by accident.... Well, you can imagine. It felt like a violation. I had to ask myself: is my protegée spying on me? Is she putting these letters in my box?"

"I'm dumbfounded," Leela said. "But I do know you were spying on *me*."

"I had my eye on the contact of a contact. I had to ask myself: is Leela the go-between?"

Leela could feel her breathing turning ragged. "I can't believe this."

Mentor and former graduate student faced off, warily, across the sheaf of grant proposal.

"How did you meet him?" Berg asked.

"Under the circumstances," Leela said, "I think you should explain how *you* met him, and what grounds you have—"

"I haven't *met* him, I've observed him."

"Where?"

"There was some vandalism in my apartment building, run-of-the-mill stuff at first. The mezuzah would be ripped off my door. At first once every few weeks, then more often. Shit smeared on my *New York Times*. Scratches along the side of my car. Tires slashed. I didn't connect this with the mail at my office at first, because if you live on the northern side of Cambridge, stuff like this just happens. Though not usually as frequently."

"It just happens at MIT, too. I've had trash outside my office door. I've had rude notes on my bulletin board. Did you fail someone? Give them a D?"

"Ds and Fs come and grovel and beg and sob for higher grades. They don't send hate mail."

"I'm not sure that's true. One unsigned note on my bulletin board said: *To the Bitch from Dixie.*"

"The Bitch from Dixie?"

"From a Yankee who got a C or a D is my guess. It's not an insult another Southerner would make." Leela smiled grimly. "Southerners are unfailingly courteous, especially when angry. And when Southerners stab someone in the back, they always wear clean white gloves."

Berg stared at her. "I suppose that's meant to be funny," he said. "But I don't find death threats funny."

"Sorry. Lousy attempt to lighten the mood."

"I started getting threats at my apartment. In the mailbox. They hadn't been sent through the mail, they'd been put there. *Your son's kibbutz has been targeted.* Math Department letterhead, same font, same format, one line in the middle of the page, business envelope." He picked up the framed photograph of his son's wedding. "Then there was a laser copy of this photograph, with a hole through my son's face. So it has to be someone with access to my mailbox key and to my office."

"You can't seriously have thought I was involved."

"I didn't know what to think. I thought you might have been used."

Leela could feel a chill beginning at her toes and fingers and creeping along her limbs. She closed her eyes.

"I had to find out who it was," Berg said. "I outfitted myself with a disguise. Canvas drop sheets, white coveralls, cap, paint, rollers: the real thing. A house painter. I arranged subs for my classes. I was ready for however many days it was going to take."

Bizarre images bounced around inside Leela's head: Berg in paint-spattered coveralls and surgeon's coat performing post-mortems.

"I repainted the entryway walls in my apartment building," Berg said. "And the stair risers and the railings. Primed them. Painted them. Repainted them. The landlord owes me. High-hiding-white primer, semi-gloss finish, high gloss on the trim. It's amazing, frankly, a real eye-opener for an academic. You're invisible, day after day. No one even looks at you. You're part of the wall."

"I'm trying to imagine this," Leela said.

"Third day, I see one of my undergraduates, a bright intense kid named Ali Hassan. He sees me, well, he sees a man painting the stairs. He doesn't even bother to see if I'm watching or not.

I don't register. He opens my box with a lock pick. He leaves one of his charming notes."

"Did you get him on camera?"

"Didn't want to alert him. I just wanted to know who he was. I began to watch him in classes, I began to follow him. He meets contacts at that Moroccan coffee shop on Mass Ave."

"Café Marrakesh."

"That's the one. Your boyfriend is often there at night."

"He's a musician. He plays there two nights a week. It's a moonlighting gig."

"Where he hangs out with anti-Semitic thugs."

"He doesn't *hang out* with—Why would someone Jewish—?"

"Perhaps he's not. Not really."

"He is. His grandparents are Holocaust survivors. After the war, they got to Australia."

Berg turned his hands palm up in a gesture of mystification.

"Scads of people hang out at Marrakesh for the coffee," Leela said. "And for the live music at night. They sit at a table with strangers and start talking. They don't necessarily know who they're talking to. It doesn't mean anything at all."

"Hassan only ever meets with the same few people, most often with a contact named Jamil Haddad. Sometimes your boyfriend arrives with Jamil Haddad."

"Jamil Haddad!"

"I found out his name from a waiter. He didn't know who your boyfriend was, but he knew Haddad."

"He's the suicide bomber."

"What?"

"Yesterday. Jamil Haddad blew himself up in the subway."

"How do you know that?"

"I guess it was on the news."

Berg was stunned. "I don't know how I could have missed that." He kept smoothing his hand across the top of their grant proposal, pressing down, ironing it in four-four time, wiping a smear from its skin. "What exactly was your boyfriend's connection with Jamil Haddad?"

Leela said miserably: "I don't know."

"Don't you think you're playing with fire? Look, I'll be blunt. When you were a student, the rumor was you'd pick up anyone in Harvard Square and take him home for a fuck."

Leela stood abruptly and caused a small landslide of books. "How dare you?"

"Don't shoot the messenger. I hear stuff. Students, guys pissing in the bathroom, staff gossip. I'm not making judgments. I'm just telling you what I hear and that you have a bit of a reputation—"

"It's out of date," Leela said coldly.

"I just thought a warning might be in order. If you pick up trash, you might catch more than an STD."

Leela said icily, from the door, "I'll get the rewrite to you by morning."

"Oh shit," Berg said. "Look, I apologize. I was out of line." He moved between Leela and the door and closed it again. He returned to his desk. "Sit down," he said. "Please." He picked up her proposal essay and tapped it, one side after another, on his desktop, in pursuit of perfect alignment, all edges straight as a die. "Look, if I was out of line—and I was—it's because no one can take hate mail lightly. Not me anyway. Not these days. Every time there's a bombing—"

"They just make me feel numb now," Leela said. "They don't seem real any more."

"They seem real enough to me. I wish I knew where all this would end." Berg rubbed his eyes. "The truth is, I invented a reason to get you in here today. I had to know if you were part of this. I just had to know."

"I'm not. I swear to you, I'm not."

"And your boyfriend?"

"I don't know. It doesn't make any sense and I can't believe... but I just don't know."

"I believe you, though I'm not sure why. Because I want to, I guess. In fact, your proposal's fine. You don't need to touch it. I'll FedEx the whole thing off tomorrow."

"Thank you."

"I'm confident we'll get this. It's big money. I'm looking forward to working with you on the project."

"Thank you."

"But I have to hope, with respect to... you know, that you'll be careful."

"I'll be careful."

BOOK IV

Promised Land

1

THAT FIRST SUMMER after Leela-May crossed over, fifteen years back, Maggie used to spend late afternoons waiting out by the gatepost on Rural Route Three. She was watching for a sign from Leela-May. This was when Maggie believed—she still had reason to believe—that Leela would come back from the other side. It was the summer before Maggie's last year in middle school and her sister's transfiguration, not to mention the turbulent front of Maggie's own future moving in, smoked like haze at the crest of the hill. The haze was shot through with shimmer and gold, a cloud of gorgeous and tantalizing nothing, but Maggie could not see through it.

She would bring a book and sit cross-legged in the grass, her back against a fence post, but she could never concentrate. She would shade her eyes and squint until she could just make out the hump of the Hamilton house, which she was able to do by lining up her thumb with two pines and then looking slightly to the left. Beyond the Hamilton house the rural route dipped toward swamp, but long before the mailman's white-and-blue van came over the crest and floated onward like a galleon in fog, Maggie would see the tell-tale halo of dust beyond the Hamilton chimneys and she would abandon her book and start running.

The house, built in the old plantation style, had been derelict for so long that sections of Hamilton veranda had come adrift and jutted like wreckage from a honeysuckle sea. Maggie climbed on the rusted gates—the crossbar of the H was her lookout point—until she could make out the driver of the van behind his wheel. Then she would start shouting. "*Hey*, Mr. Boykin! *Hey!*" She would spread her wings and loft herself out from the H and crash-land on the unpaved road. "Is there a letter, Mr. Boykin?"

"One day you will either break a leg or get yourself run over, Maggie-Lee."

"Is there a letter from my sister?"

"There's something here from the County Council," Mr. Boykin might say. Or: "I believe I've got your utilities bill."

"But have you got one for me?"

"Well now," he would say, making a great show of searching through the canvas bag on the seat beside him. "I don't believe so, Maggie-Lee."

"But there *has* to be, Mr. Boykin. It's been a week."

"Well, there *is* one here for your daddy." He would hold the envelope at arm's length and squint. "Can't rightly read this handwriting, but I think it says—" He would squint some more and make a performance of deciphering the script with difficulty. "*Mr. Gideon Moore, Rural Route 3, Promised Land, South Carolina.* Yes, that's what it says, but I don't have nothing here for Miss Mary-Magdalene Lee Moore herself."

On such jackpot days, Maggie would stand on tiptoe and lean into the van and throw her arms around the mailman's neck. "Don't tease, Mr. Boykin, it's mean. Just give it me, please, pretty please."

"It's against the law," he would say. "It's a *federal* offense.

I have to put this letter in the box at your gatepost, and nowhere else, or the sheriff might could string me up."

Maggie would whisk the letter from his hands. "He can string me up instead," she would call. "What's he gonna do? Shoot me?" She would run alongside the van to the double gates and then race up her long dirt drive, gasping, laughing with excitement, leaping over pot-holes and nettles, clutching at the stitch in her side, and hand the envelope to her father—"It's here, Daddy. It's come"—but the summer of that year was not propitious.

"How many letters does this make, Mary-Magdalene Lee?"

"Um, five, no six now, Daddy. Four that we've read and the one that you wouldn't—"

"Six. This is her sixth."

Gideon Moore studied the envelope, inspecting postmarks and stains. He turned it over and held it up to the light. Maggie chewed her fingernails. Minutes passed.

"Look at this, Mary-Magdalene Lee," her father said somberly. He pointed to the spidery postmark. "Read it out loud."

"June 6," Maggie read. "Cambridge, Mass. 02138."

"Six, six, and this is your sister's sixth letter. What does that tell you?"

Maggie knew what three sixes told. "Mark of the beast in the Book of Revelation," she said sadly, and her father nodded and they both contemplated the sorrowful off-white object. It looked, Maggie thought, like a pigeon shot with a BB gun. It looked like a stricken dove. Then Gideon Moore spat on the Yankee stamp and peeled it off and put it in his mouth. He chewed and swallowed.

"Daddy," Maggie begged sadly.

"It is not that which goeth into the mouth that defileth a man; but that which proceedeth out of the mouth, Matthew fifteen, verse eleven."

He dropped the letter on the barbeque pit beside the screen porch and struck a match on his shoe and bent to set the paper on fire. He and Maggie watched Leela-May's words burn and curl. Black shavings twisted in the air and Maggie lifted her hand and let scorched words settle there, fragile as feathers. She closed her fist over them.

"We are going to pray for Leela-May Magnolia," her father said.

Maggie pressed her lips to the ash in her palm. She pressed her palm to her forehead.

"Here and now," her father said, kneeling on the stony weed-crusted ground, and motioning for Maggie to kneel beside him. Maggie, in cotton shorts, surreptitiously brushed at pebbles with one hand. "Now if Leela-May had mailed this one day later," her father said, "that would have been a whole other story. Of course, if she had mailed this one day later, it would have been because she had been stopped on her road to Damascus and she would have written a different kind of letter, first sentence to last, than a letter mailed on the sixth. Seven is the Lord's favorite number. How do we know that, Mary-Magdalene Lee?"

"Because God created the heavens and the earth in seven days," Maggie said. "And because there were seven years of plenty in Egypt, and seven years of famine, and seven priests with seven trumpets marching around Jericho, and seven seals in the Book of Revelation."

"And because the Lord said we must forgive our brother seventy times seven, Mary-Magdalene Lee. Could you forgive your sister seventy times seven for crossing over and leaving us to manage by ourselves?"

"I'd forgive her seven *million* times," Maggie said fervently.

She understood that her father did not only mean his older daughter's going north, though no one else in the family, as far back as they knew, had ever crossed the Mason-Dixon line. Crossing over into wickedness was what he meant, and this, Maggie knew, was something Leela-May had done long ago.

"Daddy, the next one will be her seventh letter."

"Let us pray," he said. He bowed his head but raised both arms in supplication, hands open, offering proof of cleanliness to God above. "Lord," he said, "we thank thee for speaking to us in thy secret ways. Thou revealest that which is hidden."

From under the curve of her lashes, Maggie watched the secret swirl of ants. They moved in paisley code beneath the grass. She saw things she had agreed to keep hidden and things her sister didn't know that she had seen: Leela-May and Richard Calhoun in the back seat of his car; Leela-May and the Barnwell boys in the crawl space under the church, Leela-May with Benedict Boykin, the mailman's son, smoking cigarettes and kissing behind the school, Leela-May and Cobb Slaughter lying on the Hamilton veranda with arms and legs tangled like an octopus tying itself in knots.

"Lord," Gideon Moore prayed, "all things are known to thee, and thou knowest that thy daughter Leela-May Magnolia has crossed over, but thou art the Good Shepherd."

Maggie heard the quaver in his voice. "Daddy," she said gently.

He's only got us, Maggie, was the last thing Leela-May had said at the gas station where the Greyhound bus stopped. *He's held together with duct tape and the Bible and magic numbers and us.*

And his letters, Maggie reminded her sister: his letters to the President, to senators, to congressmen, to the Pope, to assorted world leaders.

Well, yes, his letters. But we never mail them.

Sometimes he mails them himself.

You mean he's onto us? That's a bad sign.

Maggie reached out and laid her hand on her father's wrist.

"The good shepherd," Gideon prayed, his tone part plea, part reproach, "*searches* for the lost sheep—"

"Daddy."

Her father's sorrow was frightening to Maggie because she did not know how to shift it. He was a web of such delicate parts, of such improbable and contradictory tracery: body strong as a back hoe, fixations like flint, faith like a bonfire for heretics, compassion infinite, generosity to those in need boundless, spirit frail as a dragonfly wing.

"Let loose thy Holy Spirit as bounty hunter, O Lord," Gideon Moore prayed, "that the conviction of sin may fall upon Leela-May."

Maggie could see her sister in the glowing embers of the barbeque pit. Leela-May was tied to a stake. She saw her father—on fire with muddled love and bewilderment—lighting the pyre.

"Let thy Holy Spirit seize her and shackle her and return her to thy path and to thy faithful servants because thou knowest, O Lord, that Mary-Magdalene Lee is not a very good cook, nor can she be when there is summer-school homework that must be done and when the housekeeping tasks are rightfully those of Leela-May Magnolia. In Jesus' name we ask it, Amen."

"Amen," Maggie said.

*   *   *

Every day, Maggie washed down his truck. She hosed off the dust, she smeared beeswax paste, thick as corn mush, on the scarred metal flanks, she buffed till the rust holes looked dignified and till the faded red bodywork took on a holy glow.

The logo on each cabin door—professionally done, bartered for plumbing work, designed and executed by master sign writer Boykin—nephew of Boykin the mailman (Vietnam vet) and Boykin the roofing man, all Boykins being members of the African Methodist Episcopal church in Promised Land—was growing faint. *The Sword of the Lord and of Gideon*, the sign said if one knew what it said.

"It should say *Gideon and Daughters*," Leela-May had rashly protested once, before crossing over, before startling everyone except her high-school math teacher and Cobb Slaughter, her Math-Prize rival, by her ascent into Ivy-League heaven, before giving up on her after-school and weekend goal of perfecting the sharpening of blades: mower blades, scythe blades, rotary tillers, her sassy tongue.

"It *means* Gideon and Daughters," her father said. "It means the Lord will provide. It means ready for all emergencies. Read your Bible, Book of Judges, chapter seven."

THE SWORD OF THE LORD AND OF GIDEON.

SHARPENING AND FIXING.

WE WORK MIRACLES.

IF IT'S HOPELESS, BRING IT TO US.

And people did. From the white Pentecostal church and from the black AME church, they brought that which was broken or blunt. Baptists, Methodists, Presbyterians, even white Episcopalians, all made processional pilgrimage along Rural Route Three in their beaten-up or gussied-up cars because Gideon Moore had a gift. Not only from Promised Land did they come, but from the farthest points of the county. They came bearing offerings—lawnmowers, vacuum cleaners, outboard motors, busted tools—and they laid them before the sword of the Lord and of Gideon Moore. The floor of the barn-turned-garage was strewn with parts. In well-oiled machinery, Gideon saw Intelligent Design. He knew the universe ticked like a clock.

"In a gear shaft that works," he told his daughters, "you can see the fingerprint of God."

Maggie stood in the doorway of the shed with a wet chamois cloth in her hand.

"The van is clean as a soul just baptized, Daddy. Mrs. Donaldson needs you to come fix her air-conditioner. She says if you don't get there quick, she'll be no more'n a puddle on her porch."

"Got to go by the Rileys first, fix one of their cars, then I'll get to the Donaldsons. You call her back and let her know."

"Daddy, while you're gone, can I read Leela-May's letters again?"

"We already have their true meaning," he said.

Maggie wanted the other meaning, the surface one, the paragraphs that shimmered with Boston accents and strange Yankee idioms and amazing news, with accounts of the fish market and Quincy Wharf and Old North Church where Paul Revere had hung his lantern and the underground world of subway trains and music students who played for tossed coins in Harvard Square, but those letters had been annotated and hidden away. Her father had sliced up each letter with his pencil, marking off seventh letters and seventh words, calibrating the thinning out of his daughter's soul. Sometimes the marked-off letters had needed rearranging to make clear the code of the Lord; and sometimes advanced divination had been required. Sometimes every seventh sentence had to be marked, and only then did the seventh word of each seventh sentence make everything clear.

Rushing... underground... music... Harvard... foreign...

"She is bound at full speed on a downward path," Gideon concluded. "She is lost—she is temporarily lost—but the Good Shepherd findeth his wayward sheep."

Maggie knew her father pined for the letters. She knew he feared them. "Open it, Daddy," she begged as each missive arrived. Then the trembling in his fingers would start.

"You do it," he would say. "You read it out. You've got young eyes."

While she read, her father rocked on the porch swing in small slow arcs, his hands on his knees.

Dear Daddy and Maggie-Lee:
My room is on the top floor of one of the dorms in Harvard Yard. It's hot as grease on a griddle up here, just under the roof, but I love it. It's so private. I can watch the world without the world watching me. Private. Isn't that a strange new thing? Nobody knows anybody else's business up here. In Promised Land, where everyone knows everything about everyone else, we can't even imagine such a thing. I think about this a lot. Everything is so foreign here, and I am a foreigner. I love that. I love it that no one knows who I am.

That was the third letter. The fourth letter went to the stake. After the fifth letter, Gideon worked on a busted tractor for many hours without a break.

* * *

When the seventh letter came, Maggie did not run from the Hamilton house to her drive.

"You hurt your leg bad?" Mr. Boykin asked.

"I just feel like walking, is all. Don't tell Daddy you gave me a letter. Don't spoil the surprise."

"I didn't give you," he said. "You snatched. You want a ride back?"

"No," Maggie said. She inspected the date carefully and pondered it as she walked. This one was safe. It had been mailed on the fourteenth of June.

"Daddy!" she said, handing it to him. "It's her seventh letter and it was mailed on the fourteenth and that is a multiple of seven."

Her father balanced the letter on the tips of the fingers of both hands, assessing its true weight and moral worth. He swayed back and forth on the porch swing, eyes closed and head bowed. He prayed for guidance. Maggie closed her eyes and prayed too. She prayed for sevens. She prayed for seventy times seven. The porch swing creaked as it moved.

"It has to be burned."

"But it's her seventh one, postmarked fourteenth," Maggie protested. "That's triple perfect."

"It bears Satan's mark."

"Where? How?"

"God is a mathematician without error and by the power of the Holy Spirit, we can discern the meaning of the messages he sends."

"We *pray* for her," Maggie pointed out. "If we pray, we have to have faith. Satan can't touch her."

"Look at this date, Mary-Magdalene Lee. When you add up all the digits, month, day, and year, what do you get?"

Maggie's lips moved. She marked off sub-totals with her fingers. "Twenty-four," she said.

"No. The whole year, the whole year. You have to add on two for two thousand."

"Twenty-six."

"Which is double thirteen, the Devil's number."

"I'll be thirteen next birthday," Maggie dared to protest. She put her hands on her hips. "Does that make me bad?"

"It makes me worried," he said. "It makes me afraid for you."

"Oh Daddy, you don't have to worry."

"I'm worried but I also trust in the Lord. Leela-May cannot outrun the grace of God and nor can you, though Satan will do his best."

"Daddy," Maggie pointed out, touched with the sudden bright fire of the Spirit, "look at her zipcode. It's Cambridge, Mass., 02138. That adds up to fourteen, a double seven."

The porch swing rocked back and forth, back and forth. The late afternoon turned dark. There was a deafening percussion of cicadas. The letter, pale as communion bread, lay on the fraying white wicker of the swing. Under the weight of Gideon's right hand, it glowed—or so it seemed to Maggie—giving off radioactive light. She could see the bones in her father's hand.

Mentally, she rehearsed asking *Daddy?*—trying out various tones—but the risk was too great. She counted junebugs instead. She thought that Leela-May would know the equation for measuring the onset of dark: x fence posts by y minutes equals z twilight shadows. Leela-May could have told them: in seventeen minutes, the pines along the drive will disappear. Stars began to be visible and Maggie marked them off in groups of seven in case this meant something, because Leela-May had told her that the seven sisters in the Pleiades had guided ships in the ancient world. There are really *hundreds* of stars in the Pleiades cluster, Leela-May had explained, but the naked eye can only see seven because the naked eye wants to see patterns it already knows.

These were the patterns Maggie knew: that God whispered numbers, in code, in her father's ear, and that Leela-May followed algebraic clues and math symbols along quite different trails, picking up numerical crumbs and magic as she went, pressing on toward the heart of the labyrinth and the radiant answer to some vast riddle.

Maggie was allergic to numbers. She did not trust them.

She thought her father had fallen asleep. She imagined how she might slide the letter from under his fingers and steam it open and read it and slide it safely back under again.

She took two quiet steps toward the swing and reached for the letter but Gideon stirred and opened his eyes. "What are you doing, Mary-Magdalene Lee?"

"You fell asleep, Daddy. You should go to bed."

"Yes," he said. "I should go to bed."

At the screen door, he paused and said: "Sometimes the Lord speaks different ways to different folks."

The screen door banged shut. The letter lay on the swing.

Maggie's finger was shaking as she wormed it under the flap and tore the envelope.

Dear Daddy and Maggie-Lee:
I'm in seventh heaven because the Honors students have met for some Early Bird seminars, pre Labor Day. It's like math summer camp. Afterwards, we sit around talking and arguing and making up problem sets for one another.

*We call ourselves the Pythagoras Club and our motto is
All is Number, which was the motto of the secret society
of the students of Pythagoras himself. I thought you'd
find it interesting, Daddy, that a mathematician born on
the Isle of Samos in 580 BC or so agrees with you on this
point. This is what he believed: that the clues to all the
mysteries of the world are encrypted in numbers. Also
that we should bring body and soul into alignment—into
perfect mathematical alignment—with the movements of
the planets and stars. We need, he believed, to be in tune
with the music of the spheres. He believed the planets
sing as they move, and this is what blows my mind: since
the Hubble telescope has been recording the humming
from Deep Space, physicists have known that he was
right.*

The screen door creaked. "Mary-Magdalene Lee?"

"Yes, Daddy."

"You do not need to tell me what she says."

"She says you are right about numbers."

"She had to go away to college at the end of the world to
learn that? Lock the door when you come in."

"She says the stars sing. She says there's some telescope—"

"*Who is this,*" Gideon demanded, "*that darkeneth counsel
by words without knowledge?* The Book of Job, chapter 38.
*Then the Lord answered Job out of the whirlwind and said:
Where wast thou when I laid the foundations of the earth…
when the morning stars sang together, and all the sons of God
shouted for joy?*"

"And what about the *daughters* of God?" demanded the
voice of Leela-May so abruptly and loudly that Maggie had to
press the letter against her mouth.

Gideon flinched, as though hit by a small sharp stone from a sling. "Did you say something, Mary-Magdalene Lee?"

"Daddy, if you stand there with the screen door open, the bugs will get in."

Gideon stepped out on the porch and let the door swing shut. He swayed a little in the dark but then righted himself and felt his way toward the column at the top of the steps. The wood was soft to the touch in several places and he let his hand explore gingerly until it found a length of railing where he could lean. Beyond the dark massy crowns of the pines, the black dome was spangled with glitter. "*Canst thou bind the sweet influences of Pleiades*," he murmured, "*or loose the bands of Orion?*"

"Leela-May says there are really hundreds of stars in the Pleiades," Maggie offered, "but mostly we can only see seven because we want to see the patterns—"

"When I was little," her father said, "I used to lie awake and watch the stars from my bedroom window. I was in love with the Milky Way. I tried to count the stars I could see." He rubbed his eyes with the back of his hand. "But we can't get there. There are more than any numbers we can reach." Maggie joined him at the railing and slipped her hand into his. The back of his hand was wet. "Your mother used to stand here, Mary-Magdalene. On this very spot. Your mother and I. We used to count the stars and count our blessings."

"Daddy," Maggie said. She pressed her cheek to the back of his hand.

"Where were *we*?" he asked his daughter. "Where were *we* when the morning stars sang?"

A pale disk of moon mounded up at the edge of a cloud and suddenly Maggie could see the shape of the barn and the hulking shadows of mowers waiting to be fixed. She could see the truck crouching in the dark. She could almost see the silver snail-trail of the sign: *The Sword of the Lord and of Gideon*. One by one, she touched the hard little row of calluses on Gideon's palm. What does five mean? she wondered. Her father squeezed her hand so hard that it hurt. He said gruffly, "There are more mysteries and more blessings in this life than there are stars, Mary-Magdalene Lee."

Maggie thought there was a kind of sadness that almost made you happy. You could drown in it the way you could drown in the moon. It was just right for Gideon and daughters, she thought.

2

EVEN BEFORE MR. BOYKIN answered the phone, Maggie imagined she could hear the joyful hubbub that always swirled through his house. There were always children: nieces, nephews, grandchildren, second cousins, the friends of second cousins. There was always laughter. There was always someone singing Gospel at the top of her lungs.

There were always, at any one time, at least three people eating, two cooking, four peeling or shucking or chopping. The sink was always crammed full of collard greens draining, and on the stove was a cauldron of grits. Small invasions of family and friends were always imminent. And Mr. Boykin was always praising the Lord. He no more ran out of reasons than did Gideon Moore, though Maggie learned very young that God was in a more lighthearted mood at the Boykin house than he was at hers. Mr. Boykin and God were on teasing terms. They joshed one another. They shared the same jokes.

The relationship between Maggie's father and God was more austere.

Maggie had never forgotten the night—she was four and Leela was ten—when someone shot holes in the Boykin house. The windows were shattered. The hot-water tank was a pin-cushion fountain and the main water pipe from the well to the house became a geyser. Benedict, who was Leela-May's age, had arrived breathless on the Moore's front porch. "Leela-May," he had gasped, "can you ask your dad to come quick?" He could barely speak for crying. He was shivering in spite of the heat. "We've been shot at. Daddy says we need a fixit man real fast for the plumbing or we're gonna be drowned and then dry."

And when the four of them—Gideon, Leela-May, Mary-Magdalene and Benedict Boykin—had jolted up the Boykin drive in the dented old Sword of the Lord and of Gideon, they saw a spectacular jet of water, and they saw a dozen children in nothing but shorts, or in nothing, hollering and laughing and running into the waterspout.

"Bet you ain't never seen a fountain like this, Gideon," Mr. Boykin said. He was laughing too, watching the children, though at first Maggie thought he was sobbing, the sounds coming from his throat were so strange.

It's the way you laugh so you won't cry, Leela told her years later. *He didn't want the children to see him break down.*

I thought he was crying, Maggie said, *but Benedict thought he was laughing, I remember that.*

How could you remember that? You were four years old.

I remember being frightened when Benedict banged on our door.

We were all frightened.

And I remember the waterspout and the children dancing and Benedict running away. Tell me what else, and there were many retellings, so many that Maggie could see herself watching the Boykin children, she could hear Mr. Boykin say, "Ain't this a sight, Gideon?"

And Maggie's father had said: "This ain't right, Esau, that someone would do this to you. This don't sit right with the Lord. What you going to do about this?"

"Well, first thing," Mr. Boykin said, "what I already did, I gave thanks to the Lord that no one was hit. And second thing, I prayed about it, for the Lord to show me the silver lining, which he is showing me. Will you look at those kids? And third thing, I sent Benedict over for you and I gave thanks that I have a good neighbor I can trust. And fourth thing, I'm gonna ask you to fix my plumbing and my windows and ask if we can pay you by Latisha coming over every weekend to clean your house."

"Deal," Gideon said. "But Esau, how come these things never get you down? How come I don't never ever see you down?"

And Maggie remembered the way Mr. Boykin's eyebrows shot up—yes, she could replay the scene exactly—she remembered how he looked puzzled. "Well," he said, frowning a little, "that's a strange kind of question from you, Gideon. We got the same God and there is not a sparrow falls to the ground. Things get me down. Those gunshots sure got me down. I just never had any reason for *staying* down. Not once I look to the Lord. Not so far, anyways."

Maggie also remembered the way Benedict had clenched his fists and glowered at his father. "It ain't right not to be angry," he had shouted, and he had pummeled his father with his fists, and then he had run off and hid.

Gideon Moore had laid a gentle hand on Esau's arm.

"That's the worst of it," Esau said sadly. "What it does to our kids."

Times had changed since that night. Black families were no longer shot at in Promised Land. Benedict had been in harm's way in the Middle East and Leela could have been killed in a bombing on the subway in Boston.

"Mr. Boykin?" Maggie said when he answered the phone. "I finally got hold of Leela-May, and she's okay."

"Praise the Lord," Mr. Boykin said. "We been praying. I heard forty-some dead on the news. Could have been a lot worse, they said."

"She could have been on that train but she walked home instead. She doesn't really know why she walked home."

"This is the Lord's doing and it is marvelous in our eyes. Same way he keeps Benedict safe in Iraq."

"Can I come and talk to you, Mr. Boykin?"

"Any time you want to drop by, Maggie-Lee."

Mown grass was what Maggie could smell, and the profligate scent of jasmine run amok. The Boykin house was only a couple of miles from the house of Gideon Moore. Maggie borrowed her father's pickup and had the window down so that her hair was whipped about her face. The car tracks were unpaved and the jolts were sometimes extreme. It was always both a shock and a pleasure to emerge from the long and winding driveway and see the front porch and the porch swing and Mrs. Boykin's flower garden and the children on the tire swing and the dogs and the chickens and the sense of unbridled joy. The minute Maggie braked and stepped from the pickup, dogs and children hurled themselves at her legs. "Hey, guys," she said, laughing, "let up!"

Latisha Boykin came out to the porch and hugged Maggie. "You gonna be teaching three of my grans at DeLaine Elementary, I hear. You got the blessings of the Lord on your head, Mary-Magdalene Lee, and you better believe you got mine. You want some sweet tea?"

"Thanks, Mrs. Boykin."

"We are all planning to drive up to Columbia for your graduation," Latisha said. "Be your cheering squad when you come up on stage."

"Latisha's gonna conduct," Esau said. "She's winding us up in rehearsals. We are gonna hoot and holler to bring down the roof of the University of South Carolina."

As though on cue, the children shouted in unison: *You go, girl! You go, Mary-Magdalene Lee!*

Maggie laughed. "You'll have me thrown out."

Latisha said, carefully, "Leela-May coming down?"

Maggie sighed. "I hope so. But you know Leela-May. I have to keep working at it. I was planning to ask Benedict for his help."

"He's been shipped back to Iraq already."

"Oh." Maggie sipped her tea. "Did he say much about his meeting with Leela-May?"

"He said he'd seen her, that's all," Letisha said. "He didn't get down here, you know. Said there wasn't enough time. He doesn't tell us too much these days."

Esau said nothing.

Maggie thought about Leela-May and Benedict: the swimming hole, the Hamilton house, the flag demonstrations. She said: "I still remember when your house got shot up."

"Yeah," Esau Boykin said. "Things sure have changed."

"Hmm," Latisha said. "*Some* things have changed."

"Confederate flag's come down off the State House," Esau said.

"One time Leela-May showed me the drawings that got pasted on her locker," Maggie said. "When she and Benedict were going on those flag protests. She took them down but she kept them in a folder."

"Ugly stuff. Hate's ugly."

"Very ugly. But Leela-May never got scared."

Esau smiled. "Benedict used to say: Leela-May's so strong you would swear she was black."

"That girl is as fearless as they come," Latisha said. "Just like your daddy."

"She *is* like Daddy in a funny way, isn't she? She gets angry when I tell her that."

"I remember when our church was burned down," Esau said. "Back before you or your sister were born. Your daddy showed up at the Rebuilding Bee. He was the only white man who came. I said to him: 'How come you're here and not wearing a white hood, Gideon? There's people whose mowers you fix who did this.' And your daddy just said: 'I know it, Esau, and I don't understand it, but *inasmuch as they have done it unto one of the least of these my brethren, they have done it unto me.*'"

"That's Daddy. He knows the Bible by heart."

"He's a strange man, your father. And Leela-May got the fearless gene from him. Ain't nothing or no one can frighten that girl."

Maggie turned and turned her glass of sweet tea as though she were winding up a clock. She fidgeted with the gingham tablecloth. "That's kind of what I wanted to talk about," she said. "There's something wrong. Leela's scared."

"It's that bombing."

"I suppose so. But it seemed like that hardly registered with her. She seemed very strange, very jumpy, but she wouldn't explain, and it scares me because I'm not used to Leela-May being scared."

Maggie thought back to that night, fifteen years ago, the first night after Leela-May had left home. Maggie and her father sat side by side on the porch swing, not saying a word. They sat there for most of the night. Maggie was wide awake, too frightened to switch the porch light off. At some point, faint snoring disturbed her and she eased herself off the swing and went inside for a quilt. She covered her father gently, but the movement and the sound of the screen door woke him.

For several minutes she stood over him with the quilt and he stared back from the swing. "Well," he said at last, "we'll just have to fend for ourselves, Mary-Magdalene Lee."

"Yes sir," she said.

"We'll have to look out for each other."

"Yes sir."

"The Lord will provide," he said. "We better get inside and get some sleep."

"You got the fearless gene too, Maggie-Lee," Esau Boykin said.

"No," she said. "I don't. But Leela-May does, and when *she's* scared...."

"But don't you think it's the bombing?"

"I think it's got something to do with Cobb Slaughter. She's just seen him again."

Esau shifted uneasily. "Benedict never much liked Cobb Slaughter. Never trusted him either."

"What really happened with Cobb's mother?" Maggie wanted to know.

Neither Esau nor Latisha seemed to want to discuss this issue.

"People blame ol' Calhoun," Esau said at last, "but it's not that simple. Like most of us, he came back *different*. He never drank like that before. He never got violent. I guess it wore her down and one day she just couldn't take any more."

"What did Cobb's father actually do in Vietnam?"

"Not much I can tell you about that," Esau said. "Everyone fights his own war and they're all different."

Latisha brought another pitcher of sweet tea. "Leela-May and Cobb were always kind of close, weren't they?"

"More than that," Maggie said.

Esau and Latisha raised eyebrows.

"I saw them sometimes," Maggie said sheepishly, "on the Hamilton house veranda. I used to spy on Leela-May. I used to watch her with boys."

With Benedict too, she did not say.

"Hmm," Latisha said. "Benedict always thought Cobb looked daggers at him. He thought it was because of politics. Because of the flag. I always thought it was because of Leela-May, but I never said anything. I didn't want to put the thought in his head. I was afraid of trouble."

"Leela-May would never be frightened of Cobb Slaughter," Esau offered categorically.

"She's scared of *something*," Maggie said.

"I've seen a look in Cobb Slaughter's eye a time or two," Latisha said, "when he was watching Benedict shooting hoops in a high school game. I didn't like that look one little bit."

BOOK V

Mishka

Musical hallucinations were invading people's minds long before they were recognized as a condition of malfunctioning neural networks. Plenty of composers have had musical hallucinations.... Toward the end of his life, for instance, Robert Schumann wrote down the music he hallucinated; legend has it that he said he was taking dictation from Schubert's ghost.

New York Times, JULY 12, 2005

It is a great shame to ban music but there are worse things you can do to it: turn it into muzak, for example.

IAN BEDFORD,
The Interdiction of Music in Islam

1

FROM THE MOMENT he left the apartment, Mishka had a sense of massive risk. His life was in danger. He knew it as surely as he knew how to play Beethoven: that is to say, without giving the matter any thought. His hands knew what to do. The knowledge was stored in his body. He knew he was a marked man. Simultaneously he knew this phobic dread was clearly absurd, it was neurotic, ridiculous, shaming, yet the intuition was extraordinarily intense. It was so intense that he was unable to cross Massachusetts Avenue. He stood transfixed by the newspaper stand at the corner of his street and Mass Ave. A man was propped against the stand, watching him.

"Uncle Otto," Mishka whispered, and the moment he spoke Uncle Otto disappeared and the *Boston Globe* fixed him with its headline through the drop-glass gate: BOMBER IDENTIFIED. Below the headline, Jamil Haddad, with his habitual smirk, stared out of cold black eyes.

Mishka had to back away from the curb.

"Hey. Are you okay?" someone asked.

Mishka leaned against a shop front and fought back the urge to be sick. Cars were coming at him every which way. There was a bull's-eye painted on the front of his shirt.

"You look as though you need a doctor," someone said. "Should I hail you a cab?"

"I'm fine, I'm fine." Mishka waved the man on. "Thanks. It's nothing. Just a dizzy spell."

He had change in his pockets. He dropped quarters into the slot and pulled the glass door of the newsstand toward him. He reached in and extracted the *Boston Globe*, then he turned the paper around and put it back. Now the lower half of page one, inverted, faced the street. He let the glass door swing shut. He leaned on the stand.

He had a class. He was responsible for teaching an undergraduate class, but he could not get himself across Massachusetts Avenue. Every driver had a bead on him. Twenty minutes ago—could that be right? Could that have been only twenty minutes back?—he had answered the phone and spoken to Dr. Berg, Leela's colleague. Dr. Berg had been angry, ostensibly about Leela, though Mishka had the illogical impression that the hostility was directed at him. He had never met Berg. Was Berg jealous? Was that it? Was there something between Leela and Berg? In any case, Mishka had handled the matter. He had been courteous. He had spoken as an adult speaks. He had sounded normal. He left Leela a note.

Where had Leela been all last night?

What was happening to him?

He could not cross Massachusetts Avenue, which seemed to him as lethal as a booby-trapped DMZ in a movie. He could not teach a class. He was not capable of standing in front of a group of people and speaking. He walked south, hugging the store fronts. Car horns made him jump. He crossed quiet side streets, steeling himself against panic, until he reached Harvard Square. He took the subway to Central. At Café Marrakesh he made a phone call, and then he waited for Sleiman Abboud.

"I am ready to meet him now," he said on the phone. "I have to see him." He felt as though he had said: *I have to see him before I die*, and having said that, or having thought it, the terrible pressure inside his rib cage eased and he unclenched his hands and thought to himself with amazement: It was just that. It was the need to acknowledge my want, my desire to know the Abukir side of myself, the X in my identity, no matter what it turns out to be. His body felt lighter, relaxed. He felt almost jovial. It had nothing to do with premonition or death, he told himself. It was the collision of desire and of fear.

"I have to see him," he said again when Sleiman joined him in the smoky café. "As soon as possible."

"Arrangements will be made," Sleiman told him. They ordered Turkish coffee and sweet bread. "Wait for my email," Sleiman said. He wrote something on a paper napkin that bore the Café Marrakesh logo. "Here's the contact number. I wouldn't advise calling from your apartment. Your phone may be tapped. In fact, I wouldn't advise calling from anywhere in the States. Call when you get to Beirut."

Mishka could not stop himself from asking: "Did you know about Jamil Haddad? Did you know in advance?"

"Don't ask questions," Sleiman said. "And don't come here again before you leave."

"When do I leave?"

"Two days, three at the most. We have contacts with certain airlines. You will leave as soon as our contacts can get you a seat. Don't go back to your apartment before you leave."

"But I have to go back for my things."

"There's nothing you need. Buy some changes of clothes and a suitcase. You'll be reimbursed."

"If I don't go back, Leela—my girlfriend—will call the police."

Sleiman frowned. "All right. Go when you know your girlfriend is out. Be gone before she gets back. Leave the kind of note that will reassure her, so she doesn't go calling the police or anyone else."

The sound booth in the Harvard Music Lab was like a womb. All day Mishka had walked the streets of Cambridge in some sort of a trance. He had been in and out of the apartment while Leela, presumably, was parrying Berg's irritation in his office. He left another note:

> *Dear Leela:*
> *I'm off to the west coast for a week. Have lucked into*
> *incredible job opportunity. I'm flying out for interview.*
> *Wish me luck. Will call to let you know how it goes.*
> *Mishka*

He had taken a suitcase and his oud and there had been an awkward moment when the tenant on the floor below, pausing on the landing, had said: "That's quite a load, Mishka. Are you off on a concert tour or something?"

"Audition on the west coast. Job interview," Mishka said. Auditioning a family, he thought. Auditioning for the role of member of the family tribe.

"Good luck then. Not easy carting that Persian thing around, I imagine. You look a bit like a walking piñata. I assume you won't try to get to Logan on the T."

"I'll hail a cab on Mass Ave."

"Have fun."

Fun, Mishka thought sourly. A funny thing happened on the way to Beirut.

He had walked to the Music School and stashed suitcase and oud in his office, and then he had walked around the city until it grew dark, and then he had holed himself up in the

Music Lab like a nocturnal creature in its burrow. Now he was calm. He had his bearings.

The sound booth cradled him. There was white fluorescent tubing to simulate day, but Mishka preferred to light a candle and sit in the dark. He supposed he must have been happy in the nine floating months before his birth. He supposed contentment must also have bathed his mother in that time when she could rest a hand on her belly and she and her son could converse in code, tapping out musical notations in the blood. He remembered also the womb-like contentment of the first six years of his life. He knew this was why the small dark space of the sound booth and the wick's nimbus and the music and the sound of his heartbeat all added up to an addiction. Cradled by the felted walls, headphones on, Mendelssohn's *Violin Concerto in E Minor* or Gluck's *Orfeo* or Saliba al-Qatrib's classical Persian meditations on the oud seemingly emanating from inside his head, from inside his blood vessels, from the underside of his skin, Mishka was in a state of perfect peace. He was also, simultaneously, at his grandparents' dining table in the house made of silky oak and mahogany and black walnut—the house where he was born—with the rainforest pressing in close.

The house was a curio along the middle reaches of the Daintree, a crocodile-thick torrent that hurled itself down the coastal range and into the Coral Sea. *Where the rainforest meets the reef* ran the brochures luring tourists and real estate buyers to the north-eastern corner of Australia. Visitors could go crocodile hunting up the Daintree or they could take the catamarans out to the coral cays that littered the Pacific or they could rent diving equipment to gawk at the wrecks of schooners and clippers and American battleships impaled on coral claws. If they made their way upstream into tunnels of jungle in a recycled Army Duck, a guide would certainly point out the unlikely dwelling that locals called Bartok's Belfry or Reffo Castle, though postcards in Port Douglas and Cairns identified the place, tongue in cheek, as Chateau Daintree.

There were normal aspects to Chateau Daintree. Like all equatorial habitations, the house rested on twelve-foot stilts so that cooling breezes and cyclonic floodwaters could pass beneath. Above the stilts there was more outdoors than indoors: more covered veranda than walled rooms. All this was proper and acceptable, and the dining table was where it was supposed to be: on the covered veranda. Everything except the corrugated iron roof was made from rainforest timbers—the walls, the floors, the furniture—and this too was as it should be, the wood grain extravagantly gorgeous and gleaming like tea-tree oil.

Everything—house and furniture—had been made with his own hands by Mishka's grandfather in the late 1940s when the house was one of the few dwellings between Cairns and Cooktown, and this was when the abnormalities had crept in. Perhaps because there were no other houses, no templates, for Mordecai Bartok to copy, he had created his own idea of refuge, fusing details well suited to equatorial wetlands with Hungarian memory and dreams of safety and imperial Hapsburg fantasies. There were anomalous European flourishes that had nothing to do with adaptation to the tropics. There was, for example, a second story above the main living area—which was itself perched high on its tree-trunk stilts—and that extra floor was adorned with a turret and gabled windows, so that someone in a pontoon with outboard motor, rubber-nosing a route upriver between estuarine crocodiles and mangroves, would be startled by the triple-decker rising out of forest scrub and epiphyte creepers like a fantasy in a child's book of wonders. The staghorn ferns and rainforest undergrowth that were rampant between the stilts seemed intent upon swallowing the house, and indeed there were tree orchids that climbed up the veranda posts and kept climbing and trailed across the roof and up the turret and hung down again across the gable windows like bunting. No one had ever seen such a building except in picture books in the Children's Room of the Cairns public library.

On the top floor behind the gabled windows, it was rumored, the reffo family slept. Mishka did not know, until he began attending the regional school in Mossman at the age of six, that he was a reffo. He was born in the Daintree. His mother before him was born in the Daintree. But his grandparents had arrived as refugees from a concentration camp in 1946 and the Bartoks were still a reffo family.

There were good reasons for this. Strange things happened at Chateau Daintree, strange sounds and strange smells wafted up and down the river from Bartok's Belfry where the nightly after-dinner menu rotated from Gluck to Monteverdi, from Beethoven to Mendelssohn and Bartók, and back. From the first note of Gluck or Mendelssohn, the sound booth off Harvard Square became rich with the aromas of goulash and *pogácsa* and cinnamon-scented *kipfel* and mud-strong coffee. Small wildlife would skitter across the desk top and the white tablecloth. Sometimes Mishka would hear the tiny feet of glider possums on the lab equipment, and if he moved, the creatures would freeze and regard him warily from their black liquid eyes. There was always a vein bleating visibly in their necks and their bushy tails would twitch and shiver like the skin of a river under wind.

Beyond the veranda posts—and the veranda posts always materialized in the sound booth and the rainforest pressed up against them—beyond the veranda, iridescent against the violent orange and mauve of sunset, there would be green flashes of parakeet wings and the strange harsh calls of scrub turkeys and pink-breasted lorikeets.

Mishka's grandfather was always at the head of the table, his grandmother at the foot, his mother across from him. After dinner, when the dishes were cleared away and the nightly recital began, all four heads were bowed slightly, all eyes were closed. All four listened raptly, while upstairs Uncle Otto played.

Uncle Otto would never join them for dinner.

Every night, as the family sat at table, Mishka's mother would be sent upstairs to ask Uncle Otto to come down.

"Devorah," Grandpa Mordecai would say, "will you ask Otto if he will join us?"

Mishka loved this ritual. His eyes lingered on the soft swirl of his mother's skirt, the way it fluted itself around her legs. He loved the *pad pad pad* of bare feet on the wooden stairs. He liked the soft silence as she vanished into the upper rooms. *The upper rooms.* That was the family term for the story that was not supposed to exist in north Queensland. At the table, his grandparents would watch the stairs with rapt faces. Then his mother would reappear.

"Uncle Otto does not wish to join us, Papa," she would say. "He will eat later. But he will play for us after dinner."

"Good, good," Grandpa Mordecai would say, his smile benign across the table. "He will play for us later."

And then Mishka's grandmother would bring out the steaming paprika-scented bowls in spite of the fact that the wet air pressed down on the dishes and on the diners like the hot towels that Grandma Malika placed on Mishka's chest when he was sick. It did not occur to anyone that the meal was not entirely appropriate, but certain changes, certain concessions to climate, did creep in. Instead of *kipfel*, there might be sliced mango or pineapple before the coffee, and often, during the wet season, when the rain would begin before the first course was done, Mishka would lean from the veranda railing with a pitcher, which would brim over in a minute or so, and they would all drink the rain from crystal goblets. They would laugh and toss it over each other because there were two seasons, the Wet and the Dry, and the downpour meant the Wet had begun and living in the house was like living in a grotto behind a cascade.

The rain was splendid and thrilling music, drumming against the iron roof. Palm fronds and silky oak branches thrashed the sides of the house and quandong berries pelted the verandas like hail.

"In the old country," Grandma Malika would say, laughing with wonder and rubbing at a bruise on her arm, "in the winter, we would be snowed in. In a strange way, it was like this."

"Like this," Grandpa Mordecai would concede, "but very different."

Usually the power would fail for an hour or two, and the ceiling fan would stop and the wet air would settle like a layer of damp on the diners who moved a breeze back and forth across their faces with woven reed fans. Grandma Malika would light the candles, and Mishka thought of himself and the three people he loved as figures inside a music box, leaning toward each other over the white linen cloth. They were inside the light, inside the golden circle, and just beyond the table, on all sides, were the heavy drapes of rain, folds of water flashing white and silver like roped silk.

"Otto will have competition tonight," Grandpa Mordecai would say, having to raise his voice over the heavy percussion of the rain. "This he never had to contend with in Budapest."

"Snowstorms," Grandma Malika would murmur dreamily and Mishka would know she was back in that other place where frosted powder, cold as whipped ice-cream and as unimaginable, was piled high against the windows until the house was blanketed in white. "This reminds me of blizzards," his grandmother would say, indicating the little cocoon in which they were suspended, cut off from the world, "except it was cold outside instead of hot, and the air was so dry, if you touched someone, little blue flames would leap up." She reached out to touch Mishka's wrist by way of demonstration and the damp left a wet band on Mishka's arm.

"Snowstorms, yes," his grandfather said. "I remember a concert in Budapest, let me see, I think I was ten years old, so 1930, and Otto was eighteen, performing already since seven years, giving concerts, a child prodigy he was, just like Mozart and Mendelssohn. Béla Bartók and Zoltan Kodály, they were both teaching at the Academy in Budapest, and they told Otto he had great promise and they were present at this concert and the drifts were four feet deep in the streets. The people who managed to get to the concert hall came in horse-drawn sleighs, Mishka. This was the only way. It was so cold that we kept our overcoats and boots on during the concert, and Otto had to play with gloves on his hands with the fingertips cut out."

"Mishka," his mother would say. "Look at the way the light moves in the rain."

And he would see, in the fluted wall of water beyond the veranda eaves, the shredded rainbows of moonlight and the ribbons of candle-glow that were tossed and tangled about.

"Isn't it beautiful?" his mother asked, fanning herself and then setting the fan down on the table and taking hold of her cotton shift at both shoulders and lifting the garment slightly away from her body and shaking it, ventilating herself. She lifted and lowered, lifted and lowered her dress. She picked up her fan and waved it languidly back and forth. "When light is scattered," his mother said, "it multiplies itself."

"Like music," his grandfather said. "When I was your age, Mishka, when I was five, we thought music was much more important than food." He laughed. "A good policy, since we had more music than food. When we didn't have enough to eat, our mother would say: Let's eat music. And she would sit at the piano and Otto would play his violin and we all would sing. And our mother would say: think of the notes as *pirogi* and fill yourself up. And we did. And afterwards, I didn't feel hungry. And now look: we have real food and real music," indicating the laden table and the drumming on the roof and the sweet antiphony of the wall of rain.

"The promised land," his grandmother murmured. "This is where we escaped to, Mishka: the promised land." And it *was*, Mishka thought: the roar and push of the rain, the candlelight, the family, the night creatures, the forest, what more could anyone ask for? Mishka did not have a name for the feeling which flooded him, and at the time he did not know any other way to be. Many years later, when he could summon up that same feeling—when he was addicted to summoning up that feeling again—he would attempt to label it: safety, belonging, connectedness, the promised land, but the feeling did not readily translate into words. The feeling was made up of a mélange of sounds and sensations. In that time, inside that feeling, he had no sense of where he ended and where his family or the forest or the night creatures began. This was before he had started school, before he knew other children, before he learned he was different and peculiar, before he knew the Bartoks were reffos, before he noticed that he did not have a father. He did not have a name for the feeling, but he could *see* it and *hear* it, and it was a river that rose and rose in its banks like the Daintree in the Wet season until it washed his body with warmth and rushed all around him, foaming and splashing him with Gluck and Mendelssohn and Uncle Otto's violin and bird cries and fragrant night-blooming flowers.

"And now, Devorah," his grandfather would say as the coffee was served, "will you tell Otto we are ready?"

And Mishka would listen again to the soft shushing of his mother's feet on the stairs. She would carry a candlestick and the light would lick up and down the polished treads like tongues of fire.

"Tonight, because of the rain," his mother might say, "he will play Bartók. The 1921 concerto."

"The 1921," his grandfather would say. "That is good. A good choice. Full of lightning and as loud as the rain."

And the four of them would huddle close to the candle's halo, heads bowed, rapt, and listen as Uncle Otto played.

2

WHENEVER DEVORAH SAID, "Tonight, he will play Beethoven, the *D Major for Violin*," Mishka knew they would hear the third movement, since that was Uncle Otto's favorite. Once upon a time, Grandpa Mordecai said, there had been many recordings of Otto's concerts and no doubt, here and there throughout the world, there were music-lovers who still owned their original copies, but all copies owned by Otto's own family had been lost or destroyed in the war. Nevertheless, through a broker in Cairns, Grandpa Mordecai had been buying second-hand copies, often damaged, one by one; and other more modern recordings of Otto's favorite concerti were so constantly played in the Bartok tree-house that Mishka knew entire works by heart. This was why, even when the nightly deluge drowned out the music, the listeners heard each note as it fell from Uncle Otto's bow. Mishka could close his eyes and feel the river welling up inside him, pressing against the levee of his skin with such urgent rapture that he would feel it could not be contained.

There were framed photographs of Uncle Otto on the walls. The photographs had a brownish tinge as though they had been steeped in tea or soaked by Daintree overflow in the Wet season or as though the lens of the camera were looking at Uncle Otto underwater. Because of this, Mishka once had a strange dream.

In his dream, Uncle Otto fell overboard on the voyage to Australia and drowned, but Grandpa Mordecai dived into the ocean and saved him. On the deck of the ship, he applied mouth-to-mouth resuscitation. Uncle Otto's face was as white as a fresh-caught fish slit open, but after a while his blue lips kissed Grandpa Mordecai back, and he sat up and played his violin. All the sailors and refugees cheered.

Uncle Otto wore high white starched collars and waistcoats and trousers that buttoned close at the ankle, so that Mishka often wondered, especially during the season of the Wet, if Uncle Otto might not be covered in heat rash from head to toe.

He had asked his mother about this, but his mother had a way of not answering when he asked about Uncle Otto.

"Can I watch when he plays his violin?" Mishka begged.

"Uncle Otto likes to be undisturbed," his mother said, and indeed, the door to Uncle Otto's room was always closed. "He prefers night time, when we're asleep."

"Like the night birds," Mishka said. "And the night bloomers."

"Like the moonflowers," his mother agreed.

"Will you ask him," Mishka begged, "if I stay up very late, would he teach me the second movement of the Mendelssohn?" because Mishka's grandfather also played the violin "though I cannot hold a candle to Otto," his grandfather said, and he was teaching Mishka on a custom-made half-size instrument especially ordered from Sydney and shipped to Cairns. "From where," Grandpa Mordecai declared, "they must have sent it by carrier pigeon or given it to one of the larger fish," but it did eventually reach the Daintree post office and Grandpa Mordecai drove Mishka down to collect it.

"It is acceptable," Grandpa Mordecai said, bouncing the bow on the strings, "though barely. It is better suited to the size of your fingers, Mishka, but the sound is not as lush and rich as it should be." He shook his head in distress. "You must make up your mind to grow quickly, especially your hands, so you can play on my violin, though mine is also, alas, a very second-rate instrument." His grandfather sighed. "I bought it after we came to Australia. It is to Otto's Guarnerius as the Daintree community hall is to the concert hall of Budapest. If only Otto would teach you," his grandfather said. "You have his touch and his musicality already. Like Otto, you are a genius, Mishka. You could play for the Empress Maria Theresa herself."

"Can we ask Uncle Otto to teach me?" Mishka begged.

"I will ask him," his mother promised, "but Mishka, darling—" and his mother stroked his hair, his mother had in her eyes that look that in later years, when he was outside the charmed circle of Chateau Daintree, Mishka would think of as the "going away" look, a look to which both his mother and his grandparents were susceptible, a look that made him think they were watching him through the wrong end of a telescope and were reaching toward him, momentarily, from a different world—"you can listen to the recordings and teach yourself."

And Mishka did listen to the recordings. He listened to them over and over. He listened to Beethoven, Mendelssohn, and Bartók. He knew them by heart.

"The interesting thing about Bartók," his grandfather told him, "to whom we are not related, except in spirit, is that he was not Jewish. Maybe his great-great-grandfather converted, who knows? But we do know this. He felt himself an outsider, like us. In Hungary, they accused him of being unpatriotic because he was interested in the folk music of the Slovakians and the Romanians. When he was a child, they were all part of the Austro-Hungarian empire, but after the First World War, the Slovakians and Romanians were foreigners. Like Beethoven, Bartók believed passionately in the brotherhood of mankind. In 1919, he and Kodály were suspended from the Budapest Academy by the fascist regime. And in the 1930s, he refused to perform in Nazi Germany. He refused even to let his work be broadcast there. He moved to America in 1940, while we were, you know, still wandering in the wilderness"—this was the closest Mishka's grandfather ever came to mentioning Auschwitz—"and I didn't learn that he was in America until after all that bad time was over and Australia took us in. But Otto played for Béla Bartók in Budapest in 1930 and he was proud to play Bartók in 1940 when Bartók was unfashionable and 'inappropriate' and he is happy still to play Bartók today."

There were many versions of Béla Bartók in his grandparents' house: the three violin concerti—the 1921, the 1922, and the 1938—and the six string quartets, interpreted by Jascha Heifetz, by Yehudi Menuhin, by Itzhak Perlman, by David Oistrakh, by many others. By the time he was five years old, Mishka could identify the work and the performing artist after five bars. So on the rain-thundering nights, when Uncle Otto played his favorite movements, the listeners sat around the candle one floor below and closed their eyes and heard every note.

The violin was the first love of Mishka's grandparents, but they had other loves too, especially opera and the music of the early Renaissance and the ethereal arias written for the counter-tenors of the sixteenth and seventeenth centuries. Recordings arrived by mail order with some frequency, and the crocodile hunters on the river reported in the pubs of Mossman and Cairns that the reffo family must get some very strange visitors: blokes who sang like sheilas at the top of their lungs, blokes who sang as though they had been kicked in the you-know-where.

There was one aria in particular that Mishka's grandparents loved as much as they loved Otto's playing: the counter-tenor aria from Gluck's *Orfeo ed Euridice*.

"It is a song of the utmost grief and pain, Mishka," Grandpa Mordecai explained. "Orpheus has found Eurydice in the Underworld and then lost her forever and he does not think he will be able to live without her. But when he sings his grief, he touches her again."

Whenever the aria—*Che farò senza Euridice?*—was on the record-player, Mishka noted that the going-away look settled on his mother and grandparents and that they wept silently, and so for him the song evoked simultaneously their sorrow and the musky happiness of his closeness to those he loved.

This was before Mishka himself knew loss.

By day, Uncle Otto kept to his room and Grandma Malika made bread and made everyone's clothing and made European seedlings grow incongruously in the rainforest shadow, and Grandpa Mordecai made cabinets and tables and chairs from mahogany and silky oak, red cedar and teak. Once a month, he loaded his goods onto a large flat-bottomed barge and took them downstream to the Daintree ferry crossing. There he met a man who had come up from Cairns with a truck. The man bought the cabinets and tables and chairs and took them back down to Cairns and then shipped them to Brisbane and Sydney and Melbourne.

Grandpa Mordecai also spent many hours of each day with his violin. "I cannot hold a candle to Otto," he told Mishka, "but he has always liked to hear me play. When I was six and he was fourteen, he taught me the Bach Double so that we could play it together, the Brothers Double Bach we called it."

When Mishka was five, and the special half-size violin had arrived from Sydney, Grandpa Mordecai began to teach Mishka the Kreisler exercises and the Mendelssohn and the Bach Double which they finally performed together in a gala concert for Mishka's mother and for Grandma Malika and Uncle Otto when Mishka was seven.

Grandpa Mordecai told Mishka that Uncle Otto was moved to tears.

By day, Mishka's mother worked on the veranda at her drawing board. She clipped a large sheet of art paper to her easel, and on a small table at her side she placed an arrangement of the leaves and flowers and fruit of some exotic plant that she and Mishka had gathered in the forest.

Mishka watched as his mother drew the leaves and tasseled flowers and blue berries of the quandong tree. First she drew in pencil, and then she used watercolors. Her work was slow and meticulous because she had a contract with a Sydney publisher for *An Illustrated Botanical Encyclopedia of the Rainforest*. Mishka waited for her paintbrush to turn the fallen leaves of the quandong bright red and the quandong berries their vivid cobalt blue. The flowers were golden tassels on a slim green stem. At the bottom of the sheet, with a very fine brush and black paint, she wrote in cursive script: *Elaeocarpus angustifolius (Blue Quandong)*.

"You should put lorikeets and parakeets in there, Mummy," he said.

"This is a plant book, Mishka darling, not a bird book. This will become the Blue Quandong page."

"I know," he said, "but there are *always* birds in the quandong trees."

"This is the way the publisher wants it. Birds don't belong on the page."

This made no sense to Mishka. It seemed to him that not only the birds but his grandparents and his mother and himself and Uncle Otto's music and Gluck's aria and their house also belonged on the page. He understood the business of dissecting and naming. He could draw and identify stamens and axils and pistils and sepals and bracts, he could label them, he could list them in categories, but bees belonged with sepals, and birds with seeds, and everything seemed to him to flow into everything else and to be on the same page and to be part of the river of feeling without a name that welled up inside him and pushed against his skin until he would believe that the pressure of so much beauty would lift him off his feet and loft him into the rainforest canopy, and at night, when the moon hung low between the veranda posts, he really believed he could fly and he could join the lorikeets in the quandong trees. It was entirely logical to him that the brilliant birds with trumpet voices would like noisy colors. They would cry and chatter and he would respond on his violin and they understood one another because they could all speak without words, and Beethoven's *D Major* rose up from the quandongs in a dense flutter of strings.

"When I grow up," he told his mother, "I am going to write a concerto for quandongs and parrots."

When Mishka was six years old, he began to go to the closest public school, which was in Mossman, forty-five minutes to the south on an unpaved road. His grandfather drove him down when the morning lay like gold leaf on ocean and on cane fields and on the steep forested slopes. Last night's rain was always steaming up from the road so that Mishka saw hundreds of wraith-cobras performing for the snake-charmer sun. After school, and after the after-school sports, his grandfather drove him home again under black skies that were low and heavy with the nightly deluge that politely waited for six o'clock. His grandfather's car was a dowager Buick, old but well preserved and full of dignity, so that among the two or three other cars on the deck of the Daintree ferry, the Buick presided like a queen.

In those days, before the fruit-cropping time, before sugar gave way to avocados and passionfruit and mangoes, the cane stood to attention in green and purple-plumed ranks each morning and saluted as Mishka arrived at school. The cane marched to the very boundaries of the buildings and yard, an invading force, every day gaining ground, every night sending out advance reconnaissance troops, so relentless that children playing cricket or soccer would stumble over spiky green shoots the next morning. This was the growing time. Once the cutting and crushing began, once the cane trains were trundling along the narrow steel tracks to the mill, the air was so heavy with a mist of molasses that the drowsy children would brush soot from their arms and lick sugared air from their lips.

The first days at school were a wonder and a terror for Mishka, since he had never known—had never before talked to or played with—other children. He had seen them occasionally, on those rare journeys to Mossman or Cairns to pick up mail-order parcels or to buy something that could not be grown or raised or built at Chateau Daintree. Once in Cairns another child had approached him and asked, "Where did you get those funny shoes?" and Mishka had lowered his eyes, too shy to speak.

Alone at the gates of Mossman State School, as the Buick retreated, Mishka thought of the way crows would swoop down on an injured scrub turkey and peck it to death. There seemed to be hundreds of children who flew at him.

"Who are you?" they asked him.

He said in a small voice: "Mishka Bartok."

"What's your favorite TV show?" they demanded, but Mishka did not know how to answer this question.

"What's your favorite hit song?"

Hit song? Mishka puckered his forehead, mystified. Hitting music? What would that be?

"Your favorite song," someone said, and that one was easy.

"*Che farò senza Euridice,*" he said.

The children blinked and stared.

"Or maybe the second movement of Mendelssohn's *Violin Concerto in E Minor*, except that isn't a song with words."

The children looked at one another and then at Mishka. "What?" they said.

"And my next favorite," Mishka said, "is the 1921 Bartók concerto."

There was a shuffling of feet in the shadows of the high wall of cane.

"Are you loco, or something?" a tall boy asked. "Wha'd'ya say your name was?"

"Mishka."

"Mishka the fishka," the tall boy said, and the others all laughed.

Mishka also laughed.

"What are you laughing at?" the tall boy asked.

Mishka said nothing.

"You have to do what I tell you," the tall boy said. "You have to answer questions if I ask them. I'm Tony and my father is the police chief for Douglas Shire. Why did that old bloke in the funny car bring you here?"

"He is my grandfather," Mishka said.

"I know who you are," Tony said in a burst of enlightenment. "You're the reffo boy. How come you live up the Daintree? And what does your father do and how come he shot through?"

Mishka did not know how to answer any of those questions, so he said instead, "My grandfather is a cabinet-maker and he also plays the violin. My Uncle Otto is a famous concert violinist. My mother is a botanist."

"Fuck a duck," Tony said.

Thus began Mishka's years in a Queensland state school. This was not an auspicious beginning.

I do not belong on this page, he concluded. He wanted his mother to paint him somewhere else.

At home, in the cocoon behind the waterfall, after Uncle Otto had played the final movement of Bartók's second concerto and Mishka was in bed and his mother was climbing the stairs to kiss him goodnight, Mishka rehearsed ways to ask the following questions: What does my father do? Is my father a cabinet-maker like Grandpa? Is my father a violinist like Uncle Otto? Did my father run away and leave us? Where is my father?

But when his mother leaned over him and he felt her soft warm lips against his cheek, he could not ask any of his questions. He could feel them low in his throat, wet and sticky, but they were trapped there. They did not want to come out.

My father.

The words were so strange and new that he began to shiver. He pulled up the sheet. Above him, the ceiling fan turned only sluggishly, moving wet air, redistributing the heat, but he felt cold. He could hear the high hum of the generator singing *Where has your father gone?* He could hear the drumbeat of the rain on the iron roof: *fa-ther fa-ther fa-ther*. It was as though some great bird he had never seen before, an eagle with a wingspan that stretched from the Daintree to Mossman, weirdly feathered like a parrot in emerald greens and blue-blacks and vivid orange, with a sharp curved beak, had swooped down and was pecking at his heart.

When Grandpa Mordecai put Gluck on the record player, Mishka suddenly knew what the aria meant: *What shall I do without my father?* It seemed to Mishka that the great bruise inside him, the hole where his father should have been, crept out into the music like a wounded creature from its cave and cried piteously: *Look at me. How shall I live without my father?*

Mishka could no longer hear Gluck without weeping.

He tried to imagine what his father might look like and he imagined him in tea-soaked browns like Uncle Otto in the photographs. He imagined his father in a high white starched collar and vest, with striped trousers that were held close to his ankles inside something that looked like socks that buttoned up the side. He imagined playing the Bach Double with his grandfather while his father sat in the shadows of the veranda and he imagined his father clapping and being as impressed as Uncle Otto had been.

Mishka shivered himself to sleep and when sleep came it came with the rise of the river. Dark water was lapping at his window then flowing in a tidal wave across the sill. His father and Uncle Otto, looking like twins, slipped into the room like fish. They splashed in water and shook themselves. They gave off silver. They picked up Mishka's violin and his grandfather's. They played the Bach Double.

During his early years at Mossman State School, Mishka thought of his father the way he thought of Uncle Otto, except that his father was in a different closed room in a different house.

He told Tony Cavalari at school that his father was a violinist who was traveling all over Europe giving concerts.

"Fuck a duck," Tony said.

On a late Friday afternoon years later, when Mishka was in Grade 4, and parrots were falling out of trees, and gunshots were peppering the air, a rubber police dinghy with a loud outboard motor moored itself amongst the mangroves in the lee of the Bartok house. Two policemen and a boy got out.

"Hey, Mishka!" the boy called out.

"G'day, Tony," Mishka said.

He and his mother and his grandparents were leaning over the veranda railing.

"G'day," one of the policemen called out. "Sergeant Cavalari, chief of police for Douglas Shire. We got word of marijuana crops up here, north side of the Daintree. Know anything about that?"

"No, sergeant," Mishka's grandfather said.

"Mind if I poke around your garden a bit?" He turned to his son. "Tony, why don't you go on up into the house and play with your little school mate for a bit."

"Wow," Tony said, when he joined Mishka on the veranda. "Reffo Castle is really weird, it's really super. Can I go up in those pointy things?" He gestured at the turret and the gables.

"Okay," Mishka said, though it was alarming to have Tony in the wrong place. He took Tony to his own bedroom with its gabled window-nook and window-seat.

"Fuck a duck," Tony said, standing on the banquette and looking out on the rainforest canopy and down at the brown snake of the river. "You can almost see down to Mossman," he said. "Can we go in that round pointy thing?" The turret was what he meant, though he found the inside of the little tower a disappointment, an anticlimax. He had imagined something exotic, a torture chamber with chains, a closet for witches, but all he saw on the inside was a small round sitting room equipped with books on shelves and two armchairs. "I never seen round bookshelves before," he said, salvaging an element of strange. "Hey, what's this?" He opened a closet door into the eaves and yelped at three glowing pairs of eyes.

"Possums," Mishka explained. "They live there."

"Fuck a duck!" Tony ran from room to room, excited, whooping like a TV cowboy. He reached for the handle on the door of Uncle Otto's room.

"No!" Mishka shouted, appalled. "You mustn't open that door."

But it was too late.

"Why not?" Tony asked, his hand still on the knob of the open door. He was staring into the room.

Mishka was almost sobbing. "You're not allowed, no one's allowed except my mother."

"Fuck a duck. Why not?"

"It's Uncle Otto's room. You'll upset him. You've got to close the door."

"There's no one in here," Tony said. "There's *nothing* in here."

Mishka could feel a pain in his chest. His heart was beating so fast that he thought it might burst. He joined Tony at Uncle Otto's door. The wood floor was completely bare but the walls were covered with framed photographs.

"We can't go in," Mishka said with sudden and absolute authority. "Come on." He pulled Tony with him and shut the door.

From below, Sergeant Cavalari called out: "Tony! Come on down, mate. We're going," and when Tony pelted downstairs, followed slowly by Mishka, Grandpa Mordecai was saying to the policemen: "There are some hippies living further up the river. We see them going past in their boat."

"Thanks for the tip," Sergeant Cavalari said. "Quite a place you got here. Come on, Tony."

Later, when darkness fell, the Shabbas candles were lit on the veranda. The Shabbas meal ended and Mishka's grandfather said: "Devorah, will you tell Otto that we are ready?"

Mishka's mother climbed the stairs and Mishka heard her knock on the door of the empty room. She came down again, her bare feet on the treads like drumsticks muffled with velvet. "He will play the Mendelssohn," she said. "The second movement." The rainy season was over, the air hushed except for the skittering of small creatures and the night birds' cries. For the first time in his life, Mishka did not close his eyes while Uncle Otto played. He watched his grandparents as they listened, the way they smiled, the way their bodies moved with the phrasing. He watched his mother and he saw how her body was slack with something for which he had no word, something that frightened him. Years later, in the Music Lab off Harvard Square, when he replayed this night for himself, he saw that the name for what his mother felt was resignation, that she was suspended in some high narrow place of great stillness, with sorrow on one side and the surrendering of hope on the other. It was as though the smallest movement would take her over the lip of the abyss. Even so, it seemed to Mishka that she could hear Uncle Otto: the way her head was tilted up toward the music, the way her right hand sometimes moved as though she were conducting. Mishka himself listened to the loudest silence he had ever heard.

There was the sudden sound of the police boat passing back downriver, though Mishka could see from the three other faces that the motor did not overwhelm the sound of the violin. He had a sensation of falling the way a shot parrot falls, falling into the river and on down through the river bed and down and down below it to where a vast underground cavern opened up and he felt that his falling would go on and on without end.

3

"YOUR GRANDFATHER WASN'T always like that," Mishka's mother said. "He remembered Otto's death only too vividly when I was young, but he couldn't talk about it. He never spoke about the camp. It seemed to get more and more painful over time, and then one day he simply un-made the past." She and Mishka were walking along the esplanade in Cairns. The night was warm but blustery. "Your Beethoven brought tears to your grandfather's eyes tonight," his mother said. She reached up and brushed Mishka's cheek. "You are like Otto restored to him. We are so proud of you."

It was a warm night in December, end of the school year, the night of Mishka's high school graduation. He had been showered with prizes, he had won a scholarship, he would be heading south to the university in Brisbane.

A sharp breeze was barreling along the seawall and the palms were groaning and tossing their multiple arms like windmills in rage. Lower branches, the ones hanging vertically against the trunks, discards already, simply waiting for their shedding number to be called, were falling on all sides with soft booms that sent seismic vibrations along the esplanade. Mishka felt the thump and tremble against the soles of his feet, and the buffetings seemed to him heralds of change as well as warnings.

"Do you mind waiting here for a minute, Mum?" They had reached a bench that looked out to sea. It was late, and there were no other strollers in sight, but the esplanade was well lit. "I'll just nip into the hostel and leave my violin in my room. Then we can walk."

His mother smiled. "Take your time," she said. Already he could see the going-away look settling on her like the salt mist that came off the bay. She is preparing herself, he decided, and the thought was like a heavy suitcase that would have to go with him. When he had kissed his grandparents goodnight at the hotel further down the esplanade, his grandfather had held him and said: "I will not see you again, Mishka, not after Hanukkah, I mean, but I give you to the world. Give the world music."

And Mishka had felt almost ill with love and irritation in equal parts. "Grandpa," he said, "of course you will see me again," though even as he said it there lay between them the unspoken fact that his weekend trips back to the Daintree had grown further and further apart.

"Mishka," his grandmother said, "a little gift, so you will not forget us," and she pushed something tissue-wrapped into his pocket.

"Grandma," he said, "how could I possibly forget you?"

He left his mother on the bench by the seawall and ran two blocks down a side street to the hostel where he had been boarding for his four high-school years. He put his violin case on the bed and took stock of the room that had been his chrysalis, his private cocoon. Very soon, in a matter of days, he would spread his wings and never see it again. He had never let anyone visit. The room was small—a bed, a desk, a chair, a music stand, books: that was all—but he could see palms and passionfruit vines from his window, and from the small balcony he could see the bay.

He had taken music lessons privately as well as at Cairns High, and he had spent all his spare time in the practice rooms at the school. He was solitary. He did not know what to say to fellow students. He did not know how to be with them. He had quietly accustomed himself to the knowledge that the three people he loved were peculiar and perhaps quite mad in a harmless kind of way, and he felt an immense protectiveness and tenderness for them. He thought that very likely he too was crazy and therefore it was important to conceal his condition. For one thing, there was the matter of shame. For another, it was possible that madness was infectious and therefore he had a moral obligation to keep his distance from other people. It was important to be crazy as discreetly and privately as possible, and this seemed to him not so difficult since the strange and beautiful house of his childhood existed outside of ordinary time and ordinary space. He himself continued to live in this limbo of not-here and not-now, and for this reason he knew it might never be possible for him to be certain of what was real and what was not.

He took off his evening jacket, since the night was very warm, and felt the slight bulk of his grandmother's tissue-wrapped gift in one pocket. He took it out and unwrapped it. It was a diptych, a small hinged frame in a hand-crocheted cover. When he opened it, he saw two photographs. On the left, sepia-toned, was Uncle Otto, aged fourteen, and Grandpa Mordecai, aged six. On the right, in black and white, was a family portrait dated 1956: his grandparents, looking youthful, seated in wicker chairs with banana palms behind them. On the grass at their feet was his mother, aged six. They must have had photographic copies made in Cairns, he thought, since he knew the originals were among the most precious things they owned. He knew that the frame itself, of oiled silky oak, would have been made by his grandfather. He stroked its intricate crocheted cover, his grandmother's handiwork, with one finger. The cream silk was as soft as the tassels on the quandong flowers. Mishka pressed the totemic object to his heart and gave himself to the warm rising waters of the river of emotion within him. It had not taken him in flood this way since he moved to Cairns, putting all of one hundred kilometers between his hostel room and Chateau Daintree. He did not know how long he stood there, swept by love and grief and obscure unidentified pain, before he placed the frame like a half-opened book on his desk.

When he returned to the sea front, his mother was not on the bench, though her shoes were. He scanned the esplanade, but could not see her. The tide was going out and the sand flats were littered with shells and kelp and jellyfish and small crabs that skittered back and forth. Then he saw his mother, far out with the receding tide, her skirt lifted up to make a pannier, barefoot and ankle-deep in wet sand, no doubt gathering seaweed specimens. He cupped his hands, megaphone-style, and called to her and she straightened up, startled, and stood there like a seabird, delicate and watchful. Then she seemed to remember where she was and who was calling her and she made her way back toward the wall.

The concrete levee below the steel railing was four feet high, and Devorah held the pannier of her dress up to the level of the esplanade. Mishka took the antlered and parsley-like sea plants, one by one, and laid them down on the grass beside the bench. "For my book on water plants," she explained. "I started with rainforest pools, but I'm going to do saltwater plants too."

"How will we carry these?" Mishka asked. "I'd better take them to my room until we're ready to go back to your hotel."

He extended his hand and pulled his mother up the concrete wall until she had a foothold on the esplanade and then she clambered between the steel rails. "I'll use my scarf," she said, unknotting the silk square from her neck and gently placing the sea plants in it and tying the corners.

Misha stood at the railing to watch the cruise catamarans coming in from the outer reef on a path of moonlight. "So when exactly did Grandpa bring Uncle Otto back to life?" he asked.

"Uncle Otto?" his mother repeated vaguely. "You know, I still don't have any red seaweed. It's much harder to find."

Mishka said patiently: "You said Grandpa decided to unmake the past. When did he do it?"

"Oh." His mother brushed at her eyes as though insects were bothering her. "It happened while I was away in Sydney," she said. "I was gone for nearly ten years and when I came back, things were different."

"Was it because you went away?"

His mother suddenly picked up her silk bundle by its knot and began to walk along the esplanade as though she were late for an appointment. Mishka had to run to catch up. They walked for fifteen minutes before she spoke. "They never tried to stop me. I know they were proud of my fellowship. My father kept saying: 'Otto went away too, to the academy in Budapest. It's a necessary thing.' But they believed they would never see me again."

"That's what Grandpa said to me tonight. *I'll never see you again, Mishka.* I told him that was ridiculous."

"Of course you will come home with us tomorrow," his mother said.

"Or in a day or so."

"And you'll stay until Hanukkah."

"Of course. So why did Grandpa—?"

"In case you don't."

They walked for another five minutes without speaking.

"It was the look on their faces," his mother said, "when the train pulled out of the station. I should never have gone by train. Trains are difficult for them. I shouldn't have let them come to Cairns to see me off."

"We should turn back," Mishka said.

"For ten years it haunted me, and for ten years it kept me away. I was afraid if I came back, I'd never get out again." She turned to him and made a gesture with her hand that might have meant resignation. "I was right about that, wasn't I? I tried to get them to visit me in Brisbane, and then in Sydney. I mailed them train tickets, but you know how it is. They don't like to leave the house. It's where they've escaped to."

"We should turn back. It's not so well lit here."

"Do you know that the Queensland government has tried to farm quandongs? Tried to grow them commercially? But it hasn't worked. They won't grow outside the Daintree. The rainforest ecology is so intricate that its plants can't survive outside it. They don't transplant. We're the same, Mishka. Our family."

Mishka shivered. An icicle of fear, sharp as a dagger, nicked his heart. "People are not plants," he said, annoyed. "How come we have photographs of Uncle Otto? I thought they lost everything."

"They did. In the fifties and sixties, your grandfather wrote to the music academies in Budapest. He tapped into a network. People in Europe sent him the photographs. What he wanted more than anything was to get hold of Uncle Otto's recordings, and he's managed to get a few, as you know, although they're not in good condition. His real dream was to find Uncle Otto's violin, because he's certain it must still exist. No one, not even a Nazi officer, would destroy a Guarnerius. But he's never found any trace."

"Do you know what happened to Uncle Otto?"

"More or less. I put it together from bits and pieces. My mother told me some of it. She told me Otto kept his little brother alive. The camp commandant was a music lover and he used to bring Otto in to play at dinner parties for his guests. Of course, Otto's Guarnerius had been taken when they were first rounded up, but somehow the commandant tracked it down and Otto sobbed when it was put in his hands. That's what he told his brother, and that's what my father told my mother. Your grandparents met after the war, on the ship to Australia. They both lost everyone else. They have me and they have you. It's a heavy load for us."

"It's heavy," Mishka agreed.

Otto, his mother said, was given extra food for performing, and he stole leftovers when he could. He was shot for stealing. No one knew what had happened to the violin.

"Once I started school," Mishka said, "and I heard about Santa Claus, I thought of Uncle Otto like that. He was Santa Claus. Kids know he's not real, but they believe in him just the same."

And that is how I think of my father, he did not tell her.

"Yes, it's like that," his mother said. "For a while, I believed my parents were invisible to everybody but me. Since I was about ten, I've thought of them as gifted children. I had to protect them."

Mishka almost said: That is how I think about you.

"When you went away," he said, "when you were in Brisbane and Sydney…."

"I was mostly lonely, but I was passionate about botany and

that saved me. I buried myself in my work, and as long as I was working, I was okay."

"You've never told me anything," Mishka said.

"You've never asked."

"Do all families avoid talking about the things they think about most?"

"I don't know," his mother said. "I don't know anything about other families."

"I don't either," Mishka said. "It doesn't matter as long as I'm practicing or listening to music or composing."

"I know," she sighed. "I would have liked to make it different for you if I knew how. Maybe it's history, or maybe it's because we both grew up in that house, or maybe it's just in our genes."

"Or maybe all three," Mishka said. "How old were you when you left?"

"Eighteen. End of high school. Same as you. I had a Commonwealth Scholarship. I went to Brisbane first, to Queensland Uni, then on to Sydney for my master's."

"Why didn't you stay there?"

"I did. I stayed away for ten years. I worked for a publisher, the same one I work for now."

"But then you came back."

"Yes. And when I did, Uncle Otto was playing after dinner every night."

"Why'd you come back?"

"Because I was pregnant with you and I was desperately lonely."

So now he would ask.

Who was my father? he would say. Where was he? Where *is* he? Does he know I exist? As soon as his heart stopped jumping like a fish on a hook, he would ask. There was a sharp pain in his chest and very suddenly he swung himself over the steel railing and jumped down onto the sand flats and began running through the brackish salt water of the outgoing tide. He called back in a strangled voice: "I can see some red seaweed. I'll get it for you." He ran, chasing the tide, his feet pressing deeper and deeper into the wet sand, great fans of water spreading like wings from his ankles. The tide-line was far out now, and he ran as though he could retrieve something essential to his survival if he could just catch up with the sea and stop its retreat. He ran until he was at last knee deep in ocean and could feel the pull of the undertow. He was out of breath and he had a stitch in his side. He bent over and splashed salt water on his face. He turned back and could barely see the white smudge of the concrete sea wall, though a path of moonlight shone on the wet sand like a bright white line joining him to the figure he could no longer make out on the shore.

He turned back to the Pacific. He thought he would probably have to walk another kilometer before the water would be deep enough for swimming. If the tide were not so far out, he thought he would simply start swimming and keep swimming until the void swallowed him. Instead he turned and followed the path of light to the esplanade.

His mother was waiting. She was leaning on the steel railing watching him.

"Mishka, I'm sorry," she said.

"We should turn back."

"Your clothes are sopping wet."

"Tell me about my father."

"Yes," she said in a small voice, as though he had pressed on a bruise. "I know I should have."

"Where did you meet him?"

"We were students together, I don't mean in the same field. He was Lebanese, doing a degree in civil engineering. We were both very lonely. We used to do what lonely people do in Sydney: ride the harbor ferries a lot. That's how we met. For weeks, we would see each other every day and smile and nod but never speak. And then one day we made conversation, and we began having coffee at Circular Quay when the ferry docked. It became a daily ritual and I would wake up every morning looking forward to it. I told him about the rainforest. He told me about Beirut. And we both loved music. He took me to a concert that some Middle Eastern students put on. He was one of the performers. He played the oud. It's a Persian stringed instrument that looks like a lute and the Persian word for it is *barbat*. It's the ancestor of the lute. It came to Spain with the Moors, though not to the rest of Europe until the Crusades. His oud was a beautiful thing, a deep-bellied wooden instrument inlaid with ivory. And he sang. He had a beautiful voice.

"Afterwards he took me back to his apartment in a taxi. I sat up front. He had to share the back seat with the oud." They were passing one of the esplanade benches and his mother sat down and set her silk bundle of seaweeds on the bench beside her. She folded her hands in her lap and studied them like a penitent. "That was the night we became lovers," she said.

"Did you...?" But Mishka did not know what he wanted to ask.

"Mishka," she said. She was pressing her hands against her chest. She spoke as though in considerable pain. "I'm afraid to remember it. I'm afraid to fall back down that well. It took me so long to climb out."

There was a fallen palm branch beside the bench and Mishka pulled off several fronds and began braiding them.

"When people are starving," his mother said. "When they are really starving.... My father told me that after the liberation, when they were offered food, real food, chocolate bars, by American soldiers, they couldn't eat it. It made them sick."

Mishka twisted his braided fronds into a circle and knotted them. He placed the bracelet on his mother's lap.

"That is what we were like," she said. "We were famished. We were voracious. But we didn't know how to manage so much feeling." She put the palm bracelet on her wrist. "I was frightened." After a while she said: "You were conceived in great passion."

Mishka pulled more fronds from the palm branch and began shredding them furiously with his thumbnail.

"After a while he moved in with me. He and his oud. We lived together for several months."

"He wasn't Jewish."

"No."

"So you didn't—"

"What was strange though... he used to play in the evenings after dinner."

"Like Uncle Otto."

"Except of course I would watch him."

"And hear him."

"I used to hear Uncle Otto," his mother said quietly.

"And except he wasn't Jewish."

"He came from a Muslim family, but he wasn't anything. He was secular. We were intellectuals. We didn't believe in belief systems, we used to say."

"What was his name?"

"His name was Marwan Rahal Abukir."

Something like a small muffled explosion at the base of his spine shook Mishka and traveled in shock waves throughout his bone cage. He felt giddy. His sense of balance had gone. Michael Abukir, he thought. I am Michael Abukir, son of Marwan Rahal Abukir, oud player.

"What happened?" he asked coldly. "Did he leave you?"

His mother studied his face in the moonlight. "King David was an oud player, Marwan said. When King David sang the psalms, he accompanied himself on the oud. Marwan used to sing something in Arabic that reminded me of that beautiful psalm, *By the rivers of Babylon I sat down and wept....* Uncle Otto used to play that in the camp."

"Did he leave you?"

"I suppose that is what happened."

"What's that supposed to mean?"

"When I told him I was pregnant, he said we would get married but first he had to go home to tell his parents. He never came back. I never heard from him. I was numb. I lived in a fog."

"He doesn't know I exist."

"Three months later I had a letter from his brother to say he'd been killed in a car crash. That's when I decided to come back to the Daintree. I didn't think I could manage living anywhere else."

"So you have the name and address of his brother?"

"The postmark was Beirut. There was no return address."

"Have you still got the letter?"

"Yes."

"Do you have a photograph of my father?"

"He did not like to have his photograph taken, but I do have one," she said. "It was taken by a street photographer at Circular Quay, the ones who used to prowl around and take pictures of tourists. We had just come off one of the ferries and the flash went off in our eyes. The photographer handed me a card with the date and a number and a studio address. Months later, after I knew he was dead, I found the card in my drawer and I went to the shop and they still had the proofs, so I bought a postcard-size print. I've had a copy made, and your grandfather has made a frame. I'd planned it as your going-away present, but I'll give it to you tomorrow when we get back to the Daintree."

Mishka leaned on the railing of the seawall. He had the sensation that he was falling, falling right through the day when Tony Cavalari opened the door to Uncle Otto's room, falling again like a shot parrot down a black hole with no bottom to it. And then something stirred in the black nothingness below and came rushing up to meet him like an oil gush coming in. It almost swept him over the wall, and he held the railing so tightly that his fingers turned white.

"We should go back to the hotel," his mother said.

"You go in. I'll walk for a while."

"You're getting a cold," his mother said. "Your voice sounds throaty."

"It's just the night air." He was already walking away.

"Mishka," she said after him. "You look like your father."

"Good night," he said. He did not turn back. He could not bear to look at her. He walked for miles and miles as though he were drunk. The thing that was surging and roiling within him was an anger so terrible that it frightened him.

He walked all night.

Just before dawn, he went back to his room at the hostel and wrote a note to his mother. He left it at the desk of her hotel. There was no salutation.

I won't be coming back to the Daintree, the note said. *Had an offer to play dinner music at the resort on Green Island and have decided to take it until I leave for*

*Brisbane. Please mail me the photo, care of Green
Island Resort. Mishka.*

He walked back from her hotel to his room, collected his
violin, a duffel bag of clothing and the framed diptych and
walked to the wharf. He took the morning's first catamaran to
Green Island. He stood on deck and watched the green water
curling away from the twin keels like shavings of mango peel.
He watched as the dark green gave way to the turquoise lagoon
around the island.

In the room assigned to him at the resort, he set the diptych
given to him by his grandparents on the dresser. He sat on the
bed, the pillow at his back, his hands behind his head, and
studied it.

"So, Uncle Otto," he said aloud. "It turns out I'm a bit
of a mongrel. What do you think of that?" He realized that
he did not know if his mother had ever told her parents
about Marwan Rahal Abukir. Then he realized that of course
he did know. She would not have told. They would not
have asked. His grandfather would have made a tiny frame to
his mother's specifications, but he would never have seen
the photograph she planned to insert. "So, Grandpa," he said
aloud, "I'm an Abukir, not a Bartok. What do *you* think of
that?"

Uncle Otto and Grandpa Mordecai gazed back impassively,
mournfully, from their tea-colored faces.

"You are right," he told them. "Even at Chateau Daintree,
I don't belong."

When the little parcel with a Daintree postmark arrived, he
let several days pass before he opened it.

It was a diptych in a wood frame with a hand-crocheted
jacket: a twin to his other graduation gift.

To the left of the hinge was a black and white photograph of a young man and a young woman. The woman, his mother, was beautiful, her lustrous black hair like a shining weight on her shoulders. The man had dark curly hair that fell across his brow. There were hollows below his cheekbones: a sculpted face. His lips were full and sensual: one might have thought they were the lips of a woman.

Mishka studied his own face in the mirror.

This might have been a photograph of himself.

On the right side of the diptych was a miniature watercolor: red leaves, blue quandong berries, tasseled flowers. *Elaeocarpus angustifolius (Blue Quandong)*, ran the delicate script beneath.

This was the mighty tree, Mishka grimly reminded himself, that could not survive beyond the rarefied ecosystem of North Queensland rainforest.

Inside the package, there were also two envelopes. One was frail and curled and yellow. It was addressed to Mlle. Devorah Bartok, 25 Willow St., Sydney, NSW, Australia. It bore a Beirut postmark. Inside was one sheet of paper with a brief message written in baroque swirling script in fountain pen:

June 17, 1977
Mademoiselle Bartok:
I have the sadness to inform that my brother Marwan
Rahal Abukir has been killed in car accident some month
ago. I have found your address in personal papers.
I am, mademoiselle, your respectful servant,
Fadi Rahal Abukir.

Mishka picked up the photograph of the father who had died before he was born. "You are less real than Uncle Otto," he told the image.

There was also a sealed envelope, addressed simply: *Mishka*, in his mother's handwriting. He could feel several pages of a letter inside. He did not open it. He kept it on the dresser for several days and then he dropped it in the incinerator behind the resort kitchen.

A month later, he left for Brisbane.

4

In the sound booth off Harvard Square, the candle flickered and Mishka leaned into the music and watched the way that small golden moons seemed to rise from the wick and float into the dark. One of the moons floated over Brisbane and settled there and those years became glowing and clear to him. They were not much different from the years in Cairns, except for the luminous bubble of Mr. Hajj's apartment in Kangaroo Point, and the moon settled over that apartment and the apartment was enveloped by the light and that time was so ineffable, so rare, so out of time, that it floated free, it had nothing to do with Brisbane at all.

Except for Mr. Hajj, the Brisbane years were a blur. They had the shape of hostel rooms or of the practice rooms at the university. They had the texture of total immersion in work. They had the odor of frugality, which did not bother Mishka in the least. His habits were ascetic. He survived on his scholarship money and he put some aside. He was saving his airfare. On the advice of his professors, he was applying to graduate schools in America. He wanted to be somewhere unknown. He wanted to be nowhere. He wanted to be gone.

He supposed he must have known fellow music students in Brisbane. He supposed he must have been at a party or two. He had trouble remembering.

He remembered the pieces he had composed, a diary of sorts. *Green Island Largo. Rainforest Gigue. Sonatina for Quandongs and Parrots. Homage for Uncle Otto. Night Music for the Brisbane River.* He could hear these from first note to last in his head. He could mentally finger the chords, he could relive his bowing technique.

He could remember and date precisely the convulsive encounter that produced something altogether new in his musical vocabulary and in his compositional diary, the fork in the journey of his life that gave birth to so many pieces that his professors described variously as "problematic" or "disturbing" or "daringly original": *My Road to Damascus; The dream of the man with the oud: Trio for violin, oud and tabla; Elegy for Uncle Otto and Mustafa Hajj; Message for Uncle Fadi.* The path to these compositions began with two separate advertisements he had placed in the newspaper under separate category headings.

WANTED TO BUY: Persian stringed instrument known as oud.

WANTED: teacher of Middle Eastern classical music.

Both had been answered by the same person, a man with an elegant but slightly accented voice, who called the number given for both ads. "I am Youssef Hajj," he said. "I teach Persian classical music and I can import for you from Damascus a custom-made oud." He gave an address in Kangaroo Point, the inner-city loop of the river where apartment blocks huddled beneath the Storey Bridge. "You must come in the evening," Mr. Hajj said. "I teach only at night."

When Mishka found the ugly concrete block of flats under a harsh yellow street light and pushed the buzzer for number 3A, a gnome-like man came to the door.

"Mr. Hajj?"

Mr. Hajj bowed by way of acknowledgment. "Youssef Hajj."

"Michael Abukir." Mishka had not planned to say this. He had not thought to rehearse what he would say, but he was only mildly surprised by this spontaneous reinvention of himself.

"Come in, come in," Mr. Hajj said. "You are Lebanese."

"Uh... partly."

"But not raised Lebanese." Mr. Hajj put a gentle restraining hand on Mishka's chest. He was looking at Mishka's feet, his eyebrows raised. "May I request that you remove your shoes? In Syria, this is our custom. In Lebanon too."

"Sorry." Embarrassed, Mishka unlaced his shoes. "You are right. I was born and raised in Australia."

When he passed through the front door in socked feet, he stepped into a jewel box. The floor was thickly covered, wall to wall, with overlapping Persian rugs in rich shades of crimson and peacock blue. Cushions in silks and satins were strewn about. There was no other furniture. Propped against one wall were three stringed instruments, big-bellied, the richly grained wood sensuous to the gaze and to the touch. Mishka held his breath. Without being conscious of his action, he moved toward them as toward long-lost family members or lovers. He stroked the great pregnant bellies of the instruments, he traced the outline of the sound holes, he caressed with his fingertips the ivory inlay, he ran the palm of his hand along the neck—there were no frets, he observed—and lightly plucked the double-coursed strings. Two of the instruments had five double strings; the third had seven.

"Beautiful," he murmured. "Beautiful woodwork." Mahogany, silky oak... his grandfather would die for such instruments. "My grandfather is a cabinet-maker. He would love these. Why does this one have seven strings?"

"That one is antique Persian," Mr. Hajj said. "In Persian, it is called a *barbat*."

"May I hold one?"

"Of course."

For Mishka, this was an act of reverence. He had a sense of touching simultaneously his father and his Grandfather Bartok. "How do you hold the instrument? Like a guitar?"

"I will show you."

Mr. Hajj sat cross-legged on his rug and rested the instrument in his lap.

"More like a lute," Mishka said. "Will you play for me?" He sat opposite on the floor, legs crossed.

Mr. Hajj began to play and Mishka closed his eyes and imagined himself in Ali Baba's cave. He saw dark-eyed girls in diaphanous silks with veiled faces. Rainforest intruded, but with cedars of Lebanon instead of quandongs, peacocks instead of parakeets, minarets where Uncle Otto incongruously played the oud and Marwan Rahal Abukir, sitting opposite, played the violin. Grandfather Bartok whittled at big-bellied ouds emerging from silky oak boughs.

Perhaps hours passed by, perhaps no time at all.

"You are weeping," Mr. Hajj said.

"My father used to play the oud. He died before I was born."

"Ah," Mr. Hajj said. "And you wish to learn to play?"

"Yes."

"To honor him?"

"To know him, I think. To communicate with him."

"You have studied Western music?"

"I play the violin. I am a music student at the university. In composition."

Mishka could see a quickening of interest in Mr. Hajj. "I have entertained for some time a little dream, of duets for violin and oud."

"That would definitely interest me, but first I want to learn to play the oud."

"Yes, yes, of course, but you understand that the system is completely different from the Western system of music."

"I understand."

"I have two students for the oud. One is Syrian, as I am. The other is from Iran. And I have a student who plays the tabla. You may join this class. You may learn on one of my instruments until you obtain your own."

Mishka used half his airfare money to buy an oud, which was shipped from Damascus, a transaction that took some time and involved convoluted connections and customs arrangements. The city of Damascus, Mr. Hajj told him, crafts the finest ouds in the world, but for reasons of history and politics, Mr. Hajj had to negotiate with Damascus via a contact in Beirut. When the shipment came, it was addressed to Mikael Abukir.

Mishka lived in two worlds, traveling between alien planets like an astronaut. By day, he was Mishka Bartok who lived in Brisbane, took his classes and played his violin. In his hostel room and in the practice rooms at the university, he composed for the violin. By night, he was Mikael Abukir, a man who spent hours in Ali Baba's cave and played the oud. The rhythm of movement between his two worlds felt natural to him. His childhood had trained him for such a life, which was not unlike the movement from Chateau Daintree to school in Mossman. Mishka knew the rules for living parallel lives: keep things separate. Render unto Ali Baba the things which are Ali Baba's, because everything you needed to know to function in Ali Baba's world was counterproductive to survival in the world of a Brisbane university student.

And vice versa.

Once, in mid-afternoon, hungry for the onset of night, he had taken the city catamaran—the Rivercat—downriver from the university dock to Kangaroo Point and had gone walking through the maze of back streets beneath the bridge. He had stopped at a greengrocer's barrow to buy an apple and found himself, to his astonishment, face to face with Mr. Hajj.

Mr. Hajj smiled. "You are surprised, Mikael?"

Mishka, overcome with embarrassment, could think of nothing to say.

Mr. Hajj laughed a little. "One cannot pay the rent by teaching Persian classical music in Brisbane," he said. "I am a greengrocer by day."

Mishka felt that he had done something gross and improper. "I'm sorry," he said. "I'm so sorry."

"I am not sorry," Mr. Hajj said. "I am grateful."

"But in Damascus—"

"Yes, in Damascus I was a famous musician and professor of classical music."

"It's not fair," Mishka said. "It's not right."

"Many things are not fair," Mr. Hajj said. "In Damascus, my brother Mustafa was a very well-known lawyer. But he represented a client whom President al-Assad did not like."

Mr. Hajj was polishing tomatoes and arranging them in his barrow. He would take two at a time from a crate behind him, wipe them with a damp cloth, and then place them in his display case in neat rows.

"What happened to your brother?"

"He was tortured and then executed. The body was returned to the front door of our family house."

"Mr. Hajj," Mishka said in anguish, but what was there to say?

"I escaped," Mr. Hajj said. "I am grateful."

"My grandfather," Mishka said, "lost a brother. The circumstances were... similar. And very painful."

"Your Lebanese grandfather?"

"No. The... my other one. Hungarian. He escaped to North Queensland."

"For loss, we have music," Mr. Hajj said. "And that is why we have music. For love and for devotion and for sorrow. Tonight, bring your violin."

That was the beginning of *Elegy for Uncle Otto and Mustafa Hajj*, a duet for violin and oud.

Thereafter, however, Mishka knew that his two worlds were night and day, and he kept them apart.

In his day world, he had won some university prizes: plaques, certificates, checks. He had signed the checks over to his mother and had mailed them, along with the plaques and certificates, to the Daintree. He included a card with the plaques: *For Uncle Otto*. He signed the card: *Mishka*.

He knew there was cruelty involved in his refusal to write letters, to send news, to make phone calls, to go back for the High Holy Days. He loved his mother and his grandparents—they must know that; he was confident they took such knowledge as a given—but his love was on the far side of a roiling crevasse of anger. He knew his anger was illogical and unjust, and he did not understand it. He feared it, but he could not cross it. It was elemental and volcanic. It was like the turbulent rivers of hot lava beneath the earth's crust. He was afraid of stepping into it. He was afraid of fault lines and fissures through which it might erupt.

Instead he busied himself with applications for graduate school: the forms, the transcripts, the reference letters, the fees. It seemed that every American transaction required a fee that gobbled Australian dollars. He skipped lunches and gave up the buses to make ends meet. He used his student pass on the Rivercat or he walked along the path beside the river. The daily walking calmed him, four miles each way, from campus to city.

When notification of acceptance with fellowship came from Harvard, he had no one but Mr. Hajj to tell, and Mr. Hajj said only: "I will miss you." Mishka made a photocopy of the letter from Harvard and mailed it to Chateau Daintree. What followed was the bureaucracy at the American consulate, the airline reservations, the special packing arrangements for his violin and his oud, the flight. After that, what he remembered was a blur of jetlag and disorientation and meaningless formalities and much playing of his oud in secret in his room, and much playing of his violin, much playing of Gluck and Monteverdi in practice rooms and sometimes—because of the resonance, because the shadowy underground made him think, incongruously, of the rainforest—in the subway.

He finished his first year, his second, his third. He remembered only the pieces he composed. And then: disruption. Two meteors turned his life upside down. One meteor was named Leela Moore; the other was Jamil Haddad.

Long minutes before he and Leela stood face to face for the first time, he sensed her presence. He sensed her as the pressure of air ahead of a subway car. He sensed her as he used to sense Uncle Otto waiting in the closed upper room when his mother climbed the stairs in Chateau Daintree. All his nerves stood on tiptoe. His skin read barometric changes in the air. He knew a major disturbance was moving in.

When she was there, in front of him, speaking to him, all he heard was static. His pressure gauges went wild. There was a moment when an image came to him of his mother and his father at a boat railing as a harbor ferry docked at Circular Quay. He was standing in Harvard Square at the hub of a cacophony of car horns and swooping traffic and he had that old childhood sense of warm rising floodwater that was rushing him to some secret ecstatic place where he was part of the rainforest and the lorikeets and the parakeets and then there was simply the sense of joyful drowning in Leela's kiss or of falling into a vortex of light, terrifying, but exhilarating too. He had given himself to the flood. He had been swept beyond all hope of return.

Famished people are unable to eat sensibly, his mother had said. He remembered that. Something like that. *I am afraid to remember that time*, she had said. *I am afraid of falling back down that well.*

He had not forgiven her then for her sheer indifference to consequence.

He understood now.

In the sound booth off Harvard Square, the day after the subway bombing, surrounded by Uncle Otto's music, he had an urge to dial a telephone number in Australia. "Mum," he would say. "I understand now." Simply that. "I understand about you and my father." And then he would say: "Something terrible's happened. I had nothing to do with it, but I'm involved. I don't know how to climb out of this well."

That's the way it is with us, Mishka, his mother would say.

"Mum," he would say. "There's something else. I've met someone who knows my father. He says Marwan Abukir isn't dead."

In the silence that came over the line, he would feel the bruise spreading over her body. He would hear her footfall on the stairs. She would look back over her shoulder. *Marwan is in the upper room*, she would say, *with Uncle Otto. We preserve our lost ones however we can, Mishka. We preserve them as we knew them. We survive. We go on.*

Then the line would go dead and he would be back there at the moment when he first met Jamil Haddad in Professor Siddiqi's class. Professor Siddiqi had just introduced them: "Mishka Bartok... Jamil Haddad."

Jamil Haddad had stared. "You are an Abukir," he said.

Mishka had a sensation of cyclonic disturbance in his head, of a storm surge rampaging up the Daintree, of huge black waves. He had a memory of shot parrots falling. He reached for the wall.

"Are you one of the Saida Abukirs," asked Jamil Haddad, "or the Baalbah Abukirs?"

"I don't know," Mishka said.

"Why do you whisper? I can't hear you."

Mishka felt as though he were shouting. "How did you know I was an Abukir?"

"How do I know a cat is a cat? You look like one. You are Lebanese."

"My father was Lebanese."

"Speak louder."

"My father was an Abukir."

"I am Lebanese. I know your family."

"I believe I have an uncle in Beirut," Mishka said.

"Many of the Baalbah Abukirs are in Beirut now. What is your uncle's name?"

"It is Fadi Rahal Abukir."

"I have not met your uncle, but I know his name and reputation. I also know the reputation of your other uncle, Marwan, who is a hero to me."

Mishka remembered the way the room turned upside down and began to spin like palm branches in a storm. He remembered the way the floor came to meet him. He remembered the thump on his head.

* * *

Jamil Haddad did everything violently. He spoke in blunt flashes
of certainty. He gestured furiously. In the seminar on Persian
Classical Music, he argued constantly with Dr. Siddiqi. He
launched into long verbal attacks. There was ferocity in his
hatred of music. Once, to Mishka's horror, he kicked at the oud
in Dr. Siddiqi's office and Mishka gave an involuntary cry of
pain.

"I don't understand," Mishka said. "Why do you take this
class? Why do you study music?"

"I do not study music," Jamil Haddad said scornfully. "I am
studying engineering. I study the pollution of Islam by the West.
I am taking Siddiqi's course on the history of corruption from
the fourteenth century onwards, when European contamination
began. Music is licentious. It is forbidden."

"But what about Rūmī?" Mishka asked. "What about the
saints and mystical poets? I thought in Islam, music is always
religious, it's always devotional."

"Not in pure Islam," Jamil said. "There is no music."

"But you sing the Qur'an in the mosque."

Jamil was furious. "The chanting of the Qur'an is not
music. It is *tajwid*."

Something came off Jamil Haddad: an aura of hot intensity,
a kind of white light. "Long live the Islamic Nation," he would
say to Mishka by way of salutation. "Allahu Akbar," he would
announce at the start of Dr. Siddiqi's class. *God is great*. "Long
live the Islamic Nation."

Dr. Siddiqi would say mildly: "This is a seminar in the history
of Persian Classical Music, Jamil. Not in politics or religion."

"All of life is religious," Jamil would say. "Every statement
is political."

"In this seminar," Dr. Siddiqi would say, "we will restrict ourselves to the discussion of music."

"He is not to be trusted," Jamil confided to Mishka. "He is a Sufi, and he has been further corrupted by his life in America. He is not like your Uncle Marwan, who burns with a pure flame."

"My Uncle Marwan plays the oud," Mishka said. "He is a singer and a musician."

"That is a lie. Marwan Rahal Abukir abhors music."

"Perhaps this is a different Marwan Abukir. What does he do, the one you know?"

"I don't *know* him. It is his reputation I know."

"What does he do?"

Jamil lowered his voice to a whisper and recited in a weirdly rapid melodic chant: "Islam is our aim, Qur'an is our constitution, Jihad is our path, War till victory; God is great, Allahu Akbar!"

Mishka choked back a spasm of laughter. All he could think of was rugby games and Cairns high school: the spectators huddled, faces painted in school colors, the chant of team war-cries, the mock-epic rivalry, the mimicry of blood sport. The enforced warrior intimacy had always seemed to him silly and juvenile and distasteful, but he was wary of it too. He had seen too many games turn into brawls. In his experience, a chanter of war-cries could turn savage in the blink of an eye.

"Marwan Abukir has trained in Afghanistan," Jamil said quietly. "You understand? He is preparing himself. We are all preparing ourselves."

Now the swallowed laugh felt to Mishka like a hot pepper. He almost choked. His instinct was to get away, to run, to dive into salt water and wash himself clean. He had an image of himself leaping over the seawall in Cairns and running to catch the receding tide and the shadow of his dead father's name. The memory was so intense that he could smell kelp, his pounding feet were sending up spray—

"So what is this Bartok business, anyway?" Jamil demanded.

"What?" Mishka blinked. He was astonished to find he had not moved.

"Did your mother marry a Jew?"

"Uh… no," Mishka said, truthfully.

"I know one of your uncle's sisters lives in London, but she married a Lebanese man. Bartok is not a Lebanese name."

"No. It's Hungarian."

"Marwan Abukir's sister married a Hungarian?"

"I never knew my father. He died before I was born."

"That is good. That is Allah's will. You must reclaim your family name."

One day, after Dr. Siddiqi's class, Jamil Haddad told Mishka: "There is a man who lives in the Back Bay who is a Saudi. He is a very wealthy man. He knows your Uncle Marwan personally. He is in contact with your uncle. If you come to the mosque, I will introduce you to this man."

That was the first time, though the meeting with the man who knew Marwan Abukir took place before they ever reached the mosque. It took place at Café Marrakesh in Central Square.

"This is Sleiman Abboud," Jamil said. "The man who knows your uncle."

The man who knew Marwan Rahal Abukir had piercing black eyes. The moment he saw Mishka, he said: "You are your uncle's double." He held Mishka's chin between his forefinger and thumb and turned his head first one way, then the other. "Amazing," he said. "Amazing. Very useful."

Mishka's heart was jumping about in his chest.

"Your uncle and I met in Afghanistan," Sleiman Abboud said. "But now he is back in Beirut. We cooperate. You understand what I mean?"

Mishka made a vague gesture with his hand. He was afraid to speak.

"Visas. IDs," Sleiman Abboud said. "What is your citizenship?"

"Australian."

"You have an Australian passport?"

"Yes."

"You have a Green Card?"

"No," Mishka said. "A student visa."

"That might be useful. I will let Marwan Abukir know we have met. Perhaps a meeting will be arranged."

Mishka felt as though he were being sucked into Sleiman Abboud's black eyes. His sense of balance had gone, though perhaps that did not happen when he was talking to Sleiman Abboud; perhaps it happened when he submerged himself in the multi-celled organism of the men on the floor of the mosque. He had an eerie sense of becoming one particle of water in a wave that crested and poured itself out, crested and prostrated itself, over and over again. Mishka felt that he could not breathe. He felt that he was trapped in a rugby huddle. He had a sense of being trampled by a mob, of being dragged and held under a wave.

Allahu Akbar, Allahu Akbar, Allahu Akbar moved like an ocean about him.

He did not think he would leave the mosque alive.

Night after night, like an addict, he returned. He returned to Café Marrakesh and he returned to the mosque. He returned to hear Sleiman Abboud's stories and prophecies and rants. He was searching for nuggets of his father. He discarded the rant like rind.

"Marwan Rahal Abukir is a brilliant structural engineer," Sleiman said. "He has built bridges in the most difficult terrain in the world."

"Where has he built bridges?" Mishka asked.

"In Jammu and Kashmir. One of his bridges was blown up two months ago by the Jaish-e-Mohammad group."

"How terrible," Mishka said. "Was my uncle—?"

"Was he hurt? Of course not. His planning is perfect."

"I meant, was he devastated?"

"On the contrary," Sleiman Abboud said. "Marwan Abukir is the magician who knows exactly which card to remove. You understand me?"

It was important, Mishka thought, to meet Sleiman Abboud's gaze steadily but inscrutably until Sleiman Abboud himself looked away, which he did, finally, with a brash smile, by waving a twenty-dollar bill at a dancer. At Café Marrakesh, there was always a belly dancer. She moved, she *flowed* toward their table, the garlands of cheap silvered coins at her wrists and hips tinkling.

"Make these young men happy," Sleiman Abboud ordered, gesturing at Mishka and Jamil Haddad. The gesture was intended, Mishka thought, to provoke. It was intended to humiliate. Why was it, Mishka wondered, that people mistook reticence for weakness? He kept his eyes on Sleiman Abboud.

"You remind me of someone I knew at school in Australia," Mishka said. He calmed himself by imposing Tony Cavalari's face on the shoulders of Sleiman Abboud. The belly dancer was wreathing Mishka's head with a silk scarf. She let the silk trail over his cheeks, around his neck. A glass jewel was pasted in her navel and gold stardust glittered across the tanned amplitudes of her skin. Her belly moved like a separate live thing, dimpled and twitching, and she thrust it closer and closer to Mishka's lips. As though unaware of her gyrations, Mishka smiled at Sleiman Abboud until Sleiman Abboud stood abruptly and left the café. Only then did Mishka realize that his own hands, clasped below the level of the table, were shaking.

He dreamed that night that he was with his mother and his father on a ferry that was passing beneath the Sydney Harbour Bridge. There was an explosion, and he saw in slow motion how the bridge, like a spectacle of shimmering firecracker beauty, sent girders and cross-braced steel spinning like wheels in the sky. He watched the whirring spark-spitting ascent of half a ton of curved metal, coiled like a white-lightning snake. It hovered. It began to fall like a spent rocket. It torpedoed the ferry and the ferry went down without a splash.

At Café Marrakesh, there was nightly entertainment: belly dancers and performing musicians who played tabla and oud. Mishka went night after night for the music, and he went also to hear the rambling anecdotes of Sleiman Abboud. He could not begin to explain this to Leela. He could not speak of the precious but ominous thing he had found: his father's existence. It was like one of those double-edged treasures in Scheherazade's tales: a jewel that brings death to the finder.

He left Leela notes.

I'm working on a new composition. Can't blame you if you're sick of living with a monk, but you know what I'm like. I'll be obsessed till it's done. Working late in the sound lab again. Don't wait up. Love, Mishka.

One night, when the regular oud-player was ill, Mishka took his place on the dais at Café Marrakesh. He was conscious of the disdainful eyes of Jamil Haddad. He was conscious that the eyes of Sleiman Abboud never left him. Even during the tabla solo, it was Mishka whom Sleiman watched. After the musical interlude, he beckoned, and Mishka responded as though on a leash. Sleiman Abboud tugged; Mishka went. *Until I know all I need to know about my father*, he told himself. *Only until then.*

"We must walk," Sleiman Abboud said.

They walked the back streets of Central Square. "I have been in conversation with Marwan Rahal Abukir," Sleiman said. "He wants to know if you are his son."

Mishka reached out to steady himself against a wall. He could not speak.

"Marwan Rahal Abukir had a relationship with a woman in Australia," Sleiman Abboud said. "The relationship shamed his family. He repudiated the woman and her unborn child, but if that child was a son, he says *Allah be praised*. He says the will of Allah has been revealed."

Mishka leaned against the wall of a building.

"He would like to meet his son," Sleiman Abboud said. "Does the son want to see the father?"

Mishka was unable to reply.

"When you are ready," Sleiman Abboud said, "we will provide an air ticket to Beirut."

5

IN THE MUSIC Lab, the candle had guttered out. Mishka sat in the dark, cocooned between earphones, and listened to Mendelssohn. He was playing the *Concerto in E Minor*, one of Uncle Otto's favorites, and he listened in spite of interference. He turned up the volume. He filled every cranny of thought with the lush sound of Yehudi Menuhin and the Philharmonia, but still a rogue drumbeat interfered, arrhythmic, jarring, discordant, the blaring headline intruding, BOMBER IDENTIFIED, BOMBER IDENTIFIED, BOMBER IDENTIFIED, and below the headline, like counterpoint from an out-of-tune instrument, the picture of Jamil Haddad.

Jamil Haddad grew louder and larger, ballooning out of the sound system like a *jinn*. Mishka switched on the light to dispel him.

From his briefcase, he took the envelope he had collected from the Music Department's receptionist one hour earlier. First there had been a phone call. "The receptionist has a message for you," someone said. He had recognized the voice of Sleiman Abboud. The envelope had contained an e-ticket link and flight itinerary: Air France, round trip, Boston to Beirut, via Paris. The outbound flight was two days away. There was also a typed message.

Don't go to Café Marrakesh again, the message read. Don't go to the mosque, don't go back to your

apartment before you leave. A room has been reserved
for you at the Airport Marriott. In the lobby is a booth
for the taking of passport photographs. You must have
a photograph taken. A sealed envelope will be delivered
to you at the Marriott. It will contain a Lebanese
passport made out in your real name: Mikael Abukir.
Attach the photo in the appropriate place.

Tonight he would sleep in his office, his head on his desk.

He pulled from his pocket the paper napkin on which,
earlier in the day, Sleiman Abboud had written his father's
phone number in Beirut. There was a logo on the napkin, an
oud and a crescent moon, with CAFÉ MARRAKESH written below.
He studied the phone number scrawled above the oud in
ballpoint pen.

Suppose he were to dial that number now? At the mere
thought, his blood knocked against his temples like a drum. He
heard his heartbeat, thump thump, like heavy footfalls on stairs.
He felt small and fragile, like a child waiting for his mother in
the dark.

He sat with his left hand resting lightly on the receiver. He
closed his eyes, and the phone number of the house in the
rainforest was visible to him as though written in blue
quandong berries on the leaf-strewn ground. It would be
already tomorrow morning along the Daintree. If he called, his
mother would answer, or his grandfather would. He imagined
his own voice like some mythical creature in Ovid, a
changeling, caught in the act of metamorphosis, translating
itself from sound to electronic pulse. His voice would travel in
sine waves that Leela could calibrate and graph, it would coil
into the whorls of his mother's ear and spill out again, slipping
along the veranda with glider possums, wafting itself up the

stairs and across the landing and slinking under the door of the upper room.

But suppose his grandfather answered. Suppose he heard his grandfather say: "Hello? Hello…?"

Grandpa, it's me, Mishka.

Suppose he heard his grandfather say, "Hello? Is anyone there?"

They will have moved me into the upper room, Mishka thought. That's why I saw Uncle Otto this morning, leaning against the newspaper stand.

He picked up his pencil and scribbled furiously at the draft of his score: *Incident in a Nightmare.* He wove in the strains of Uncle Otto's violin: Beethoven, Mendelssohn, Bartók. He wrote the sound of the gunshot to Uncle Otto's head. He wrote in the ferry on Sydney Harbour. He wrote in Marwan Abukir's oud.

Two days ago, he had said to Jamil: "There must be two people with the same name. The Marwan Abukir who is my uncle plays the oud. He sings. He loves music."

And Jamil had spat on the sidewalk. "Marwan Abukir," he said, "testified in the blasphemy trial of Marcel Khalifa in Beirut."

"Who is Marcel Khalifa?"

"A musician, a singer, a darling of the degenerates. He performed a song that included words from the Qur'an. We demanded his death."

A day later, Jamil Haddad had blown himself up.

Approximately thirty hours ago, Jamil Haddad had blown himself up and he had blown up Mishka's life too.

In the margin at the bottom of the page of *Incident in a Nightmare*, Mishka wrote a note to himself. *The Marwan Abukir who testified in the blasphemy trial of a musician cannot be the Marwan Abukir who is my father.*

He lifted the receiver and dialed the international access code. He dialed the 61 for Australia. He dialed the 7 for Queensland. He paused.

What would he say?

Mum, I'm flying to Beirut to meet my father. I don't see how he can be my father but I think he is. I'm afraid he is. He's no longer the man you loved. He hates music. He's become a fanatic.

He replaced the receiver. What right did he have? Better that Marwan Abukir stay dead for his mother. Better that his mother lock her memories upstairs with Uncle Otto. He lifted the receiver again. He knew exactly what he wanted and needed to say.

Mummy, I'm frightened, but I have to know. I have to meet my father, but I'm afraid of what I'll find out. I'm taking my oud and I'm going to play for him. I want to know if he'll play for me.

Everything depends on the oud. That's how I'll know.

He replaced the receiver. He had no right.

He wanted comfort. He wanted Leela. She would be asleep in their bed; or perhaps she would be sitting up, wide awake, waiting for him, or not trusting him, or thinking of someone else.

He wanted to call their apartment. He wanted to speak to her. He wanted to touch her. *Che farò senza Euridice?* He wanted to look at her again, but if he went back now, if he looked back, he feared she would disappear forever. Those were the rules.

But he could speak to her, surely? There was no interdiction against speaking.

Are you still there? was what Orpheus must have called out, and when there was no answer he made his fatal mistake. He looked back over his shoulder.

There must have been a moment, Mishka thought, a single

moment when he caught one radiant glimpse of his love before
he lost her.

Mishka picked up the receiver and pressed it against his
chest. He began to dial his own number. It was after midnight,
but what would Leela care? She might in fact be sick with worry.
Or she might be thinking of someone else, a childhood love just
re-found. He stopped and hung up. He was afraid. Suppose the
line was busy? Suppose she was not at home?

That morning, after Berg called, he had written a note. He
had stood at the edge of their bed for whole minutes and studied
Leela. She slept like a child, defenseless, her cheek crumpled
against one arm. He had wanted to take off his clothes and
crawl back into bed beside her. He had wanted to lick her, head
to toe, the way a cat licks a kitten. He did not know how he
could go back to living without her.

He understood why Orpheus had gone mad.

He pulled out a yellow-lined legal pad and began to write
Leela a letter. He would mail it from the airport. She would get
it after he had gone.

Dear Leela, he wrote.
*I lied on the note I left earlier today. I'm not going to
the west coast, I'm flying to Beirut. The only
auditioning I'll be doing is auditioning for the role of
long-lost son. I think it's possible I've located my father.
I never realized how much I needed the answer to this
riddle.*

Who am I?

*It seems likely that I won't want to know. It seems
likely that my father will appall me. It seems likely he is
a fanatic and a terrorist. I still have to find out. I still
need to meet him face to face.*

I don't know if I hate him or love him.

There are some things that I need to ask him to his face: Why did you abandon my mother? Why didn't you ever have the slightest curiosity about me?

Leela, I realize now that you must have known about the mosque. I was in search of my father, that's all. Jamil Haddad, the suicide bomber who was in one of my classes, introduced me to a man who knows my father. I don't know why I couldn't talk about that, but it has something to do with panic and something to do with shame.

I have a premonition that things may go wrong. This is probably stupid, but just in case....

I'm taking the oud with me. I want to play it for my father.

If something goes wrong, will you call my mother and my grandparents in Australia? If you slide the photograph of my parents out of the diptych, you will find the phone number of their house in the Daintree Rainforest on the back. I want you to meet my family. I want my family to meet you.

If something goes wrong, I would be very grateful if you would ship my violin back to the Daintree. Tell them I'll move in upstairs with Uncle Otto. Tell them I will watch over them from wherever I am.

Leela, if anything goes wrong, I would like to leave the diptyches to you. Next to my violin and my oud and the pieces I have composed (which belong to anyone who loves music), these are the most precious things I own.

I have never owned you, but you are even more precious to me than music and I would play my violin

or my oud till Cerberus wept in order to keep you if that
would work.
    Love,
    Mishka.

Before he cleared security, he mailed the letter.

He would use his Australian passport until he reached Beirut. He had only one small suitcase. Checking in the oud as FRAGILE—HANDLE WITH CARE had required considerable paperwork, but he had seen it move off at last, safely, with his suitcase. He watched until the conveyor belt took them from sight.

It was not until his flight was called, at his gate, that he felt compelled to go to the pay phone. The message on the answering machine had not been changed.

Hello. You've reached Leela and Mishka. We're not available at the moment, but if you will leave your name and number and a brief message after the tone, we'll return your call as soon as we can.

"Leela," he said. "It's me. My flight's been called. I should only be gone a week or so. I'll call you when I get to Beirut....

"Uh... I miss you, Leela. I wanted to say goodbye, just in case.... They're boarding and I have to go now."

BOOK VI

Cobb

1

WHEN THE LAST few pieces of the puzzle showed up on Cobb Slaughter's screen and meshed perfectly, his hands on the keyboard shook. His breathing turned quick and shallow. He could feel a jazz skip and then a lurch in the beat of his heart and then syncopation. Stop. Suspension. For what seemed like an age, he heard no heartbeat at all, and then he heard racing arpeggios.

Hugo was the odd word that came to him, involuntarily, and he found that he had not only said it aloud but that the spelling was visible in front of him, floating in the room like a thread of alphabet cloud. He examined the letters curiously, and with some alarm, before they faded. Perhaps they were an after-image of a too-bright word on his screen. Hugo? Then he realized—and was fascinated by the intricacy of his neural retrieval system—that the apparent non sequitur was a *bodily* memory, intense and visceral. What he felt as the last jigsaw piece fell into place was weirdly similar to the quiver of pressure—on skin and eardrums and heart—that comes just before a hurricane makes landfall. Cobb's body remembered this: the euphoric sense of *rush*, the awareness of exceptional danger, the eerie calm before exhilaration and risk collide head-on. He had been in junior high when Hugo battered the Carolinas. The hurricane had blown into Charleston on the

autumnal equinox with a twenty-foot storm surge on top of
abnormally high tides. Wind speed topped 150 miles per hour.
Charleston was flattened and drowned. McClellanville and the
barrier islands were washed away. Promised Land, thirty miles
inland and therefore marginally better off, had clung to survival
on the tips of its nerves. Cobb's body itself retained the imprint
of the storm's Category 4 imprecations.

Hugo's message was this: Significant Death or
Transfiguration.

Monitoring the incoming data on Jamil Haddad and
Sleiman Abboud and Marwan Rahal Abukir and Michael
Bartok, Cobb felt that Hugo-like *frisson* against his skin. He had
joined up the dots. They mapped transfiguration. The blood-
pumping muscle behind his rib cage raced and skipped beats and
raced again. He experienced sharp pain—too much sudden
oxygen—in his lungs. He had to rest his head in his trembling
hands.

He had, in effect, defused a ticking bomb.

He would prevent havoc that was already planned.

He would be vindicated.

He imagined the shocked face of Leela Moore: *I've been
sleeping with the enemy.*

Would she, at last, taste fear? Would she be anxious? *Leela-
May Magnolia Moore, you are hereby charged with giving aid
and succor to an alien and to terrorist organizations.* Would she
have bad dreams?

He imagined also how the look in Benedict Boykin's eyes
would change. There was Benedict's former look, which
haunted and goaded Cobb, and there was the way that Benedict
would look at Cobb in future. Cobb saw the old look
everywhere, on faces in the street, on grunts in the army, in
dreams, the look that infuriated him, the one that was lowered

and guarded and falsely modest but which nevertheless issued a challenge. The look said this: *My moral credentials are impeccable; yours are slimy. My great-grandfather was a slave; yours owned slaves. Anything you do, regardless of courage or principle, is tainted by the dirty fact of your past; anything I do is hallowed by mine.*

The memory of his last encounter with Sergeant First Class Boykin—his last face-to-face encounter—still filled Cobb with turbulence.

You wanted to see me, Sergeant Boykin?

Yes, sir.

At ease, sergeant. What did you want to see me about?

Interrogation procedures, sir.

You did your duty in that regard, sergeant, in reporting to me. And I did mine. Objective achieved. I passed the photographs on to my superior officer, and interrogations have been taken out of our hands. They are the task of local militia. We are not involved.

Yes, sir. That is the problem, sir. There is evidence of torture. Some detainees that we handed over are dead.

That is very unfortunate, sergeant, but we are at war and local militia are not under my control.

They are operating on our premises, sir. They are doing it here.

Strictly speaking, sergeant, these premises are theirs. We are guests and advisors.

Some of our men took photographs afterwards, sir. In the cells. Of mutilated bodies. If those photographs get out....

I see. Yes, that is indeed a problem, sergeant. We will make taking photographs a punishable offence. Do you have any copies?

Some, sir. The ones I confiscated. They're in this envelope.

Thank you, sergeant. I'll keep these, and I'll issue orders accordingly.

Yes, sir.

And then, since Sergeant First Class Boykin continued to stand there, continued to refuse to lower his eyes: *You are dismissed, sergeant.*

Sir, we are ghosting them. We bring them in and hand them over. We keep no records. With respect, sir, it seems to me that this does not absolve us of responsibility. It only means that our abdication of responsibility is not on record.

Thank you, sergeant. Your opinion will be taken under advisement. You are dismissed.

Yes, sir.

But Sergeant First Class Boykin remained for one beat, two beats longer, and his eyes accused: *What will you do about it, sir?*

Cobb's voice had been steely: *You are dismissed, sergeant.*

Yes, sir.

The salute, Cobb thought, had a challenging edge and it rankled. Moral superiority is cheap, he wanted to say to Benedict Boykin, when it doesn't cost anything. There is the issue of military protocol. There is the delicate issue of diplomatic relations. There is the prickly matter of the autonomy of local troops.

There is the issue of borderline insubordination.

He slid the photographs out of the envelope and fanned through them.

"*Jesus God!*" he whispered.

He resealed the envelope and put it in the bottom drawer of his desk. He locked the drawer. He felt a compulsion to wash his hands. He could see stains on the pads of his fingers and on his palms, and there was a burning sensation on his skin. Something toxic must have been on the prints. His hands were smeared.

An orderly came in and said "Sir?" The orderly sounded nervous.

"What is it?" Cobb glanced up from the sink. He was scrubbing at his hands with a brush.

"You're not answering your intercom, sir. I've been buzzing on and off for ten minutes. Your hands are bleeding, sir."

Cobb stared at his hands. "Contamination problem," he said. "It's been attended to."

He dated the onset of bad dreams from that day.

He did not send the photographs on. When he left the army, he took the sealed envelope with him. The photographs remained like toxic sludge at the bottom of a box in his safe.

2

WHAT SURPRISED EVEN Cobb himself—or almost surprised him—was the way he had so accurately intuited the facts about Michael Bartok before he had proof, before he had any hard evidence at all.

He had read a magazine article once about identical twins, Korean twins, who had been separated at birth. Both had been adopted in the late 1950s, in the wake of the war, by American families, though those families were radically different. Twin A, adopted through an international agency by anthropologists— Jewish New Yorkers whose collaborative field work was based in far-east and south-east Asia—had grown up in Chennai (which Twin A's grade school certificate still called Madras), and was fluent in English, Hindi and Tamil. He had been accepted at the London School of Economics and was passionate about his life's cause: viable systems of third world development.

Twin B was adopted by a former GI who had fathered a child in Korea but whose sweetheart and baby had been lost to a bombing raid. The father was Southern Baptist and full of guilt. By way of atonement, he and his American Baptist wife— to whom he had confessed his wartime fornication—adopted Twin B and brought him home to Alabama. Twin B grew up in a blue-collar suburb of Birmingham that was full of conventional, law-abiding, church-going, Republican voters. To the mixed pride and consternation of his god-fearing parents, Twin B gave his time to inner-city Baptist mission work: the rescue of drug addicts, the homeless, all the lost for whom Jesus had died. Thus it was that his local congregation raised the money to send Twin B to an international evangelical conference entitled "Rescue the Perishing."

Neither set of adoptive parents knew that the baby they brought home in infancy had a twin, yet both adoptees, it transpired, had always fantasized a shadow half. The twins met, by chance, in the transit lounge at Heathrow airport in London. They found themselves standing side by side in the men's bathroom, pissing simultaneously, identically dressed in beige pants and blue shirts and beige linen jackets. Each subsequently reported a sense of absolute inevitability in the meeting: a small shock of surprise, an adrenalin rush, and then déjà vu: a meeting that had already happened over and over in dreams and fantasy, a docking with the mother ship, the smooth interlock with a missing part.

This was how Cobb Slaughter felt as the data he always sensed he would find appeared on his screen. The dossier on Michael Bartok/Mikael Abukir was by no means the first manifestation of Cobb's gift. He had a sixth sense. Before the first wire tap, he felt vibrations. He had never been wrong.

Hugo. Switch-flow. Ferment. An excess of white heat was rampaging through the highways and byways of his blood. He felt intoxicated. Every time, it was like this. He had never been wrong.

To celebrate, there was a particular kind of bar he would go to, whatever city or country he was in. Every city had this kind of watering hole. The bar would be dark. There would be young women in sequins and gauze whose services went beyond serving drinks, young women who flowed and swayed like

exotic fish through the dimly lit murk. The young women held
aloft trays of drinks and the drinks were bedecked with cherries
and paper parasols and tiny flags. When customers touched the
young women, or stroked them, or introduced certain kinds of
provocation between their legs—cell phones, perhaps; hundred-
dollar bills; cubes of ice—the girls giggled fetchingly and
suggestively and leaned toward the customer with their trays.
They accepted payment for drinks in original and
unconventional ways.

Cobb would sit in a corner and sip his whisky and watch
other men make asses of themselves. Observing loss of control
in others—reading the predictable stages—was his specialty. He
himself would take an old round tin for loose-leaf tobacco from
his pocket. Under cover of his bistro table, he would open the
tin and stroke the sand dollar inside. The glittering young
women would come and go. They would sit at his table and
offer him a drink on the house, or they would ask if he would
buy them a drink. He would be courteous but non-responsive.
He would be detached—and therefore increasingly desirable—
until a woman with the right kind of eyes came along. The
woman would meet his gaze evenly, or perhaps with a certain air
of challenge, but not lasciviously, not with blatant sexual
invitation. He preferred that the woman be black.

The woman would sit at his table and order drinks.

"Something is making you sad," she might say. She often
said that.

"On the contrary," Cobb would reply, meeting her eyes.
"This is a private celebration."

"Ah. Then perhaps I can help you privately celebrate."

"Perhaps you can."

There were always back stairs in such bars. There was
always an upper floor with shuttered windows and red-shaded

lights. Always, he would place the tobacco tin under the pillow. That was essential. The sex would be acrobatic and slightly violent and would last for hours.

"You are one wild man," the woman would say.

When Cobb left, he would request something personal, a little kinky, a little odd. If granted, he would promise, the bit of theater would result in a doubling of the fee. The role-playing involved a chair, a sheet, and the ceiling fan. Part of the task belonged to Cobb. He would twist the sheet into a rope and sling it over a blade of the fan. He would knot the rope around the woman's neck. She was then required to stand on the chair. "I'll leave the money on the bed," he would say. He was generous. "Best if you don't move," he would say, "until someone comes. I'll send the manager up." He would exit the room and leave the woman standing naked on the chair.

On the night the last jigsaw piece on Mishka Bartok fell into place, he left the dive that was on the waterfront in Charlestown and took the subway to Harvard Square. He walked through Harvard Yard and up Oxford Street and along the street where Leela's apartment was. He stood opposite, in shadows, and watched the light in her gable window for some time, and then he walked on up Massachusetts Avenue to his own apartment near Porter Square.

IN HIS APARTMENT in Porter Square, Cobb unlocked his fireproof portable safe and took out his files. He did not take out the file marked *Baghdad/Photographs/Boykin*. He never opened this file. He never touched it.

The folder he removed was labeled *Calhoun Slaughter 1968*, a date some years before Cobb was born. The folder was thick with photographs, and the photographs were eight by ten inch in size, some black and white, some in color. They were newspaper and magazine reprints, all taken by the lone journalist who happened to be in Ambush Alley on the Tay Ninh-Dau Tieng Road when Calhoun Slaughter's M113 armored personnel carrier blew up.

Two of the photographs had moved like a lit fuse around the wire services of the world: the explosion of the lightweight armored vehicle; and the one of Calhoun Slaughter apparently firing at point-blank range into the back of the head of a prostrate body.

Other photographs—the crew before, the crew after, Calhoun Slaughter kicking corpses—had appeared in assorted Sunday supplements and magazines. Context meant nothing to newspaper editors; visual drama was all. Cobb, on the other hand, kept the images in chronological sequence and always examined them in order.

The first photograph was from Before, and showed the four-man crew atop Mr. Blue, the vehicle's nickname scrawled in fat brushstrokes across its flank. There were the commander, the driver, the two side gunners. Cobb's father had been a side gunner. He had taken off his helmet and was mopping at the sweat on his face with his sleeve. He was also laughing, as was his driver, Sergeant Leroy Watson, another Southerner, a black giant of a man from Alabama. They had just shared a joke. The four-man team was close-knit, though the other side gunner was a Yankee, and the commander was a Midwestern college boy who'd failed a year at agricultural college and lost his student deferment and been drafted. Leroy and Calhoun, the Southerners, had a non-stop bantering routine. "That Leroy," Cobb's father used to say when drink and reverie claimed him, "he could crack me up in a skinny minute. Leroy could've made Westmoreland himself crack up."

If it were not for the nature of the vehicle, the rice paddy on one side, the wall of dense tropical forest on the other, the red dust blowing up from the road, if it were not for these props, one might have thought the men were at a tailgating party and that a football game was getting underway.

Cobb loved this picture of his father: young, handsome, full of bravado and courage, straight man to Leroy's comic line. He had had a photographic studio crop this image and frame it. It was one of three photographs he kept on his night table or beside his bunk at assorted bases around the world. There was also a snapshot of his parents' wedding (his father in uniform; his mother fresh as Confederate jasmine in a street-length dress with a gardenia in her hair). The third photograph was of Cobb Slaughter with Leela-May Moore, first- and second-place winners in the high school Math Prize.

Cobb studied the face of his father atop Mr. Blue. Suppose nothing had happened to erase the laugh? Suppose what happened in the next few minutes had never happened?

Ambush was what happened.

The Reuters photographer caught the moment of impact. The hail of sniper fire hitting the flank of the APC was visible on the second image as tracer arcs, manifest as a disturbance on the lens like vapor trails in the wake of a plane. Laughter had been erased from the faces. It had been blown from the frame. Cobb thought the vapor trails must contain the dispersed atoms of mirth. The eyes of the crew were wide and shocked, the mouths tight in grimace. The white blur was the hand of Calhoun Slaughter as he reached for his helmet. Holes were visible in the APC's flank.

The third photograph showed the APC veering toward the clump of jungle, guns blasting. A covey of men was caught running from the trees like quail flushed out of cover by a dog.

In the fourth frame, there were seven bodies on the road and four men on top of the APC, still standing, their rifles trained on the bodies, watching.

Frame five: three of the crew had relaxed their stance. Side Gunner Slaughter was in the act of dropping to the road.

Frame six: explosion. The entire APC was an inferno, a core of fire in a cloud of red dust. No figures were visible.

"Those M113s," Calhoun Slaughter would explain—he would expound on this *ad infinitum*, to his son or to strangers in bars, in rambling and interminable lectures, especially when the whisky wound him up—"those M113s were fucking death traps. Tinfoil hulls!" He would crush a beer can in his hand to demonstrate. "Lightweight, so that aircraft could bring them in." He would draw diagrams with his finger in spilled beer. "Caseless ammo to cut down the weight. Might as well have sent us out in a tinfoil powder keg with a burning fuse."

Frame seven: the still-burning tank filled the upper third of the image; the bodies, face down, filled the foreground. Calhoun Slaughter, blackened, scorched, uniform in ribbons, face and legs darkened with blood, one arm dragging like dead meat, was between the two, crawling toward the camera and the bodies.

"Half a second before this photograph, I saw that fucking corpse—this one here"—jabbing with his finger—"lift his head and lob something at the APC. I heard it whistle over my head. 'You're done for, buddy,' I screamed. 'You're meat, you're Vietcong stew.' Then my eardrums burst and Leroy... Leroy was the man in the sun."

Frame eight: this shot was the one seen round the world. An American GI, with his booted foot on a body, firing at the back of its head. A series of further images showed a systematic kicking of the bodies. "I wasn't taking any more damn chances," Calhoun said. "Every one of those fuckers, for all I knew, was playing dead."

There was, of course, no image of the dead photographer. "A sniper got him, and I got the sniper. They were still out there, in that frigging pocket-handkerchief of jungle, watching us, the bastards. I fired off my whole belt's worth into those trees. Would I have called the fucking base if I'd shot the journo? Would I have handed over his fucking camera?"

There was no court martial. A military inquiry ascertained that none was warranted. There was no trial, except in the media and the court of public opinion. Cobb's father should have been awarded a purple heart, but the award was withheld to avoid stirring up further negative attention, and Calhoun Slaughter came home to averted eyes and silence. He had only partial use of one arm. He had a pulpy hole in his cheek. He lived on his disability pension from the VA and sat on his front porch and drank. He screamed and shouted in his sleep. Awake, he was unpredictable. When drunk, he ranted; but there were other times, there were other times...

"Don't peek," his father said. That was probably what his father had said, though the memory was in fact made up of sensations, not words. Cobb could smell tobacco and the damp wool of his father's sweater. He could smell the funky leathery stink of his father's boots. He could feel rough skin on the hands pressed over his eyes. He was three years old and this was his earliest memory. It was Christmas morning. He remembered how his father's fingers scraped his cheeks like sandpaper as his father's hands slid away to let him see the surprise. He remembered the tricycle, gleaming red, and the smile on his mother's face. He could never see his mother's face distinctly. He could see only radiance, as though his mother's face were the source of light. He remembered feeling nothing but joy.

"Meant to have it done for your third birthday," his father had told him over and over, years later, in the maudlin hours of each anniversary of Cobb's birth. "Didn't quite make it. But I did have it done for Christmas."

"I remember that Christmas," Cobb would say. "It's my earliest memory. I loved that tricycle, Dad."

"Found it at the dump, did I tell you? Rusted all to hell, mangled front wheel, no seat."

"You fixed it up good."

"Sanded it, painted it. Your mother made a little padded seat. We called it the Red Racer and we could hardly get you off of that thing. You would have taken it to bed if your mother had let you."

One year his father had told him, "Night before your third birthday, I went on a bender."

Cobb made a non-committal sound. His father always went on a bender on his birthdays.

"Accidentally ran over the damn tricycle," his father said. "Your mother cried so much, I was ready to run over her too. Kinda scared me, so I took off for a couple of days. Had to start from scratch to fix the damn thing up. Got it good as new in the end."

"It was beautiful, Dad."

"You used to ride that Red Racer as if you were king of the world."

Cobb still had the Red Racer. He kept it wrapped in a mover's quilt in the loft of his father's garage. He would climb up there on every trip home and look at it and dust it off. He planned to give it to his son if he ever had one.

There were other images, their sequence random, which he ran like videotapes, fast forward, rewind, fast forward again, a blur of sensation: his little legs pedaling, pedaling, red dust rising, his compass set for the porch where his parents leaned on the railing, watching; his parents as lighthouses, giving off safety and warmth; his head on the pillow through which came a night noise, a creak-creak-creaking, and he was padding barefoot, the hallway floor cool to his feet, to where he could see them: his mother and father floating on the porch swing, his father's fingers stroking his mother's face.

Cobb thought of his addiction to the past as akin to his father's benders. After the hangover, he returned to the right ordering of now.

Fact: In the blown-up train on the Red Line, identifiable body parts had been found: a head and two legs, no torso, sure sign of a suicide bomber. The head was that of Jamil Haddad, graduate student in engineering at Harvard, registered auditor of a seminar in Persian Music, frequenter of the mosque in Central Square.

Fact: Various members of the mosque in Central Square had expressed sympathy with radical jihad. Their intemperate statements were part of the public record.

Fact: There was a history of association between Jamil Haddad and the Australian music student whose passport bore the name Michael Bartok. They both frequented Café Marrakesh in Central Square and they both frequented the mosque.

Fact: In visits to aforesaid Middle Eastern bar and to the mosque, Michael Bartok assumed a different name, that of Mikael Abukir.

Fact: A search of the apartment of Jamil Haddad, following his death, had revealed computer files with lists of contacts and names. This list included a cluster bracketed together: Mikael Abukir, Marwan Rahal Abukir, Fadi Rahal Abukir, Sleiman Abboud.

Fact: Intercepted email communication between Marwan Rahal Abukir and Sleiman Abboud indicated that the former believed Mikael Abukir to be his son.

Fact: Marwan Rahal Abukir had been on extended training stints at jihadist camps in Afghanistan, but had recently returned to Beirut. Intercepted emails and cell phone calls between Marwan Abukir and Sleiman Abboud indicated that Abukir was actively recruiting young Muslims with American citizenship or with Green Cards and student visas.

Fact: In the four days since the explosion on the Red Line and since Cobb's interrogation of Leela Moore, Michael Bartok had not returned to the apartment he had been sharing with his lover, but was registered at an airport hotel.

Fact: Air France had a reservation in the name of Michael Bartok for a round-trip ticket via Paris to Beirut.

Fact: Cobb was dedicated to forestalling acts of mayhem; Cobb was also dedicated to making Leela understand the gross errors in the choices she had made.

So: the musician would be permitted to fly the coop. He was bait: the little fish who would hook the whale. The Abukir phone line in Beirut would be tapped. After contact was made, the meeting would be under surveillance and a rendezvous of a different sort would be arranged.

Cobb passed on his intelligence to several relevant bodies, military and federal. He listed options. The father would of course be apprehended. He could be held for interrogation on substantive grounds. The son could be allowed to return and then arrested by Immigration at the port of attempted re-entry in Boston. He could be charged: he had met with known terrorists. This method would be the least troublesome, politically speaking, and entirely legal.

But suppose Bartok/Abukir made no attempt to return?

Suppose his father were recruiting him for deployment elsewhere, for a bombing in Australia, perhaps?

It was clear to Cobb that kidnapping and detention of both men in Beirut, on the grounds of forestalling major threats, was the only safe option. There was a risk that the Australian government would lodge a protest—international protocol frowned on the kidnapping of citizens by a foreign power, especially since Lebanon was not a combat zone—and this was why it was essential that no official unit, encumbered with national identity and sanction, be involved.

The action could be officially disowned.

It would be due to rogue elements.

Cobb, in his outsourced element, would arrange the containment incident. He would transfer his pigeons to Baghdad. There, Marwan Rahal Abukir, hub of a lethal network, would be transferred direct to U.S. Military Intelligence. The son, whose role was as yet unclear, would be held until Cobb Slaughter arrived.

Cobb wanted to sift the truth of this one for himself.

4

"THOSE FUCKING BANDITS," Cobb fumed. "What do you mean, you don't know where he is?"

"Sir, we contacted Military Intelligence the way you wanted. We arranged to hand over the father—"

"The *father*," Cobb barked. "I told you to hold the son until I got there."

"Special Forces barged in and took over, sir. They took both men."

"You should have stopped them. They have no jurisdiction in Beirut."

"But they do here, sir, in Baghdad. In the war zone."

"They hate having their miserable intelligence failures shown up." Cobb punched the desktop with his fist. "They wouldn't have either man if it weren't for us. Find out where they are."

"I tried, sir, but they were ghosted. There's no paper trail. There's no way to trace them."

"There's always a way. Talk to the rank and file. Find out from barracks gossip where they went."

"I've already done that, sir. For what gossip's worth, the rumor is rendition. Egypt for the father, no one's sure about the son. Probably still in Baghdad is the word, but turned over to certain Iraqi militia who know what to do."

"Find out."

"Yes, sir. Military Intelligence says we'll get a commendation, sir. The father's a very big fish."

"They're trying to buy us off."

"Yes, sir. But we *have* pulled a major terrorist out of the game. We can all sleep better."

Cobb did not sleep better. He slept fitfully and a phone kept ringing in his dreams. Sometimes it was Benedict Boykin, sometimes Leela. *Iraqi militia who know what to do*, they both accused.

With respect, sir, Benedict Boykin said, and kept saying like a badly cracked record, *it seems to me that this does not absolve....*

Cobb, Leela said, *what have you done? Did you listen to the messages he left me? Mishka's a lost soul looking for his father.*

It's not my fault, Cobb pleaded. *The Iraqi militia wasn't what I planned. I was planning to handle this myself. I play tough but I don't play dirty.*

He unplugged the phone but it kept on ringing.

BOOK VII

Underworld

1

THE SACKING SMELLED like night soil and when Mishka breathed in—when he *could* breathe in—he felt grit and hair fibers on his tongue. His tongue seemed abnormally large and soon it would not fit in his mouth. Soon breathing would be impossible. Mostly he was not conscious of breathing but he was conscious of something that felt like hot skewers in his shoulders. His wrists were tied together, crosswise, and held in a carpenter's vise. Someone was tightening the vise.

The pain came and went.

There were moments of sheer sweetness, moments when he could not remember where he was and then knew he was where he wanted to be.

He had found his father.

Or perhaps he dreamed he had found his father.

In some of the dreams his father embraced him. In others, his father smashed his oud. In still others, his father brandished a scimitar and slashed Mishka neatly in two from head to toe.

The pain was like a crowded city street. So much was happening that he could not translate the danger, could not distinguish mere agony from life-threatening risk. There seemed to be buses, cars, trucks, road tankers, dumpsters, eighteen-wheelers, all bearing cargoes of torment, all emptying their loads on his body, all threatening to crush him, and the shouting drivers, buffeting pedestrians, horns, screaming tires, policemen's batons were blurred into one vast cacophony of peril. He wanted to shout *Wait, give me a fighting chance, let me face one lethal collision at a time*, but the turnpike of pain was too foreign, the traffic was coming too fast, it was too... it was too... and then, unpredictably, it would switch to slow motion and a detail would flicker and pause and loom huge and close inside the sacking. For example: a car would brake, he would hear the scream of its tires, or perhaps the scream was his own, and one time he saw the face of a child pressed against the window of the car. It was the face of a little girl and he saw her in extraordinary detail: her wide frightened eyes, the freckles on her cheeks, the red barrette in her hair.

Mishka, her lips mimed soundlessly, and he realized he was just inches away from his mother. What are you doing here? he asked, confused, because she should have been safely tucked in the family album, aged six or seven, behind the window of his grandfather's car. He could see the down on her neck.

Neck, she echoed, nodding and nodding, and now he could begin to translate. He could identify one strand of the pain. He became conscious of a savage chafing where the hood was tied. His mother rolled down the window of the car. Mishka, she said, let me help, and he left his body and climbed through the window and she slid her cool fingers beneath the rope. You must identify each thread, she explained. You must isolate and catalog and name. When you are finished, the car can drive us away and we can leave your body behind. Look, she said. See? It isn't you. It's just a stage costume and you can climb in and out.

He joined his mother at the window and they stared at the effigy wearing the costume of his body. It was swinging by its wrists from a hook. Its feet did not quite touch the floor. Apart from the hood, it was naked. The light changed, the car moved, and Mishka left his effigy behind.

He could hear screams.

He wondered which were the screams of his effigy and which were coming from the next cell.

The car—it was no longer his grandfather's car, it was a limousine, and the driver was dressed entirely in black—drove into yesterday. Where are we going? Mishka asked the driver. My instructions are to monitor the arrival of your flight from Paris, the driver said. Mishka recognized the airport in Beirut. Very smoothly, very cleverly, the car cruised onto the tarmac and onto the plane and up a side aisle and stopped at Seat 36A. Here's your row, his child-mother said. She was still with him in the back of the limo. You have to get off here, she told him. I'll wait in the car till you need me again.

Mishka disembarked with the other passengers. He cleared Customs and Immigration. He took a cab from the terminal to the Beirut Dunes Holiday Inn and checked in with his small suitcase and his oud. Then he sat by the telephone and smoothed out the paper napkin which bore the logo of Café Marrakesh, Cambridge, Massachusetts. He read the phone number aloud. Three times his nerve failed him. He drank two miniature bottles of scotch from the mini bar and stood on the balcony and let the breeze off the harbor buffet him until he grew calm. He was on the sixth floor and the Mediterranean stretched as far as the eye could see like a shimmering crystal shawl.

He went to the telephone. He dialed the number of his apartment in Cambridge. He got the answering machine.

"Leela? It's me, Mishka. I'm in Beirut. I'm safe, I'm fine, I'm at the Holiday Inn, the Beirut Dunes Holiday Inn. I was afraid to tell you where I'd be staying in case things went wrong, but everything's fine. I had no trouble at all. I should be meeting my father today. I'll call you later, after we've met. I love you, Leela."

He hung up. He took three deep breaths. He dialed his number in Cambridge again.

"It's me again, Leela. Look, just in case something goes wrong.... This is silly, because the worst that can happen is my father will reject me, or he'll turn out not to be my father, or he'll be my father and I'll be horrified by him, and I'm already braced for all of those possibilities, but I have this... I have a premonition, I have a feeling of dread. I suppose it's just nerves.

"Anyway, in case something does go wrong, I'm going to mail you a postcard today. It'll have the phone number of my father on it, I mean of Marwan Rahal Abukir, who's probably my father. It seems silly not to read it to you right now, but there are reasons I can't. I don't want you to do anything unless something goes wrong. And I'll also send a letter for my mother, but I don't want you to mail it on unless, you know....

"I'll call back later tonight or tomorrow, after I've met him."

He opened the drawer of the desk and found the stationery folder. There were two identical postcards: *View of Beirut Harbor from the Holiday Inn.* He wrote the phone number of Marwan Rahal Abukir on the back of one card and scrawled: *Leela, This is the number. Love, Mishka.* He wrote a letter to his mother on hotel stationery and sealed it in a hotel envelope and addressed it: *Devorah Bartok, c/- Daintree Post Office, Queensland, Australia.* He placed both the postcard and the sealed letter inside another envelope which he addressed to Leela. Then he went down to the reception desk and asked for an airmail stamp to the States.

"We can take care of that for you," the receptionist smiled.

Back in his room, he felt safer. He dialed the number Sleiman Abboud had given him.

A voice answered in Arabic.

"This is Mikael Abukir," Mishka said. "I would like to speak to my father."

Someone was tightening the vise on Mishka's wrists and lifting him. His feet were not touching the floor. His shoulders were burning. A black wave, tidal, engulfed him and he was floundering, but his father was floundering too and a great access of energy made itself available to Mishka. He could have swum, if necessary, from Beirut to the heel of Italy. Certainly he could swim across the lobby of the Holiday Inn which was under black water. In the spaces between manta rays and sharks and armed soldiers he could see himself in a time-lapse image and his swimming arms pulled at the waves, stroke after stroke, and he was there.

His father embraced him. "My son," he said. "Allah be praised."

Mishka was sobbing and could not speak. What word should he use? Dad? My father? When he managed at last: "We do look alike, my mother said that we looked alike," he could see that his voice was a shock.

His father, agitated, turned away and covered his face with his hands. "You have an Australian accent," his father said, and Mishka thought his father was weeping. His father's accent was British boarding school but there was an overlay of Aussie diphthongs, a faint hint of surf beaches and Aussie pubs.

"It brings back a lot of memories," his father said. "Your accent."

"Where did you learn English?" Mishka asked.

"School. A British school here in Beirut. My father paid for the best education for his sons." His father seemed nervous in the lobby. He kept looking behind him. "Shall we walk on the beach," his father asked, "and pretend it's Bondi?"

"Can I show you something first? In my room?"

Mishka felt an intense urgency to display his oud, to play the oud for his father. He felt that something decisive would be learned.

"In your room?" his father said. "Why in your room?"

"Why did you go to your room?" the voice demanded over and over. It was booming very large inside the hood. It was the voice of a hostile schoolteacher and Mishka was being caned again and again and he could see the sugarcane fields and the Mossman schoolroom and the expanse of Beirut Harbor and the strange indecipherable look on his father's face when Mishka showed him the oud, but he could not see the right answer to the question and the teacher was enraged and was shouting and striking and pushing and his mother came by in the car again and they drove into the dark.

His mother must have dropped him off near the Holiday Inn because he was walking with his father along the boulevard, the Mediterranean on one side, the canyon of high-rise hotels on the other. "It's very beautiful," Mishka said. "Beirut is a beautiful city. Very different from what I expected."

"Does it remind you of Sydney Harbour?" his father asked.

"It reminds me of Queensland beaches. Surfers Paradise. Noosa. The esplanade in Cairns."

"I never visited Queensland," his father said. "But this always reminds me of Sydney Harbour. And Sydney Harbour reminded me of Beirut. I rode the ferries every day, sometimes for hours, because I was homesick. I met your mother that way."

"Yes," Mishka said. "She told me."

They left the boulevard and walked along the beach. Without thinking about it, Mishka sat on the sand and removed his shoes. He tied the laces together and slung the shoes over his shoulder. His father watched without comment, but did not remove his own shoes. They walked for a long time without speaking.

At last his father said: "Is your mother still living?"

"Yes."

"How is she?"

"She is well," Mishka said.

"She has married?"

"No. Never."

"Your mother was a beautiful woman."

"She is still beautiful," Mishka said. He counted one hundred steps in the sand before he said: "The last time I saw her, we were walking along the esplanade in Cairns, beside the Pacific. The tide was out."

"We used to take the ferry to Manly," his father said. "We used to walk on the beach."

"My mother loves shells. She loves gathering seaweed and shells."

"I remember that." His father stopped to pick up the black empty wings of a mussel. "I felt passion for your mother, but I am no longer the young man I was in Sydney. She would understand."

"She did not know what to think. She believed you were dead."

"It seemed less cruel that way."

Mishka said nothing. He walked diagonally, moving closer to the water. His father followed. Mishka crossed the wet sand and let the tide splash around his ankles. He kept walking. There was a distance between his father and himself.

"I was already betrothed before I went to Australia as a student," his father said. "I came back to dissolve the betrothal honorably. That was my intention, but it was not possible. Family honor required that I marry."

"I see," Mishka said. He wanted to ask: *And were you never curious? Did you never wish to know anything about your Australian child?* But he was afraid to know the answer to this. Instead he asked: "Do I have half-brothers and half-sisters?"

"You have five half-sisters. I have no other sons. That was my punishment, the will of Allah."

Mishka kept walking into the water until the waves were at his knees and then sharks or predators, or perhaps fishermen with poles and sharp hooks, were tearing at his flesh and black water closed over him.

The sack over his head was like a night sky.

Floating lights, like small moons, came and went. Mishka floated. Perhaps he was flying. Perhaps one wing was ripped off. He felt as though one wing had been ripped off. The pain was excruciating, but it came and went. Sometimes the moons disappeared completely and the sky was so black that Mishka wondered if he were in fact not part of the sky at all but sunk deep in the ocean, below light. There were long stretches of nothing and he would wonder where he had been. Sometimes a great bird—an eagle, a vulture—tore at his liver with its beak.

The bird would fix him with its basilisk eye, demanding answers, and he could see the eye through the hessian sack. The eye burned him.

Yes, Mishka confessed. Prometheus. That is my name.

He confessed that he was in possession of hidden knowledge and he was keeping that knowledge hidden from the gods, though he understood it would be plucked from him.

Sometimes he said: "My name is Orpheus," and then he realized that the snarling shapes in the room were Cerberus and his fierce brood of pups.

He tried to explain that he had not descended into the dark world of Cerberus to steal secrets. Love had brought him. He had wanted to know if he could love his father and if his father could love him. He had come to call love to himself with his oud. If he could play his oud, if he would be permitted to play for Cerberus....

His answers were always wrong and brought punishment.

He tried to remember the secrets he had filched. This was required. Yes, he confessed, he knew of incidents. He knew about the bombing in Boston. He knew many details: the Park Street stop, the train after his, the bodies, the torn limbs, the severed head of Jamil Haddad. What more did he know of Jamil Haddad? He knew much. He knew that Jamil was an engineer. He knew that Jamil hated music. He knew that Jamil Haddad knew Sleiman Abboud.

Cerberus snarled and growled and continued to tear at Mishka's flesh. Mishka's wings—he was still suspended in flight, his wings caught in a tree perhaps, or in a net—were dislocated along the muscle where his feathered limbs were attached to his back. If he gave names, Cerberus promised, the pain in his wing sockets would be eased. He gave the name of his father and Uncle Fadi. He gave again the name of Jamil Haddad. He gave the name of Dr. Siddiqi who had introduced him to Jamil Haddad. He gave the name of Sleiman Abboud. He gave the name of Mr. Hajj, his music teacher in Brisbane, Australia, who had taught him to play the oud.

Cerberus paused in chewing gobbets of Mishka's flesh. His ears pricked up. He was particularly interested in Dr. Siddiqi and Mr. Hajj. These were new names. They were not on previous lists and Cerberus sniffed them with excitement.

Tell me about them, he snarled, but Mishka's tongue was dry and swollen and moved clumsily and he felt his wing tendons giving way. He would soon drop away from his wings.

Cerberus snarled and growled. He commanded: "Tell about Mr. Hajj."

Mishka told how Mr. Hajj had Damascus contacts. Mishka told about the shipping of ouds. He confessed it was possible that Mr. Hajj and Dr. Siddiqi were involved in the same Middle Eastern network, that their business was ostensibly music. He admitted that the booby-trapping of ouds could be part of their plan. When pressed, he spoke freely of Damascus. He spoke of the craftsmanship, he discussed the finest oud-makers in the world. He explained that Mr. Hajj, for political reasons, had to order through contacts in Beirut. He could not name the contact in Beirut, though he acknowledged that a global network existed (Damascus, Brisbane, Beirut) and he would try to remember the contact's name, and yes perhaps it was Marwan Abukir or Fadi Abukir but they knew nothing of Mr. Hajj so a connection seemed unlikely but perhaps it was so.

If he could play.... If he could play, yes, he would show what Mr. Hajj had taught him and he would promise to tell everything he knew.

He could not see because of the hood, but his bare feet were touching the floor. He might have been sitting, but it was difficult to tell because too many messages were coming from his body. They were coming too fast to translate. His wings drooped at his sides. They felt strange to him. He could not lift them, and when his oud was given to him, at first he did not recognize it because his hands were so clumsy.

Nevertheless he embraced it, he stroked it, he recognized its voluptuous curved backside, he wept to touch it again. His fingers were like thick vegetables and they would not do as he wished. He could barely spell out the notes against the neck of the instrument. He had not been given a *rishi* so had to pluck at the strings with his thumb. Nevertheless a song of Rūmī began to flutter upwards like a flock of small white doves in the room and Mishka was overwhelmed with its beauty. He sang the Arabic that Mr. Hajj had taught him and then he sang the translation:

> *The reed and the oud charm us because they are echoes,*
> *They know the notes of the planets and stars,*
> *They delight the souls of angels,*
> *They remind us of the gardens of Paradise,*
> *Our souls fly there to rejoin their loves.*

He could not remember where he was, but perhaps the Holiday Inn, yes, his room at the Holiday Inn because his father was still agitated by the song. His father was telling him to be quiet. A Sufi song, his father told him, and his father spat on the song. Heresy, decadence, contamination by the West, his father said. It was like a virus, a canker, spreading out from the fourteenth century and that heretic mystic, Rūmī. The infection had to be cauterized.

"But the poem and the music are beautiful," Mishka protested.

"Beauty is dangerous," his father said. "It is a trap."

Mishka closed his eyes and played and sang until his father fell silent.

He opened his eyes, but kept playing. His father was sitting in the armchair by the window. On the small table beside the chair was a vase of frangipani and his father had pulled one flower from its stalk. His father was shredding the petals with his thumbnail, he was killing the flower.

"My mother told me that you were a musician," Mishka said. "You used to sing to her. You wooed her with music. That is why I learned to play the oud. I wanted to know you. I wanted to touch you this way."

"All that is an abomination to me now," his father said. "Music is like the sexual power of a woman. It is evil because man has no resistance against it. It must be crushed before it destroys."

The fragrance of the bruised frangipani was extraordinary and Rūmī rose from Mishka's oud and from his lips in defense of beauty. *Everything loathly becomes lovely*, he sang, *when it leads you to God, and when it leads you to your Beloved.*

"Be silent!" his father shouted and his father snatched the oud from Mishka's hands but it was not his father who smashed it because they were walking on the beach and the oud was still in his hotel room and then they were walking along Boulevard Saeb Salaam and then the black limousine stopped and the driver said that Sleiman Abboud was waiting for them, but that was not true. From that moment onwards, Mishka was unsure of what happened because of the hood and because of the jagged colored shapes that moved like a turning prism in his head. He did not know what happened to his father. He thought he himself was on a plane again, but he was not sure. And now there was Cerberus and the smashed oud. He could feel the splinters, he could see the broken neck of the oud in spite of his hood, or perhaps it was his own neck, and he watched himself sobbing, curled up like an infant on the floor, naked, with a sack on his head.

Then the oud miraculously reassembled itself and rose up like a Being of Light and spoke to him, and its wings were like the wings of a great seabird and were as white and blinding as the sun. I am the messenger of the Lord of Music, proclaimed the Radiant Oud. Cerberus has lain meek at my feet and has licked my ankles. I have parted the Red Sea and led captivity captive and my power is so great that none can resist me and I cannot, I cannot be destroyed. Do not weep by the rivers of Babylon, but seize my power.

Then Mishka seized hold of the radiant being and wrestled with him and music arose from their struggle and Mishka said I will not let thee go except thou bless me and the oud touched the hollow of Mishka's thigh and Mishka was in very great pain and then he was in the absolute radiant embrace of the sun and the music of the spheres was all around him and he felt no pain at all.

2

LEELA READ THE letter mailed to her from Logan airport. She played and replayed her answering machine.

She dialed her own office number. She left a message on her own machine.

"Cobb," she said, "This is Leela. I hope you're still listening in." She was willing her voice to sound calm. She spoke in a rush. "I know you know Mishka's in Beirut. I want you to see a letter he sent. It explains the mosque, it explains everything. It's all personal, he's not any kind of terrorist, I can prove it to you.

"It's like what happened to your father, Cobb. It's the same kind of thing, photographs read the wrong way. Please call me, Cobb, and let me explain."

"But he called me," Leela explained from a pay phone in Harvard Square. She spoke to the reception desk of the Beirut Dunes Holiday Inn. "He called me yesterday from one of your rooms. He must be there."

"We have no record of a Michael Bartok."

"Uh... Bartok is his—it's possible he checked in under his Lebanese name, which is Abukir."

"Let me see. Yes, we did have a Mikael Abukir, but he checked out yesterday."

"He checked *in* yesterday."

"He checked out yesterday afternoon."

"Why would he check out yesterday afternoon when he'd only checked in that same day?"

"Yes, it is curious," the girl at reception said in excellent English. "But sometimes it happens. Probably friends or relatives invited him to stay at their house."

"Mishka himself checked out?"

"Mishka? I am sorry, I do not understand."

"Sorry. I mean Mikael Abukir. Did he himself check out? I mean did the same person who had checked himself in check himself out again hours later?"

"That I cannot answer," the girl said. "I was not on the desk yesterday. I do not know what Mr. Abukir looks like."

"Do you have video cameras in reception? Would you have a record of Mr. Abukir checking in and checking out?"

"Yes. We have video cameras. We have a record."

"Could you confirm for me if he himself checked out, or if someone else claimed to be checking out on his behalf?"

"I cannot give that sort of information over the phone. It can only be given to next of kin or to the police."

"I'm next of kin."

"You will need to file a report to the police with documentation—"

"This is urgent. I'm afraid something terrible has happened. He would not have checked out without letting me know. He had reason to fear that someone... that something very alarming.... What do I have to do to get that report?"

"Where are you calling from, madam?"

"Why do you need to know that?"

"I mean, from what country?" the girl asked.

"From the USA."

"Then you must contact the American Embassy who will contact our local police."

Embassy, yes, that would be the quickest and most reliable route, but not the American one. Leela dialed information. Washington, DC, she said; Australian Embassy; yes, she would like to be put through.

When she heard the accent, she was unprepared for the sudden grief. Her voice wavered. "I wish to report that an Australian citizen has gone missing in Beirut," she said. "I think something terrible may have happened."

Five days later, Leela found an envelope with a Beirut postmark in her mail. She knew the handwriting. She had to sit down and breathe slowly. Her hands were shaking as she slid a knife under the flap. Inside was another sealed envelope and a postcard. She stared at the view of the harbor. She held the letter up to the light.

She called the Australian Embassy again.

She had called every day, but the message was always the same: inquiries were being made; no information was available at this time.

"The letter was mailed from the Holiday Inn in Beirut," she explained. "They have their own metering machine. Their logo is stamped on the postage. Michael Bartok has sent the phone number of the person he was going to meet. He had reason to believe he was in danger. He promised to call me after that meeting but has not been heard from again. The Beirut police should be given this information. It's urgent."

Leela was put on hold.

Someone new came on the line and Leela explained again.

She was put on hold.

At last someone from Passport and Visa Information introduced himself. The embassy had made due inquiries, the passport official said. Michael Bartok, holder of an Australian passport, had departed from Boston, but no Michael Bartok had entered Lebanon or had registered at the Beirut Dunes Holiday Inn.

"That is true," Leela said. "I have explained that. He used his Lebanese name."

She explained and she re-explained.

Her explanation had been noted, the passport official said, but the Australian Embassy had no record whatsoever of a Mikael Abukir. There was no evidence that Mr. Abukir carried an Australian passport. Mr. Abukir was therefore beyond the scope of the embassy's responsibilities. The Beirut Holiday Inn, the official said, had confirmed that Mikael Abukir had produced a Lebanese passport at check-in.

"But if I can prove to you," Leela pleaded, "that Michael Bartok and Mikael Abukir are one and the same?"

An Australian traveling under a false name and possibly forged documents, the official said, had put himself beyond the reach of diplomatic aid.

3

It would be morning in Australia, tomorrow morning. This seemed ominous. Leela was placing a call to the future. She imagined the house where the phone was ringing (where the phone would be ringing tomorrow?). She imagined parakeets pausing in flight, bright colors ashimmer. She imagined furry gatherings on the veranda beyond Mishka's room—possums, tree kangaroos, scrub turkeys. She imagined their watchful eyes. She imagined Uncle Otto tuning up behind his closed door, the torrent of the Daintree below.

The bunting of Mishka's descriptions hung thick as lianas in her mind.

A woman answered on the fifth ring. "Hello?" The voice was tentative, surprised, as though unused to a ringing phone.

"Can I speak to Devorah Bartok?"

"I am Devorah Bartok."

"Ah... Ms. Bartok, you don't know me. My name is Leela Moore and I'm calling from Boston."

"Boston!" There was a register of alarm in the voice. "Something's happened to Mishka! What's happened?"

"Uh, actually, I don't know what's happened to Mishka, that's why I'm calling."

"Yes?"

"I'm Mishka's girlfriend. We've been living together for some time."

"I see." The voice became subdued, barely more than a whisper, as though it had no right to alarm. "We didn't know. He doesn't…. He hasn't…."

"I know. But he's talked about you. He has your photograph on the dresser in our room. I have a letter for you from Mishka."

"A letter for me?"

"He mailed it from Beirut, but he's been missing for several days. He said I should send—"

"Beirut!"

"He was going to meet his father."

"I don't understand. His father died before he was born."

"He thought his father might still be living, but he wasn't sure. He gave me instructions on what to do if things went wrong and I think they've gone wrong."

"Things have gone wrong." It was a statement of known fact. The voice was as faint as an echo.

"He's asked me to send you this letter. He also wants me to send his violin.

"Ms. Bartok…?"

But the line had gone dead.

Dear Devorah Bartok:
I am so sorry to have upset you, but I thought you would
want to know. Mishka flew to Beirut six days ago to meet
a man he thinks might be his father. He called me from
the Holiday Inn when he got there. He promised to call
back after his meeting but he never has. Supposedly he
checked out, but I don't believe it. I believe it was
someone claiming to be Mishka.

He mailed a letter just before his meeting and it reached me today. I enclose a photocopy of his postcard which gives the phone number of Marwan Rahal Abukir, who might be his father. There are steps we can take and they are urgent. I'm enclosing his letter to you, plus all the information I have, including an audio cassette which is a copy of the calls Mishka left on my answering machine. I'm sending by international courier. I'm hoping you can get a lawyer or your State Department to make inquires with the Australian Embassy in Beirut or with the Beirut police. Foreign nationals can't just disappear in another country without a trace. Your government can demand an explanation.

My phone number is above. Please call me. However, since I think my phone is tapped, please simply leave the following message and I'll return your call from a pay phone. Just say: I'm calling about the quandongs. (I have seen your beautiful miniature drawing on the diptych on Mishka's desk.)

Sincerely,

Leela Moore.

Leela dialed the country code for Lebanon and the area code for Beirut. She dialed the number Mishka had written across the back of a blue harbor on a postcard. She felt as though she were dialing underwater.

A male voice answered and said something guttural in a language Leela did not know.

She said: "Is Marwan Rahal Abukir there?"

There was a silence.

Several seconds passed. Leela thought she heard breathing. Then she heard a click and the line went dead.

* * *

It was because I failed to respond, Leela thought, because I doubted, because I spied on him. That is why Mishka vanished. It was because I didn't answer when he begged to be reassured. I turned away from him. I froze him out.

That was clearly Eurydice's error.

Are you still there? Orpheus must have called over his shoulder.

And why didn't Eurydice answer?

Was she irritated? (*He knows I'm here. What is this incessant need to control? Does he file reports on* his *absences?*)

Was she frightened? (*Where the hell is he taking me? Where are these pitch-black tunnels leading? Isn't that Cerberus ahead?*)

For whatever reason, she never answered, and Orpheus, apprehensive, looked back.

Game over.

4

"I'LL PUT YOU through to Dr. Siddiqi's office," the secretary said.

"Siddiqi here."

Leela studied the Music School from a telephone booth across the street. "Dr. Siddiqi, you don't know me. My name is Leela Moore and I have a post-doc and a teaching position at MIT, but the reason—"

"Your name is familiar. Mathematics and music? Renaissance violins and lutes, yes? This interests me, because of the Persian connection. I've heard something about your work—"

"Yes, that's…. I'm surprised that you've heard. I'm flattered. But that's not why I'm calling. Forgive me for interrupting, but this is urgent. I'm calling about Mishka Bartok."

"Ah. This is all so terrible, so terrible."

"You know what's happened?"

"I am in shock. Yet I cannot say I was totally surprised."

"Dr. Siddiqi," Leela said with alarm, "could I come and see you? I'm very close to the Music School. Could I come and see you right now?"

"Nothing in the Qur'an forbids music," Dr. Siddiqi explained. "It is only in *hadith*, the commentary."

"*Hadith?*" Leela repeated.

"Something like *midrash* in the Jewish tradition. Scholarly commentary. Debate. *Hadith* is used to argue both sides of the case. I explained this in my seminar, I explained it to Jamil Haddad, but fanatics are not interested in facts. They have no interest in history. They do not understand the evolution of beliefs and customs. For them, what is, *is*, and has always been that way." Dr. Siddiqi sighed heavily. "A student like Jamil Haddad is poison. He can infect a whole class. When I learned he was the suicide bomber, I felt ill but I was not truly surprised. Do you know what I felt next, after horror and nausea? I am embarrassed to tell you. I felt relief. Now I am rid of him, I thought."

"I never met him," Leela said. "I know nothing about him. I'd never even heard his name before I learned he was the bomber."

"Michael Bartok never spoke of him?"

"Unfortunately, no. There was a whole.... There were things he could never talk about. It was too confusing for him, too painful."

"I was distressed by Jamil Haddad's hold over him, but I saw it begin. I saw the very moment when it began. It was because Jamil knew the Abukir family and he recognized Michael as an Abukir. It was as though he had hit Michael with a stun gun. But I know nothing of his personal details apart from that moment. We always talked music."

"I knew something had happened. He changed. He was moody. There were absences, more and more of them, always unexplained, so one night I followed him. He went to that mosque in Central Square. I think he must have gone often."

"Yes. He did. I also go to the mosque in Central Square. It is not only jihadists and suicide bombers who go."

"It has a very bad reputation."

"It takes just one rotten fish to make the whole barrel smell. Many people who are proud to be good Americans and good Muslims worship at the mosque in Central Square."

"You said you knew what had happened to Mishka."

"I did?"

"On the phone. You said it was terrible but you weren't surprised."

"I was talking about Jamil Haddad. He had the jihadist's obsessive cunning. He would use anyone to further his cause. I've been afraid he might have used Michael Bartok. I haven't seen Michael since then."

"He's disappeared in Beirut."

"Beirut! He fled the country? That is not a good sign."

"It's going to look like that, isn't it? I don't think that even crossed his mind."

"You knew he was going?"

"No, not beforehand, but he left me messages. He was going to meet his father. Dr. Siddiqi, do you have any contacts in Beirut?"

"I am Iranian by birth, not Lebanese, but yes, I have some contacts in Beirut."

"Thank God. Mishka checked into the Beirut Dunes Holiday Inn a week ago. He called me twice from his room. I have his voice on my answering machine. His check-in was recorded on videotape at the hotel. A few hours later, supposedly, he checked out, or someone checked out in his name. The hotel will only give videotape access to the police. Do you think—?"

"I think I could."

"I've made a copy of all the information I have, including the phone number of Marwan Rahal Abukir, the man Mishka

thinks is his father. Also transcripts of Mishka's phone calls. It's
in this envelope."

"I'll do what I can, Dr. Moore."

"Leela."

"Youssef."

"Will you call me as soon—?"

"I will."

"There's another problem," Leela said. "My phone's being
tapped so when you call, if you'll just say the music's arrived—"

"Your phone's tapped? I think mine is too."

"Yours too?"

Dr. Siddiqi shrugged. "I go to the mosque in Central Square.
Jamil Haddad was in my class. I'm Iranian, though I had to
leave Iran years ago. I'm used to surveillance."

There was a message on Leela's answering machine. It was
Youssef Siddiqi's voice. "Your music can be picked up tomorrow
morning at 10 a.m."

In the music library at precisely ten o'clock the next day,
Leela could scarcely breathe. "What have you found out?"

"I have a friend who has a friend who is a policeman," Dr.
Siddiqi began. "He has seen the tapes and he's sending me
copies. He says the person who checked out is not the same as
the person who checked in."

"I knew it. When do you think—?"

"The tapes are coming express."

"Not that we're going to recognize the person checking out.
But it will be something to go on. Some evidence to report to the
embassy and the government."

"Another thing. The policeman friend of a friend traced the
Abukir address from the phone number. He put the place under
surveillance. Marwan Rahal Abukir has also disappeared. His

brother Fadi blames the son. The family believes the so-called son was a scam, a CIA set-up to kidnap Marwan because Marwan recruits suicide bombers."

"I'm sorry, but Dr. Siddiqi is not in his office today," the secretary said.

"I'm puzzled," Leela said. "I've been expecting a call for a week now. He should have a package for me. It's rather urgent."

"We're puzzled too, Dr. Moore. He hasn't called in sick and he hasn't even collected his mail. We've called his home and no one answers, and he doesn't answer his cell phone either. We think there must be a death in the family."

Leela stood in the phone booth across from the Music School. It felt familiar.

She dialed the number of the house in the rainforest in Australia and let the phone ring ten times. There was no answer.

5

THE WEEKS MOVED heavily and slowly.

There was a note from Berg to say they had got the grant. Leela should have felt pleasure. She felt nothing.

There was a note from Berg to say they needed to meet. She sent an answer back through campus mail:

Dr. Berg: Am working on something interesting: the years at the dawn of the thirteenth century when the oud was becoming the lute. Investigating the density of the wood and the curvature of the ribs in construction. The math's provocative. May seem like I'm off on a tangent, but I believe it's related to the structure of the early violins. Too involved to be interrupted at this point. Will get back to you when I've got more data. Leela.

For the Nth time, she called the Music School.

"We still haven't heard from Dr. Siddiqi," the secretary said. "We can't understand it. I'm afraid you can't leave a message because his voicemail's full."

Leela felt drugged. She wanted to sleep all the time. She felt as though she were living in somebody's dream.

The forsythia had long ago turned from gold to green and the oaks were in dense full leaf when she came home, late one night, to the fast red blinking of the signal on her answering machine.

She hit PLAY.

She heard a female voice with a strange accent. She had to replay the message to catch the words.

I'm calling about the quandongs, she heard.

6

FROM THE PHONE booth in Harvard Square, by the subway entrance, Leela could see the beginning again: a couple, indifferent to crowds, kissing passionately; a street musician or two. She watched the couple, book bags pressed awkwardly between them, heedless of trucks careering close and of the buffeting of students as they passed. Just so had she so brashly, so recklessly kissed Mishka. That was a lifetime ago. On all sides, time fell away steeply. She felt dizzy and leaned against the wall of the booth. When someone answered the phone, she could not speak.

"Hello?"

"It's Leela," she said, she rehearsed saying, she intended to say. "I got your message."

"Hello?"

"Your message about the quandongs," Leela said.

She heard static. She heard underground rivers, she heard the wash and shush of the Pacific, she heard the Daintree in full cyclonic flood. She was stranded on an island in the middle of nowhere with crevasses on every side. How would any message get through?

"Is anyone there? Is that Leela?"

"Yes. It's Leela. Is that Devorah?"

"Leela?"

"I got your message, Devorah. Can you hear me?"

"Leela, it *is* you. I've got good news."

Leela closed her eyes. She could feel the overspill of the Daintree on her cheeks. She could feel floodwater rising. I've been stranded, she wanted to explain. Siddiqi's vanished. The air is humid with menace. I can't reach Cobb, he won't contact me, and he's the only one who might know what's happened, who might help. When I called you weeks ago, no one answered. I'm lost. I'm flotsam. I'd given up even dreaming of rescue.

She could not speak.

"I've been in Sydney," Devorah said. "My publisher has a friend who's a lawyer. She's with Human Rights Watch."

Leela could hear music. On the sidewalk, there was a man with a guitar.

"I gave her everything you sent me," Devorah said. She spoke of tapes, the Holiday Inn tapes, the Beirut tapes, which the lawyer had managed... and the man who checked out of the hotel, who had claimed to be Mishka but wasn't, who had been identified.... She spoke of the American ambassador in Australia, who had been deeply embarrassed, Devorah said. He had promised to intervene.

Leela listened but all she could hear was Gluck. The phone booth was full of Gluck and there was good news. She was watching the man with the guitar. He sat cross-legged on the sidewalk. There was a felt hat in front of him and pedestrians were dropping notes and coins as they passed by. A dollar bill fluttered and drifted away. The man did not notice. He looked blue. Everything looked blue. Leela could not see the blue man's face.

"In Baghdad," Devorah said.

"In Baghdad?" Leela tried to concentrate.

The man with the blue guitar was no longer playing Gluck. Leela could not quite hear what he played. She pushed the door of the booth open a few inches and mostly heard the hubbub of traffic interlaced with a thin thread of song. The tune sounded vaguely Middle Eastern. Baghdad Blues, Leela thought. The Baghdad Rag.

"Apparently procedural errors," Devorah said, and Leela was conscious of a lack of mathematical diligence on her part. If she could calculate the angles of divergence, if she could measure precisely the gap between the dastgah system and the Western tonic scale....

"Major embarrassment to the Americans at this point," Devorah said. Extradition proceedings, she explained. Extradition proceedings were under way. "Though this will take time," Devorah said.

The man with the guitar stood up. He was saying something. He made exaggerated words with his lips as he moved toward Leela. He rapped on the glass door of the telephone booth. He was mouthing a message through the glass.

"Still under heavy suspicion," Devorah said. She said something about conditions... extradited on certain conditions....

"What?" Leela asked the man who was rapping on the door.

"He will be kept in detention," Devorah said. "The Australian Government has to guarantee...."

Taking far too long, mouthed the man with the guitar.

"Going to take time," Devorah said. "We don't know how long. But the main thing is, he's alive and they're sending him home."

"He's alive!" Leela called through the glass. "They're sending him home."

She felt laughter descend like a great bird that sank its talons in her shoulders and shook her. The man with the guitar looked alarmed.

"Leela?" Devorah said.

"How long...?" Leela asked. The words choked her. Another bird, the sobbing bird, had come.

"We don't really know. Two weeks, the ambassador thinks. He's promised to take a personal—"

The man rapped on the door with a coin.

"Two weeks," Leela told him. She shouted. "Only two weeks!"

The man with the guitar shook his head. He tapped his finger against his skull. *Crazy*, he mouthed. He made a sweeping gesture with one arm, an ironic and elaborate bow.

"Leela?" Devorah said.

"I'm coming," Leela said urgently. "I'll fly out. I want to be there when he arrives. I'll bring his violin."

"I'll meet you," Devorah promised. "Call me as soon as you have your flight."

The man with the guitar was writing something with his finger on the glass. He turned. He was walking away, but he had left his hat full of money by the curb.

"Wait!" Leela called. She felt panic.

She hung up and raced after the musician. "Wait!" she called.

The musician looked over his shoulder. "What the hell's the matter with you?" he shouted, startled. "Quit following me!"

7

LEELA'S EYES WATERED. She was jetlagged. She could remember the sequence—the flight to Sydney, the meeting with Devorah, the flight on to Adelaide together, the interminable drive through scrub and desert—but she could not remember what day it was. She felt groggy. She had never seen such a sun-bleached landscape, so full of nothing.

"This is the place," the lawyer said.

"This is nowhere."

"That's the idea. This is Camp Noir."

"Camp Noir?"

"That's what I call it."

Devorah touched Leela's arm. "Mishka's in there," she said. "We're going to see him."

"I have to warn you," the lawyer cautioned. "This is going to take time. We have several levels of security to clear."

Sharp lines of light—the sun striking the razor wire—buffeted Leela like a shower of bright arrows. She shaded her eyes. The light crisscrossed the steel mesh and threw motley on the five of them. They were in something resembling a cage of chain-link steel.

"Second level," the lawyer explained, as the steel gate behind them rolled shut. There were closed gates ahead. On all sides, they were wrapped in steel mesh. Above, the sky was cloudless blue. The blinding disk of the sun burned Leela's skin. "Don't touch the wire," the lawyer warned.

Leela watched shimmering diamonds and shadow diamonds ride in harlequin formation across her arms and across the faces of the two men whom they did not know and across Devorah and the lawyer who had told Leela and Devorah, "Call me K."

"Kay who?"

"Just K. As in K for kangaroo court. K for Kamp Noir. This is an off-the-record assignment, and K's my off-the-record name."

Leela was curious. "What are your on-the-record assignments like?"

"Same. But we operate on multiple tracks and some of my methods and contacts are definitely not on the record. The less you know about me, the less trouble for all of us if things don't work out."

They were waiting for the guard to push the button that would open the next set of gates.

"How long do they leave us here?" Leela asked.

"As long as the whim strikes them," K said.

"They place bets on us." The tall man with the bruised eye mimed the tossing of a coin. He caught the invisible disk with his right hand and slapped it against his left arm. "They bet someone will get tired enough to lean against the fence." He barked with laughter and made a mushroom gesture with his hands. "And then pouf! Barbequed Aussie."

"We're broiling already," Leela said. "This heat is unbelievable." She was engaged in a futile attempt to ventilate herself with her shirt, flapping it out and in, fanning her skin. "We should have worn hats or brought umbrellas."

"They would have taken them back there anyway." The man gestured over his shoulder at the first security building. He must have been in a brawl, Leela thought. There was a swelling purple contusion around one eye. "Those guys up there in the towers have no objection to heatstroke in the cage. Cuts down on the nuisance factor, which is us."

"Believe me," K said, "it can be a lot worse. I've stood here in a thunderstorm. I was afraid I'd get fried by lightning."

"What happened to your eye?" Leela asked the man with the bruise.

"I made a mistake back there." The man touched his cheekbone tenderly, experimentally. "I tried to stop them confiscating my glasses."

Leela was shocked. "Can you see?"

"Things are blurry."

"Bastards," K said. "I deal with this all the time. You'd think I'd get used to it."

"Can't we report them?" Leela asked.

K and the tall man laughed. Leela felt light-headed with the heat. The tall man's laughter rose like a dandelion puff and floated up to the ceiling of the cage.

"Security at detention camps is outsourced," K explained.

"No one's accountable," the tall man said. "I'm Kareem, by the way."

"Leela. How come you have an Australian accent?"

"Because I'm Australian," Kareem said. "Born here. This is Rashid. He wasn't."

"Hi, Rashid."

Rashid raised his eyes for a moment and lowered them. He half nodded.

"Rashid's stopped talking," Kareem said. He mouthed a word at them: *Depressed.* "His brother Abu's in there. Been there three years now. No charges." He mimed elaborate sewing actions with his fingers and an invisible needle and thread. He mouthed more words: *Sewn his lips together.* "I'm related to both of them by marriage. We're second cousins, or something like that. Who're you trying to visit?"

"My son," Devorah told him. "My son Mishka. Why do you say *trying* to visit?"

"Because that's the routine. We wait one hour, maybe two, maybe three. We get X-rayed, we get body-searched. And then we may or may not get to see Abu."

"Oh," Devorah said, stricken.

"Look!" Leela said. There was someone coming out of the desert, walking steadily and swiftly toward them, his feet barely touching the sand. He was wearing a loose white shirt that drifted about his body like smoke. He was carrying something.

"Look at what?" K asked.

"That man," Leela said. "And it's an oud."

"What are you talking about?"

"The man with the oud."

"Mirage," Kareem offered. "Happens all the time in desert air."

The man in the white shirt, the man with the oud, kept coming closer.

"I can see him," Kareem said. "Man with a shotgun. He's real enough, mirages always are. But he could be fifty miles, a hundred miles from here."

The man in white was almost at the wire. "Mishka!" Leela called.

"Don't touch the wire!" Kareem shouted.

Leela blinked. The man in white was no longer there. "Mishka *is* here, isn't he?" she asked K. "We *will* see him."

"Technically, yes," K said. "That's my information. He's been extradited, he's arrived, and we'll be able to see him. Eventually. Though not necessarily today. Nothing happens fast in this system."

Devorah put a hand over her mouth.

Leela pulled down a shutter in her mind. On the long flight out, she had shoved all her sensory memories in a trunk and pushed them down hard and turned the key, but the trunk had sprung leaks. She woke from a dream of making love and Mishka's smell was on the travel pillow and in the air. How is Mishka? the Qantas steward asked, and there he was in the seat beside her but when she touched him, he turned into someone else. He was seeping across the edges of every frame. He was always coming towards her. He always vanished when she touched him. Expect nothing, she warned herself.

She wrote a zero in the dust with her sandal.

She erased the zero with her foot.

Beyond the next guard house, where the visitors had to take off shoes and belts, where they had to pass through another scanner, they were directed to an outdoor waiting area surrounded by steel-mesh walls. The walls were high and topped with jagged harm that caught the light. Picnic tables and benches were scattered about, all seats taken. Kareem and Rashid squatted, Middle Eastern style. Devorah and Leela sat on the ground, cross-legged. K remained standing.

"You can't sit," Kareem warned. "Ants. They're vicious biters."

"I don't care," Leela said. "I'm too tired to stand," but within minutes she was leaping up, frantically brushing at her thighs.

"Here," someone called from a table. "We'll make room."

"How long have you been waiting?" Leela asked.

"All morning. Not counting the time in the cage."

"I don't know if I can stand much more of this," Leela said.

"You will," said the person who had made room. "You'll learn. You don't have a choice."

"None of this matters, Leela," Devorah murmured. "It's worth the wait."

Two names were called.

Leela watched the people who went forward. She noted that they did not permit themselves excitement. They disappeared through a door.

The rest waited.

There were more names called and there was waiting.

Kareem and Rashid were called.

"Good luck," Leela said.

"Thanks," Kareem said. "You too."

There was more waiting.

Devorah said, "I've just remembered something funny and sad. When Mishka was little, he had an imaginary friend. I think he must have been four, and by the time he was five, yes, once he got his violin, the friend disappeared. But I would find him sitting on the veranda staring into the trees. He'd put his finger to his lips and say *Ssh! If you make a noise, Yixel won't come.*"

"Yixel?"

"That was the name of his imaginary friend. And then he'd warn me: *Yixel won't come if you're with me. He only comes when I'm all by myself.* I'd watch him from inside the house and he could sit there for hours. I'd see him smiling. I'd see him talking to Yixel."

"Visitors for Michael Bartok," the megaphone announced.

A small cry escaped Devorah's lips.

"Don't show emotion," K warned.

Leela told herself: *Stay calm. If we behave ourselves, we'll be rewarded.*

The man at the desk beyond the steel door looked them over. "Michael Bartok can't see you today," he said. "He's too ill."

"I need to talk to Colonel Shulton," K said.

"Colonel Shulton's not available," the man said.

"Will you let the colonel know I have a message for him?" K persisted. "I believe he would consider it urgent."

"Oh right," the man said. "You're on chatting terms with the colonel."

"Something like that."

"How do you know Colonel Shulton?"

K smiled. "I'm not sure the colonel would like me to answer that in public."

The man on the desk looked at her warily.

"May I borrow a page of your notebook there, and your pen?" K asked. She reached for them and the man did not stop her. She scribbled several sentences down. "Could I have an envelope?" she said.

"What?"

"It's a private message. I know the colonel wouldn't appreciate your taking it to him unsealed. Thank you." K licked the flap. "I think he'd be grateful if you would deliver this now."

"The colonel's ex-military," K explained, sotto voce. "Earns twice as much managing this joint as he ever got in the army."

"How do you know him?" Leela whispered.

"I don't. I know people who do."

"The thing is," Colonel Shulton said, facing them across his desk, "he's not in the best condition for visiting."

"What does that mean exactly?" K asked.

"A certain amount of PID. He's under medical care."

"What is PID?"

"Post-interrogation disorder. From before he was shipped to us. He had some crucial information and they got it."

The colonel seemed to change shape. He was a balloon man. His mouth opened and closed. Devorah fainted. Leela and K helped her to a chair. There was a window behind the colonel's desk, a black glass square. Leela could not see through it but she was certain that Mishka was there. She could hear the sound of a violin.

K produced a letter. "The American ambassador has taken a personal interest," she said. "I think you had better let us see the prisoner. Mistakes have been made."

"Well, hmm," the colonel said, skimming the letter. "He's in the infirmary. I could perhaps let you visit very briefly. You will have to be escorted by armed guard."

"We accept," K said.

There was a body under the sheet. The head was bandaged and the face was turned to the wall. Tubes from a drip feed were taped to one arm.

"Mishka," Devorah said, and there was a slight movement of the arm. The fingers halfway made a slack fist and then went limp. Devorah touched the shock of hair above the bandage that covered both ears.

Leela watched the hand flinch again, watched the fingers curve and then droop. She reached for them. It was as though the hand had no bones. She laced her fingers through those of the hand beside the bed. "Mishka," she whispered. She pressed the back of the hand to her lips. She felt for the hard little circles on the pads of Mishka's fingers at the chord-playing tips. She frowned. There were no calluses.

She leaned over the bed and the figure groaned and turned. Devorah cried out. "This isn't Mishka," Leela said.

8

WATER CURLED ITSELF away from the ferry's prow like a green fin edged with cream lace. Behind the boat, the V grew wider and wider, lapping the forecourt of the Opera House and imperceptibly touching the pylons of the bridge itself before leveling out entirely and merging with the sun-flecked skin of Sydney Harbour.

"It's beautiful," Leela murmured, leaning over the railing, transfixed. It was mesmerizing, looking down into the water. A red streamer of silk swooped by and she heard a child at the railing cry: "*Mummy, Mummy, my scarf!*" She watched the silk buck in the air like a bird, then drift, then settle on the water and darken and disappear. She wondered how much was lost down there. She imagined wrecked boats, drowned bodies, lost scarves beneath the keel. "Mishka told me you liked to ride the ferries."

"Yes. When I was a student. I did it for whole afternoons. We're approaching the Heads now. You'll notice the water turn choppy."

"You're right. That's so sudden."

"It's the Pacific pushing in," Devorah said.

"The harbor's far bigger than I imagined. It's like a sea."

"That's what it is. A sheltered sea."

Wind buffeted them and their hair streamed out behind their heads like flags. Their eyes watered and rivulets of damp crisscrossed their cheeks. Devorah was hunting for something in her shoulder bag.

"Here." Leela offered a tissue.

Devorah shook her head. "No, that's not...." She found what she was looking for and held it tightly in her fisted hand. She stared down at the pleated wake. "I know how Mishka would score this," she said. "I can hear it in my head. Rondo for wind and water. He was like Mozart, you know. It was amazing, the pieces he composed when he was little. And then by high school, well.... He won a scholarship. Of course, you know that." She opened her fist and showed Leela what looked like three vivid marbles, cobalt blue. "Quandong berries," she explained. "I was planning to give them to him." She smiled mournfully. "I got them through all those levels of security." She extended her arm over the railing, the berries in her open palm, as though making an offering to the gods. Then she tipped her hand and let the berries fall into the water.

They did not sink.

They were tossed high in the froth like lottery tokens and then they bobbed backward inside the wake, three small buoyant dots.

Leela slid her hand along the railing and placed it over Devorah's.

"I do not understand anything," Devorah said. "I do not understand how the Marwan I met on these ferries could become what they say he has become."

"How does anyone know?" Leela murmured. She did not understand how Cobb could have become what he seemed to have become. She did not really believe it.

"Mishka's letter said his father had become a music-hater," Devorah said. "At least, that's what he'd been told. That's what he feared. But I don't know how that would be possible. It's like asking me to believe that trees can swim. Mishka couldn't believe it either. He was certain that once he played the oud for his father...."

Below them, the dark green water of Sydney Harbour made soft slapping sounds against the hull. The wind skimmed music from the waves.

"I wonder if Mishka got the chance," Devorah said. "It is very strange." She put her hands over her face. "To have gone on loving a man—the memory of a man—who hates music. It means there's something defective about me."

"It doesn't mean any such thing," Leela said. The scent of honeysuckle, of Cobb, of Mishka, were all in the air. Love was a predator, she knew that. It roared around like a hurricane and blew anyone in its path to kingdom come.

They both stared into the water.

Leela could hear a low antiphonal chant from the ferry engines and the wake: *Cobb must know, Cobb must know, Cobb must know where Mishka is.*

"K said that poor boy, the one we saw, was actually an American," Devorah said. "K told me he died. They had to ship the body back to Arizona."

"'I know. She said it's not the first time. It's chaos in Iraq, bodies get mislabeled and lost."

They stared into the wake.

"I'll put Mishka's violin in Uncle Otto's room," Devorah said at last, "until he comes for it."

"I keep thinking I hear him playing. It's usually Gluck, but sometimes it's his own compositions. I don't just mean in dreams. I really hear him. Either I'm going mad, or it's a sign."

"I think there's a sorrow gene," Devorah said. "I think I inherited it. I think I passed it on."

Leela moved closer, so that body warmth flowed between the two women. "My mother died when I was very young," she said. "It was like a black hole I had to keep filling."

"You could have Mishka's room," Devorah offered, "if you want to stay until we get news."

"This is what we know," K told them. "We know Mishka and his father were picked up together. We've got witnesses who saw them get into a black limo on the main drag beside the harbor in Beirut. It was done in broad daylight.

"We know they were then flown to Baghdad. We know that within an hour Marwan was put on a flight to Cairo.

"We know Mishka arrived at an underground prison in Baghdad—it used to be one of Saddam's—later that day. We know he was still alive three days later when the man in the next cell got released. His name's Ali. He talked to Amnesty's field workers. The prison's run by local militia and there was torture."

Devorah closed her eyes and began rocking back and forth like someone in pain or at prayer.

Leela managed to ask: "How can you be sure it was Mishka?"

"He told Ali his name. Sometimes he'd sing. Ali had been held for two weeks and then released.

"After Ali, we lost the trail. We think Mishka's a ghost in American hands, but we can't be sure. Even they aren't sure. He could be a ghost in Shiite militia hands."

"A ghost."

"No records kept. So there's no way to trace him. The ambassador tried, the Red Cross tried, the Australian Government tried. They honestly believed they'd found him and got him repatriated. And at least some American military sources thought they'd got rid of an embarrassing mistake. I can tell you, everyone's nervous. Everyone's hedging bets and trying to cover their arse. Either nobody knows where he is, which is definitely possible, or the people who know can't afford to let it be known that they know."

"What do we do now?" Leela asked.

"I've activated every feeler and every antenna that I have," K said. "And my feelers are hooked up with other feelers, here, in the US, in the Middle East. Eventually we're going to hear something. Someone else who was in detention with him will be released and will talk. Guards talk. Guards and soldiers take photographs. Someone has photographs of Mishka. Gossip travels on the internet these days. We're going to learn what happened to him and where he is. That's a hundred per cent sure wager on my part. But I'm not going to lie to you. It could be years before we know. Or we might know tomorrow. He might be alive, he might not be. But in the meantime, you should both go back to your lives. There's nothing else you can do."

Leela called her own number in Cambridge, Mass. She left a message on her answering machine.

"Cobb," she said, "this is Leela. I'm in Australia. There's been a horrible miscarriage of justice." She had a wild hope that Cobb would be listening in, that he'd cut in, that he'd respond. "I'm sure you know what I'm talking about." She waited. She heard the hum of her empty apartment. She almost gave a call-back number but thought better of it. "I can't believe this is what you want. I won't believe it." She lowered her voice. "This isn't you, Cobb. It just isn't you. If you know where Mishka is...." She closed her eyes. "You could leave a message on my answering machine," she said. "I can check by remote." She waited. She wanted to believe in magic. She dropped her voice to a whisper. "We're blood brother, blood sister, remember?"

* * *

"Wherever he is," Leela said on the wide veranda of the house above the Daintree, "this is where Mishka is in his mind. This was his perfect retreat. I think that's why he was afraid to come back. In case it had changed."

"It is changing," Devorah sighed. "Developers are coming closer. They've cut roads through virgin-growth rainforest. They've sold lots."

Mordecai cradled Mishka's violin in his arms. "After all these years," he said, "it has come back to the family. It is Otto's. I'd know it anywhere."

"They live more and more in the past," Devorah murmured. "They've moved back to Hungary before the war. There's no snow and there are parrots, but they don't notice little differences like that."

"Oh, the parrots!" Leela gasped. "Mishka told me, but I didn't have the faintest idea—"

"It's because we've got food on the veranda. They've become quite shameless."

With a brilliant whirring of wings—there were flashes of crimson, emerald, cobalt, gold—birds settled on Leela's head and shoulders and arms. "If Mishka could see me," she said.

"He used to say that when he grew up he'd write a concerto for quandongs and parrots."

"He did," Leela said. "Except it's a sonatina."

"Devorah," Mishka's grandmother said. "Will you ask Otto to play?"

BOOK VIII

Unheard Music

1

"... and I can see him," Leela said, "just feet away from me, but there's this *airlock*, this force field, some sort of resistance between us." She reached out, miming the impasse of an invisible barrier, her palms flattened against its sheer surface. "He's singing the aria from Gluck."

Berg put a hand on her arm. "Where are you?"

"Is someone watching?" She looked about nervously, knocking her wineglass over. "I know Cobb is probably listening, but he won't get in touch." She stared at the rivulet that dripped from table to floor. "Did I do that?"

"Forget it. That's the least of your worries." Berg reached for a napkin and mopped at the spill. Leela trailed her fingers through the puddle of chardonnay, bewildered. "Just explain to me where you've been," Berg said. "Explain why you disappeared. I'm sure you realize you almost cost us the grant."

Leela played the words back to herself. She wrote them in the spilled wine and studied them. "None of it makes sense," she said.

"No," Berg said, "it doesn't. You don't answer emails, you don't answer your phone, you disappear for a couple of months just when we've won a major grant, and then suddenly you show up but you keep tuning out."

"He was singing an aria from Monteverdi."

Berg took a deep breath. He said carefully: "I thought it was Gluck."

"Monteverdi's *Orfeo*."

"Gluck's *Orfeo ed Euridice*, you said."

"Sometimes the Gluck, sometimes Monteverdi." Her hands tested the air in front of her, surreptitiously, but the imaginary wall was unyielding. She pressed her fingers against it.

Has she been practicing this? Berg wondered. Does she practice against a mirror? She was still floundering in the tunnels of her nightmare, yes, but the thought crossed his mind that she could moonlight as a mime artist. He could almost see her wall. He could almost feel it between them. She was agitated. She was looking through him, at someone else. Her distress spoke in ballets of restrained elegance and for some reason he needed to locate the right word—the exact word—to describe her strange gestures. Fey? Delicate? Courtly? *Courtly*, yes. He gulped at his scotch.

Of course, she could be slightly deranged. She could be on drugs. Pressure did that: competitive pressure for grants, for prizes, for research breakthroughs. Marriages—his own, for instance—went down the drain; children—his own, for instance—moved out of the country or grew estranged. He was not unfamiliar with the phenomenon. One former student had lofted himself from a balcony ten floors up and had flown to his death, arms tracing slow curves as he plummeted. ICARUS, ran the student newspaper headline, FLIES TOO CLOSE TO SUN. Icarus had already won a major research grant. He'd been working on aerodynamic forces, computing the velocity profile for nonsingular arcs. He'd run into a snag.

So. Berg knew where students—especially the brilliant ones—could go.

"He has blood all over his face," Leela said in a low voice, "and I call out to him, *Mishka, Mishka!* He looks around as though he hears something, but he can't see me. I can tell he's in an interrogation room. It's as though I'm studying him through one-way glass."

"The way you study everyone."

"Pardon?"

"Look, it doesn't matter."

"Do I? Do you think that's true?"

"It doesn't matter. We understand numbers, not people. Go on."

"He's cradling his smashed oud. He holds it out to me—or to someone in the interrogation room, someone I can't see—but when I reach for him"—she leaned forward against the invisible wall—"when I try to offer comfort, there is always this obstruction. Sometimes I pound on it till my hands are bloody, but it's useless." She offered her hands as proof, extending them first as fists. She opened them. She displayed the veined backs, the unblemished palms. "I'm afraid to think what that wall might mean."

"You keep having the same dream."

"Almost every night. I'm scared to go to sleep."

"Well, the absent are always wrong," Berg consoled.

Leela rested her crossed arms on the table and leaned forward to nest her face in them. Berg wondered if she practiced this posture in front of her bedroom mirror. He imagined how she might lean slightly this way or that to get the spill of her shoulder-length hair just right. When it brushed the table, soft detonations of her perfume were released and the fragrance buffeted him in a succession of slight but pleasurable shockwaves. Perhaps she rehearsed her movements. He had begun to cultivate this kind of uncharitable thought about Leela to neutralize the fact of his desire and to tamp down his anxiety about the state of her mind.

In between their recent encounters—and how should he think of them? as rescue attempts? as random mentoring sessions?—he had begun to dream about her. In his dreams, he studied her through one-way glass. Last night, for example, a man was painting her portrait. A man, he thought grimly, was *executing her likeness*. The man wore a Red Sox baseball cap and a white T-shirt that said MISHKA across the front. The man was singing a jingle at the top of his lungs, singing in the style of Pavarotti, *o mio spaghettio, o mio pomodoro*, and he was taking liberties with his model, flicking chunky tomato sauce at her from his paintbrush and licking it off as he worked. Berg, watching through one-way glass, was greatly offended. He smashed the screen—after all, *technically*, Leela was still his protegée, his former graduate student, his junior colleague, and he had manifest responsibilities. He woke in a shower of glass splinters, brushing crumbs and dried pasta from his sheets.

"You are wrong about absence," Leela told him.

Berg sucked in his bottom lip and bit on it and thought about the painting in his dream, an act of rank plagiarism since the original hung in the Boston Museum of Fine Arts and Berg often studied it on Sunday afternoons. *Lips That Have Been Kissed* it was called. Berg was in love with the porcelain face and the mane of coppery hair. He wondered if Leela had seen the painting. He could ask her if she liked the Pre-Raphaelites. He could start with that. He could mention Rossetti casually, Dante Gabriel, he would say, the one who was obsessed with a particular model, and did Leela know that one of the finest examples, etcetera, and he could suggest next Sunday afternoon.

"The absent accuse us all the time," Leela told him. "If I'd trusted him, if I hadn't frozen him out when he needed me most, he might never have gone to Beirut."

Berg watched Leela trace an M with her index finger in the puddle of wine and felt a jealous rush, baffling and humiliating.

"Syllogism one," he announced, professorially. "Primary premise: the absent accuse us. Secondary premise: absence of the plaintiff in a court of law renders the charges invalid. Conclusion: the absent are wrong, and the defendant inflicts the charges on herself. Yes, a tab," he told the bartender. "And another glass of white wine for my young colleague, unless she—yes, another glass."

"You don't understand," Leela sighed.

"I'm trying to," he said. "And I do understand irrational guilt. It requires our collusion."

"What about actual guilt?"

Berg thumped the table and a small wave of scotch crested above the lip of his glass and pooled by his coaster. "You are not responsible for what happened to Bartok."

"I think dreams can mean something," she said earnestly, "that we don't have equations for. Sometimes they can. There's no reason why you would believe that. I wouldn't have, before this happened."

"Do you know how many people, in this city alone, claim after every bombing incident to have had a dream that predicted it? There've been articles. It's a syndrome: not just the prevalence, but the predictable categories. One of our colleagues, well, Dowell, I think you took a course with him, Dowell did a statistical sampling at Student Health Services of sleep disorders reported post 9/11, then again after the Park Street bombing, and the mathematical spike—"

"Don't you concede—"

"And again after that Chicago incident three weeks ago, which is nowhere near us."

"Don't you concede that it's at least possible, at least a possibility, that someone close to us, someone *in extremis* who has been kidnapped—"

"*Kidnapped* is not a neutral—"

"Isn't it possible, even in a universe governed by the laws of physics and math, that such a person could make psychic connection?"

"But you see, when you say *kidnapped* you're revealing that you've already told yourself a certain story, that you've already established a certain explanation for why your boyfriend decamped. I did warn you to be careful, given the company he kept. The truth is, you have no idea what he was up to in Beirut. You really don't. The story you've constructed informs your dreams."

She leaned toward him, her hands clasped. She might have been praying. It was her controlled intensity that Berg found so alluring and so dangerous. He imagined a glass safety wall between them. "But I do know what happened," she said. "I did find out. Well, not precisely, but we do know…. Amnesty has a deposition from someone who was in the next cell…." She opened her hands and pressed them lightly against the invisible wall. She clasped them again. He watched the way her knuckles turned white. "I can't talk about it."

"You've been talking about it non-stop."

She put a hand over her mouth, embarrassed. "I shouldn't drink."

"It's not easy to make sense of what you've said."

"I shouldn't have said anything at all. I don't want to talk about this any more."

"Okay," he said. "Let's talk about something else. Our grant. Your stalled post-doc project."

She opened her eyes then, met his briefly, and studied the surface of the table. "I'm not sure it's possible," she said in a flat voice. "I'm not sure I'm capable any more." She tapped her forehead with an index finger. "Something got broken."

"Most scholars go through stages like that. Let's look at it this way: what led you to mathematics in the first place?"

"Is that relevant?"

"It might be. And I'm curious. It's still rare to get a female colleague of your caliber."

"I grew up with numbers. Crazy numbers, Bible codes, hidden messages from God in Social Security numbers, in dates, in whatever, completely nutty, but weirdly enough I did get addicted to numbers."

"Hmm. Well. We're all number junkies. Nothing unusual there."

"And I was lucky enough to have a fantastic teacher very early…. Even though she…."

"Yes?" Berg prompted. "Your teacher?"

"She was Cobb's mother…." Leela looked behind her. "I have an ominous feeling he's watching but he won't get in touch."

"You've lost me."

He watched Leela press against her glass wall.

"Your math teacher," he said, breathing hard. "What about her?"

"What? Oh. Nothing. She got me hooked on math. I loved solving equations, I loved pinning down the unknowns. I loved taking on a problem set and not letting go till I'd untangled it."

"And that's the way back. We've got some knotty problems sitting waiting. Start untangling them."

She shook her head. "Won't work any more."

"Why not?"

"Because it's different now. Because back then...."

Her silence went on so long that he had to nudge her again: "Back *when*?"

"Back then, before Mishka... before what's happened, math made sense of everything. It was so *pure*, it was just so beautiful, it was so...." She shrugged. "It was an addiction. It was my beautiful cocoon."

"Mathematics constructs an ideal world," Berg said, "where everything is perfect but true."

"Yes. Exactly."

"I was quoting Bertrand Russell."

"I guess I still believed—just like my Dad, I suppose, which is a sobering thought—that there was some underlying key, some great secret code, and I was deciphering it. My father's code was magical but mine was scientific truth."

"And you want to give up the search."

"I no longer believe there's any code. It's just static. It's scrambled noise and scrambled numbers. Nothing makes sense to me."

"That's the starting point for every mathematical breakthrough in history. You slam into a wall and you blast a new doorway. That's probably the real meaning of your dream." Berg leaned across the table, excited, and seized her wrists. "You've hit a wall. You're dazed. It's part of the process. You know, every year I get one student, or sometimes in a good year two, who makes me say to myself: this one is going to change the rules of the game. That's if he doesn't go astray, or if she doesn't fall off the world. I can't tell you how pleased I was, how relieved, when you came back looking for me."

"I didn't come looking for you. It was you who came after me."

Berg narrowed his eyes. "Only because you came to my office first."

"I came to your—? No."

"Three weeks ago. The day after the suicide bomber in Chicago. You told the department secretary you needed to see me."

"No I didn't."

"You're on our security camera. I checked it in case the secretary got the wrong name."

"I don't remember doing that."

"I could play you the tape. By the time I came out of my office, you'd disappeared. On the tape, you pace around the department office like a caged tiger and then you leave."

He was still holding her wrists. Leela looked at his fingers curiously—they were symbols that had to be decoded—but she made no move to disengage. "I know I'm not in great shape," she said.

"Your hands are shaking."

"I have trouble concentrating—"

"Are you on medication?"

"I don't know. I mean, no. No, I'm not. I'm not on medication." She seemed to be struck, for the first time, by the sheer strangeness of the two of them—former dissertation supervisor and former graduate student—sitting in the induced twilight of a bar, holding on.

"I know anxiety attacks when I see them," Berg said. "Well, everyone's on edge. We're all waiting for the next bombing. But whether you're conscious of it or not, you've been sending me SOS signals."

"Have I?" Leela said. "Well, I suppose it's because of the way you followed me down into the subway last week. I keep half-believing Mishka will reappear there and when you tapped me on the shoulder, I had this mad hope...."

Berg frowned. He laid her wrists down in front of her, neatly, one on top of the other, and released them.

"And you were out of breath," Leela said, "so I knew you'd run after me and that was so...."

Indeed, Berg thought. So unexpected. So unwise.

She had burst into tears and he had instinctively put his arms around her. She had sobbed on his shoulder and he had buried his face in her hair.

"You must have thought I was a lunatic," she said.

"Not at all. You were clearly in shock. You needed to talk."

"Did I talk very much?"

"For hours, but you didn't always make sense."

"Can I just go back to the idea for the moment, for the sake of argument, that Mishka is making contact with me through dreams—"

Berg sighed. "You're *stuck*, you know. Whatever happened, you're stuck there. You go over and over the same fragment like a cracked record and I think you've got to try to dislodge yourself. So I'm going to say something brutal: the chances of psychic contact are just about zero because you never really knew the man. I mean, you had to stalk him to find out he was going to that mosque."

"I shouldn't have done that. I should have trusted him."

"Look, I admit I'm prejudiced. I have a low opinion of someone who hangs around with thugs who send me hate mail."

"Is that still happening?"

"No, thank God. But then the probable instigator blew himself up, didn't he?"

Leela turned and turned a coaster in her hands. She began tearing it, carefully, precisely, purposefully, in a spiral. "I'm making a strange loop," she said. "In math, we accept strange loops."

"You're code-switching. Invalid analogy."

"We accept conclusions that don't make sense. I'm in a strange underground loop with Orpheus."

"Orpheus. Right."

"I mean Mishka. He's a musician. He's gone into the underworld and hasn't come back. It's not supposed to happen that way."

Berg looked away. He had to be careful. He did not want her to disappear. "Orpheus in the underworld," he repeated, neutral. What was it with mathematicians? Did it help to be crazy? From Newton onwards, a case could be made.

Could he seriously consider himself unscathed?

"I'm the one who's been trying to rescue him," Leela said. "It's supposed to be the other way around."

Berg wanted to shake her. He kept his eyes on the torn coaster in her hands. "Don't you think this fixation on an underworld might be something you need to know about yourself?"

"What I know about myself," Leela said slowly, "is that I know very little, and I think very little can ever be known with certainty, and I am frightened."

Berg ignored all the warnings then. He leaned across the table and held her face in his hands. "It will be all right," he said. "Whatever's happened, it will be all right. This is temporary. It's shock, it won't last."

"What I'm frightened of," Leela said, "is the glass wall in my dream. I'm frightened of what it means."

"These things pass," Berg promised, "they pass. And I've got boring but simple advice. Start coming in to your office. Start looking over work you've already done. Start *doing*, instead of brooding. I know what I'm talking about. I've been where you are now, after my marriage broke up. And no matter what happens, life goes on."

2

THE VOICEMAIL ON Leela's office phone at MIT was full. Every single message was from Siddiqi. *Your music has arrived*, the messages said. Leela played all the messages back and then she went to a pay phone and called the Music Department in Paine Hall.

"When can I pick up my music?" she asked.

"It's been here for weeks," Siddiqi said. "Where have you been?"

"I could ask you that."

"Better if you don't. You can pick up your music at two."

"So I'm drifting," Leela explained. "I've been back a few weeks, but I'm a mess. I haven't been going to my office. I can't concentrate. I can't even read. I have bad dreams. I keep thinking I see Mishka. I make a fool of myself running after people and tapping them on the shoulder. When they turn around, they don't look like him at all."

"Grief's a wild animal," Youssef Siddiqi said. "So is fear. If you tremble and cringe, those two will tear you apart. You have to ride them."

"Is that what you're doing?"

"I hope so. I've put it behind me. I was picked up, I was let go, it's done with. That's not what I want to talk about."

"But I do. How long were you held?"

"A few weeks."

"You had a lawyer?"

"Eventually."

"Not at first?"

"No. But then I got one, and then I got out. And here I am."

"You're a citizen. This isn't supposed to happen."

"My lawyer's handling that. I was afraid I'd be picked up again after the Chicago incident, but I wasn't."

"Aren't you outraged?"

"I was," Siddiqi said. "But rage is like picking up a burning coal to throw at someone. You're the one who gets hurt. And the good news is that the mosque has issued a statement, did you see? Haddad's been condemned as un-Islamic. So things are improving and Muslim moderates are speaking up."

"But Mishka," Leela said, anguished. "What about Mishka?"

"That's what I've been asking myself. What can we do? What can I do, as an American and a Muslim and a musician? And I came up with something, but I'll need your help."

"I'm listening."

"Michael composed a piece called *Elegy for Uncle Otto and Mustafa Hajj*."

"Yes."

"We played it one afternoon, Michael on violin, myself on the oud. It was after a class when we both got badly rattled by Haddad, who had a pathological hatred of music."

"I never met Jamil Haddad. I'd never even heard of him before the bombing."

"Jamil was a walking time bomb. I've never known anyone more angry. Michael and I talked for hours about what hatred of music means, and we decided it's an inverse compliment to music's power. Michael talked about Mr. Hajj and Uncle Otto, and he went to his office and got the score of his *Elegy* and we played it."

Leela could picture this: she could see Mishka, his eyes closed, his body an extension of his violin. She could imagine Youssef Siddiqi and his oud.

"This was more than a month before the bombing," Siddiqi said. "It was one of the things I kept thinking about. When I was being interrogated, I mean. It was one of the ways I got by. I passed the time trying to remember the whole piece. I was playing it mentally. And suddenly the thought hit me that we always have tapes running in the practice room. So after I was released, that's the first thing I did. I hunted back through the files and I found our performance. I made copies. Here's one for you."

Leela held the cassette between her hands as though it offered the chance to rewind time.

"And then I got another idea," Siddiqi said.

He was excited. Leela sensed his excitement as something exotic and strange, like a moon landing, a rare and impressive achievement but light years beyond her reach.

"The music department's got copies of some of his compositions," Siddiqi said. "And you must have others at your place. We could have faculty and students perform his work. We could have a concert in Sanders Theater: *Elegy for Michael Bartok*."

"*Elegy!*" Leela said, alarmed.

Youssef reached across the table and laid his hand over Leela's and Leela saw Mishka as she kept on seeing him in dreams: on the other side of a glass wall. *On the other side*, she thought. She could imagine herself performing in the subway, a slightly deranged woman with a hat at her feet who was always singing *a capella*: *Che farò senza Mishka Bartok?*

"*Homage*," Youssef corrected himself. "*Homage to Michael Bartok*. Sorry. I was picking up on the title of his piece."

Leela said flatly: "You think he's dead."

Youssef sighed. "I don't think that. We can't know, can we?" He began chafing Leela's hands, as though she were a blizzard victim who needed warmth. "There's one thing we can be certain of: his music is alive."

All Leela could hear, however, was the slow beat of a drum and the notes, in a minor key, of an elegy.

3

In Leela's apartment, there was a message on the answering machine: two full minutes of silence.

Leela played the message over and over. She thought the silence sounded like Cobb. From the back of her wallet, she pulled the old photograph, dog-eared, taken years ago, a lifetime ago, on the day of the Math Prize in high school.

She pressed the photograph to her lips.

She slipped a tape into the cassette deck. It was the tape that Youssef Siddiqi had made. She turned off the lights. She closed her eyes. She imagined Mishka standing by the window, the tree behind him, the neon aura backlighting the tree. She could see him clearly through her closed lids. When the warm sound of his violin and of Youssef's oud filled the room, she said aloud, "I knew I was right about Cobb."

Mishka lowered his violin and met her eyes. What makes you think you can trust him? he wanted to know.

"Because I know him better than he knows himself. I always have."

The telephone rang.

"You see?" she said. She watched Mishka watching her hand as it traveled toward the receiver. She watched how he moved his bow to make words float up from the strings. He played a phrase from Bach, the St. Matthew Passion: *Tell me where you have laid him.* "He will tell," she promised. "I know he will." She cradled the phone against her cheek and the curve of her neck. "Cobb? I knew you'd call," she said. "Where is he?"

"Leela?"

"..."

"Leela?"

"Who is this?"

"Leela, where have you been?"

"Is that Maggie?"

"You have to come home, Leela. Daddy's dreadfully ill. The doctor says it's a matter of weeks."

4

Cobb had never seen such a labyrinth.

"How far beneath Baghdad does this extend?" he asked.

"We don't know," the warden said. "There are corridors we can't use because they've caved in. We think we lost some detainees that way."

"What do you mean, you *think* you lost some? Aren't you keeping records?"

"Not for these ones. We used to. We had orders to shred." The warden paused at an intersection. He shone his flashlight down the tunnel ahead—no end was in sight—and then down the cross tunnels, which were extremely narrow, more like sewers than walkways. The floors were damp. The walls wept slime. There was a dank smell of mold which triggered a breathing crisis for the warden. He pulled an inhaler from his pocket and closed his mouth over it and pumped. "Happens every time," he gasped, raking air into his lungs. "Just give me a minute."

Cobb's eyes were adjusting. He could now see the small barred openings, one foot square, that at intervals gave onto darkness.

"I'm okay now," the warden said. "Let's go. I hate coming down here."

Moans could be heard, and furtive rustlings. The warden pointed his flashlight at the sounds. "Damned rats," he said.

"We've tried everything." The beam of light fell on a white arrow crudely brush-stroked on the wall. "It's down this way."

"How can you tell?"

"We painted those signs. Got lost once when my battery gave out." He clicked the off-switch to demonstrate.

"Shit," Cobb said. "It's black as pitch. What'd you do?"

"Had a panic attack. Yelled until relief guards came but they thought I was a prisoner gone berserk and did the ice water thing. I thought I'd had it." He groped for Cobb's hand and pushed it against the battery pack in his jacket. "Feel that? Now I always carry a spare."

"How about switching your flashlight back on?"

The warden laughed. "Sure. Notice how quiet it is? It's like they turn into spiders, watching us. After a while, they see in the dark."

Cobb studied the small barred openings just visible beyond the glow of the warden's torch. He could see nothing. There was nothing behind the black holes. Then he thought there was. He thought he saw eyes, burning bright like the eyes of cats. He began to see them all around him, moving like paired fireflies in the dark.

"They're watching us," the warden said. "Their hearing gets more acute too. You wouldn't believe how many claim they can tell a spider from an ant."

"How many detainees have you got here?"

"No idea."

"They're all ghosts?"

"All ghosts, and we get new ones every day."

"Where do you find the space?"

"Revolving door. It's musical cells because most of them get released. Eventually."

"How long is *eventually*?"

"Could be a few days or a month. Depends on interrogation. That's the beauty of ghosting. If we registered them, we couldn't just let them go."

"And you'd run out of space."

"Hard to know, to tell you the truth. There's miles of cells we've never used. We think Saddam left people here who've never been found. We do have maps. We found them on parchment in a section the archaeologists say was a library."

"Was this the sewer system?"

"Hell no. That's a few centuries lower down. This wasn't built underground. This *was* the city before one of those floods, tenth century, fourth century, I can't remember which. We have to let the archaeologists poke around—it's part of the deal—and they tell us this stuff. Apparently they've lost count of the number of times the river flooded and the number of times the city's been rebuilt on top of the mud. We're walking on an ancient street. Here's the cell."

"Wait," Cobb said. "Who's in charge of interrogation?"

"Can't answer that. Beyond my scope. We're private, see. We won the contract. We just manage the place."

"For whom?"

"For whoever. Iraqi militia, army, NSA, CIA, interpreters, interrogation squads, they all come and go."

"Who's on these interrogation squads?"

"Who knows? They wear masks. I get the transcripts and I'm responsible for passing them on."

"Passing them on to whom?"

"Sometimes a courier picks them up."

"And you're permitted to read them?"

"Not officially, but I run a little sideline in copies, as you know. It's how I learned this is your boy. Speaking of which—"

"You'll get the rest of your money."

"I have to warn you, your boy's a weird one. He hums a lot. Sometimes he sings."

"Was there any intelligence at all?"

"They couldn't shut him up. But you know that. I already gave you the transcript."

"You call that intelligence?"

"Hey, I warned you. But who asks me? The squads say they get what they need but you have to separate the wheat from the chaff."

"The transcript was babble. Oud makers, oud teachers, violin techniques...."

"Code names, the analysts say. They're working on it."

"Working on it?"

"Deciphering."

"You've got to be kidding."

"They think he might be talking strategy. Violin *techniques*, get it? That's what the analysts say. Booby-trapping musical instruments. The squad told him they got that much from his father. He pretty much went crazy and confessed."

"There's nothing about that in the transcript."

"The squads don't tape Level 3 interrogation. They make an oral report."

"You said most ghosts get cleared and released."

"Not this one. Too valuable as leverage with the father. Sorry I can't leave the flashlight but we're short of equipment. Here's a candle and matches."

"Hey, wait!" Cobb said, but the warden was gone. He turned a corner and extinguished himself.

Cobb had not felt the dark as something so alive and malevolent and soft-fingered since the night when his mother died. He heard humming and stood transfixed. Trembling, he tried to strike a match. Something thumped against him, almost knocking him over, something soft and bulky and large. He tore another cardboard match from the pack and struck it. As it flared, the body hit him again like the clapper of a bell.

"Oh Jesus," Cobb whispered. He held the match higher. "What the fuck have these idiots done?"

BOOK IX

Promised Land

1

COBB WAS FLOUNDERING in the tunnels again. They reached out for him no matter where he was and sucked him in. He got lost every time. The body he was looking for was always in a different cell but he always found it.

It turned lopsidedly. Suspended by its wrists from a hook attached to a pulley, arms twisted up behind its back, it resembled a body hanged in effigy, more a parody of itself than an actual human form. A gurgling sound, like water moving in a clogged drain, came from inside the hood and the sound so terrified Cobb that he cried out and his shocked breath extinguished his candle.

A frenzy of activity gripped him.

He re-lit the candle—his hands were shaking and he had to strike a second match—then he held the candle between his teeth and force-fed a dangling tail of knotted rope toward the pulley. The body crashed down without warning. It was a dead weight, snuffing the candle, knocking Cobb to the floor. With dread, he pushed at the body and rolled himself free. He lit the candle again and fumbled with the knots on the hood. A sheet, twisted tightly to make a thick soft rope, had been used to tie the hood around the neck.

Cobb was all thumbs.

He could still hear the guttural rattle.

He loosened the sheeted knots. He ripped off the hood.

He was staring at the face of his mother.

Cobb's terror was absolute. He backed off frantically but he was tangled, hobbled, snared in the corded sheet. He stumbled into blackness and fell.

"Help me!" he shouted. "Help!" He pounded on the floor of the cell. He was desperate for an inhaler, he could not breathe. He could see his high school pennants on the wall. He could see the trophy for second prize in math. He could see a worn pair of running shoes, much too small, beneath his bed.

"Cobb!" called a querulous imperious voice. "Stop yelling and come here when I call."

"Stay away from me!"

"Goddammit, Cobb." It was not his dead mother's voice, it was his father's. "You wake me up with your goddamned hollering, you can damn well come when I call."

Cobb's heart was still thumping.

"Goddamned bed's leaking," his father shouted. "It's sprung a leak. You get yourself here on the double."

"Coming, Dad."

The hallway between his own bedroom and his father's was narrow. Cobb felt his way. He could barely see the warden up ahead. He could hear rats under the house. He lifted his father from the bed and carried him out to the porch. His father was as light as a child. It was not quite dawn and the stars and a pale rind of moon were still in the sky.

Cobb was fully awake now.

He remembered the email from the VA hospital: *Your father discharged himself after surgery. Insists that he wants to die at home. Condition critical.* Cobb had flown from Baghdad to Paris, Paris to New York. He had rented a car and driven south. Two days ago, he had reached Promised Land.

For a moment, before settling the old man into the rocker, he savored the fact of cradling his father in his arms. "I'll change your sheets, Dad. And I'll get you some dry pajamas."

"Get these damned things offa me first. They stink."

"Okay. Sure." Cobb tugged at the sodden pants. He was shocked by the pallor of his father's thighs, by their frailty, by the birdbone ankles. "Here," he said, taking off his own pajama jacket. "Cover yourself with this while I get you dry pants."

"Who the hell's gonna see me?" His father batted the shirt away. "I'll piss on anyone who comes on my porch."

Cobb smiled. "Better than shooting them, Dad." He felt almost light-hearted. *It was a dream. It was just a bad dream.*

"And bring me some Jack Daniels," his father said.

"Dad, you haven't had breakfast yet."

"Jack Daniels is breakfast."

"The doctor said your liver's shot and you're diabetic. You're killing yourself."

"That'll break a lot of hearts," his father growled.

"It'll break mine," Cobb said.

"Bullshit." His father mustered enough energy to goad the rocker to creaking motion. The muscles in his skinny shanks tensed. His limp penis flopped against the rocker's pine seat. "I'll break more than your heart if you don't bring my whisky."

"Dad, I came home to look after you and keep you alive. The doctor said you won't obey medical orders, and you refuse to have nursing care."

Cobb's father, naked from the waist down, heaved himself out of the rocker and took a step toward the door before collapsing.

"What the hell are you doing, Dad?"

"I'm going for my shotgun is what I'm doing. If I don't get my whisky, I might as well put a bullet through my head.

Take your pick. You can bring me my Jack Daniels or my gun."

"Okay, Dad, you win. I'll bring your whisky." Cobb carried his father back to the rocker on the porch and went into the house.

"And by the way," his father called after him, "in case you haven't heard, that crazy Gideon Moore's got cancer. Never let a drop touch his righteous lips and he's gonna beat me to the grave, is what I hear. So don't you go giving me shit about Jack Daniels."

Cobb reappeared in the doorway, the sodden pajamas still in one hand. "That's a shock. How long's he had cancer?"

"Who the hell knows? They don't go to doctors, those Pentecostals, because God's s'posed to look after them. The younger one, the little sister—what's her name? I can't remember names any more—she defied her daddy and got a doctor to come, but that was after her daddy turned yellow. Pancreatic cancer, the fastest downhill trip you can get. He'll be lucky to see Christmas, stupid bugger."

Cobb leaned his forehead against the door jamb. He could feel too much past bearing down. "He was always kind to us. He never charged us, remember, that time the pipe in the kitchen burst."

"We never had a pipe go bust."

"Yes we did, Dad. Don't you remember? It was right after—" *Right after I found my mother. Come to think of it, you were blind drunk and I had to run all the way to Leela-May's house and Gideon Moore drove me back in that crazy beat-up truck and the whole way back he was praying out loud and I was terrified he might shut his eyes while he was driving but he fixed that pipe and he told me I could stay at their place whenever I needed to, but I never did. I was afraid of sleeping in the same house as Leela-May*

with only a wall and a door in between. I was afraid I'd go up in
smoke. I was afraid I'd catch fire and their house would burn
down. "Maybe I dreamed it," he said.

"You dreamed it, and you're daydreaming now. I gotta wait
for my whisky all day?"

"Sorry."

When Cobb brought Jack Daniels and dry pajamas, his
father took a deep swallow and said: "I know I'm a grumpy old
bastard, Cobb, but you turned out okay anyway, no thanks to
me. I musta done something right."

Cobb busied himself with getting the pants over his father's
ankles. He kept his eyes low. The rough warmth was so
unexpected that he was afraid some inner rampart might give
way. He knew this would embarrass and infuriate his father. He
managed gruffly, "You did okay, Dad."

"I did lousy."

"You drew a rotten hand. I don't forgive Uncle Sam for
withholding your purple heart."

Calhoun Slaughter, shifting his bony ass to wriggle into the
dry pants, was so startled that he wet himself again. "Shit," he
said. "Fucking useless pisser's done broke." He kicked the clean
pants off his ankles and used them to mop at himself. "Shit, son,
don't go wasting your juices on that. If you knew how many
men deserved medals but never got 'em…. Well, you *do* know,
of course you know. It's a total fucking lottery, war. No one
knows what the hell they're doing, and afterwards no one can
remember what happened, and what does it matter? The way I
see it, life's shit, you have bad dreams, then you die."

"It matters," Cobb said fiercely. "In war, there's right and
there's wrong."

"Yeah, there's right and there's wrong," his father said. "But
when you're trying to stay alive, it ain't easy to tell which is

which, especially in the heat of the moment." He gulped at his whisky. "Never knew it was something you got so worked up about."

"Dad...." Cobb was stunned. How could his father not know? "It's always upset me. You got punished when you should've got a medal."

"Is that why you're hollering in your sleep?" his father asked.

"I'm hollering in my sleep?"

"To wake the dead."

"Sorry. Bad dreams."

"Join the club," his father said. "But don't have bad dreams about me."

"They're not about you."

"A Bronze Star in Afghanistan. Special Forces. Major, heading for colonel. And then you suddenly go and quit the army. Tell me why."

"I told you, Dad. I moved sideways. Private unit. Lots of guys are doing it."

"Why?"

"Better money, for one thing. More autonomy. And some stuff can be done better this way. There's more leeway, less oversight. I'm still in intelligence, but I'm freelance."

"So why are you hollering in your sleep?"

"Because something went wrong. Fucking turf war."

"Something always goes wrong. There's always turf wars."

"This was my own stupid fault. I've got stuff on my conscience."

"Cobb, all these years I been thanking my stars you took after your mother, not me. That you ain't got a demon on your back. Ah, shit." His father clutched at his side. He gritted his teeth in sudden pain. "This is killing me, Cobb.

Thank you, Jesus, I been saying all these years, and you gotta know I don't think about Jesus a whole lot, but my boy got a Bronze Star. When I got to bragging about you at the VA hospital in Columbia, they had to put a bag on my head to shut me up."

Cobb pressed his fist against his mouth and bit down hard on his hand.

"Now you're telling me I passed the poison on?" his father said.

Cobb turned away and stumbled toward the porch steps.

"Hey, dammit, you come back here, boy," his father ordered, "or I'll shoot you stone dead."

From lifelong habit, Cobb paused and turned. He even managed a weak grin. "You sure know how to hand out compliments, Dad."

Come here, his father's hand signalled. Obedient, Cobb returned. *Here*. His father pointed to the floor at his feet. Cobb sat on the weathered boards and laid his head against his father's naked thigh. He could feel the bone. His father put his hand on Cobb's head. They did not speak for the longest time.

"I had bad dreams," his father said, "so you wouldn't have to. Shit happens. It's not your fault. Don't lose any sleep."

"This *is* my fault, Dad. Whereas you, you never did anything wrong."

"Are you nuts? I did a million things wrong. You gotta understand this, Cobb. I didn't do anything wrong the day the APC blew up, but I did plenty of other things wrong. The worst one... I *should've* been court martialed for that."

"Court martialed? For what?"

"I never told anyone. I probably should've. I should've told your mother. If I'd told her, she would've understood.... She probably would've understood." The old man clutched at his side and grimaced. "*Unhh... unhh...*" he gasped.

"*Dad*, don't distress yourself."

"If I'd told her, everything might've been different."

"It's okay, Dad. It doesn't matter."

"It does matter, dammit. There's something you need to know. I need to pull the pin on this before I shove off. Stand by for the rubble."

"Dad! *Dad*! Don't get so worked up. You're going to give yourself a heart attack. It doesn't matter. Truly, it doesn't matter. You've always been a hero to me, I swear to God."

"It's like a stuck videotape. I never stop firing that shake'n'bake mortar. I never stop thinking that hut's full of Vietcong but only children run out, nine, ten, maybe thirteen children. Who'm I kidding? I know exactly how many. I counted the bodies. Thirteen. They're burning to death in Willie Pete before my eyes. No photos, no journalists, no one ever knew. But me, I never stop seeing those kids.

"So here's something you gotta understand, Cobb. I should have told you. I should have explained. The APC thing, the shooting a guy in the back of the head, the corpse-kicker thing, all that hate mail, I was *grateful* for it. It was like hush money. I had this fuckin' great boulder of guilt to carry round and every hate letter, it took an ounce off."

"Dad. There's no way you're guilty. You couldn't have known."

"I know I couldn't have known. Doesn't make any difference to how I feel about dead kids. If I'd told your mother...."

"No one can talk about the worst stuff."

"She was pregnant."

"What?"

"When she killed herself. She was pregnant."

"Jesus, Dad."

"When she told me," his father said, "I freaked out. I couldn't handle it, Cobb. I just couldn't handle it. I knew there'd be hell to pay. I'd freaked out the first time too, when she told me you were on the way. I hit her, Cobb. I don't remember doing it, but I saw the bruises. I never believed you'd be born alive or born normal, and when you were, I knew the leg-trap was still out there somewhere, waiting to snap its jaws shut. I knew it wouldn't let me off twice. So I told your mother to get rid of it. I ordered her to."

"Jesus, Dad."

"That's why she did what she did."

"Jesus, Dad," Cobb said again, and the rampart did give way then, for both of them.

They held each other and for the first time in his life, Cobb heard his father weep.

"When you're hollering in your sleep, Cobb, what are you seeing?"

"I can't tell you, Dad."

"Haven't you been listening to me, boy? If I'd had the sense to tell your mother—"

"This is different."

"How?"

"It's so much worse."

"How could it be worse than killing children?"

"It just is."

"Can you fix it?"

"I'm trying to. I can't figure out how."

"Don't do nothing, like I did. You're smarter than me. You'll figure it out, and while you're figuring, you can bring me another Jack Daniels, and by the way, I've been meaning to tell you, crazy Gideon's older girl, the wild one, has come back to see her daddy before he dies. Don't look as though you've seen a ghost. It's natural, ain't it? Even runaways like you and her come home for the last goodbye."

"She went to Australia," Cobb said.

"That so? Well, now she's right back here in Promised Land."

"You've seen her?"

"Came to visit in the VA last week without so much as a by-your-leave, and me all hooked up to tubes and pissing into a plastic bag. I wanna be seen like that? I says to her, 'You're lucky I don't got my gun underneath my pillow, Leela-May. Kindly get your ass out of my room.' You know what that heifer said?"

A shadow of a smile crossed Cobb's face. "I can imagine."

"No, you can't imagine. Something's knocked the sass out of her." Calhoun Slaughter mimicked Leela-May's voice: "*I do apologize for bothering you, Mr. Slaughter, but it's very important. I'm begging you to tell me how I can get in touch with Cobb.* Couldn't believe my ears. If I'd said, 'Crawl under this hospital bed first and lick my shoes and then I'll go get him,' I do believe she would have done it. Someone's cut that heifer down to size. Now you go and get yourself down the road to pay our respects to Gideon Moore."

"I can't do that, Dad."

"What d'you mean you can't do that? Where's your Southern manners? You go and give that crazy old nutter our respects. Tell him I know that him and me ain't going to end up in the same place, but if he's willing to put in a good word for me, I'd take it kindly."

"Dad, I can't."

"What's the matter with you? You've had the hots for that girl since she got that prize you should've won. And it's my belief she's always had them for you. She sure wants to see you real bad."

"It's not for that sort of reason, Dad. She's always been otherwise engaged."

"Then go fight for what you want."

"I can't. The thing that went wrong concerns her. It isn't something she'll be able to forgive."

"Bullshit. Not forgiving takes too much energy, people can't keep it up. Believe me, I know this. There's not a single bastard I can be bothered hating any more. So you go see that wild woman and make things right."

2

LEELA SAT AT her father's bedside and held his hand. There was a convulsive movement in his fingers before they went limp. His eyelids fluttered.

"He's heavily sedated," Maggie said.

"Why didn't you take him to emergency sooner?"

"He wouldn't go. You know how he is."

"He's the color of summer squash."

"That's when I got the doctor to come. When he started to turn yellow."

"That's too late. That's way too late. How could you have left it so late?"

Maggie sighed. "What would you have done if you'd been here? Kidnapped him? Forged power of attorney? Trussed him and gagged him and driven him to the hospital and signed him in?"

"Sorry," Leela said, chastened. "For such a kind man, he always was stubborn as a mule."

"Listen to who's talking," Maggie said.

"I used to get so exasperated with him. Now all I can remember is how gentle he was."

Maggie rubbed her sleeve across her eyes. "You finally noticed."

"He never recovered from Mama's death."

"I can't comment. I never knew her. And neither of you ever let me ask questions."

Leela stared at her little sister. "You wanted to ask me stuff?"

"Of course I wanted to ask you stuff."

"I'm sorry. I guess I was preoccupied with staying afloat myself."

"I figured that out. And I managed."

"You can ask me stuff now."

"What were they like together, Daddy and Mama?"

"I remember them on the porch swing, holding hands."

"I like that. What else?"

"I remember one night...." The memory agitated Leela. She left the bedside and paced the room. "It was not long before you were born." She leaned her forehead against the window and stared out.

"Leela?"

"Passion," she said. "They had that. Mama used to put fresh-picked lavender on his saucer with his morning coffee. She used to put it on my pillow at night. She said it gave you sweet dreams."

"I remember finding lavender on my pillow when I was little."

"Me too. I believed Mama came back and put it there. I guess it was Daddy."

Their father stirred and opened his eyes. "Helen?" he said.

"We're here, Daddy," Maggie assured him. "Leela and me, we're both here."

"I thought I heard Helen," he said.

"Mama's waiting for you, Daddy," Maggie promised.

Gideon smiled and closed his eyes. He floated back to his in-between place.

"I'll pick some lavender for his pillow," Leela murmured.

"There's something else I've been wanting to ask."

"Ask away."

"The numbers thing. Was he always like that?"

"I was only six, remember? I can't be sure. But I think it started after Mama died."

"I suppose it made him feel safer."

"I understand that now," Leela said. "I went to a tarot card reader in Boston a few weeks back. Can you believe that? A cynic like me."

"Is this about Mishka?" Maggie asked.

"When life's out of control, you grab at straws. You *want* to believe."

"Why haven't you said anything about Mishka?"

"You're touching a bruise."

"So I figured," Maggie said. "You want to talk?"

"I don't know if I can," Leela said.

"What did the tarot reader say?"

"She said: *Your heart's desire will come to you but you will have to pay costly dues.*"

3

Cobb stood with his duffel bag on the porch steps. "I'll miss you, Dad."

"Bullshit," his father said.

"I wish you'd let me stay and look after you."

"I don't need looking after. I've never let anyone tell me what to do and I ain't gonna start now. Besides, you need to go fix what you've gotta fix."

"It can't be fixed."

"I don't believe you."

"Well then, I don't know how to."

"You'll figure it out. This freelance intelligence thing—"

"I'm through with that. I'm going to quit."

"You gonna get back in the army? The real army?"

"Hell no. I'm thinking of teaching math, maybe." *Like my mother*, he did not say.

"Like your mother," his father said. "You could do worse."

"Thanks."

"Just don't you leave Promised Land without stopping by Gideon Moore's."

"I told you, Dad. I can't do that."

"Then you are too damn stupid for your own good, son."

Cobb shrugged. "Damage's done by now. Too late to change."

"You heading up I–95?"

"Yeah. Thought I'd stop by the old Hamilton house first, if it's still standing. I'm sentimental about the place."

"It's covered in kudzu and part of the roof's fallen in, but it's still there."

"Bye, Dad."

"Bye, son."

As soon as Cobb's rental car was out of sight, Calhoun Slaughter made his unsteady way to the phone and dialed the number for Gideon Moore.

Cobb parked opposite the Hamilton house. His father was right. The kudzu was rampant and the roof had caved in, but through the wrought iron gates, he could still see the ghost of the veranda. He remembered lying there, side by side with Leela when they were seven years old, decoding water stains on the ceiling. It might have been yesterday.

Why *was* that?

How was it that a memory from so far back could be more intense, in all its particulars, than last week? He could smell the Confederate jasmine. He could smell the ivory soap on Leela's skin.

I can see a parallelogram, she said.

It's not a parallelogram. It's a coffin.

I'm so sad about your mama, Cobb.

He could feel Leela's breath against his cheek, hear her slightly off-key voice singing in his ear, *Hush, little baby, don't you cry.* He had been so afraid he would disgrace himself by crying that he pushed her away. He had locked his mother's death inside a box and buried it. It seemed to Cobb that a shadow life, a life that might have been his, was buried under the Hamilton veranda.

He left the car and crossed the road. Someone—probably someone from the sheriff's office—had placed a padlock and chain on the rusted gates, and the old hole in the wall that they used to climb through was overgrown with dense Cherokee rose. He pushed his way into the Cherokee, head down, arms protecting his face. The matted runners were so unyielding that he had to return to his car and take a tire iron from the trunk. He hacked a passageway into the grounds. The thorns raked him and blood trickled across his cheeks and his hands.

Beyond the wall: further impasse. There was no hint of the former sweep of lawn. The once graciously landscaped grounds were scruffy second-growth wilderness. With the tire iron, he pried loose a path between azaleas and hollies gone berserk until he found the front steps. The house made Cobb think of a Southern belle after too many mint juleps at a ball. She had collapsed in on herself. Her hooped skirts of veranda had slumped into underbrush, the pillars were askew, most of the veranda roof must have blown away at least one or two hurricanes back. The three steps were still in place but when he climbed them and stepped onto the remains of the veranda, his foot went through a soft board. He sank into a quilt of weeds and kudzu and simply lay there.

This was where he'd found Leela toward the end of their senior year. He'd become a regular watcher by then. He had a list of the boys she'd grappled with and the ones who'd taken her panties off.

He had been surprised to find her alone that day, lying more or less where he lay now.

He had crept out of his hiding place behind the azaleas and climbed the three steps and leaned against the veranda railing, arms folded. She was lying on her stomach, her head on her crossed arms, staring down through the boards.

"Waiting for someone?" he'd asked coldly.

"Oh Cobb! Don't do that! You gave me a scare."

"Guess I'm not the one you were expecting."

"I wasn't expecting anyone. I came here to be alone."

"Really?" he said. "I thought you came here to fuck."

She sat up then and hugged her knees and simply looked at him.

"The slut of Promised Land," he said.

She held his gaze. She did not look embarrassed or shamed. She did not look brazen. She did not look like a slut. Her eyes were open and direct, meeting his.

"I come here when I'm sad," she said quietly. "I wonder if my father would have been different if my mother hadn't died. I wonder if I would have been. I wonder what you would have been like if yours hadn't. I think about how we used to come here together when we were kids."

It was a knack she always had: the ability to slither between him and his anger, the ability to look at him and dissolve every defense he'd so carefully built up against his yearning. And suddenly they were tearing at each other's clothes and biting and sucking and kissing. Their lovemaking was violent and desperate, and afterwards they lay on their backs and played their childhood game of reading stains.

"I can see a map of Massachusetts," Leela said. "See? There's Cape Cod."

"That's not Cape Cod, it's Chesapeake Bay."

"I can see wings," Leela said. "I want to fly a lot further than Chesapeake Bay."

"You're glad to be getting away."

"Yes, I am. I won't ever come back."

"I can see a ball and chain."

"No one will ever chain me down," she said. "And no one's chaining you down either, Cobb."

"The chain's got your name on it and the ball's Promised Land."

She rolled toward him then and pressed her face against his chest. "Don't say that. I'd rather die than not get away."

He buried his lips in her hair.

"I don't mean away from you," she murmured. "I mean from here. Don't you wonder who you'll be somewhere else?"

"We'll drag Promised Land with us," Cobb said. "We'll never be able to cut loose."

"I don't believe that. Promise me you'll visit me in Boston?"

But in Boston she had indeed become someone else, someone who forgot about Cobb, and now there were no stains to be read and no veranda ceiling whatsoever. The rotting floorboards dipped close to the ground and Cobb rolled over and lay on his stomach and pressed his face into the weeds.

"Cobb?"

"You never meant it," he accused. "Out of sight, out of mind, once you got there."

"Why haven't you called? I know your eavesdroppers must have passed the message on."

"Leela!" He jackknifed himself up. "What are you doing here?"

"Your father called me. He said you wanted to see me. This was where you'd be waiting, he said."

"Shit!" Cobb said, sucking his hand. "I've got a splinter."

"Hold still. I'll get it out."

"Don't touch me."

She ignored this. She held his hand steady and pinched the splinter between her teeth. She licked at the puncture and pressed the ball of her thumb against it. "I'm not asking for anything but information, Cobb. If you know where Mishka is, just tell me. Just tell me if he's dead or alive."

Cobb turned his head away. He tried to stand, but the soft uneven boards made him lose balance. He had to move like a dog, on all fours.

"*Please*, Cobb." She was crawling after him. It was like an obstacle race: missing boards, kudzu, chunks of roofing. "I understand the surveillance. I don't hold any of that against you. I know you have to do what you have to do. But you're *decent*, Cobb, and he's innocent. All I'm asking is if you know where he is."

"Leela, I can't—I ca—"

"Please, Cobb, I'm begging you. It's not knowing that's so unbearable. I think I could handle any kind of news, but I need to know."

Cobb could not get air into his lungs. He half turned back, thumping on his chest.

"Cobb, what's the matter?" There was alarm in her voice. She pitched herself across a fallen pillar. "What's happening to you?"

He was gasping. He was blue in the face. He was on his feet now and running and stumbling toward his car. Leela ran after him. He locked himself into his car.

Leela leaned across the windshield and mouthed through the glass, "Please, Cobb, *please*," but Cobb revved the engine and she slid from the hood as he drove off.

4

COBB DROVE AS though the devil, with blue lights flashing and sirens whooping, were behind him. He kept to I–95. From time to time, his eyes caught a state trooper's car lurking in the median strip behind trees and he dropped back to within ten miles above the limit. He crossed North Carolina and was well into Virginia before he stopped. He filled up with gas and then, quite suddenly, when he got back behind the wheel, he found he was afraid to drive on.

He could see Leela sprawled on the hood of his car, her face distorted by the curve of the glass. He knew she was not really there. Her eyes seemed abnormally large and close. His hands were shaking. My God, he thought, what's happening to me?

It's not knowing that's so unbearable, Leela's eyes said. *I'm begging you, Cobb.*

He had finally done it.

All his life, he had wanted her to know precisely this: the shameful suck of hopeless wanting, the dead weight of things that nothing could change.

And now he had got his wish.

He thought he had never seen anything so terrible or so frightening.

He wound down his window. "Leave me alone!" he shouted. "Life's shit. Get used to it, the way I've had to."

He saw the motorist at the next pump looking at him strangely.

He managed to start the car. A mile down the road, he had passed a Motel 6. He drove back, in the slow lane, at forty miles per hour. He checked in. He closed the blinds in the cheap and horrid little room and pulled the blanket over his head.

Cobb could see in the dark. He could hear spiders foxtrotting up the walls. The cotillions of ants sounded different: a little soft shuffle here, a slide there. He could see the fine crosshairs of sacking inside his hood.

"You received photographs," the interrogator said.

"I do not recall receiving photographs."

"Bullshit. I gave them to you."

"Is that Benedict Boykin?"

"Surprise, surprise. Answer the question. Did you receive photographs?"

"Yes."

"Did you study them?"

"I couldn't bear to."

"Did you pass the photographs on to your superior officer?"

"The first time, I did. Nothing happened. The second time, I didn't pass them on."

"Do you still have the second set?"

"Yes."

"Where are they?"

"I have them with me. I always have them with me. I never dare leave them anywhere."

"Do you ever look at them?"

"I can't bear to."

"What are you going to do with them?"

"I can't do anything with them while my father's alive. I can't make him go through that again."

"Through what?"

"Hate mail. Slander. Lies about his military record."

"Call the witness," Benedict Boykin said. "Calhoun Slaughter, do you swear to tell the truth, the whole truth, and nothing but the truth, so help you God?"

"I do," replied the voice of Calhoun Slaughter.

Cobb twisted violently on his pulley. "Take this fucking hood off me," he screamed.

"Shut up," Benedict Boykin said. "Calhoun Slaughter, is your son being honest?"

"Maybe," Calhoun Slaughter said. "Probably partly. But he's also yellow. He's afraid of hate mail. He's afraid of having his Bronze Star spat on."

"I can't breathe," Cobb gasped. "I can't breathe. I can't do this to my father."

"Bullshit," Benedict Boykin said. "It's yourself you're worried about."

"It wasn't my fault."

"You're the only one who can fix it," Benedict said.

"Dad," Cobb pleaded, "if I let these photographs out of the box, you know what they'll say? Like father, like son, they'll say."

"That's the way it plays," his father said.

"I won't do this to you or to me."

"You'd rather live with not fixing it?"

"Isn't there any other way, Dad?"

"Probably not, son. You're going to be crucified."

"That's garbage," Benedict said. "There's a failsafe way," and Cobb saw that yes, there was. He could let the cat out of the bag and no one need know who had done it.

* * *

Cobb called his father from the motel.

"Dad?"

"Where you calling from?"

"Virginia. I'm in a crappy motel. I've changed my mind. I'm going to go back to Baghdad. There's something I think I can do. Wanted to let you know just in case."

"In case what?"

"In case things don't turn out. In case there's shit."

"There's always shit."

"I mean serious shit. I've got some photographs."

"What sort of photographs?"

"Dirty photographs. Torture."

"Not our guys," his father said. "We don't do that."

"Not our guys. But our guys know about it."

"Shitheads," Calhoun Slaughter said. "Military trash. Should be court martialed. What you gonna do with the pics?"

"I'm sending them to the newspapers." Cobb heard a whistling intake of breath. He heard his father gasping for air. "*Dad*!" he said, alarmed.

"You can't do that, son," his father said. "First you gotta send them upstairs. Those are the rules."

"I did that, Dad. Nothing happened."

"Shit."

"You think I shouldn't do this?"

"I don't know. A few bad apples. Maybe the dirty stuff's stopped."

"It hasn't, Dad. I saw stuff myself. Our guys know about it. Some of them watch. Some of them took these pics."

"This'll get nasty, son."

"No one's gonna know who mailed the photos."

"I wouldn't count on that. You ready for what could happen?"

"I guess I'll find out," Cobb said. "What about you?"

"Don't you worry about me."

"The photographs are only part one. Part two is I got a rescue mission in the works. Wish me luck."

"I wish you luck. You see Leela-May this afternoon?"

"Yeah, you sneaky old bastard."

"What happened?"

"This is what's happening."

"You're gonna drive me to prayer. Stay safe."

Cobb dialed Gideon Moore's number but when Leela answered he lost his nerve.

"Hello?" she said.

Cobb held his breath.

"Is that you, Cobb?"

On the wall across from the motel bed and the phone was a framed photograph of a football game: the Virginia Cavaliers against the VMI Keydets. Cobb squinted and searched for sweater number fourteen, his old number, on the VMI team. The photograph, in color, was faded and stained. It looked decades old, perhaps a glory memory of the motel manager's youth, a distant victory in a cheap plastic frame.

"Cobb," Leela said quietly. "I've never understood what happened to us. We were so close when we were kids. Blood brother, blood sister."

He could feel her blood thumping through his veins. He could see sweater number fourteen in the thick of the scrum. What year was that game? He needed to know. Was it possible that he himself was there? He could smell ivory soap. He sniffed his own skin and smelled Leela. When the Keydets won a game, he used to call her Boston number from his dorm. He never spoke. *Are you a deep breather?* she would ask. She was flippant back then. She had never known fear or want.

"Where are you, Cobb?" she asked gently. "Are you on the road or back in Promised Land? Can I see you?"

Cobb walked toward the photograph, the coiled cord unsnaking behind him, the receiver still pressed to his ear. He read the fine print on the matte: *Championship Game, Virginia Military Institute.* He squinted, his eyes close to the glass. He had played in that game.

"It's strange," Leela said. "I can't stop thinking of all those times, those other times, on the Hamilton veranda.... I remember the week your mother died. That was the time we traded blood."

Now that he was close to the photograph, he could see how fly-blown it was. Insects had left needle tracks. Mold was mushrooming up from the turf. He peered at the figure in sweater fourteen. Its face had been eaten away. There was a stain like a parallelogram where the goalposts were. There was a smear of blood on the frame.

Cobb Slaughter, he thought. Blood brother bloodied. Former VMI football player, erased.

"I can see a parallelogram," Leela said.

She could not have said that. He knew she had not said that.

"You don't even have to say anything, Cobb. I know it's you. I'm glad you called, whatever it means."

"It's not a parallelogram, it's a coffin," he said, shocking himself. His words were jammed up in the mouthpiece like sludge.

He heard a sound like that of a small bird in the mouth of a cat. He listened to Leela's breathy silence.

"Say something," he begged.

"Are you telling me Mishka's dead?"

I heard him humming, he wanted to say.

"What are you telling me, Cobb?"

He wanted to tell her: the warden says he sings.

"Is Mishka alive?"

He spoke then. He managed to speak. "As far as I know, he's still alive. It wasn't supposed to happen this way, Leela. Things went wrong."

"Where is he, Cobb?"

Atonement. That was what he was hungry for. "I'll bring him back," he promised.

"Oh Cobb, oh Cobb." He could not tell if she was laughing or crying. She was babbling. He closed his eyes and listened to her sweet noisy breathing for several more seconds and then he hung up.

He could drive again now.

He knew exactly where he was going.

5

At Gideon's bedside, the nurse adjusted the morphine drip.

"I'll be back in the morning," she told Leela. "He'll be free of pain till then. You should try to get some sleep yourself."

"I've got a pillow. I'll doze in the chair," Leela said. "Maggie sat with him all last night. It's my turn."

"He's in a deep sleep. It'll last for at least six hours."

"I know that." It was easier to talk to him then.

"I believe they hear everything you say," the nurse offered. "They just can't answer back."

"I have this memory," Leela said. She spoke aloud. She stroked her father's arm, which was ochre-colored, withered as a prune. The skin was so papery and dry that where the edge of the sheet chafed his forearm, his capillary veins leaked blood. "It's this room. It's full of my memory." She put her head on the pillow beside her father's. "I must have been nearly six. I heard noises in the middle of the night." Her father's breath was medicinal and sour. He was exhaling death. Leela moved slightly, so as not to breathe him in. "I tiptoed to the door of your room. Of *this* room." There was a moon like a yellow plate hanging in the window. There was a little heap of clothing on the floor. She could see her mother's blue nightgown, her father's striped cotton pajamas. She kept looking at the soft pile of cloth because she knew she was not supposed to see her parents naked. "Mama's stomach was huge as a balloon," she said drowsily. Her father was kissing it. Her father put his ear against his wife's belly and his hand was playing with the beard between her legs and he kissed her there too. And then he held himself high up over her and pushed against her. Leela remembered the sounds her mother made and she remembered how she felt heavy between her own legs. When she crept back to bed, she was strangely excited and frightened and she touched herself the way she had seen her father touch her mother. She imagined Cobb kissing her there. She wanted him to.

"I was afraid that's why Mama died when Maggie came, Daddy. I was afraid it was because I'd seen."

She wanted to tell Cobb, but never did.

She wanted Cobb, but would settle for almost any boy. She always pulled them down. She always had a mad itch between her legs and she always wanted someone's mouth or someone's prick to ease it.

"I wanted Cobb for years and years, Daddy," she murmured, "and now I want Mishka."

"Is there something you want?" the night nurse asked.

Leela opened her eyes very wide and closed them again. "What are you doing here?"

"I let myself in. Why did you press the night-call button? What do you need?"

"I need Mishka."

"I can't help you there," the nurse said. She wrapped a black cloth around Gideon's arm. She pumped the gray rubber ball which was attached. She took a blood pressure reading. She watched the monitor beside his bed. "I'm afraid it won't be long," she said. "The music's a good idea. The dying are aware, I believe. I believe he hears that. What is it?"

"It's Gluck," Leela said.

"It's very beautiful. It's making him smile. He looks so peaceful. He knows you're holding his hand."

"He's going to get better," Leela said.

"He won't get better. In fact, I think you should wake your sister up. I think it's time."

"Now?"

"I think there's no time to be lost."

The hallway was longer than it used to be and Maggie's bedroom was very far away. Leela walked and walked and then walked faster. The hallway was thick with Gluck. There were more doors, many more doors, than Leela remembered. She stopped at each one. She knocked. She put her ear against the wood and listened.

Che farò... she heard Mishka singing behind a blue door.

The door was locked, but when she hefted her shoulder against it, it gave way like a cobweb and she was inside a very small room. The room was empty but picture frames jostled each other on the walls: simple wooden ones, ornate ones, gilt filigree, carved oak. There were photographs of Mishka with Uncle Otto, Mishka with his mother, Mishka with his grandparents, Mishka with Leela. There was a photograph of Mishka and Leela kissing in Harvard Square. There were others, taken in their bedroom, steamy scenes. Cobb must have donated them. There were photographs of Mishka with Jamil Haddad and of Mishka outside the mosque in Central Square. There was Mishka with Youssef Hajj. There was a photograph of Mishka in the Holiday Inn in Beirut.

There were three entire walls of photographs.

The fourth wall was black plate glass. Leela could not see through it, but from beyond the glass, she could hear Mishka singing a lament. She could tell he was singing in pain. She could hear an interrogator's voice. She thumped her fists against the glass and the moment she did so the glass turned clear.

Mishka was huddled, cross-legged on the floor, cradling his smashed oud in his arms. He wept as he sang.

"Mishka!" she called, drumming on the glass. "Mishka!" But he could not hear.

It was when she leaned against the glass, sobbing, that the glass gave way. It did not break. It stretched like a membrane and she walked right through, pulling the glass with her like the skin of a balloon.

"Mishka," she murmured, ravenous. She was unbuttoning and unzipping as she went. She peeled the wetsuit of glass from her body and stepped out of it. She lay down beside Mishka on the floor. He turned to her then and smiled and she pulled his head down between her legs.

6

IN NEW YORK, mere hours before his flight, Cobb sorted through photographs. He imagined Benedict Boykin at his shoulder. *This one, not that one*, Benedict signaled. Cobb made copies, and on the copies he blacked out faces with a magic marker pen. He blacked out the face of anyone who wore combat dress. The other figures—not always naked—wore hoods that were tied at the neck. On a sheet of white paper he wrote: *Confiscated from US soldiers in Iraq*. He signed nothing. He put the copies and the sheet of paper in a brown manila envelope which he addressed to the *New York Times*. He dropped the envelope in a mailbox on East 42nd. From the mailbox, he could see the clock on Grand Central Station and the time was twenty-three minutes past nine.

He thought he knew what to expect.

He was wrong.

Back in Baghdad, he drank coffee with Iraqi militia groups. He slipped money to Shiite policemen and to Sunni drivers of cabs. He hung around bars with American wardens and guards. He reassembled his team. He watched, he listened. He was mapping out Operation Underworld.

He heard barracks talk about photographs, whistle-blowers, traitors. He monitored internet gossip. Blogs fumed and smoked on his laptop, websites smoldered. There was speculation. There were vows to run the whistle-blower down.

FIFTH COLUMN: ARMY SABOTAGED FROM WITHIN.

TRAITOR TOO YELLOW TO SHOW HIS FACE.

Cobb busied himself with strategy. He told his team there would be no second chances. They had to get it right the first time.

On the blogs, detectives were rampant. Conspiracy theorists weighed in. Landmarks in the photographs were enlarged: this area of the city and not that. There were lists: who was stationed in Baghdad when, which units were where, who was known to be back in New York on the postmark day. Vectors were drawn and in a very short time the quarry was named.

LIKE FATHER, LIKE SON, Cobb read. MILITARY DISGRACE RUNS IN FAMILY.

EVIDENCE THAT FORMER SPECIAL FORCES MEMBER WAS DOUBLE AGENT.

MERCENARY: FIGHTS FOR MONEY, NOT PATRIOTISM.

On the talk shows, which Cobb picked up in streaming video, there were officers, now retired, who had been in Afghanistan. There was always considerable murkiness, they said, about Major Slaughter's Bronze Star.

A soldier who had served in Slaughter's unit revealed that his former officer was morally depraved. "He visited brothels," the soldier said. "I cannot reveal on family television the things he made women do."

SLAUGHTER CUTS AND RUNS, headlines proclaimed. He was nothing more than a highly paid gun-for-hire and it was rumored that he was now immersed in further mercenary stunts.

It was known he had left the country.

In Baghdad, Cobb's own men averted their eyes. Nevertheless, they said, we won't tell the press where you are. *We're* not stool pigeons.

"If you want out of Operation Underworld," Cobb told them, "you're free to go."

We'll go, they said. But we won't blow the whistle on you.

There would be a Judas, Cobb knew.

Hate was a strange phenomenon, he thought. He stopped reading the blogs. He found the level of toxicity too high. Hate, he thought, was even stranger than love. Haters behaved more insanely than lovers did. They were more reckless. They lived on an adrenalin rush. That was the lure, Cobb saw.

He made contact with Benedict Boykin and they met inside the ruined shell of a house in the dangerous quarter of the city.

"You are a surprise to me," Benedict said. "I didn't think you had it in you."

"I need help. I've got my weapons, but my team has quit. I need four men. Can you get me four men?"

"Not if they know who wants them."

"They don't need to know. I'll wear a mask. Just say it's an unofficial exercise and there's money in it."

"What's the good of offering money?" Benedict asked. "You'll all be killed."

"The money will go to their families. I'm counting on you to set that up. I want the desperate ones."

"You are a surprise to me," Benedict said.

On the afternoon of Operation Underworld, Cobb went to a post office inside the American zone. He wore an electrician's coveralls and a knitted cap pulled down close to his eyes. From a pay phone, he placed two calls to Promised Land. He huddled in the booth and spoke low.

"Dad?"

"Fuck the lot of 'em," his father said. "You get a Bronze Star from me. You doing all right?"

"I'm okay. How about you?"

"Don't worry about me," his father said. "Where the hell are you? You still over there?"

"Yeah. Got one more thing to do and then I'll be home."

"You'll have to go into the witness protection program. Or I could sit on the porch with my gun."

"It's that bad?"

"We could both go live in Jamaica."

Cobb laughed. "See you, Dad."

"I'll let you stay around longer next time."

Cobb didn't trust himself to speak. By the time he had dialed Leela's number he could not see.

"Hello?" she said.

Cobb stroked the curves of the receiver and leaned into her voice.

"Who is this?" she asked. "Is that you, Cobb? Are you crying?"

Bye, Leela, he thought, and hung up.

Epilogue

LEELA WAS STILL staring, dazed, at the headlines when the telephone rang.

"Esau Boykin," the caller said. "Is that Leela-May?"

Leela nodded.

"Have you seen the papers, Leela-May?"

"Mnnh," Leela said.

"I've had a call from Benedict, and Benedict said to tell you there's good news."

Leela pressed a hand over her mouth. She was leaning against the wall beside the phone. She slid to the floor. The block letters of the headlines were wet and starry, their edges jagged.

WHISTLE-BLOWER KILLED IN BAGHDAD
MILITARY MAVERICK REDEEMED
Secret torture center exposed.

Associated Press reports that a former Ba'ath-party prison used by rogue Iraqi militia groups has been discovered. One room in the prison was found to be piled with decayed and mutilated bodies. Scores of prisoners in malnourished condition, often with severe injuries due to torture, have been found. Among them are American businessmen and contractors who had been kidnapped and held for ransom. There are also many Iraqis and foreign nationals. Those prisoners for whom there is evidence of terrorist connections—a minority, according to the present administrator of US forces in Iraq—will be transferred to prisons in the US or at Guantanamo. The remainder will be returned to their families or repatriated to their own countries.

"Never have I seen such barbarism," said the administrator of US forces in Iraq. "This is what we are up against."

The prison was liberated in a daring and carefully planned pre-dawn raid by a small force of former members of the US military who took heavy fire from rogue troops. Among those killed was military maverick and former major in the US Army, Cobb Slaughter, leader of the raiding party.

"This was entirely a private initiative," the administrator of US forces said, "but all those involved died as heroes as far as we are concerned."

Two items with Baghdad postmarks arrived in Promised Land. Both were addressed to Leela and Esau Boykin delivered them by hand. He left the mail van at the roadside and walked up Gideon Moore's long drive. He handed Leela one letter and one small package. Of the letter, he said: "That's my boy's handwriting. I can't stay but a few minutes, but I'll pay my respects to Gideon if I may."

Leela curled up on the porch swing and opened her mail.

US Army Base, Baghdad.
Dear Leela,
First things first: Michael Bartok is alive. He's in very bad shape, and it will be a long time before he can play a musical instrument again, but he's alive. Both shoulders are dislocated and his hands are badly damaged. He's to be sent back to Australia.

A few days ago, Cobb got in touch with me. He asked for my help. We always unofficially knew where the ghost prisons were. He asked me to get in touch with you if things went wrong. I promised I would. We shook hands.

That was the last I saw of him.

I'd misjudged him, I acknowledge this now. He's to be buried in Arlington. I hope to be there. I hope to see you and his father there.

May he rest in peace.

Love,

Benedict.

The other item was a small padded envelope. Inside the bubble wrap was a tobacco tin and inside the tin was a sand dollar with a seven-petalled star. A small plain card said: *To Leela: love, Cobb.*

She knew she would take the sand dollar with her to the Daintree. High in the rainforest canopy, she would sit on the veranda with Mishka's head in her lap. She would stroke his hair while the parakeets settled on their shoulders. Uncle Otto would play while they dreamed.

Leela stood at the foot of the steps to Calhoun Slaughter's front porch. The old man was in his rocker with an open bottle of Jack Daniels in one hand.

They stared at each other.

Leela thought that she should try to say something light and ironic—*Are you going to shoot me, Mr. Slaughter?*—anything to stop herself sobbing in front of Cobb's father.

He wiped the back of one hand across his eyes and held up the bottle with the other. "Want some?" he asked.

Leela nodded.

"Come here," he said.

She sat on the porch and rested her head against his thigh.

His hand, when he passed her the bottle, was wet with tears.

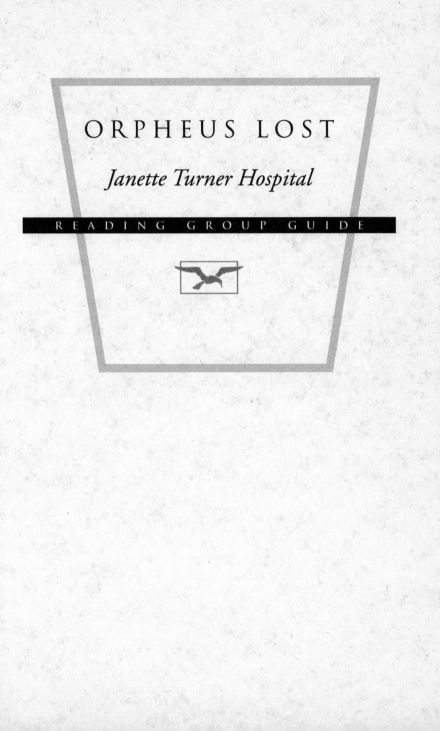

ORPHEUS LOST

Janette Turner Hospital

ORPHEUS LOST

Janette Turner Hospital

DISCUSSION QUESTIONS

1. Leela is a mathematician and Mishka is a musician, but they engage with their work in a similar, obsessive way. How do their work and their relationship insulate them from a tumultuous, outside world?

2. Leela is known as "Leela-May" in her hometown of Promised Land and Mishka's passport lists his name as "Michael Bartok." What do these different names, and later Mishka's adoption of the last name "Abukir," signify for these characters?

3. From the beginning of the novel, the author draws a parallel between Leela and Mishka's story and the Orpheus myth. How does the myth play out when Cobb Slaughter descends into the "underworld" of prison cells to rescue Leela's lover? Do you think the myth is transformed over the course of the novel? In what ways?

4. Why is Leela's patience during questioning so irritating to Cobb? What is the tenor of his relationship with Leela?

5. Why is Leela drawn to men like Cobb and Mishka? How is Cobb similar to Mishka, despite their obvious differences?

6. Why does Leela avoid returning to Promised Land? Discuss the importance of place, the past, and the difficulty of going home in *Orpheus Lost*.

7. "For loss, we have music," says Mr. Hajj, Mishka's oud instructor. How do Mishka and his family in Australia deal with loss through music?

8. Why do Mishka's grandparents bring Uncle Otto back to life? Do you see a connection between Mishka's mother's return to the Daintree and Leela's eventual return to Promised Land?

9. Do you think that Gideon's obsession with "magic numbers" is related to Leela's passion for math? Discuss the significance of Gideon's preoccupation with numbers and the divine power he believes they hold.

10. Both Cobb and Mishka wish to gain their coercive fathers' affections. What does the novel tell us about the nature of family ties and forgiveness?

11. Does Cobb redeem himself through the suicide mission that exposes the illegal Iraqi prison in which Mishka is held? Does he redeem his father?

12. *Orpheus Lost* tells a fictional story, but it brings to mind recent political issues and the U.S. war on terror. How has the novel caused you to reflect upon current events?

MORE NORTON BOOKS WITH READING GROUP GUIDES AVAILABLE

Diana Abu-Jaber	*Crescent*
	Origin
Diane Ackerman	*The Zookeeper's Wife*
Rabih Alameddine	*I, the Divine*
Rupa Bajwa	*The Sari Shop*
Andrea Barrett	*The Voyage of the Narwhal*
	The Air We Breathe
Peter C. Brown	*The Fugitive Wife*
Lan Samantha Chang	*Inheritance*
Leah Hager Cohen	*House Lights*
Michael Cox	*The Meaning of Night*
Jared Diamond	*Guns, Germs, and Steel*
John Dufresne	*Louisiana Power & Light*
Ellen Feldman	*Lucy*
Susan Fletcher	*Eve Green*
	Oystercatchers
Paula Fox	*The Widow's Children*
Betty Friedan	*The Feminine Mystique*
Barbara Goldsmith	*Obsessive Genius*
Stephen Greenblatt	*Will in the World*
Helon Habila	*Waiting for an Angel*
Patricia Highsmith	*Strangers on a Train*
Ann Hood	*The Knitting Circle*
Dara Horn	*The World to Come*
Janette Turner Hospital	*Due Preparations for the Plague*
Pam Houston	*Sight Hound*
Helen Humphreys	*The Lost Garden*
Wayne Johnston	*The Custodian of Paradise*
Erica Jong	*Sappho's Leap*
Peg Kingman	*Not Yet Drown'd*
Nicole Krauss	*The History of Love**
Don Lee	*Country of Origin*
Ellen Litman	*The Last Chicken in America*
Vyvyane Loh	*Breaking the Tongue*
Emily Mitchell	*The Last Summer of the World*

*Available only on the Norton Web site: www.wwnorton.com/guides